# THE COAT &
# THE CROWN

Joseph of Egypt

© 2010 Mary Keith Boyack

Send Inquiries to:
  Digital Legend Press and Publishing
  4700 Clover St.
  Honeoye Falls, NY 14472

See the complete library at www.digitalegend.com

For info write to:   info@digitalegend.com
or call toll free:    877-222-1960

Printed in the United States of America
First Printing: September 2010
Second Printing: February 2011

ISBN: 978-1-934537-98-5

# THE COAT &
# THE CROWN

## Joseph of Egypt

## MARY KEITH BOYACK

DIGITAL
LEGEND

NEW YORK

# Dedication

This book is dedicated to
Belinda, Barbara, Bobby, Billy, Lizzy, Amy, Becca, and Berta.

# Genealogy

Adam

Seth

Enos

Cainan

Mahalaleel

Jared

Enoch

Methuselah

Lamech

Noah

| Japeth | Shem | | Ham | |
|---|---|---|---|---|
| | Arphaxad | Canaan | Egypt | Cush |
| | Salah | | Pharaoh | |
| | Eber<br>(father of Hebrews) | | | |
| | Peleg | | | |
| | Ren | | | |
| | Serug | | | |
| | Nahor | | | |
| | Terah | | | |
| | Abraham | | Pharaoh | |
| | Isaac | | Hyksos King | |
| | Jacob<br>(Israel) | | Apophis<br>(Pharaoh) | |

Reuben / Simeon / Levi / Judah / Isacar / Zebulon / Dan / Naptali / Gad / Asher / Joseph / Benjamin

# Author's Note

Dear Reader,

How is it that a seventeen-year-old boy, torn from his roots, made to suffer every kind of cruel extremity, could still maintain faith in his God? The story of Joseph has fired my imagination and stirred my soul for my entire lifetime. I began at a young age to collect his stories wherever they could be found. Along the way, Dr. Hugh Nibley caught my attention as he taught that the phrase *coat of many colors* can also be interpreted to be *coat of many patches, pieces, or cuttings*—even marks or insignias—very likely a symbol of authority.

When I was in Egypt, I sought for clues about Joseph, but found none. Often the ancient Pharaohs destroyed any evidence of their predecessors in order to appear greater than the latter. Such obliteration would have been expected in Joseph's case since he and his Pharaoh were Hyksos. (The Hyksos, who were ruling at the time of Joseph, were Shemites.) However, the natives in the Fayoum Valley in Egypt still refer to their waterway as Joseph's (Yussef's) Canal. As far as we know of his adventures in Egypt, Joseph had no contact with anyone who shared his belief in the God Yahweh. I gave him Cephas.

Some preliminary readers have questioned the skin and hair color of some of the characters—blondes and red-heads—thinking all mideasterners should have been dark. My research shows that Noah and his sons, Ham, Shem, and Japeth, were fair-skinned blondes and red-heads. Ham's wife, Egyptus, was dark. Ham and Egyptus's offspring filled the continent of Africa and some surrounding countries. Ham's son, Caanan, settled the land of Caanan where Abraham, Isaac, and Jacob (Israel) became dwellers. The bloodlines of Israel were unmixed until Judah took a Caananite woman for one of his wives, as did Simeon.

I believe that Joseph kept a record of his own life and that it will someday come to light. Until then, this novel is my best guess as to what might have been his story. Please come along and enjoy the journey.

–Mary Keith Boyack

# Prologue

"What's the matter, son?"

Joseph looked up and quickly straightened his shoulders. The flap of his father's tent was pulled back to let in sunlight and his father beckoned to him from within.

"Nothing, Father. I'm fine, I'm fine."

"Come in and let me look at you. You are not fine. Your tunic is torn, your knees are scraped, and your face— Have you been crying?"

Joseph brushed a quick hand over his cheeks. "I don't do that. Only women and babies cry."

"Who told you that? Am I not a man who cries? Come here."

The boy stepped onto the finely woven rug—one of many that covered the dirt floor—always clean and swept. This tent was his father's best, designed to entertain visitors, and Joseph always felt a reverent awe to enter there, where he always learned as much as he could at Jacob's feet. Jacob sat in a large chair that served as a *hodaj* when strapped atop a camel. There were six such chairs, each large enough to seat two. The rest of the room was unfurnished except for a folding table that was set up to hold a lamp and his father's writings. Folded mats and blankets were stacked along the side.

"How old are you, Joseph?"

"I'll be ten soon. Maybe then I can do things better."

"Well, from what I see, you do excellently for a nine-year-old." He patted the seat of the chair. "Sit here beside me and let me tell you that men not only cry, but they also shed tears for others. Do you see these tears in my eyes? They are for you, Joseph."

The boy shook his head. "Not for me. I'm tough."

"I know you are, but God has shown me somewhat of the future and I know your road will not be easy."

"But I can do it, Father."

"Yes, yes," Jacob said as he pulled Joseph into a loving embrace. "Now I want you to speak without fear. Tell me about your brothers."

Joseph sat up. "But I can't."

"Yes, you can. I insist on it."

"Well, I do love them. But sometimes they are rough with me. Do you remember at the house of Grandfather Laban how I begged to work outdoors with them? I wanted to be with them all the time, but they acted as if they didn't like me. I think it's because Mother and the other women gave me extra food and lots of hugs and kisses. So sometimes the boys spoke as if they were angry." Joseph paused, then added, "They don't want me to act like a baby." He looked into his father's eyes. "But I want them to be proud of me."

"And now? Are they proud of you?"

"Well, on this trip they have let me help. I've learned much about cattle, how to care for sick animals and to help with lambing and feeding. Sometimes Reuben smiles at me or pats me on the back. I like Reuben. He's a good big brother to us all."

Jacob smiled. "I'm glad to hear that. But tell me why you're upset."

Today after chores, Asher made a ball out of sheepskin and they began tossing it around. I wanted to join in, so when the ball came my way, I ran to jump for it, but I tripped on someone's foot and fell flat. When I stood up, Simeon threw the ball so hard at me that it caught me in the middle and I couldn't breathe. I'm okay now, and next time I'll do better. Anyway, the boys went on playing, but Zebulon stayed with me until I felt better." Joseph looked down, unwilling to share what he had heard as he struggled for breath—taunts and jeers about mama's little baby who was going to cry.

"Thank you for telling me. I see clearly now and love you all the more for it. You are a brave man, my nine-year-old son. The Lord has great plans for you. Keep faithful, and all will be well. Now go to your mother. She needs you."

Joseph stepped back into the sunshine and took a deep breath, comforted in his father's love and happy in the surrounding beauty. Before him in the shady grove, his brothers were laughing and shouting. Beyond in a meadow, white sheep dotted the landscape under a deep blue sky. A few date palms and fig trees grew nearby, their fruit a needed supplement to the food supply. Camels and donkeys were penned close to the stream.

After washing up, Joseph went to the cooking tent.

"Shalom, dear boy," Zilpa said, echoed by the other women from the table where they worked. Bilha, Leah, and Debora, the nurse who had been sent as a gift from Grandfather Isaac, were all busy chopping and cutting to prepare the evening meal. From an animal-skin bag Leah poured a drink and brought it to him. "Here, have some kefir; you are fond of kefir."

He was not really hungry, but accepted it politely, then asked, "Do you know where my mother is?"

"She's in the sleeping tent. Being so heavy with child, she needed rest, but you may go in."

He approached the tent quietly and peeked inside.

"Come in, Joseph. Come here to me."

He ran into Rachel's open arms and snuggled there, soaking in joy. Then he sat up, looked at her smooth skin, at her brilliant blue eyes that mirrored his own and golden hair that fell along a graceful neck and said, "You must be the most beautiful mother in the whole world."

She tousled his curls. "Beauty only matters if it comes from the soul."

"I love your soul then, Ima."

"And I love yours, my son."

"Is there anything I can do for you? Are you thirsty?"

"I'll tell you what I would really like, Joseph. I'd like a song. It would brighten my day and help me rest better."

Joseph thought a moment, then fervently began his favorite song, one she had taught him. She closed her eyes and listened as though her heart would burst for love.

"Joseph," she said when he finished, "promise me something. Promise you will look after the baby when he comes, and teach him to be good like you."

"You can rely on me," Joseph said in his most grown-up voice. To himself he said, "The baby will always feel loved when I'm around."

———

Later that day when Jacob visited Rachel, she told him about her fears for Joseph. "He is so truly good, only nine and trying to be a man. I pray they won't break his heart."

"Yes," Jacob said. "And because of him I have changed my lesson plan for tonight."

That evening, after a meal of lamb stew and flat bread, Jacob gathered his children for their schooling. Last night they had skipped lessons because the day had been spent raising tents and securing pens for the cattle. The stay in this fertile spot gave the animals a chance to graze on ample vegetation and drink from the stream. When there was no meadow or stream nearby, the animals had to be fed by hand and watered from buckets. When no water could be accessed, Jacob dowsed a spot under God's direction and there they dug their own wells. Because a man's power and wealth were measured by his wells and herds, Jacob and his sons were forging a trail noted by all, and all who saw knew that God blessed this family with abundance and goodness.

When the family gathered this night, Jacob began with prayer and asked for wisdom to touch the hearts of his children. They sang a song, as was the custom, then he spoke.

"When last I taught you, I spoke of how to use words, how to speak the language of a great leader. Tonight, however, I want to tell you that a great man is not measured by his oratory or his learning. One who would stoop to help the downtrodden, speak comforting words, or take another's burdens on his own shoulders—this is a great man. God is God because he mastered all virtues. He would be the servant to us all. When we care for another, we are acting as God would act. A great man would never leave one lying by the wayside if he were wounded in body or spirit." At this, Reuben looked over at Simeon, and Simeon looked down at his feet.

# BOOK ONE

# SLAVERY

# Chapter One

## Eight Years Later
# Ahkmar's Caravan

"Put on your good wraps, Mahta. I want you to look your best for our visitors."

Mahta's spirits rose; she even smiled, having had little reason to smile since her father died. She hurried to her corner. *Maybe there will be children I can play with.* Aloud she called, "Yes, Uncle, I'm going to my pack. I'll get my clothes." She knew if she didn't obey Uncle right away, she would be cuffed on the side of her head. She found that out on the first day, the day he dragged her to his house after the funeral, when she could do nothing but cry.

"Stop that!" he had said, "or I'll give you something to cry about!" Then he snatched her by the hair and hit her hard. She had tried to swallow her sobs.

Mahta didn't know how long she had lived at Uncle Meshca's house. She had tried to be invisible, had learned to stay out of the way and not make a sound. In her solitude, she had invented a friend, a young man who looked much like her father. He was very kind to her and called her "Sweetie" and "Dear One," like her father used to. She named him Sashi. She and Sashi would whisper and giggle quietly in her corner under the covers when she thought no one could hear.

"Come, Sashi, we are going to have visitors. Make sure you don't make any noise. Just stay out of the way and wait until I tell you what to do."

When she stepped out to where her uncle waited, he just said, "Come," and led her from the house.

Mahta was delighted. "We get to visit our friends away from the house," she whispered to Sashi.

On the outskirts of town, they approached a trade caravan where a small, dark man stood in front of many wares and animals.

Mahta looked for children, and to her joy she saw some. They were small, a young girl and two little boys held close to veiled women, one with a baby who kept to the back.

Uncle and the trader must have had words previously because the man looked Mahta over carefully, cleared his throat and said, "Let it be done." Uncle took the small sack of silver and left quickly. Mahta turned to follow him, but the trader caught her by the hand and said, "Oh no, *yaldah*, you belong to me now."

"Don't worry, Sashi," Mahta whispered. "Now we have children to play with." But she found out she was wrong when she tried to approach the little girl and got jerked away as the little girl got a slap for smiling.

After her wraps and shoes were taken from her, she was dressed in rags and oriented to her new role. She walked at the back of the caravan, tied to the wagon and behind the animals. The good thing, she decided, was that she could talk aloud to Sashi.

Mahta often tried to remember her mother, and even though she had only been four when her mother died, she could remember some of her songs. Her mother loved to sing and had taught Mahta many little songs. That was Mahta's happiest memory, and now she and Sashi made up songs as they trailed behind the caravan.

———

Coming to, Cephas could hear moaning, then realized it was coming from his own throat. The more aware he became, the more pain he felt, but worse than the physical pain was that of remembering. He wanted to wipe the caked blood from his swollen eyes, but couldn't raise his arm.

Against his will his mind relived the terror—the beatings he and his family had sustained; the screams, panic, and blood; how he had thrown himself at the men about to assault his wife. The sound of their laughing with relish as they stoned him still rang in his ears. His memory mercifully refused to call up all that had happened.

He began to sink into oblivion again and welcomed the blackness. In and out of consciousness he told himself, *This is it...I'll die and join my family.* In time, however, his eyes opened and he forced himself to look on the bodies of his wife, his daughter, her husband, and his three grandchildren. *If I survived, maybe some of the others are still alive.*

He willed himself to drag his body closer to theirs, but found that he hadn't been able to save even one of them. The sight of their contorted bodies on the hot desert floor, the flies defiling them, made Cephas retch uncontrollably in nothing but dry heaves. "I'm sorry, I'm so sorry," he cried over and over, sobbing, his body void of enough moisture to make tears.

He had managed to come nearest his daughter, probably the last to go, and he closed her eyelids.

*Oh, God, why couldn't I have died? Why did I have to see this?* He realized that they must have been on the ground for at least a day, probably more. His skin was burned, his lips cracked, and he could taste blood. The marauders had taken his headdress and robes and left him in the unmerciful sun. They had, in fact, taken everything—all the clothing and food, every animal. Looking around, he decided to crawl to an outcropping of rock where the spoilers had hidden before the attack. Above all, he needed shade, but he knew he wouldn't last without water.

He grabbed at the sand in an effort to pull himself forward, every movement torture, until one arm and one leg began to respond. He found himself praying, his natural habit, but abruptly broke off. *If God were going to help me now, why didn't he help me earlier?* A darkness of spirit engulfed him and he cried out in despair. "Help me," he pleaded, and out of the void came a memory—a scene of himself surrounded by students, as he had been a high priest, a teacher. He was giving a lesson he had taught in Salem at the great house of learning:

"God is not the author of evil. From whatever source tragedy springs, it is not from Him. I know that when we experience affliction, we tend to become angry and blame Deity. Bad things happen. We do not choose misfortune, but we may choose how we react to it."

It had been easy to teach that when misfortune was not his, but this test was too hard. "Dear God, I need to believe again. If it be thy will that I live, please help me. Help me find rest; help me find water. I'm in thy hands." Then he lost consciousness.

Cephas dreamed. He was again in the Salem house, being ordained as a high priest. The man giving the ordinance was telling him what an honor he was receiving. "This station is only for the very worthy, those who have turned their lives over to God and served him faithfully."

"But I've been a high priest for many years," he tried to explain.

He awakened. Someone was holding his head up and trying to squeeze water into his mouth from a goatskin bag. He tried to swallow, but could only cough because his throat was so swollen. Finally, a few drops at a time, the fluid found its way down, and exhausted, he fell back into the arms of his rescuer. A few more times they moistened his parched throat, then left him to rest in the shade. Like cracked earth when saturated with rain, his body began to renew. *Oh blessed water.* He was finally able to thank his attendants and express his deep gratitude to God.

He took stock of the band who had saved him, a traveling merchant and his entourage who were using the scant shelter of the outcrop to set up camp for the night. He pointed to where his family lay, and the men acknowledged that they knew the bodies were there, and were commencing their burial.

Early the next morning, Cephas saw that the workers had devised a sledge to be dragged behind a donkey, and he knew they planned to take him with them. "Please, God, take care of my loved ones. I dedicate each grave to Thee, that their resting place will be watched over. In time, let each of them rise again to Thee."

———◦◦◦———

Ahkmar had mixed feelings. He had taken the girl child as a slave because he couldn't refuse—she came at such a low price. She was a skinny little thing and didn't amount to much now, but when she filled out he could fix her hair and clean her up. With pretty robes she might fetch a handsome price, especially if he saw to it that she remained a virgin. Virgins always commanded a higher price.

*But this old man may cost more in upkeep than I could ever get for him in silver. He may even die soon.*

First and foremost, Ahkmar was a money maker. He loved the challenge of using his wits to make a few shekels, so he took a chance that the white-haired man may recover and be of some use to him. He ordered his workers to make the sledge, then found a worn out tunic and a piece of rope for them to dress Cephas. He scavenged up an old rag for them to wrap round his head and another to fashion as a canopy. *This is too much. I never intended to be in the slave business. Goats are much less trouble than people.*

Each day he watched to see how much food he had to waste on the man and the girl. Finally he announced, "After this, just give them a share of the leavings we save for the animals."

Fortunately for Cephas they traveled only a couple of days until they came to a small settlement next to a river. The workers asked Ahkmar if they should bathe some of the filth off the slaves. "I don't care," he answered. "Do it if you think it's necessary."

Cephas couldn't raise himself up, so the men lowered him, sledge and all, into the water. Messa jumped in and splashed the battered face, wiping off the caked blood. At once, Cephas felt improved. He thanked them and smiled at the girl struggling to bathe in the stream.

After that, the little girl walked by his side and one day reached for his hand and asked, "Are you my friend?"

"Yes," Cephas answered, "and I hope you are mine."

"My name is Mahta," she told him.

"And mine is Cephas."

"Are you hungry, Cephas?"

"Yes, child. In this group we are always hungry."

The little nourishment and water he got, coupled with prayers and his strong will, made Cephas's recovery remarkable. It was not a week before he asked for a crutch and gave up the sling. He had also decided that the little girl, Mahta, needed someone to look after her, and he had to admit that he needed her company. Being a slave, he discovered, is a lonely concern.

After taking stock of his condition, Cephas concluded that he was blind in one eye, though the gash was healing, and that two teeth were chipped by the stones, but no large bones were broken. He might be left with a limp from a boulder that crushed his foot, but the bruises and cuts would heal in time. *I wonder what God wants of me.*

He studied those around him, having never been in a condition of contention like this one where a kind word was never spoken. Ahkmar constantly berated his wives and children, often hitting them. He barked or growled orders to his workers. *I can understand better now the effects of hate,* Cephas thought. *People can get so enwrapped in hating that they miss the whole point of life.* Ahkmar seemed so driven in bitterness that he had no chance of reforming. Messa, on the other hand, had much good in him. If it hadn't been for Messa's compassion, Cephas would be dead by now.

The small traveling group consisted of the master, his three wives and four small children, and two male servants, Messa and Kamar. Their herd was big enough to also require at least one shepherd. Nathor kept the sheep from wandering off, and looked after the lambing and shearing. In addition to sheep, Ahkmar owned camels, donkeys, and a few goats. Although animals were the main source of profit, silver was not the only means of exchange. They had taken in trade such items as baskets, jugs, rugs, and clothing. Anything surplus to his family's own needs was up for barter. Ahkmar would trade almost anything to turn a profit.

Ahkmar resembled a rat. His forehead sloped forward, his chin receded back, and his nose pushed to a point in the middle.

The way he trimmed his beard in narrow strips from his ears to his chin and let the mustache bend out like whiskers accentuated the look. His habit of sniffing the air and even the way he held his hands out like paws in front of him completed the resemblance. Behind his back his men would refer to him as *Ackbar*, the name for rodent.

Ahkmar noticed that Cephas was able to do small tasks. "Well," he said, "I see that saving your life may benefit me after all. What can you do for me, since you are so far in my debt as to owe me your life?"

Cephas, as a boy, had loved working with animals, but he had been tutored to be a learned man like his father. He knew he would one day be a high priest, but he would often go to the stables behind the great house and learn all he could about God's creatures. He loved the miracle of who they were. He marveled at how magnificent was a horse, how benevolent a cow, how curious a goat, and how peaceful and playful a lamb. He had high regard for camels and their endurance. He enjoyed talking with all of them and studying their responses. So when Ahkmar asked what he had to offer, he knew he couldn't tell him that he was a teacher or man of learning. That wouldn't agree with Ahkmar and might even be dangerous. So he answered, "I'm familiar with all kinds of animals and could be of use in their discipline and maintenance." Then he worried that he had spoken too well and wished he knew the language of a slave. He looked at the ground.

Ahkmar acted as if he hadn't noticed, as if he wouldn't admit that he could be less than superior, especially to a slave. "Very well," he said in a raised voice. "The slave, Cephas, will be allowed to help take care of the animals. Tradition decrees that he owes his life to me because I saved his. He has promised to honor this tradition, so he need not be shackled."

It was actually Messa who had saved him. All Ahkmar had done was consent to let Messa minister aid.

"I'll watch you closely, old man, and I'll use a slave whip if I see the need."

"There will be no need," Cephas said.

When Cephas was able to leave the sledge, he took the square of cloth that had shaded him and made a *kaffiyeh* for Mahta. Ahkmar had offered her no headdress, resulting in sunburned skin and lightened hair.

The caravan had no definite course as far as Cephas could tell. It wandered to whichever area offered enough traffic to sustain a bit of trade, or from necessity, it moved to a place to get supplies and water. They never knew when they would stop to set out their wares, or how long they would stay in one place.

Being a merchant and a slave owner, and especially having guessed rightly on Cephas, Ahkmar felt more self-important than usual. So the next time they needed to stop for water, Ahkmar sent Kamar and Messa ahead to a site that looked promising. Wells were most often chiseled out of limestone mounds whose features usually meant they contained water. So when a camp was in proximity to a dome-like structure, it signaled a possible well, although strangers may or may not be welcome to buy water from the owner. Messa hurried back to Ahkmar and reported.

"It was curious, Master. A young shepherd stood guarding the well, although it's dry. It seems they're keeping a boy in the hole. Other shepherds ate at a fire nearby. When they saw me, one of them hurried over and asked if you'd be interested in buying a slave."

"Well, let me see him," Ahkmar said as he swaggered toward the place, acting the role of a seasoned slave trader.

They had just drawn the lad up as if he were no more than a bucket of water. Even from a glance, Ahkmar could tell what a prize he beheld. Greed at the thought of how much profit the youth would bring made him almost giddy. *This one has real possibilities. I must be shrewd.*

Some of the other shepherds joined the one attending the well. They were all large and self-assured, intimidating if Ahkmar had dared to admit it. But there was little haggling. Their spokesman seemed eager for it to be done.

As he left the camp, Ahkmar smiled at having paid only twenty pieces of silver for a young man who was large and strong. Even though the lad was covered in mud, wore only a loin cloth, and wasn't shorn as a slave, Ahkmar felt smug and victorious.

But the new slave kept his eyes down and wouldn't speak, and Ahkmar's smile waned as he watched him. *Why were they so eager to be rid of him? Why didn't they give me more resistance in the bargaining? Maybe he's stolen, not theirs to sell. Maybe something is wrong with him.*

Ahkmar had the boy dressed in a tunic but no wrap for his head; it was obviously protected by the masses of thick curls. He sent Kamar to question the boy, but he came back saying, "He doesn't talk, Master. He just looks down. I don't think he's such a bargain if he doesn't talk. Maybe he's just stupid."

Ahkmar decided he would shackle this one and keep a sharp eye out. Cephas watched him closely also.

# Chapter Two

# Unlikely Slaves

No one but Ahkmar knew why he chose the unlikely course they now traveled. Before they stopped at the dry well and found the new slave, they had been on the regular trade route. Now he was taking them through a dangerous, rocky ravine that was nearly impossible for the animals to manage.

They needed water—did Ahkmar think it could be found here? He seemed angry, and made his workers tie the hands of the slaves but take the leg shackles off the boy. He himself took a whisk to their legs to keep them moving. Being in such a hurry, why had he chosen this impossible passage?

After some difficult maneuvering, Cephas looked up to get a sense of their surroundings and took in a quick breath to see Ahkmar handing over a bag of silver to a rough-looking man. *Ahkmar has brought us through the robber's hiding place.*

Thoughts of his family were always foremost in Cephas's mind and he wondered if the bandits who assaulted them were here. He looked around at the caves in the rocky hills where all manner of human refuse inhabited them. Were all his worldly goods in one of those caves? *Ahkmar knows these outlaws. He's paying for safe passage through here. Why?* He kept thinking of his family, finding it difficult to keep up his pace after passing the rock dwellers.

For many days after that the caravan was in a state of unease. There had been enough successful trading to satisfy the master, but everyone tended to their own business and tried not to cause any trouble.

———○●○———

When he was needed, Cephas always helped Nathor with the sheep. Of course, Mahta was also close by and eager to help. The caravan needed to stop so that some of the ewes could give birth. One of the mothers struggled in delivering, weakened from bleeding until she breathed her last. Mahta took the wet lamb, rubbed it with a rag and held it close to her.

"You'll have to give it up, *yaldah*," Nathor said. He took the tiny lamb and put it to one of the ewes who could give milk, but she rejected it, as did all the nursing ewes. "Without its mother's milk, it has little chance," he said. "We can't save all of them."

"But this lamb is strong," Mahta said. "My *Abba* told me that when I was born, my mother had no milk to give, but I lived."

"That's not the same thing," the shepherd said.

"They fed me goat's milk. Maybe we could feed this lammy goat's milk." Mahta reached out and took the baby lamb.

Cephas, seeing Mahta's concern, said, "We could devise a way to feed the poor little thing."

The mute boy was also listening and had already dragged the dead ewe away. When they lost or slaughtered any of the animals, they kept the skin and harvested every part of the animal that could be used. Skins stretched on racks to cure were often carried or dragged on a pole between two members of the party, sometimes two of the wives. While the others were still arguing over the newborn, the boy reappeared with a pouch he had fashioned from a cured sheep skin, one of the skins they turned inside out to hold liquid like the water bags. He had cut this one down so it was smaller. He showed them that they could fill it with goat's milk and feed the lamb. Mahta was delighted.

"I'll help her care for it," Cephas said.

"You won't need to." Mahta took the bag from the young man, turned her head aside and said, "Come, Sashi, we have work to do. I'll learn to milk the goat and make sure that we don't trouble anyone."

"Well, I guess the slaves have conspired to save the little girl's lamb; so be it." Nathor walked away, unimpressed.

Cephas turned to the boy and said, "You know a lot about sheep." But the lad acted as if he hadn't heard and hurried away to some other task. He still would not make eye contact.

As they walked the caravan's slow pace, they listened day after day to the child's singing. She sang the song her mother had sung to her, changing the word *baby* for *lammy*. "Balloo, Balloo, my little baby," her mother had sung.

"I'm not a baby," four-year-old Mahta had protested.

"You will always be my baby, no matter how old you get," her mother had explained.

Balloo, balloo, my sweet little lammy,
Balloo, balloo, your mother is near.
Hush now go to sleep
Let cloud cover keep,
Balloo, balloo lee, lammy dear.

Through winnowy winds I'll hold and caress you,
Nestle your woolly head to my chest.
I'll pillow you tender
In slumber's surrender,
Balloo, balloo lay, lammy rest.

Balloo, balloo, my downy wee darling,
Lark songs will wake your dreaming divine.
Come sing to the open skies,
Frolic with butterflies,
Loo balloo lay lammy mine.

Heaven will tend my little lammy.
Come warm in the sun, come drink from the stream.
He'll shepherd the hours
Through meadows of flowers,
Balloo, balloo lay lammy dream.

The company had come farther south than they had been before, and Ahkmar was in a better mood. In fact, he told Cephas, "Let the boy sleep without shackles tonight. You can keep him by you to help watch the animals."

A camel can shriek when startled, and while this may not have been the first one Cephas had ever heard, it was certainly the most startling. He had been dreaming of more pleasant times when the most ghastly outroar brought him sharply to his feet. The boy was just as quickly by his side.

Not only were the camels bellowing, but the donkeys were stamping, bucking, and braying. All the animals were agitated. Messa and Kamar came hurrying out of their tent, and Nathor was already tweedling and calling his sheep, each by his own name, to calm them. One of the donkeys had broken through the rope restraint and was trotting off towards a desolate wilderness. The young helper set out after him as Cephas spoke soothingly to the camels, trying to dodge the volley of spit the upset creatures emitted. "These makeshift pens do nothing to hold the animals," he muttered, as he tried to restore order. "I wonder that more than one didn't escape."

Ahkmar, red-faced, stumbled out of the main tent. One of his wives, holding her robe close with one hand and her veil to her face with the other, slipped from behind him and hurried into the women's quarters.

Ahkmar looked on. "What is the problem here?" he demanded.

Messa tried to explain. "I think it was a deadly sand serpent that spooked the camels, and they upset the others. The boy is chasing after a donkey that got away. The snake killed the one lying there."

Although the chaos was being contained, Ahkmar scowled and said, "When the speechless boy comes back, let me know."

"Aren't you afraid he may not come back?" Messa asked.

"Where would he go?" Ahkmar growled. "I'm going back to bed. Tell me when he returns." He went back inside.

"He may just keep running," Messa said. "What future does he have here as a slave?"

"It's treacherous out there," Kamar added as they attended the dead donkey and secured the other animals.

"He'll come back," Cephas said. "He can't speak, but that doesn't mean he's without understanding." Cephas wondered if the caravan master might not secretly wish that the boy wouldn't come back. Ahkmar had seemed nervous and fretful lately. He kept stealing glances at the slaves—mainly the boy.

They had camped that night by the great body of salt water. They occasionally did so in order to harvest rock salt for use in cooking, for the animals to lick, and for curing meat. For a great distance surrounding the sea the ground was dry and crystallized. Nothing grew within its boundaries, but the salt sparkled, and the terrain rose in peaks and mounds that were quite beautiful.

When Cephas had moved from a crutch to a walking stick, he carved himself a staff so he could help Nathor with the herd. After the boy joined the group, and the rope restraints were taken off his wrists, he had made a staff for himself also, leaving the bottom with two prongs. Tonight Cephas had seen the wisdom in this tool. When the boy saw the viper, he grabbed his staff and carefully pinned the snake in place with the forked end until Messa cut off its head. The boy then sought to save the smitten animal. Only after he saw that they couldn't save it, did he go after the runaway.

———◦◦◦◦———

The young slave was slowly gaining on the wild-eyed donkey. The moon was almost full, casting long shadows from the craggy forms. Although the ground was rough and untraveled, the sure-footed youth moved with practiced skill. "You don't know who you're running from," he said as he ran. "I'll overtake you in no time." He ignored the aching in his throat and the cutting rocks under his feet. The feel of the wind on his face and the freedom of stretching his legs felt invigorating to him. *Just a few more steps and I'll be able to reach the rope.*

He was soon alongside the runaway, but as he grabbed onto the dangling rope, the animal lurched and pulled the boy off his feet. He held on tenaciously, however, until the donkey wearied of the burden he was dragging and finally slowed to a stop. By then the boy had been dragged over a surface of salt and rocks, which scraped his elbows, arms, and legs, and left the wounds stinging deeply from the salt. The donkey panted in exhaustion while the boy also struggled to catch his breath.

The lad knew this country. He got up, stumbled a few steps, then stood still for a long time, looking in the direction of Bethlehem, tears washing his face and mingling with the salt powder that covered him. He looked to a faraway place in his mind, then down at the donkey, then away again, back and forth until he shook his head, squared his shoulders and led the donkey back towards camp. "So you want your freedom, do you?" he said to the animal. "So do I. We are both prisoners. But I have great things ahead for me." Then he began to cry again.

When camp was restored to its normal calm, the men went back to their beds. "I'll watch for him," Cephas told them. Two hours had passed since the disruption, so he took a water bag and began to walk in the direction of the chase. He was beginning to worry that he might not see his helper again when he heard a noise in the distance. He stood still beside a pedestal of salt and waited, the cool white moon lighting the scene before him. As the sound drew near, he could see the youth limping along and scolding the errant donkey. Cephas stepped out in his path, and the boy immediately assumed the pose of the senseless mute.

"You don't have to pretend any longer with me," Cephas said gently. "I heard you talking just now, well enough to know that you not only have speech, but high breeding too. Let me be your friend." He looked at the wounds on his battered body.

The boy kept his head down and said nothing. Cephas came alongside him as the boy kept walking. "Wait," he said, "we must tend to your wounds. Ahkmar would not like his merchandise damaged." He gave the boy a drink, then wet the hem of his own garment and wiped his salty stained face.

Finally the young slave looked at Cephas and spoke for the first time. "No one has to worry about me." His voice broke. "I'll still be able to do more than my share of the work."

Cephas spoke in a soothing voice. "I am not worried about your ability to work. I've seen what you can do. But I've had doubts about you." He reached inside his tunic. He had fashioned a bag that hung around his neck in which he kept odds and ends. He pulled out two browning apple cores. "These are for you. I saw you give your meager portion to Mahta."

The boy took the cores and ate them hungrily, every seed, every morsel. "Well if one like you has doubts about me, then I really must be in trouble."

"And who is one like me? Is my pretending better than yours?" The old man laughed.

"Why did you doubt me?"

"I've watched you these few days since you joined us, and even though you pretend to be slow, something shows through—a dignity. And now that I hear your speech, I perceive you to be a well-bred Hebrew."

"But if you had those thoughts, might not the others have doubts? Might not my life be at risk?"

Cephas felt empathy for the injured boy. He had the urge to protect and help him, but his ward was proud, so he said, "I like to think I'm at least a few steps ahead of these Ishmaelites."

"You and I are both too smart for them," the youth said. "But for the moment, we're the slaves and they're the masters."

"Why did you come back just now?" Cephas asked. "You could have taken the donkey and kept going."

The boy lowered his head. "I have my reasons, and it comes to more than honor. Why are you here?"

As he spoke, the boy stumbled slightly and Cephas reached over and put his shoulder under the boy's arm to support him, saying, "Here, lean on me." He then said, "I owe Ahkmar my life, and they trust me."

"I've been wondering if they have misgivings about me."

"They do."

"How do you know?"

"I've seen the master watching you. He often glances over his shoulder. I heard him talking with his men today. Ahkmar asked Messa many questions. He wanted an accounting of all you do. He again went over the details of what Messa saw before he purchased you. He mused about your being dressed only in a loin cloth, and asked if there was any other clothing in the cistern where they drew you up. After Ahkmar was satisfied that you were the only one to be sold, he boasted about his cunning bargaining. But he doubts that you are really speechless, and is uneasy about keeping you. He gave orders to watch for other caravans. He wants to unload you at the first opportunity and will use the excuse that he plans to discontinue his slaves and deal only in animals from now on."

The boy looked around and said in a lowered voice, "We must be careful. We're coming close to camp and I don't want to be heard."

"And I don't want to be caught talking with you. I'm eager to know more about you and tell you my story, but for now, we must be quiet. I'll get some oil and attend to your scrapes."

The boy reached out and gripped Cephas's arm. "Thank you, friend," he said quietly. "My name is Joseph."

# Chapter Three

# Sold Again

They intersected the new caravan about mid-morning the following day. As they came nearer, it was obvious they were a large outfit—ostentatious in their finery. Colorful harnesses and tassels decorated the animals. Men and women in the caravan were brightly dressed to attract the attention of all who passed. But the man on the lead camel was most conspicuous, costumed in the garb of the Orient. His white shirt was shimmery and full, gathered at the wrists and covered by a long vest of red and orange stripes. His flowing purple pants ballooned to the ankle, showing off his pointed embroidered shoes. Cocked on his head was a gold tasseled hat which he wore like a crown.

They had been to the sea port in the west where they had purchased goods from a trading vessel. They also had numerous slaves banded together in organized rows. As was often the case, these slaves were men who had left their homes and families to go into battle for their king. Their army had been defeated, so they were taken prisoner. The custom required that the losers in such battles be put to death, or be dealt with as the victorious king saw fit. In this case, some were kept as the king's captives, while the rest had been sold to these traders and were now to be put on the slave block in Egypt. They numbered twenty in all.

Ahkmar was pleased. He knew they would take his three slaves without too much notice. He didn't order his servants to prepare them for sale. He didn't want to appear too eager. Nor did he want the boy to look too good. The less conspicuous, the better. He prided himself on being a shrewd bargainer. He would not show his eagerness to see the foreign goods. He would wait until his counterpart made the first move.

Almost as if by a signal, the workers watched the men approach one another. From the first gestures, they knew they were in for a long afternoon.

Ahkmar bowed ingratiatingly and smiled his best smile. "Greetings. I am Ahkmar, an Ishmaelite son of Hamar from Gilead, a humble trader, willing to be of any service."

The rich merchant eyed Ahkmar, assessing his challenge. "My name is Kumash, son of Oman, a Midianite from east of the river. I have just obtained many goods. I need nothing, but perhaps I can be of benefit to you. It seems I've heard the name of Ahkmar, the trader."

Ahkmar kept bowing and said, "Yes, and the name of Kumash, the merchant, is well-known. I'm glad to have the privilege of this meeting."

The workers set about preparing the main tent. Anyone else would have had a tent made of black goat hair, like Ahkmar's. But the larger caravan pulled out one of their finest, unlike any seen before. It was a brilliant yellow, orange, green, and blue, patched together of densely-woven fabrics. The workers set about doing chores while they waited.

The two men entered the tent and sat on colorful, thick pillows while the servants brought refreshment. The head servant passed hot drinks poured from a large pot with a long pouring spout. Dense brown bread and soft white cheese were served with some dates and raisins.

The contrast between the two men was dramatic. Ahkmar had a dark complexion and small frame, while Kumash was large and rotund, with curly graying hair and beard. The two bargainers sipped the hot drink and talked about the weather, their ancestors, their circumstances and misfortunes. Eventually Kumash broached the subject of trade.

"You say you deal mostly in animals. Well, if you have some beasts to help carry our load, I could let go some of my goods in exchange for, say, a couple of camels—and I can always use a few more milking goats to help feed my camp."

"Yes, yes," Ahkmar said. "You will see what fine, fat goats we have. You may have them at a bargain, and I will let go my camels just because I esteem you so highly."

Kumash motioned for a bundle to be brought. As the layers were pulled back, Ahkmar's eyes quickly surveyed the beauty of the contents, but he wouldn't reveal his interest. The bundle held some exotic cloth goods as well as spices and oils.

"These fabrics come from the East, where people know the secrets of fine weaving. A man would be envied who walked with wives dressed in such excellence."

Ahkmar tried to show his practiced indifference. "Yes, they look rich, but I like to keep my wives humble. I don't wish to be set upon by thieves."

"Then perhaps you'd like some sturdy tent fabric, or I have many other items," Kumash said.

"I'm sure you do, and we could be here all night. But if you have nothing else as excellent as the cloth, I will have to sacrifice my animals for that since it's the only thing suitable for exchange."

Finally, they neared a settlement, and Ahkmar said, "To show my great generosity, and as a gesture of friendship in case we ever want to trade again, I will include my three slaves for only half their value. You are no doubt on your way to the slave market in Egypt. My path takes a different direction."

"You said nothing of slaves. I don't need more slaves. I already have more than I can handle." The three had been brought and made to kneel just inside the door. The boy lifted his head briefly to look at their potential owner, Kumash, who only glanced at them, then continued. "But I'll take them off your hands since you're trying to get rid of them."

"Ah, you see right through me. The truth is, I'm going out of the slave business so I can develop a more excellent herd of animals. You would be doing me a favor to take the three."

"Then let it be done."

"Yes, and may the gods smile on you."

By dawn the next morning, Ahkmar's caravan was gone, heavier by one trunk of exotic treasure.

Joseph found himself being hustled into the master's tent along with Cephas and the young girl. The three were pushed forward and made to kneel as Kumash spoke in a large voice. "So, this is the bonus I inherited from that clever weasel, Ahkmar. Here we have an old man with only a few teeth, a girl child too frail to lift a bucket, and a skinned-up boy who the servants tell me is not what he seems. What am I to make of this? Tell me more about yourselves. You, young man." He gestured to Joseph. "Stand. What do we have in you?"

Servants were not allowed to look directly into the eyes of their superiors, but this young man seemed oblivious to the fact. For the first time since he set out, Joseph now pulled himself up to his full stature and looked Kumash directly in the eyes. "I sense in you, sir, a man I can trust. My name is Joseph. I am seventeen years old. I cannot tell you more—my story is my own and it's better that you do not know it. I'm a slave. You bought me. You own me." He raised his right arm and continued. "As I live, I will serve you to the best of my ability. I am here because I choose to be. I will not try to run away."

Mahta watched the scene in awe, an audible gasp escaping her lips even as her hand flew up to cover her mouth. Here was every hero she could imagine: her father, Sashi, and now her protector, and his name was Joseph.

Kumash lifted his eyebrows, leaned back in his chair and folded his arms. "Well," he said, as he considered Joseph. "I can see there's more to you than what appears, although I can see plenty. You're very large for seventeen. You're well-taught in speech and manners. Behind the wounds and dirt, I see a handsome youth. No wonder Ahkmar was eager to be rid of you. It is obvious that you are well-born. I'm sure your story is worth knowing, but your trust is not wasted on me. I will trust you also. I accept your oath. Maybe sometime I may learn more of you. Since you were not restrained by Ahkmar and did not try to escape, I won't chain you with the other slaves. I'll give you the status of servant. I am told you are good with animals, so you will assist my other servants in the care of my animals."

Joseph bowed and masked his relief. "Thank you. I will serve you well."

"Yes, I believe you will. And it's well you didn't reveal yourself to that fox, Ahkmar. He would have slit your throat and left you to die if he had felt he was really in danger. It will be well for both of us that he sold you to me." Kumash gestured for Joseph to step aside. "And what of you, old man?" He motioned Cephas to stand.

The old man was bone thin, yet still tall and not bent. His white beard and full head of hair made him look older than his age, though his skin was hardly wrinkled. His blue eyes were bright, his manner guarded.

"If your trust is also offered to me," Cephas said, "then I will unburden myself of my tale."

"As long as it's short." Kumash smiled, holding up his hand. "We expect to do some traveling today."

"That satisfies me. I am a man of few words. In short, then, I was traveling with my wife, my daughter, and her family when we were struck down by thieves, robbed of all worldly possessions, and left for dead." His voice cracked slightly, but he continued. "I was barely alive, but I had managed to crawl some distance when Ahkmar's caravan rescued me. He fed and clothed me and sold me to you. Was that short enough?" His voice got stronger. "I am not toothless, as you said. My teeth were chipped when they beat me. And don't let my white hair fool you; I am strong and can work hard. I am willing to be your slave, for I have nothing left of my own."

Joseph looked at the old man, whose voice bore a sorrow that could not be hidden. Yet he knew the man was capable of great charity.

"Yes, yes," Kumash said. "I am surprised by your character. Perhaps in time I may know all the details of your story." He gestured to the girl. "Now you, wretched child. Arise and tell me about yourself."

She was covered with dirt, her light brown hair matted, her skin marred from exposure to the sun. That she was fair under the covering of filth was still apparent. If Ahkmar had bothered, he could have shaved his slaves' heads and cleaned them up for the sale. He had done neither.

She looked toward Cephas for support. He nodded to her, so in a small voice she said, "My name is Mahta. My mother died when I was four years old. When my father got sick, he was afraid he might die, so he arranged a marriage for me. He promised all his wealth and belongings to the groom's family if they would take me in." She stopped, swallowed hard, and again looked at Cephas.

Kumash suppressed impatience. "And did your father die?"

"Yes. My uncle was there. He said he would arrange things for me, but he didn't arrange anything and took me away to his house. He was a bad man. He sold me to Ahkmar and kept all of my father's belongings."

"So Ahkmar sold you to me, and what am I to do with you?"

"Oh, I can work. I'm strong for my size."

"May I speak?" Cephas said. "I don't need much food. If you will place her in my care, we can share provisions and I'll see that she is no trouble to you."

"And I'll help look after the two of them," Joseph said. "I promise you'll not be sorry."

"I am already sorry. I can't imagine why I agreed to take in such a threesome. But now we must waste no more time. Do as you will with them, Joseph. We will talk later. I'll have some clothes and food sent to you—you look half-starved. Now get to your tasks."

Joseph learned his duties as a servant quickly and worked quietly and well. As he worked, he wondered at having received the responsibility for these two unusual souls. They, in turn, tried to make themselves useful and stayed near Joseph, trusting in him.

This caravan differed greatly from the pitiful one belonging to Ahkmar. Kumash was a fine merchant, a trader of skill. In addition to the six men he employed to drive his twenty slaves, he also had six men who tended the animals, managed the five tents, and kept them mended. They also took turns seeing to their master's personal needs and comforts. He didn't have wives, but he had two young servant girls, whom he had given the status of concubines. Some of the men who had been with him a long time were allowed to bring their wives on this trip. The women's tent housed six. These women did the cooking, baking, serving, and weaving.

Transporting their personal goods and merchandise required the use of pack animals. With the new acquisitions from Ahkmar, they now had five camels and six donkeys. Four goats gave milk for drinking and for making cheese. Chickens provided eggs and sometimes meat. They also acquired three large ewes whose wool could be carded and their meat used as food.

───

The caravan traveled south, pushing on a small distance each day, and each day the three newcomers made themselves more useful until they had settled into a routine.

Mahta helped with the daily meals, and the women were glad to have another pair of hands. At first she brought them pots and water jugs, or bits of wood and dung to burn. She watched eagerly as they prepared the food, and was so willing to do their bidding that they gradually gave her more responsibilities. They taught her their recipes and techniques, and she absorbed new knowledge like the desert drinks water. She soon learned to grind the wheat used in meals and flavor it with berry seeds, citrus rind, and herbs. They made different kinds of breads, depending on their journey, and she helped with the flat breads and the large, leavened brown loaves. She assisted in making kefir from the goat's milk and sometimes added raisins, nuts, or honey to it. They also made cheese in different forms, hard and soft, which she especially enjoyed.

Cephas and Joseph cared for the animals. The two of them had always worked well together, and now they added their efforts and knowledge to that of the other workers. Joseph knew how to mend an animal's broken leg, and when a sheep was injured, he carried it on his shoulders for several days until it could get around on its own. Cephas knew what to do when a goat's milk slowed, or a ewe was late to birth. He was also experienced at repairing the tents, and he skillfully showed a worker how to mend them so the stitches on the elaborate, thick fabrics didn't show.

Kumash seemed relieved that the three were independent, good workers. Joseph had healed quickly and never complained of his sores and bruises. Kumash also noticed how people reacted to Joseph. *He really doesn't know how becoming he is.*

The women acted like giddy girls when he was near. The men either hated him, or wanted to be better around him. Joseph's transformation from mute to servant gave him added energy. He seemed to suddenly appear to help with an animal in need, or a person needing a hand.

In Ahkmar's service, Mahta had either held Cephas's hand or walked among Nathor's sheep. She loved sinking her fingers into their kinky wool and hanging on. As they settled into their routine, she took up the habit again. Ahkmar had insisted she could not keep her lammy, so after many tears, she resigned herself to her loss and took her lullaby to the other lambs. The few goats and sheep seemed to like her as much as she liked them.

One day Mahta's attention was diverted by a playful goat on her left, and as she watched it, she put out her right hand to resume hold on an old sheep. Saku, the slaver, thought he would play a joke. He quietly moved in where the ewe had been and bent his head to the right level so that when Mahta grabbed for wool, she grabbed Saku's hair instead. Those who had watched the deception laughed, but the child put her eyes to the ground and wished she could disappear. She looked around for Sashi, but couldn't see him.

# Chapter Four

# Khamsin—Time to Talk

The land was changing from the familiar rocky terrain Joseph knew to a flatter sandy floor. The colors were reddening. In the distance to the west were small mountains shaped like great, round loaves of bread.

They had not traveled far one day when the animals became agitated. Someone shouted, "Khamsin! Khamsin! The East Wind comes!"

The warning brought immediate action from everyone. The damaging wind storm could harm property and animals if they were not protected. Kumash called out orders and the caravan was quickly transformed into a camp. Joseph hurriedly blindfolded the animals and led them to an area they had secured with posts and ropes. Sensing the danger, the animals yielded to Joseph's proddings and huddled together. Joseph's quick action did not go unnoticed by Kumash.

Like a great curtain unfolding, it came. By the time the men had finished with the animals, visibility was fading and darkness was closing in.

Inside the large worker's tent, the men had already gathered to play gambling games, ignoring the storm and the roaring of the wind around them. They didn't notice when Cephas brought the girl, Mahta, into the men's tent and settled her in a corner beside himself. Joseph, having secured everything to his satisfaction, entered and seated himself by Cephas. Mahta curled herself up at their feet.

"I'm glad they're involved in their games," Cephas said. "This gives us a chance to talk."

"Yes," Joseph said. "We both have much to share. First, let me say how much I appreciate the way we work together. The moment I think we need something, you're there with it."

"Yes, I've noticed how we seem to think alike and how you are so quick to attend to the needs of others. Let's hope our work continues to be compatible. As long as things go smoothly, we'll have no trouble from the others."

They continued their conversation, unaware that they were being watched. Joseph looked down at Mahta, who was already asleep, and smiled.

"She's a dear child," Cephas said. "She's makes a tremendous effort working with the women, and they seem to like her. She doesn't talk to herself as she did at first. I think she's happy with us."

"Where is she from?"

"She told me she's an Ammonite—I'd like to confront that uncle of hers."

"Yes, but perhaps she's better off with us. At least for now we can watch over her. I notice you have started to clean her up. It was good of you to find her some salve to protect her skin."

"I couldn't get a comb through her hair; it's become so tangled and matted I had to cut some of it off, poor thing. What will become of her, I wonder?"

He sat silent for a few moments and then turned and looked at Joseph. "Are you ready to tell me about yourself?"

"Yes," Joseph said. "I believe the difficult part is past. Now I can face the future."

"But you have no idea what lies in the future."

"Whatever it is, I'm resolved to face it."

"How did you come to this resolve?"

Joseph leaned back and looked at the heaving sides of the worker's tent. "I had a dream. You see, I believe that some dreams are significant and that I have a gift."

Cephas smiled. "I notice you don't let modesty get in your way."

Joseph looked a little surprised and said, "If I sound boastful, it's only that I desire to speak truth. I know I need to learn to cloak my speech in modesty. In fact, I am striving to overcome many of my childish ways. I feel I have grown up very fast in a short while, so bear with me and I will try to do better."

"I'm sorry, Joseph. Go on."

Joseph looked straight at Cephas and said, "I believe that my God speaks to me in the visions of the night."

Cephas met his gaze and said, "My God, too."

Joseph looked thoughtfully at Cephas, then continued. "I have had many dreams telling me about my future. I also have a gift of interpreting."

"Yes, I understand."

"You do? You understand about my God? About my dreams?" He paused. "Cephas, do you believe in the Living God, Yahweh?"

"I do indeed."

Joseph grabbed Cephas into a big hug while they both laughed. Mahta stirred and sat up. Some of the men looked over at them from across the room, then returned to their game. One pretended to play, but kept watching the three.

Joseph spoke a little softer, although the wind outside easily covered their conversation. "There are so few who believe anymore. I had thought I would never find another believer since leaving my home. Tell me, my friend, about yourself."

Cephas began. "I am the son of Eliar, the high priest out of Jobab, out of Eber. I was born in Salem and lived my youth in the house of Shem."

Joseph leaned forward with sudden interest and asked, "You lived in the Great House of Learning? My father and his father also lived and studied for a time in the house of Shem. Did you know Eber, Abraham's fourth great grandfather who outlived him? And did you know Abraham's son, Isaac, and his son Jacob?"

Cephas looked intently at Joseph's face. "I knew them all. But now I'm puzzled, for theirs is the great covenant line—the line of the patriarchs. They called Shem the king of Salem, and truly he was. But while every leader of a walled city calls himself king, Shem would not take that title. He said that to be a prophet-patriarch and spokesman for God required constant humility, and the very name of king belied that role. The birthright responsibility of his descendants was upheld in the same way as it was passed down. Shem renewed it when he placed his hands on Abraham and pronounced a holy blessing on him. It was Eber, the great leader, from whom the title Hebrew was taken."

Cephas continued. "I loved and respected father Abraham, the greatest man I have ever known. He traveled from Babylon to Egypt and to all the countries between and taught them the mysteries of God. It was my privilege in the Great House to study the eternal principles reflected by the heavens as taught by Abraham after his great vision. So now, Joseph, how is it that you are of this royal lineage?"

"I bear the birthright given me by my father, Jacob."

Cephas sat upright, his face astonished. "Well, I won't say I don't believe you, but if we do not lie, then here in this slave tent sits the crown prince of the earth and one of God's high priests." They both laughed again.

"Oh, it feels good to laugh. It's been a long time since I had anything to laugh about. It will be good to have you as a friend, dear Cephas."

Mahta, sitting with her arms around her knees, listened intently to the men she grew more attached to each day.

The head slaver, who had been watching, now glared over at the three.

Lowering his voice again, Joseph said, "I'm not lying. It's because of my birthright that I'm here. I'll tell you my story, and you'll see why I say that, and why my dreams are significant."

"I don't doubt it," Cephas said. "And now I know what it was that I saw in you. I'm in awe. I wonder what part God has for you to play in these unlikely events."

"And I believe that before we're through, we'll know the role you're to play. I don't believe any of this is happening by chance."

Joseph and Cephas huddled and talked, unaware of their surroundings. Day had turned to night and the Khamsin had passed. One by one, the men on the other side of the tent left to prepare for the night. Mahta slipped out of the tent to go to the women's side.

After watching them, Saku saw an opportunity. He didn't like the looks of Joseph and Cephas, or the way they kept to themselves. The fact that their status was different from the other slaves bothered him, and he was jealous that Kumash had given them special attention. *What do they have to laugh about?*

He got up after Mahta left and caught up with her near the animal yard. He crept up behind her and said, "You shouldn't be out here alone, *yaldah.*"

Mahta started and turned to see the stocky slaver. His hair was red, his beard scruffy, his eyes half-lidded like a serpent's. His nose was too large for his face, and his jutting chin was menacing as intended.

Mahta cowered back. "I– I'm all right." She looked away. "I have Joseph and Cephas to look after me."

"But they're busy talking and you need someone strong like me. I can treat you like a little princess, can't I?" He stepped closer.

"No, don't come near me. I don't like you."

He brought his sneering face closer to hers. "I'm in charge of the slaves; you must do what I say."

She tried to move away, but he pressed closer, his foul breath almost smothering her. Her tiny frame was no match for his.

"Don't scream," he said, and put his hand over her mouth. "You're only a slave; I can do what I want with you."

Close behind, a strong voice demanded, "Saku, you are wrong! She is under my charge and you shall release her immediately." It was Cephas.

Saku turned angrily, but kept a firm grip on Mahta's arm. "I'm the head slaver! Get off, old man, or you'll get the whip."

Cephas reached for Mahta's arm and said, "Come with me, child."

Quick as a serpent, Saku struck repeated blows to Cephas's face. Cephas staggered backwards, blood coming from his nose and mouth, the gash above his eye reopened and bleeding again.

Suddenly Saku felt his robe tighten and his body lifted into the air. Joseph held him aloft, then slammed him to the ground.

By now, some of the other workers had gathered around. Saku regained his stance and snarled at Joseph. "I'll have you whipped! Who do you think you are that you can do this to me?"

"You will know who I am if you ever dare touch one of mine again," Joseph said.

"Oh, it's 'one of mine' is it?"

Kumash appeared through the spectators. "What's going on here? You know that the rules prohibit fighting."

"These men attacked me," Saku said.

"I've no doubt who the attacker is," Kumash said as he glanced at Mahta's tear-streaked face. He turned to the group. "You men here—how did this happen?"

"The old man started it," one said.

"That's right," another said.

Kumash looked from one to the next as each nodded agreement.

"Very well. The law of the caravan demands its due. Saku, you will render ten lashes to Joseph, and five to the old man since he is accused of starting the fight. But when you're finished, I'll see you all in my tent."

"But shouldn't it be fifteen and ten lashes?" Saku gripped his whip with one hand and began stroking it with the other.

"No!" Kumash said.

"What about the girl?" Saku said. "She should get a few stripes."

"You shall not touch the child!"

"But she does have to watch."

Kumash relented. "Yes, she must watch." He hurried away.

Mahta was held by the other slavers as the clothes were torn from the backs of her guardians. Cephas tried to be brave, but already weak from the pounding by Saku, he was unable to stifle his groans, and by the fourth sear, he cried out in agony and lost consciousness.

"That will do," Kumash shouted from the door of the tent.

Joseph, barely healing from being dragged, was stung as hard as Saku could manage. He gritted his teeth and prayed, maintaining silence through the first eight stripes, but cries of anguish followed the last two.

Mahta's uncle had trained her to hold her tears, so she held back as long as she could, then let go and sobbed uncontrollably as the flesh of her guardians was slashed. "Sashi," she cried, before she passed out.

All three were taken before Kumash, and when the slavers released their grip on Cephas's arms, he slumped to the floor. Joseph knelt beside him and made sure he was still breathing.

Saku stood, legs apart, hands on hips and a snarled grin on his face.

"Are you satisfied that the law has been fulfilled, Saku?"

"Yes, Master. As always, I'm here to do your bidding."

"Then I bid you leave my sight and this caravan. Let me never see you again. If I had proof of my suspicions, I could have you stoned."

"But— but Master!"

"Out! Throw this man out! Give him provisions, but he is to be killed if he ever comes near this camp again. And take your lying cohorts with you!"

# Chapter Five

# New Appointments

Kumash dismissed everyone from his tent except the three.

"Now that we have done justice to the law of the slaves, let me say to you, Joseph and Cephas, I'm sorry. To you I say it, but to no other. You have not betrayed my trust in you. It grieves me that this penalty had to be carried out. Joseph, I would like you to take Saku's place as head slaver."

Joseph, leaving Cephas in a kneeling position, struggled to his feet and stood before Kumash. It was difficult to speak. "Thank you for your trust in me," he said, trying not to wince. "I'll do whatever you bid. But I beg you find another to be in charge of slaves. I'll continue to serve as well as I can, but not as slaver."

Kumash, with raised brow, regarded Joseph for a long moment. Finally he said, "I see. You're afraid you might have to render the whip. Is that it?"

"Yes, sir."

"I'm sure there are others who would happily carry out the task of disciplinarian, though I've never known anyone who enjoyed inflicting pain as much as Saku. But for now, I'm announcing that the charge of the servants is in your hands, Joseph. Cephas, you shall be in charge of the animals. Now go, all three of you, and see to your wounds. I want you all strong and able. Joseph, have audience with me when you're restored." Kumash summoned the other servants to assist the wounded back to their tent.

They had been back in their quarters only a short time. Mahta had washed their wounds and applied oil when Kumash's servant, Hasaan, came and announced in a loud voice, "The master sends word that we will remain in this camp one more day."

Joseph and Cephas looked at each other. "Do you suppose he's worried about another Khamsin?" Joseph asked.

"No," Cephas said. "He probably needs to stop now and then to let the animals graze and to let the women catch up on the cleaning, baking, and sewing. The men must also hunt and gather firewood. Besides, I think he wants to give us a chance to heal."

"He has a good heart under that tough hide."

"May God bless him."

"And us."

"I'm glad for the rest," Cephas said. "We need another day to finish our talk. Are you able to sleep?"

"Yes, in spite of the pain, I'll sleep tonight."

Mahta spoke. "Joseph, Cephas, will you teach me about your God? My father prayed—he had small statues of wood and stone—but I never—"

"Of course, child," Cephas said. "We'll teach you of the One True God."

"He's your God, too," Joseph said. "He's the Father of all our spirits."

"And he loves you very much. Now go to sleep."

Mahta looked pleased. "Good night, Joseph and Cephas."

"Good night, Mahta."

---

The next morning Mahta was up early. She came back in the tent as Joseph was stirring and told the two men, "You don't need to get up. The other servants have done your work."

Cephas raised his head. "Kumash must really want us to get better."

"It looks that way," Joseph said, struggling to get up. "How do you feel?"

"Terrible. But my voice and my ears still work."

Mahta had begun to apply the healing oil to Joseph's back once again, and he shuddered at her touch even though it was gentle. His wounds throbbed and he knew the burning and stinging would continue for many days.

She lifted her hand and, trying to hide her tears, said, "I'm sorry, Joseph. I don't want to hurt you even more."

"Please continue, Mahta. Your hands heal and help. Don't be troubled. The pain will soon pass."

After the two were fed, nursed, and rested, Cephas opened the discussion again. "Joseph, I've been pondering several questions. First, why did you pretend to be without speech?"

Joseph gave a brief smile. "The day I joined Ahkmar's caravan, I refused to acknowledge that I was any part of it. I was shocked and couldn't believe that my brothers had actually sold me."

"Your brothers sold you?" Cephas asked.

"They did. I'll explain later." He went on. "I kept looking back over my shoulder, hoping to see rescuers. Then Ahkmar led us into what seemed a reckless path. He could have taken the much-traveled road through the Jordan valley, or even the less-used trail that hugs the shore of the sea. But when he led us through the valley of caves full of thieves and robbers, I knew that my brothers would never think to follow us there. But I kept hoping. I was relieved the cave dwellers didn't bother us, although at times I worried to see such wretched-looking men eyeing our supply animals. But God was with us."

"You know," Cephas said, "Ahkmar paid them to leave us alone."

"So that was it." Joseph paused, then resumed. "Now, as I look back, I see that to have taken such a dangerous route, Ahkmar must have been suspicious that the circumstances of my purchase were not normal. His plan worked, however. It took us three days longer to join the main road again. And such a twisting passage would certainly confuse any pursuers.

"It was on that first day, struggling to negotiate the difficult passage, that I realized I wasn't the only slave. I had no interest in what was going on around me, so I kept my head down. When Ahkmar's men switched at my legs, it was difficult to run with my hands tied behind me and not stumble over the treacherous rocks.

"Then I heard a stifled scream and saw the little girl child fallen on a stone and trying to right herself to avoid more lashes. It was you, Cephas, who lifted her up and took the switches in her stead.

"At first, I wouldn't talk because I was so hurt. All I could do was feel sorry for myself, still not believing what was happening. Later, I figured I was better off to keep quiet. I didn't want to bring shame to my brothers, and I felt God was cautioning me."

Cephas nodded, "That explains why you wouldn't speak. In our talk yesterday, you began to tell me about your dreams."

"That's right," Joseph said. "Remember the first night we talked, the night the donkey broke loose? Only a few nights before, I had a dream that changed my life. That day we passed within a short distance of my mother's grave in Bethlehem. It had been a practice of ours, as I traveled with my father, to visit the resting place of my mother, where I would unburden my feelings. The thoughts of my mother's burial place stirred me to break away and run to her plot, but some stronger sense within me held me back and calmed me. That night I poured out my soul to God, and He answered me with a dream.

"In the dream it was nighttime and the stars were bright. I was looking at a range of mountains and one drew my attention because it stood taller, more majestic than the others. As I contemplated its beauty and purpose, a line of stars moved down and encircled the large mountain. On its peak I noticed a sparkling crown. Then the outer stars changed into crowns and came to rest on the smaller mountains. I saw that there were twelve peaks surrounding the largest mountain, each capped by a crown.

"As I awakened and considered the significance of the dream, I reasoned that the taller mountain was my father and the twelve smaller mountains were his twelve sons. I also realized something else. I had planned to break away as we passed near my home in Hebron. But after the dream, I worried about what would happen if my father found out what his sons had done. If my brothers found me at home, would they resume their hatred of me and even try to kill me again? I would also risk being killed by Ahkmar's men if I tried to escape. The dream meant to me that twelve nations were to emerge from me and my eleven brothers. How could my brothers be God's leaders if they were not worthy, or how could there be twelve if I were dead? These disturbing questions were resounding in my head.

"I fell to my knees and asked God what I should do. For the first time since I left my brothers, I felt a warm, comforting peace. I heard, as a still small voice, God saying, 'Go on thy way, I will be with thee. My peace shall attend thee. Go to Egypt that my purposes may be fulfilled. In thee, all nations shall be blessed.'"

"That is what you meant when you said you were resolved to go through with it," Cephas said. "What a responsibility you bear. How honored I am to be a part of this. Where will this path lead?"

As the men sat quietly, a small voice said, "Please, Joseph, ask your God if I can go with you. We three can be a family." They turned and looked down at Mahta's hopeful eyes.

Joseph said, "We'll see this thing through, the three of us."

Cephas spoke again. "I think we're ready to hear more of your experience, Joseph. Are you willing to tell us now?"

# Chapter Six

# Joseph Tells His Story

I was born in Haran, in the house of my mother's father, Laban. My father, Jacob, worked fourteen years for Laban for the privilege of marrying my mother. She was a beautiful woman and he loved her dearly. Laban gave my father his two daughters—first Leah, then Rachel, my mother. Jacob loved Rachel more, but he was an upright and dutiful husband to both women.

Leah bore my father four sons: Reuben, Simeon, Levi, and Judah.

It grieved my mother that she couldn't conceive, so she gave her handmaid, Bilha, to my father to bear children for him. Bilha gave birth to Dan and Naptali, and my mother felt somewhat fulfilled with the two babies. She gave them much affection and love.

Then Leah gave her handmaid, Zilpa, to my father, and she bore two more sons, Gad and Asher. After the eighth son was born by Zilpa, Leah again gave birth—to Isacar and then Zebulon.

Finally, there was great happiness for my father when my mother conceived and I was born—the eleventh of twelve sons. Leah also had a daughter, Dinah.

All my childhood, I loved being around my brothers. They had been given certain blessings of unique promise from God. Everything they did seemed to bear out their promise. As with my father, everything they touched seemed to flourish. Our fields produced abundantly. Our herds and cattle multiplied.

My brothers were large and strong. I remember how they made sport. They wrestled and competed one with another. They could all run very fast, Judah being one of the fastest. But Naptali was more swift in a race than even Judah. He always acted as the messenger for my father.

In wrestling, it was Simeon who could not be taken. I looked up to Simeon with admiration and continually sought his approval, but never found it.

Reuben was rightfully the oldest brother because he always looked after the rest of us. He came readily to our defense and offered comfort in our need.

Judah was superb at all sports—at everything he did. Some of my brothers, like Gad and Dan, and sometimes Asher, acted as if they hated me. They were jealous of my father's affection for me. Simeon showed his disdain by ignoring me. Since Isacar and Zebulon were closer to me in age than the others, we played together as children. Zebulon loved me, and we shared much. Isacar was good, and always walked in the ways of the Lord.

We left Haran when I was nine years old. Laban was feeling threatened because of my father's abundance. It was also time, my father felt, for him to resume his duties in his birthright home. My grandfather, Isaac, awaited our return in Hebron of Canaan.

On the trip home, my father had a special confrontation with a heavenly being, which marked a place in his earthly path. After the vision, God changed his name from *Jacob* to *Israel*.

It was also on the trip home that my mother, who was again with child, went into labor. It was near Bethlehem that my brother, Benjamin, was born. My mother died giving birth. My father was inconsolable. As if to assuage his grief, he drew me closer to him. Whether because I have my mother's features, or because I was her first son, I believe my father was comforted when I was near. The baby, Benjamin, was coddled and cherished by him and loved by all of us.

In my grandfather Isaac's house I felt great peace. As head of us all, he would gather his family to prayers in morning and evening. He raised his arms in prayer and it seemed as if he talked with his best friend when he talked with God. We sang and danced in the circle of the great patriarch. We were taught the ways of truth daily. Our life was good.

My father, staggering under the weight of my mother's death, was dealt another blow. The all-important birthright of the covenant, renewed with God through my great grandfather Abraham and handed to Isaac and then to my father, was due to be handed to Reuben, the eldest of my father's sons. So when father found Reuben lying with Bilha, my mother's handmaid, his heart was broken even more. Reuben was contrite and repentant, but he could no longer receive the birthright.

At this point my father, Israel, decided to keep me by his side. While my brothers were in the fields, he daily taught me lessons—all things from the beginning: things which have been, things of the earth and of the heavens. I was taught the greatness and goodness of God, obedience, repentance, faith, and the efficacy of prayer. My heart was full. I desired knowledge and righteousness. My father and I became very close. He was a great man and taught as much by example as by precept. I loved him more than I dared reveal, so I showed my love by taking in my lessons dutifully. My brother Benjamin also remained at home. He delighted everyone, and was a joy to me as well as to my father.

During my learning period, Isaac died. Everyone mourned him. His sons, Israel (Jacob) and Esau, buried him with his father, Abraham, his mother, Sarah, and beside his wife, Rebekah, in the cave of Macpelah in Hebron.

Around the time of my grandfather's death, my sister, Dinah, was abducted and defiled by the son of the king of Shechem. My brothers rescued Dinah, and in retribution completely laid waste to the city of Shechem. This began their reputation in the land as mighty warriors. No one has ever beaten my brothers in battle. They do not seek to contend, but when they fight to defend, they always win.

As I was studying with my father, I began to tell him of my dreams. He encouraged me to pay careful attention to certain ones. He told me God would speak to his servants through dreams.

One night I dreamed we were harvesting wheat. As we were binding our sheaves, my sheaf stood upright and all the others bowed down to mine. I told my family about the dream, but it caused my jealous brothers to hate me more than ever.

Then I had another dream. In this one the sun, moon, and stars bowed down to me. I should have been careful in recounting it, but I wasn't. My father even rebuked me this time, saying, "You mean your mother and your brothers and I are all going to bow to you?"

"I don't know what it means. I'm just telling you what I saw."

"Well, keep it to yourself," my father said.

I kept quiet after that. We went on with my studies and nothing more was said of it. My brothers were sent north to graze the sheep.

As my father healed from the wrong Reuben had done him, he had to make a decision. One day he called me to him. "You know, Joseph, that Reuben lost his claim to the birthright. I think some of my other sons think they are in line for it. Simeon is second to the oldest. Dan is the first son of Bilha, and Gad is the first son of Zilpa. In some cases, any one of these would be eligible. In the strictest sense of the birthright, however, it should go to the firstborn of my second wife, Rachel—which is you. If I were to decide by righteousness, I would also choose you. I expect much from you, Joseph."

"Oh, Father, I feel so unworthy—I am so young."

"God has chosen you, son, and He doesn't worry about age. Did He not ordain Noah when he was but ten years old? He has a great work for you to do."

I was very touched—and humbled. My wonderful father then laid his hands on my head and set me apart as the next prophet and patriarch. He told me, "To go with the office, Joseph, you are entitled to wear this garment."

He carefully brought out a beautiful coat, made of soft white skins, known by me as the cloak of authority. As he handled the garment, his face bore a look of great reverence. He said, "In this vestment is the power of the birthright, Joseph. It is sacred. Wear it in worthiness."

It might have gone well with me if I had heeded that advice. Unknown to my father, however, the next day when he asked me to take supplies and go check on my brothers, I decided to take the coat with me. As I walked I imagined how surprised they would be to see the symbol of authority I now owned. I anticipated their joy at my appointment.

I went far to find them. They had moved camp north to Dotham. I put on the coat and was wearing it as I walked into their camp. They saw me coming afar off. I saw the sudden movements of disgust exhibited by Simeon. Dan and Gad ran to Simeon, gesturing angrily. Asher joined in.

Too late I realized my foolishness. Why had I thought that they would be glad for me? I tried to reason with myself. I had been kept at home to learn my father's teachings. They must have, in some part, been expecting this appointment.

I thought to remove the coat, but already Zebulon and Reuben had reached me. Zebulon was happy to see me. Reuben looked worried. "Joseph, why?" he asked.

"I'm sorry, Reuben. I thought you would be glad."

"Zeb and I maybe, but..."

Isacar and Naptali joined us. "They are very angry," Isacar said, gesturing toward Simeon's group.

Levi stood in the center of camp by the fire, slowly shaking his head as we approached. He looked at me and said, "They are using harsh language. It sounds as if they are plotting to take your life."

"Here, give me the coat," Reuben said.

"What will you do with it?" I asked.

"I don't know. They need a chance to calm down. Simeon!" he called. "Come let us reason as brothers."

"So he can tell us more dreams?" Dan said.

"And shall we bow down to him?" Gad shouted.

Simeon came with angry strides straight toward me. Zebulon jumped between us and spread his arms in front of me.

"What do you want, Simeon?" Reuben asked. "Do you want the coat? Here, take it."

"I want him," Simeon said, pushing Zeb aside.

Judah threw his arms around Simeon's middle and pulled him back, saying, "Calm down and let's talk."

"We're reasonable men," Levi said.

Reuben nodded. "We shouldn't fight among ourselves."

"Something can be worked out," Isacar said.

By this time I was crying. Zebulon was still trying to cover me and was crying also.

"I won't talk with him here," Simeon said.

"And where can we send him?" Reuben asked.

"We could lower him down into the cistern," Isacar said.

Reuben shook his head. "That's too dangerous. It may fill with water."

"It hasn't yet," Judah said. "That may be a good place. He wouldn't be able to escape and we could watch him."

Reuben tucked the coat inside his tunic. "Come, Judah. You and I will lower him down."

Reuben and Judah reassured me before they lowered me down. "We'll make peace with the others, then come back to get you." They removed my inside tunic and left me naked, but for my loin cloth.

I was still sobbing. "How can they hate me so much?"

"You brought this on yourself," Judah said.

They lowered me into the well where a thick layer of mud covered the cistern floor. With the rope still tied around my middle, they gave it slack and I fell headfirst into the mud. Snakes, spiders, scorpions and all manner of other small creatures made their homes in the cavern. I was frightened. My heart was broken. As I wept, I felt something crawling up my arms and back. I slapped at my arms but could not reach my back, so I rolled over and over in the mud. I cried out, "Help! Help me, Heavenly Father!" and the creatures seemed to crawl away from me.

Above, sprawled on the edge of the opening, was Zebulon. His head was visible. "I'm here, Joseph. I won't leave you."

I choked out, "Thank you, Zeb," but I could not stop crying.

In the midst of the putrid smell of stagnant ooze, I tried to review my relationship with my brothers in order to understand their hatred of me. In my younger years when I worked with them, hadn't I exerted every effort to show them how expertly I could drive cattle, bind a weak lamb's leg, shear a ram, or encourage a nursing ewe? Hadn't I tried to show how swiftly I could run, how high I could jump, or how nimbly I could climb a tree? All this so I could win their approval and be included in their games.

Then, after Father kept me home, they accused me of thinking myself above them. In fact, I think I really did. I had had much adulation from my mother, my nurses, and now from my father. I guess I thought he loved me more, so I became full of myself, and I'm sure I acted overbearing. They were bitter about my telling father that I had found them skinning a sheep. I had come into camp not knowing they had retrieved the sheep from a lion's mouth. My father's rule was to kill and eat the wild life and save the sheep for reproduction and selling.

Then there were the dreams. I should have been more humble in the telling. And now, the coat. Father had cautioned me to keep it sacred.

I stood up in the well, my arms outspread, my head tilted toward heaven and pleaded, "Dear God, why won't you help me?" Then I heard words inside my head that said, "Why won't you let me?"

I stopped crying, stood still, and listened.

"Did you acknowledge my help when I sent the crawling things away from you?" the voice said. "I can take your sorrow and pain if you will ask and lay it at my feet. You have much ahead to endure, still much to learn, and I will be with you, but you must always ask and pay attention. Stay close to me and I will stay close to you."

I bowed my head and sobbed, thanking God. In my heart I resolved to forgive my brothers, to ask them for their forgiveness, and begin anew to build a good relationship.

While the group argued, some of the untended sheep wandered off. I heard Naptali call, "Come, Reuben, we must be after the sheep." They ran away. Only Zeb remained.

I had sat there in the mud for hours, crying and wishing I was by my father's side, when I felt the ground tremble and heard the sound of animal hooves. Then I heard Zeb say, "No, it's a dry well...there is no water...no, I'm not guarding it."

I felt myself being lifted up. I saw that a caravan had stopped some distance from the well and two of the servants had come to find water. One of them said, "Well, what have we here? What is this? A slave?"

"No, uh, I mean...yes, I mean—" Zeb cupped his hand by his mouth and shouted, "Judah!"

Travelers were common in this much-used area, so my brothers paid them little mind until Judah, distracted by Zeb's call, turned suddenly from his argument with Simeon. Upon seeing that the traders had pulled me up, he quickly thought to save my life. "You won't need to kill him, Simeon," he said. "We can sell him to those Ishmaelites."

I had been dragged before the caravan master's servant. I stood there naked, covered with mud, streaks of tears on my face as my brothers strode over to join us. Next, Judah stood before me, offering me to the slavers who had pulled me up. Simeon had pushed Zeb aside, and I couldn't believe what was happening. I wanted to shout, "Don't do this! I'll be good!"

I thought it must be a trick and that Judah would wait until I was out of Simeon's sight, then retrieve me. I felt dejected and couldn't bring myself to say anything as I was sold to the Ishmaelites for twenty pieces of silver.

---

As Joseph finished telling his story, they sat for a moment in silence. Cephas slowly shook his head. "How tragic for you."

"Yes. I went with Ahkmar's caravan, submerged in self pity and sullenness. It wasn't until I saw the girl fall that my father's words came back to me. He always taught, 'When you think you deserve pity, find someone worse off than you are and go to their aid.' I've tried to be more helpful since then."

"But it must be difficult for you to face an unknown future in Egypt, not knowing what has been resolved with your brothers."

The three friends sat without speaking for a long time. Finally Cephas said, "It occurs to me that we each have a difficult challenge."

"To be a slave, you mean?" Mahta asked.

"No. To forgive. I was taught that no one can progress spiritually if they are tied to another by hate. We all have more than enough reason to hate."

"Do I have to forgive my uncle, and Ahkmar...and Saku?"

"That would be the correct thing to do," Cephas said. "But I wonder how I myself can ever forgive those who killed my family."

Joseph was still silent as Cephas watched his face.

# Chapter Seven

# Brothers' Second Thoughts

After Joseph had been led away by the Ishmaelites, Judah, Simeon, and Zebulon watched the caravan move out of sight.

"Finally rid of him," Simeon said.

"You aren't going to let them keep him, are you?" Zebulon said.

The others who had finished eating by the campfire walked up to the three looking down the empty road. "Have we done the right thing?" Asher asked.

"It's better than killing him, isn't it?" Gad said.

Dan gave a slight nod. "But what will become of him?"

"I hate to think of it," Zebulon said.

About four hours later, Reuben, Isacar, Levi, and Naptali returned from gathering the wayward sheep. The group in camp had gathered to their fire. Reuben said to Zebulon, "Why aren't you with Joseph?" Zebulon put his head down and said nothing.

"What's happened?" Reuben demanded. "Simeon, you haven't—"

"No," Judah said. "We saw the opportunity to get rid of him without any harm. We gave him to some traders."

"You sold him!" Zebulon yelled.

"Sold him?" Reuben cried. "Where is the money?" He grabbed the money sack from Judah and ran along the trade road until he quickly turned back and yelled, "Come, Naptali! You can overtake them faster than I can. I'll catch up with you."

Naptali and Reuben disappeared out of sight.

The men who had been the most belligerent were more subdued now and having second thoughts. No one spoke much. Everyone watched the road.

Darkness came, but Reuben and Naptali did not come. Chores were done and still they were gone.

It was close to midnight when the two men neared the camp.

"Did you find him?" Zebulon called.

"We did not."

In the firelight, Reuben's face reflected the way he felt. He loved his father very much. The seriousness of the hurt he had inflicted on the aged man weighed heavily on him. He couldn't bear to think of what losing Joseph would do to Father Israel.

"We went farther than any caravan could have traveled," Naptali said. "We searched every camp. He was nowhere to be found."

"How can we tell Father?" Reuben said, his voice subdued.

"I have an idea," Dan said. "We have the coat, don't we Reuben? Tomorrow after the hunt we could spill some blood on the cloth and tear it so it would look as if Joseph was attacked by a wild beast."

"That would kill Father," Reuben cried.

"Not as much as knowing that we sold Joseph," Levi said.

They talked into the night. Few got any sleep. In the morning the discussion was rekindled. "Very well," Reuben finally said. "I'll go along with the tale only to save Father from knowing."

"We must all pledge to see it through," Judah said.

Reuben nodded. "All of you raise your arm and swear. You too, Zebulon."

"Tomorrow we'll go to Father. Let's hope that this has taught us our lesson. The rest of our days must be spent making restitution."

That day another caravan stopped nearby. Among other things, they offered sandals for trade.

Judah asked, "What if we bought shoes with the money, Reuben? That way we wouldn't have to explain about it."

"Go ahead if you want to, Judah. I'll have no part of it."

"Nor I," Zebulon said.

Eight pairs of sandals were purchased for the twenty pieces of silver, and the merchant went away shaking his head in unbelief. Those men didn't appear to be fools, yet they had paid the first price he spoke, denying him the sport of bargaining. They must not value their silver to part with it so readily, he thought.

In the years ahead, the sons of Jacob felt little need and less enthusiasm to put on their expensive, well-made footwear. The mere possession of the sandals was a painful reminder of the sorrowful thing they had done. How could shoes, no matter how fine, ever replace their own flesh and blood?

# Chapter Eight

# Kumash Makes Offer

It was evening when Joseph was again summoned before Kumash.

"How is your pain, Joseph?"

"It will heal in time."

*But what of the pain in your heart?* Aloud Kumash said, "As you know, I'm on my way to Egypt to sell my slaves and all my goods. I make this trip about once a year. It is nearing High Bazaar time in Memphis, so our timing should be just right and I anticipate great success. I would like to keep you with me. I'll sell the other slaves, but I need someone with your abilities to be my assistant.

"My abilities?"

"Yes. Nothing seems to escape your eyes, Joseph. If an animal is having difficulty, or a person is in need, you are right there. Even though the rest of the company are cautioned to stay away from the slaves, when one stumbled the other day, swift as the wind you picked him up and steadied him until he could keep up again. I have often seen you give them part of your food and water. All in our number know of your compassion and may even come to you instead of me with their problems. It would mean that you would be my servant and not my slave. I believe we could work well together. What do you say?" Kumash folded his hands and leaned back with a smile on his face.

"You are kind, Kumash. Thank you for your high esteem. I don't know whether you can understand this, but my God has made known to me that my future lies in Egypt, not that I desire this for myself. It's just something I must do. What I'm trying to say is that you must sell me."

Kumash sat up. "You're right. I don't understand such a God. But if your faith in this God makes you what you are, I won't get in the way. I'll keep you as my assistant as long as I can. You can aid me at Bazaar. Is that to your liking?"

"It's fair and kind of you, good Master," Joseph said. "Could I venture to ask a bold favor?"

Kumash smiled. "You seem to bring out a weakness in me, Joseph. What is it?"

"When it comes time to sell me, would you insist that my two companions and I be sold as a unit?"

"I've never heard of such a thing."

"I feel strongly that we must remain together."

"Let me think about it. Now go to your rest. We travel early in the morning."

---

For many days the terrain had not changed. Barren sand dunes stretched endlessly on. The slaves and servants who walked often found themselves wading in sand, making traveling very slow. Sometimes those who rode were forced to dismount and pull the reluctant animals through the hot sand. The days were dry, and although the great sea was often in sight, they had to ration water. Their journey followed the old road that ran along the coast. Habitations along the route were usually made of palm branches, as were fence-like enclosures.

Only Kumash seemed not to notice the hardships. His spirits rose with each step. He laughed and joked and walked about, checking his merchandise. It was apparent to Joseph that his master took pride in his chosen work. As a merchant with many exciting things to sell, Kumash was eager to get to Bazaar.

Joseph saw to the duties assigned him, and Cephas and Mahta worked steadily through their given tasks, but as each day drew them closer to their unknown future, it was difficult to cloak their anxiety. During the day they worked quietly as they watched and waited, unlike the often-noisy camel drivers. At night they chose to sleep outside the tents so they could talk together.

Each night, when they were able, the band of three lay under the stars. Cephas taught Joseph about the heavens and they talked long into the night about the wonders of God and His creations. Sometimes Cephas pointed to a particular star and called it by name. "That is Oliblish, and there are greater Kokaubeam. Beyond our sight is Kolob, near to the throne of God—Kolob, the ruling planet."

Joseph called upon God continually, and in his uncertainty came to depend on Him more and more. In his prayers Joseph continued to ask God to bless his brothers and alleviate the grief of his father.

As the company met other caravans, they took the opportunity to trade and barter, some days traveling only a short distance. Normally they had little chance to talk as the caravan moved, but with the slack in pace, Joseph saw the opportunity he had looked for. He found his friend and fell in step with him. "Cephas, tell me what you know of our destination."

"I've never been to Egypt," Cephas said, "but I have studied its history as you have. Surely we'll be taken to the capital city, which is Memphis. The pharaoh rules from there."

"Yes, I suppose the history of Egypt is the history of the pharaoh."

"As I remember it, Egypt got its name from Egyptus, the daughter of Ham. When the three sons of Noah parted, Japeth went north, Shem settled the central areas where you and I are from, and Ham came south and spread his people over the country we approach."

"Yes, but also in our country. For Canaan was Ham's son also, and the Canaanites, his descendants."

"Anyway, Egyptus was the one who discovered the land. Her son, whose name was Pharaoh, became its first ruler. He was a righteous man and dealt justly with his people."

"So the name *Pharaoh* became synonymous with *ruler?*"

"Yes. Every succeeding king was thereafter called by that title. But not all the kings were good-hearted. Some were ruthless and ambitious. They all attempted powerful displays of strength. The people believed in the kings' omnipotence and submitted to them.

"The descendants of Ham were gifted and clever. They built mighty cities, great monuments and temples. Each succeeding ruler tried to build mightier things than his predecessor. As far as I know, the Hyksos were the first invaders to overtake the throne. The government probably changed internally many times before that, but the rulers were always Hamites. The Hyksos were the first Shemites to come to power."

"What do you know of the Hyksos?"

"Only that they were a large and powerful Nomadic tribe. I think they infiltrated the country gradually and occupied key positions. Then, when the invasion took place, the defenses were vulnerable and they met little resistance."

"They have been in power only about thirty years."

"Yes, and I wonder if their being Shemites has brought about any obvious changes."

"I'll be interested to see what's going on."

The two were interrupted as Kumash strode toward them. "Look to the animals and secure everything. We're coming to the border guard. There will be a check of our caravan."

A short time later the group came to a barricade manned by many soldiers. The man in charge demanded to see the leader. Kumash was already at the front and made himself known to the guard.

"What is your business in Egypt?"

"I am a merchant. I have goods as well as slaves to take to market."

"Are your intentions peaceful?"

"I desire only to buy and sell."

"Do you have any weapons?"

"I have a whip for my slaves and knives for maintenance of my company."

"We must search your goods."

After the search, the inspectors allowed the caravan to pass on its way.

"I see they are well-defended," Joseph said.

"The present king does not want to be unseated. They take precautions."

By now the road was showing evidence of its frequent use. The farther south the company went, the heavier the traffic became as more and more caravans joined them traveling to Bazaar. One series of heavy carts carried nothing but timbers from Lebanon. One merchant had camels laden with gum tragacanth, balsam, and resin to be used for embalming. Others carried wine from the vineyards of Canaan. Some would sell olive oil. Precious metals and semi-precious stones were brought from the East, turquoise and copper from Sinai.

Kumash knew some of the traders. With some he was cheerful and amiable, with others, more guarded.

Three days from the nearest Egyptian settlement they noticed an obvious change. Already tents were set up along the way. Traders were displaying their goods. Men with donkeys laden with water sacks had come out from the city to meet the parched travelers. A high price was paid for a bag of precious water.

A feeling of festivity filled the air. Those who had been to Egypt before talked about their anticipations. Joseph, Cephas, and Mahta watched in wonder at the scene unfolding before them.

Suddenly a stretch of beneficent green lay before them as if a line had been drawn to divide it from the buff sand behind them. Here, the people dwelt in huts of mud walls over-laid with palm branches or covered with dried cakes of cow dung, the dung also being used for cooking fires. Most of the houses stood close to the banks of a fresh-water canal.

"Water—fresh water," Mahta said, pointing. She looked at Joseph as if to ask, "Why aren't we stopping?"

Joseph nodded. "Kumash will stop for our needs. He knows."

Women carried fabric bundles and water-laden jugs on their heads. Men could be seen tilling their fields. Large harnessed oxen, often blindfolded, walked round in a circle, turning a vertical water wheel in the canal. Clay containers attached to the wheel would fill up with water, rise to the top and spill over into a wooden channel that directed the water to ditches and furrows, making it possible to irrigate their fields. Date palms held abundant fruit, and rows of lush shade trees stood beckoning.

By midmorning they came to a river spanned by a wooden bridge. The caravans, one by one, clapped over the trestle. Kumash broke away from the stream of traffic and led his people to a gently sloping bank of the river where they stopped to rest and water the animals. Everyone splashed and washed as much as they desired. Under the canopy of over-reaching tree branches, they ate a mid-day meal including dates Kumash purchased from a peasant.

"Ahhh," Joseph said, patting his middle with satisfaction.

"This river is the first of five such rivers," Kumash said. "They form the mouth of the mother river of Egypt, the Great River. The five rivers empty into the sea beyond. It is this waterway that helps make Egypt what it is. The people cannot depend on rain for moisture, but the Great River never stops. It overflows its banks for a season to succor the thirsty land. Where its branches reach, gardens grow. We will cross four more bridges and traverse the land south along the west bank."

The fertile area was so refreshing it lifted the spirits of everyone, adding fruits and vegetables to the diet of the traveling company.

# Chapter Nine

# The White City

Eventually they crossed the five rivers and slowly made their way south. Then one day someone shouted, "Look! Over there!"

Looming out of the desert like a great phantom stood the pyramid of Sakhara. They could see it in the distance rising on the plateau in a series of steps.

"I've heard of its splendor," Cephas said, "but one must see it to understand." They kept watching until they passed beyond sight of it.

Again someone said, "Look!" The city of their destination shone before them. "The White City–how beautiful." The pillars and spires towered above the white city walls, the high places adorned with gold. The sun, catching the tips and reflecting the light, gave it a mystical glow.

"There is our home for the next while," Kumash said cheerfully.

"For how long, I wonder," Joseph said to Cephas.

The last night before they approached the great city, Kumash gave orders to dress up the caravan. Everyone busied themselves making the preparations. The next morning, as the company set out, the animals as well as the people were arrayed in glittering showiness. Kumash led the group as they paraded proudly through the gate and entered the city of Memphis.

Joseph had often heard about Egypt. His grandfather and father each had dwelt in Egypt for a time. Abraham, well-known by the pharaoh of his day, had taught the Egyptians much. Part of Joseph's learning had been about the history and culture of

Egypt, which he had discussed with his father in the Egyptian tongue. Even so, he was not prepared for what he saw.

The city, surrounded by high walls, boasted ten gates for entrance—one main gate and nine smaller ones. Through each gate a road led to the city's center where stood towering columns of pink marble brought by barge up the Great River. The streets were paved with flat, polished stones. On one end stood the palace of Pharaoh, white, massive, and elegant. Behind the columns on either side were fine houses belonging to the members of his court. Bright artistry and many statues adorned the edifices. A huge obelisk stood in the center of the vast square where the merchants were allowed to set up their temporary shops.

Travelers poured into the city. Bazaar was beginning and festivities were at their height. At any other time on the square, one could find regular vendors who provided for the customers and traffic. But High Bazaar, held only once or twice a year, coincided with holy festivals and drew crowds from all over.

Jugglers, dancers, magicians, and musicians were performing in the crowded and noisy area. Costumes of every kind were paraded about, representing inhabitants from lands far and near. A group of seven tall black people strolled by in unadorned white robes, their hair cropped, their women without veils. They walked with long, slow strides, their bearing dignified and regal. Turbaned men in dark outfits walked ahead of their veiled women. Peasants in blousy shirts and leggings adorned their heads in loose swaths of drab cloth. Most merchants from Memphis wore red jackets, a round red hat cocked on their ample hair. The Egyptian women, unveiled, took no second place to any man and wore their rich fabrics and ample jewelry proudly, their hair a straight, even length, cut short above the eyes.

Pharaoh's guard was prominently displayed to keep order, patrolling the streets and watching for any sign of trouble.

Inside the colonnades, as far as one could see, every kind of trade was exhibited. Foods were displayed—pomegranates, melons, grapes, pears, oranges, cucumbers, and abundant nuts.

Freshly slaughtered and skinned goats could be purchased, their blood underfoot and attracting many flies.

Men demonstrated knife-sharpening, and women sat behind their few trinkets. A place had been roped off for wrestling bouts. A snake charmer sat impervious to his surroundings. Colorfully costumed men with water bags strolled up and down, selling drinks from a brass cup. Black men from the south sold incense, sandalwood, ebony, and leopard skins. Some sold monkeys. Others sold ostrich feathers and ivory. The newcomers could only gape in wonder.

Kumash's eyes flashed and his pace quickened. He didn't smile, but walked deliberately and proudly as he came into the square and went to the spot he had used before. "This is where we'll set up our shop," he said. Two camps were established, one on the square and a group outside the walls. The outsiders included the slaves and animals and those not pertinent to trading.

Soon the stall of Kumash was wedged between a bird vendor, his wooden cages stacked high, and a fortune teller adorned with scarves, veils, and jewelry. The animals and slaves were secured, trunks and boxes opened, and a fine display laid out—linens, brocades, and silks; spices, incense, and sweet-smelling oils; bright tapestry and costume adornments of tassels, beads, and gold braids.

Cephas and Mahta were allowed to help with the merchandise while Joseph was instructed by Kumash on the value of all his goods. Before evening came, they had already transacted a fair amount of business.

Near the obelisk in the center of the square stood a platform to display slaves. Early the second morning after their arrival, Kumash, eager to be rid of his shackled band, gave orders to prepare the slaves for sale. They were brought to the stall and washed, their heads reshaved.

Joseph went to Kumash. "Will you shave my head also?"

"But Joseph, I had hoped you would stay with me," Kumash said, dropping his shoulders.

"I'll stay as long as I can, but I think you should shave my head so others will know I'm a slave—I must eventually be sold."

"Very well, if you insist, Joseph. My servant Hasaan will attend to you. I'll take my slaves to the platform."

Kumash left with his slaves and his slavers as Joseph sat before Hasaan and was shorn of all his hair. Cephas next took Joseph's place; then Mahta slumped down on the stool and with quiet tears gave up the hair she had tried to tame.

Without speaking, all three went back to their duties until Kumash returned. "We had good fortune," he said. "A rich shipowner bought all my slaves at once. They'll be used in the galleys to row the ships, poor souls. Yet I'm relieved. Now I can enjoy the work I love to do. But what will become of you three, I wonder?"

They had been selling and trading with great success for several days and Kumash was happy. Joseph made a profit with everything he sold, and while he could understand only a few languages, he seemed to be able to communicate somehow with all his customers.

One day news came to Kumash that a trading vessel was beached on the coast in danger of destruction and the owners were hastily looking for buyers to relieve the ship of its cargo. Kumash saw the opportunity to pick up more merchandise. With the money he had already acquired, he decided to seek out the ship.

"Joseph, I'm going to recover some goods from that troubled vessel. I'll take most of my caravan with me, so I leave you in charge with Hasaan and your friends to assist you. I'll return as soon as possible."

The four who were left behind soon settled into a working routine, the trading smooth, and Joseph making handsome profits for his master.

# Chapter Ten

# Zelica

Potiphar was away on king's business. His wife, Zelica, stood looking out of her second-story front window. The view took in a large portion of the square below. It was Bazaar time and her excitement increased as she thought of the many new and exotic things with which she could adorn herself. She was stunning, and she knew it. Her auburn hair was longer than the traditional style, just past her shoulders. Her eyes were as green as the river, and her skin, which she pampered with oils, was fair and without blemish. Since her husband was third in rank of the officers of Pharaoh, she made sure she dressed equal to her station.

Potiphar and Zelica were Hyksos, like Pharaoh, appointed as part of the new regime.

Zelica put on a soft gold dress that was belted at the waist and trimmed in gold braid in a crisscross style across her chest. For her outing she chose a gold necklace with three emeralds to enhance her eyes, then planned her descent on the pavilion. She called her eunuch.

"Jaeb, bring my chariot to the back door. Today I'll ride through the colonnade and see if anything interests me."

The back door faced a street that paralleled the colonnade. Zelica had Jaeb drive to the far end of the pavilion so she could see all the displays and decide which booths merited her descent from the chariot. She had him shout at street-goers to make way for her, less to clear the path than to allow her to see the admiring reaction of people as they watched her pass.

"Stop here!" She exclaimed, her eyes on a sparkling display of jewelry. She stepped from the chariot and waved once to the bald proprietor, who smiled with glee and bobbed up and down with his bows. With an experienced eye, she skipped over the gaudy pieces and tried on only the finest adornments. As she turned to let Jaeb admire the necklace she held to her throat, she caught sight of some bright, shimmering fabric three stalls away—then she stared as she saw its vendor, her interest in fabrics forgotten compared with her interest in the young man who sold them.

Even from that distance she could see that his eyes were a strong blue color. She had never seen such a face. She dropped the necklace on the table and picked up the ring nearest to her. Placing it on her finger, she held up her hand as if to admire the ring while her eyes examined the young man beyond her outstretched hand. His head was shaven, but it didn't diminish his rugged yet pleasing features. His manner was smooth, yet his demeanor held innocence. He smiled at something a customer said, which brightened his countenance, and Zelica had to get closer.

She left the ring on the table and, as nonchalantly as possible, strolled into the next display. Jaeb, holding the horses, moved the chariot to the next booth, staying close to his mistress. She moved through the display, running her hand over the objects, unaware of what she was touching. Her eyes were on the young man. It wasn't just that he was beautiful; it was his ease of movement, confidence, and comfort in his surroundings. His customers seemed a little too enthusiastic to have his help with the cloth he was showing. Just then he turned in her direction, and she put her head down. She wanted their first eye contact to be on her terms. She hadn't heard the anxious vendor of the new display asking if he could be of any help. She came to herself and realized she was holding the statue of a fertility god, the vendor at her side. She replaced the statue, complimented the vendor on his display, and returned to her chariot.

"I'm going home now," she said to Jaeb, "but I'll return when there aren't so many people around. That fabric has caught my eye."

She ascended the chariot and returned home, looking over her shoulder.

———◦◦◦———

The next morning Zelica watched the square from her window. She could see the display of Kumash, but it was the young seller that intrigued her. *Where does one who possesses such beauty of frame and features come from?* She traced the outline of his shoulders with her finger in the air. *Why is his head shaven like a slave's and yet he seems educated and conducts business with the skill of a proprietor?*

She waited until just after midday when some shops shut down for rest and only a few people were still about. "We'll go now, Jaeb," she called.

The chariot stopped before the multicolored display. Zelica waited until she had the young man's eye, then stepped out of the chariot slowly, her movements studied and deliberate to show off her costly apparel and splendid figure. She kept his eyes in her gaze as she approached and said, "I see that you have unusual fabrics. Is there anything among your stock befitting the wife of Potiphar?"

Joseph swallowed hard. Standing before him was a woman of rare beauty. Her eyes, which looked into his, were the color of the river, her coppery hair and milky skin breathtaking. She even seemed to appreciate his momentary lack of speech as she smiled up at him, waiting for a response.

"We have a variety of silks and linens woven in the East by skilled artisans," Joseph said. "I think you'll find no finer."

Zelica turned to the fabrics and smiled to herself. She had gotten the desired effect. She asked about several lengths of luxurious cloth as she draped some in front of her. "Are you the owner of these goods?" she asked Joseph.

"No, they belong to my master."

She turned to Hasaan. "And who is the master?"

Hasaan took a step closer. "I'm a servant. Our master is away."

Motioning to Joseph, she said, "You mean your master lets his slaves go unshackled to roam about at will?"

"Our master doesn't chain these slaves. He trusts them."

She lifted her chin to look at Cephas and Mahta. *That may be, but they don't look like slaves to me.*

Zelica took her time buying a piece of linen with Joseph's help. She made small conversation with the young man, skillfully manipulating his attention, then returned home. She spent the rest of the afternoon pacing in her room, stopping frequently to watch Joseph from her window, trying to devise a plan.

---

The following day was High Market Day and one of the busiest. People thronged the square. Business was good. All four of Kumash's servants were kept busy attending to customers.

Out of the midst of the crowd noise, Joseph heard a loud voice. "It's them, I know it's them. They got shaved, but it's them."

They all looked to see Saku standing with his hands on his hips and the familiar snarl on his face. He looked the same, with his favorite whip wound and worn on his side. He was flanked by two ruffians, one with a crooked nose, the other missing a few teeth.

"These're the ones who lost me my position as head slaver. These are the high and mighty." Then he smiled. "But they carry my marks on their backs."

He came closer and glared around as if to examine everything. His companions moved with him. "So where is Kumash? Did you do away with him, or did you steal these things?"

Joseph stepped forward and said, "We want no trouble from you, Saku. You had your way when you whipped us. Now leave us alone."

"Is this a slave telling a slaver what to do? I'll tell you what I think of you." He spat in Joseph's face as his companions laughed.

People were gathering to watch. Quickly a member of the king's guard pushed through the crowd. "What goes on here?"

From her window, Zelica saw the crowd and confrontation between the two sides. She grabbed a thin scarf and called to Jaeb. "I'm going down there, but first, go quickly and see what the commotion is. Meet me along the road. Hurry!"

The eunuch ran out the front door and bounded around people and booths to put himself within hearing distance of the rift. Soon he was back to his mistress who was fast approaching Kumash's stall.

"The rough one is saying that the slave is a Hebrew, stolen by his owner and not really a slave at all. The officer of the guard is trying to decide what to do."

Zelica hurried toward the stall. She pushed her way through the crowd and faced the officer. "I'm the wife of Potiphar, captain of the king's guard. I am acquainted with these people and will report this incident to my husband when he returns tonight. He'll take care of it. I'll see to it."

The officer was satisfied and said, "All you people, be on your way." Then he excused himself to Zelica and escorted a reluctant Saku away as the crowd slowly dispersed.

As another excuse to gaze at his face, she asked Joseph about Saku. He explained that Saku had been sent away and was probably holding a grudge. She nodded knowingly, only half listening, yet enjoying the sound of his voice and the look of his eyes upon her. "Don't try to leave," she said to Joseph. "My husband will want to know of this." She made her way back to the large house at the end of the pavilion.

Only Cephas noticed Mahta shudder when the commotion was over and they could return to business. He patted her shoulder, and she hurriedly folded all the fabrics Zelica had strewn about, unsure whether her unease came because of Saku or because of the woman who seemed so interested in Joseph.

"My husband will be hungry and tired when he comes home tonight," Zelica said to her servants. She made sure his favorite foods would be prepared and a hot bath with soothing oils would be primed during supper.

Potiphar walked in the door just as his wife said he would. He carried his helmet to the common room and reviewed a couple of messages that had come while he was away.

Potiphar was every bit the appearance of a soldier—solid and square-jawed, his face creviced and ruddy. His brown hair was cut short to ease the wearing of the helmet he donned so often. For formal interviews and court appearances or for entertaining guests he wore a black wig. Zelica quietly set about preparing him for his meal by washing his hands and dusty feet while the food was put on the table.

When he came to the table he found it covered with his favorite meats, fruits, breads, and cheeses. After his hunger was satisfied, she led him to the tub where she rubbed his back and talked soothingly to him. When she thought the moment was right, she began.

"I hate to trouble you so soon after your arrival home, but I must tell you about something." She recounted the scene from earlier in the day. "They say he's not really a slave at all. If that's so, then we must rescue him. For if he was stolen, and we bring him to our house, the God of the Hebrews will look kindly on us. He's a comely lad and clever. He has made the merchant rich."

Potiphar sat with his eyes closed and said, "Remind me in the morning and I'll look into it." She smiled with satisfaction.

The next morning the captain of the guard, in full military dress, took his giant Nubian slave with him and approached the stall of Kumash. He came first to Hasaan and addressed him. "What is this I hear that you steal slaves from Canaan and bring them here to sell?"

Hasaan, startled by Potiphar's question, fell at his feet. "No, sir. That's not the way it is."

"Then quickly explain," Potiphar demanded as the three others came to Hasaan's side.

"I am but a humble servant for my master, who is away. He left me and his three trusted slaves to carry on his trade."

Potiphar looked at Joseph, Cephas, and Mahta and said, "I don't believe you." He motioned to his Nubian, who then stripped the shirt off Hasaan in one motion and began to hit him with a short whip.

Hasaan cried out, "Please, sir. I can't tell you anything different. What would you have me tell you?"

"He speaks the truth," Joseph said, stepping between Hasaan and the whip.

Potiphar looked at Joseph's appearance and asked, "Are you a slave or a free man?"

"I'm the slave of the merchant Kumash, who is away."

"How did you become a slave?"

Joseph flinched just slightly at this question and said, "I was bought in the land of Canaan."

"You lie! You are no slave. You shall both be punished for lying to me." Again he signaled his Nubian.

Zelica had been watching intently and saw what was coming by her husband's gesture. She immediately called to Jaeb. "Go quickly and tell my husband that he deals unjustly with this lad. If he is truly not a slave, he should not be beaten."

Potiphar's huge black man ripped off Joseph's shirt to beat him as commanded, but seeing the scars, he hesitated as Joseph moved to protect himself with his hands. The man with the whip motioned his master to look at the scars.

Potiphar asked Joseph, "Do you persist in your story?"

"I do," Joseph said.

"Then I'll have to imprison you until I have proof of what you say."

Jaeb arrived at the booth just as Potiphar ordered that Joseph be detained in a cell which adjoined the captain's house.

Zelica met her husband at the door after Jaeb had run home to tell her the news.

"Why are you doing this?" she asked. "Surely you can see that this boy is well taught. He should be treated with respect. We should have him as a guest in our house so that he may be honored and waited upon—not imprisoned."

"If I leave him on the square, there will be more trouble," answered Potiphar. "It's not the custom of the Egyptians to take that which does not belong to them, so I can't free him as long as there is a chance he really was sold. There were scars from previous beatings across his back. I'll detain him until the merchant returns. I'll need to see a bill of sale." With that, the matter was closed.

Zelica went daily to the cell and talked to Joseph through the door. Rather than have the guards feed him, she made sure her servants prepared meals for him. She didn't talk to him as one would a slave. She told him about everything she thought would be of interest to him, such as her friends and her children, or the lavish parties at the palace. She tried to get him to tell more about himself, but Joseph was guarded in his disclosures.

"Tell me about your mother," she said on one occasion.

Joseph shrugged and said, "My mother died when I was ten."

"Oh, you poor child. How lonely it must have been for you," she said sympathetically. "I lost a baby boy. He died right after I gave birth."

"I'm truly sorry," Joseph said, thinking of his little brother, Benjamin.

"We must take comfort in each other," Zelica said. "Perhaps I can give you a small portion of motherly attention from time to time."

After she left, Joseph sighed and wondered about this mysterious, exotic woman.

---

Kumash was gone twenty-four days. Upon his return and hearing about Joseph's situation, he went immediately to Potiphar's house. Joseph was released to Kumash when the bill of sale was verified. Back on the pavilion, the young slave was welcomed by his friends. They were relieved to see that he hadn't been abused while imprisoned.

Kumash motioned Joseph to the back of the booth to talk to him. He spoke in hushed tones. "While I was away I heard of a man in Canaan of great influence and power—one who is favored of God and man. He is said to have lost a son. The man's name is Israel, and his son's name is Joseph. The whole country knows of the terrible grief this father feels. They say he will not cease lamenting, nor give up hoping that the boy may be alive."

It took all the composure Joseph could summon to remain calm. His heart was pounding in his chest. With his head bowed he said, "I think it's time for you to sell me."

"No, Joseph, there has to be some other way."

Joseph looked up and said, "I can think of no other choice, Master. I'm sorry."

Kumash opened his mouth to say more, but Joseph shook his head. Seeing the resolve in Joseph's face, the master dropped his hands by his side and returned to his selling. Joseph kept himself busy the rest of the day sorting and arranging the goods and avoiding the crowds. Mahta and Cephas left him to himself, thinking he needed time to adjust to having his freedom taken away again.

That evening Joseph talked to his friends and told them what he needed to do. Cephas and Mahta still wanted to remain with Joseph. He tried to encourage them to stay with Kumash, who was kind and fair, but they were determined to stay by his side.

Joseph didn't sleep that night. He lay silent, his heart drawn out to God as tears fell.

# Chapter Eleven

# Slaves on the Block

The next day the three slaves prepared themselves for sale. They reshaved their heads, washed, and put on clean, simple garments. Believing in Joseph and in the path chosen by God, they looked at each other wordlessly and gave brave smiles. Then they went to Kumash and asked him to take them to their future.

Zelica rarely left the window now. Her desire to watch Joseph and know his every move consumed her thoughts. She saw Kumash and the three walk across the square toward the slave platform. Most of the platform was obstructed from her view by selling booths, but she noticed right away the new appearance of the three slaves and quickly perceived what they were doing. She ran frantically to Potiphar and burst into his room where he was preparing to leave for guard inspections. "We must buy the boy!" she said.

Potiphar looked up, distracted until understanding came to his face. He frowned and shook his head. "We don't need any more servants."

"But I have grown attached to him," Zelica said. "He will keep me from being lonely while you're away. Besides, he's so clever, he could make your work easier."

Zelica was used to having her way, ambition her driving force. She had schemed to win Potiphar and had strategically planned to get him the appointment as captain. Until now she had never let her emotions get in her way.

As he took his slaves to the stand, Kumash gave them instructions. Turning to Joseph he said, "Whatever you do, if the people ask questions, don't tell them you're a shepherd. Egyptians hate shepherds. Let me do the talking."

A few people had stopped to look curiously at the three slaves when the captain of the guard appeared out of the crowd and spoke to Kumash. "I'll buy the boy," he said as he pulled out his pouch. "How much?"

Kumash cleared his throat. "I'm selling all three together. If you take one, you take them all. You can have them all for just fifty pieces of gold."

Potiphar looked at Kumash in disbelief. "I've never heard anything so absurd." He tried to reason with Kumash to just let the boy go, but Kumash held firm to his first offer. Potiphar left in disgust, knowing his wife would not be satisfied.

"I can only do so much for you, Zelica!" he shouted as he entered the house. "I don't need an old man and a little girl. I don't even need the young man!"

Zelica pouted at the window all day, watching the reactions of people as they passed the slave platform. Many stopped and gazed for a while. A few even approached Kumash but left shaking their heads.

The next morning Potiphar was off on another mission for Pharaoh. As he kissed his wife goodbye he said, "If you can buy the boy yourself, do so."

As soon as he was gone, Zelica sent Jaeb down to bargain with Kumash. Jaeb came back with the same story—they all go together. She paced the floor and stopped at every turn to look out the window.

A well-known proprietor of the local pleasure house had stopped abruptly when he passed the slave platform and saw

Joseph. He kept his eye on the youth as he approached Kumash and began to bargain with him.

Zelica screamed for Jaeb. "Go down and buy them at any price. Don't come back without them."

The pleasure house owner went up to one hundred gold pieces for the three of them. With sweat on his brow, Kumash considered the offer. The money was more than generous, but he couldn't leave Joseph or the others to such a fate.

By the time Jaeb reached the platform, the owner of the pleasure house had retreated. Kumash was glad for Jaeb's interest and quietly sold all three slaves for eighty gold pieces.

---

As Jaeb led the three slaves to the large house, Joseph exclaimed quietly, "But this is the house where I was imprisoned." Mahta gasped, and Cephas looked at the house in wonder. It was large and covered with gray marble. Wide winding steps led up to the front entrance, which was covered by two ornately carved wooden doors. Flanking the entrance were two large cat-like statutes. Next to the statutes, a row of palm trees stood at attention across the front of the house. Cephas glimpsed someone looking out one of the spacious front windows overlooking the square.

Jaeb led them around the side where the building ended and a large wall adjoined the house. They followed the wall until they came to a small gate through which they entered into an immense open yard and stared in awe. A large vegetable garden lay in a far corner, the captain's private stables in another. A lovely fountain surrounded with marble benches lay in the center where colorful flowers grew in pots behind the benches. Children, watched by servants, played in an enclosed area near the house.

They entered a door in the back wall, which led into a long hallway, and Jaeb pointed out the spacious kitchen where they would eat their meals, a pantry and storage area, a children's learning room, and a nursery. He took them through a double open doorway into a large room with many beds. Here, the eunuchs and single men were housed. Jaeb gave Joseph and Cephas bedrolls and showed them spaces on the floor that they could claim as their own, not far from another doorway. From the second doorway they could see a staircase that went up to the main part of the house.

They were taken up the staircase to a wide hallway decorated with ornate wall hangings and marble pedestals holding animal-like statues that Joseph recognized as Egyptian gods. From the hallway they entered a large common room adorned with tapestries and expensive rugs, oversized soft cushions, and carved wooden benches.

On one of the benches sat a beautiful red-haired woman who looked familiar to Cephas and Mahta. Joseph tried to understand what was happening as once again the three friends found themselves before a new owner—the mistress of a great house. She stood, her blue caftan flowing about her, and the three knelt before her.

She smiled. "Hello, Joseph." To the others she said, "Your new master is Potiphar, captain of the king's guard. He doesn't think we need more servants at this time, but when I saw you put on the slave block, I took pity on you. From the kindness of my heart, you are in my home. You might have been sold to one of the pleasure houses and subjected to many atrocities. You are fortunate that I developed a motherly concern for you, Joseph. It is well for your friends that the slave master practiced trickery in his method of selling. Now I must decide what to do with you."

She turned to Mahta. "You, young girl, I'll place in the nursery to help watch over the children." Mahta looked pleased. As the mistress spoke, she walked back and forth, pausing to emphasize a word here and there. "My husband's head concubine, a disagreeable woman, has charge of the nursery and you will assist her. You must give special treatment to my two little girls over the children of the concubines. If I'm happy with it, I'll keep you there." She faced Mahta and said sternly, "You still might be sold to a pleasure house." Mahta put her head down.

Zelica sat on a bench facing them and said, "Perhaps you can tell me, Joseph, what I'm to do with the old man."

Joseph seemed to light up. "Cephas is an aide you'll come to prize, Mistress. He works hard, and in the service of Kumash, he cared for the animals. He could serve you well in your stables, but you might rather keep him as your personal counselor. He's a learned man. He can read the stars. You would be envied among the other wives in court if they knew you had such a wise advisor."

Zelica looked at Cephas with new eyes, and he turned to meet her gaze. "Very well," she said. "I shall try him as an advisor. As for you, Joseph, I don't know what my husband will want to do with you. For now, you may do general household tasks and assist Jaeb in carrying out my orders."

"Thank you, Mistress," he said as he bowed his head. Cephas and Mahta echoed his response.

Zelica addressed her eunuch. "Jaeb, show these three to their duties. I'll expect a report later regarding their usefulness. That's all."

After they left, she lay back on a cushion and let a deep sigh of relief and pleasure escape her. Then she giggled to herself.

---

For the first few days in the new house, Joseph spent his time following Jaeb about, learning everything he could. If he saw something that needed to be done, he set about doing it. He sought God to guide him at all times. After he learned the layout of the property, he tried to learn all he could on his own.

One morning he spent in the yard, talking with the gardener and learning about the types of vegetables and herbs grown there. He helped with the weeding and mulching and enjoyed working in the soil again. He also learned about the flowers—what kinds the mistress liked—and rotated varieties throughout the year.

Another time he inspected the stables with Jaeb, admiring the horses and asking questions about the daily routine of the workers. He learned from where the horses were purchased and which horses were used for certain occasions or chores. One horse was docile enough for the children to ride.

The captain also had a small cattle farm just outside the city walls. He raised beef for personal use and sometimes for sale in the marketplace. Joseph spent one morning at the cattle farm, viewing the master's holdings and property. He was impressed with the knowledge of the steward but noticed that the farm could be expanded and made more profitable.

Mahta was well-received by the children. She seemed content working in the nursery. She loved the little ones, and they warmed to her right away.

Cephas sat in the library upstairs and studied. The library was a small room with shelves on two sides for scrolls. Hanging on one wall was an oversized skin with lines etched into the hide depicting a map of Egypt and her surrounding neighbors. A table and three stools stood in the middle of the room. Empty scrolls and ink were kept under the table. As Cephas sat, he often wondered how he could possibly give advice to a woman like Zelica.

Twice a day Joseph and Cephas could meet in the large kitchen to eat and talk briefly. Mahta had her meals in the nursery with the children.

"Whatever am I supposed to tell that woman?" Cephas asked Joseph at the evening meal.

"I don't know," Joseph said, shaking his head. "Tell her what she wants to hear."

"But she probably wants one who charts the stars, not one who studies the heavens. I'm not a soothsayer."

"If she listens to you, you could, in truth, advise her wisely." They both considered that thought, then smiled. "But you're right," Joseph said. "The truth is probably not what she wants to hear. Just do your best, Cephas."

# Chapter Twelve

# The Designing Woman

One night after retiring, Joseph lay on his bed considering his situation when he heard the voice of his mistress. She had come to the top of the stairs and called him. "Joseph, I'm sorry to disturb your rest, but I need your help."

Joseph moved quickly to his feet. "Yes, Mistress, how may I serve you?" he said as he followed her up the stairs.

She walked down the hallway away from the common room and motioned for him to follow. "I'm lonely for my husband. This day has been a trying one, and I'm feeling the loss of my boy child. Will you come to my chambers and speak words of comfort to me?"

"If I can be of comfort to you, of course I'll come."

Inside Zelica's chambers, she crossed the room and sat on a long, softly-covered bench next to her spacious bed, which was turned down. A large embellished lantern burned on a table next to her bed. The window coverings were open wide, and light flowing curtains moved slightly in the breeze.

She motioned Joseph to sit next to her on the seat and asked, "Joseph, when you think of losing your mother, and realize you're alone in a strange land, where do you find solace?"

"In my God," he said with sincere innocence.

"Come here, Joseph." She motioned him closer. "Let me hold you as a mother holds her son. Help me, Joseph, help me find solace also."

In submitting to her embrace, Joseph felt warmth run through his body and he began to relax in her arms.

"There, doesn't that feel right?" she said. "It's right that we should comfort one another."

As she spoke, Zelica ran soothing hands over Joseph's arms and back. She continued to speak tenderly and soon her lips were on his brow. Joseph found himself sinking into a blissful state of submission. He remembered how Bilha had rocked him and sung to him, how comforting it felt.

As Zelica cooed her soft words, her lips came close to his ear, brushing it ever so lightly.

Suddenly Joseph felt a sense of danger. The hairs prickled on his neck and he realized that this was not maternal nurturing. He pulled away abruptly. "I— I must go," he stammered, then ran back to the servants' room, fell on his mat, and prayed. "Forgive me...help me...what should I do?" he cried over and over again.

After some time, these words came into his head: "Peace be to your soul, my son. You have withdrawn from the designing woman, and you must continue to resist her. Her temptations will be difficult to overcome; nevertheless, my Spirit shall attend thee. Stay near to me."

Early the next morning Zelica found Joseph alone in the library going over the figures of the house. When she entered, he stood at the table, across from her. She slowly started toward him and in her most beguiling tones asked, "Why did you run from me, my dear? Didn't you enjoy my arms?" She moved around the table toward him. "Am I to be rejected by my surrogate son?"

"You were kind indeed, Mistress." He moved slowly around the table, away from her. "I didn't mean to insult you. I was running from my own feelings."

She smiled and continued toward him. "Were they not good feelings?"

"I had no right to have such feelings, Mistress." Now he was opposite her, closest to the door.

She put both hands on the table and leaned toward him. "Don't be ashamed of those feelings, Joseph."

"Excuse me, Mistress," he said, and he turned and quickly left the room, hearing her laughter behind him.

Joseph went to his morning meal where he met Cephas, who instantly sensed something was amiss. They sat together at the end of the table, but Joseph just looked at his food. Cephas waited for him to speak, but the meal went on in silence.

Finally Cephas asked, "Why do you look so troubled, my son?"

Joseph awakened from his speculating, considered how to answer, then said quietly, "There is...a war going on inside me."

Cephas looked thoughtful, then finally said, "Is it the woman?"

Joseph seemed relieved at his friend's perception. "I have absolutely no desire for her. Being anything but her servant is the farthest thing from my mind. But she doesn't make it easy for me, Cephas."

Cephas agreed, shaking his head. "No, indeed."

"I've decided to fast today and strive to do my best."

Cephas nodded his approval and patted Joseph's hand. "May God be with you, my boy."

Joseph stood with his portion of food and carried it into the street. There he found a beggar to whom he gave his meal, and many meals thereafter.

---

"I want an accounting of everything that has happened regarding the household since I left," Potiphar said to Jaeb. Jaeb stood before his master, who was reclining on a seat in the common room. He told him about buying the slaves. Potiphar shook his head. It wasn't what he'd dictated to his wife, but things seldom went his way with her.

"For how much did you buy them?"

"One hundred pieces of gold, Master."

"And how goes it with them?"

Jaeb told of the assignments of the slaves and all the affairs of the household. He reported the things he'd been teaching and showing Joseph, mentioning the questions and suggestions Joseph had made under his supervision. Potiphar listened with interest, then dismissed Jaeb and sent for Joseph.

"Come here, Hebrew, and tell me about yourself."

Joseph stood before the soldier and master of the house and wondered whether he should stand or kneel. He decided to remain standing.

"I came from Canaan, as you know, sir."

Potiphar closed his eyes, and Joseph paused slightly, then continued. "I was sold to Kumash, who assessed me as a loyal worker and put me in charge of his caravan. I supervised his servants and the care of his animals. When we arrived here for Bazaar, he gave me the charge of his shop on the square. When it came time to part from my former master, I was sold, along with my companions, for eighty gold pieces."

Potiphar opened his eyes. "Are you certain it was eighty pieces of gold?"

"Yes, sir."

"Jaeb! Come in here," Potiphar called, and Jaeb entered. "How is it that you said the slaves cost one hundred pieces of gold when it was really only eighty?"

Jaeb's face was expressionless. "Maybe someone made a mistake, Master."

"Yes," Potiphar said, "and I fear the mistake was mine—in trusting you."

Potiphar summoned his Nubian and had Jaeb whipped as Joseph looked on with sympathy and sadness. He also looked at the face of the Nubian, curious to see discomfort in his eyes as he administered the stripes.

"Lock him in the cell until I decide what to do with him," Potiphar commanded. "You stay here, Hebrew. You see, don't you, that I'm a hard taskmaster, one to be feared."

"May I speak plainly, Master?" Joseph asked.

"I command it."

Joseph hesitated only slightly. "I see much fear in this house, also much pain. When you were away, I saw contention among your servants and concubines."

Potiphar stood up. "Show me the trouble and I'll cure it with the whip of my slave."

"I know I speak boldly," Joseph said, "but perhaps the whip is not the cure. Perhaps your slave dislikes using the whip."

Potiphar looked hard at Joseph, trying to decide whether he was being impertinent or sincere. He sat down again and found himself talking to Joseph as an equal. "About my slave, you may be right. When I first got him, his voice had already been removed. He's of mixed breeds, and you can see he's almost a giant. I make the best use of his features and keep him with me always—he is my might. Such might is effective in my office and in discipline, but not here. I can trust few servants. I waste too much time sorting out who is being deceitful. But how else can I control my household?"

Joseph, encouraged by the master's honest demeanor, replied, "Perhaps showing mercy and respect would have an influence for good on your servants."

Potiphar considered this a few moments. "And my concubines?"

"They want to be treated with respect, also. They're jealous of their mistress and would respond to kindness.

"You expect skills I do not have," Potiphar said wearily. "I come home from battle spent and disquieted, and I find trouble in my house. Only my wife gives me pleasure and comfort. I require her to run things for me in the household, but I suspect I put too much weight on her shoulders."

"Yes, I see that."

"You were in charge for your last master, and he trusted you. How old are you, Joseph?"

"Eighteen years old, sir."

"But wise and outspoken for your years." He paused while considering something, then said, "I have an idea. While I'm away this next week, I'll put you in charge of my household in place of Jaeb. If I see that things have improved, I'll consider the position for you permanently."

Joseph bowed and said, "Your trust will not be misplaced. Thank you, Master."

# Chapter Thirteen

# Joseph in Charge

Joseph spent the following days getting to know everyone in the large household and asking them questions about their areas of stewardship. The number of servants varied with the temperament of the owners. At this time, Mahta and two women served in the nursery, two men in the stables, two women and two men in the kitchen (one the gardener), three eunuchs, besides Jaeb, to maintain the house and garden, two workers and a steward at the cattle farm, one counselor in the library, and Joseph, the overseer, to run everything. The Nubian traveled with the master.

Potiphar often returned from a battle with a band of prisoners. Once captured, the prisoners became the slaves of the captors. Pharaoh's palace held numerous slave servants, as did Potiphar's. Most of the slaves were sold on the block. Once in a while one was kept. Some were castrated and made eunuchs, the servants most preferred by the Egyptian aristocracy.

Joseph went to Zelica. "What will become of your eunuch?"

"Oh, I don't know. I never pay attention to such things—except in your case, Joseph. Perhaps he'll be moved to Pharaoh's prison."

"Is it possible that he might be reinstated?"

"I don't think it's ever been done before in this household, but you're in charge, Joseph. Do with him as you will."

Joseph had Jaeb brought to him, told him he was being released, and apprised him of his situation. "You are to be given a second chance."

Jaeb was grateful. He couldn't run fast enough or serve too much. He was Joseph's helper at all times and was eventually given back to Zelica as her personal servant.

All the servants liked Joseph. He listened to them when they spoke and seemed to sincerely care.

Zelica noticed a change in the atmosphere of the house. One day she went looking for Joseph and found him taking stock in the storeroom. She entered the room and closed the door. "You seem to have time for everyone but me, Joseph," she said. "Will you please put your duties aside for a moment and talk with me?"

Joseph nodded once toward her. "I'm your servant, Mistress."

She frowned. "Don't be so stiff, Joseph. Aren't we friends?" She moved closer to him. "Haven't I shown all manner of kindness to you?"

He looked down at a list he had made and answered without looking up. "You are kind."

"Do you find me beautiful?"

He answered quietly. "You are beautiful."

She was next to him now. "Did you enjoy my arms?"

Joseph looked up at the room, unseeing and silent.

She went on. "Do you yearn to be in my arms again, as I yearn to be in yours?"

He continued to look straight ahead of him. "I can do no such thing."

"I don't understand," she said.

He turned slightly and looked at her. "My God does not approve. I've been taught since my youth that to lie with a woman who belongs to another is wrong. My master has entrusted you to my care. How could I offend him by betraying his confidence in me?"

Zelica smiled. "He doesn't need to know."

"I cannot betray my master."

"Have you ever been with a woman, Joseph?"

He didn't answer. Then he asked, "May I go now and attend to my duties, Mistress?"

She turned with a start and pouted. "Go. Go and take care of everyone but me!"

———————

Zelica sought Cephas in the library. "Old man, I need some advice."

Cephas stood before her, braced himself, and prayed. "I'll do my best to advise you, Mistress."

"What should a woman do when she aches with a heavy longing heart?"

"Is the woman grieved?" he asked.

"The woman is in love," she said impatiently.

"Is the husband away so long that the woman can't find peace on his return?"

She looked hard at Cephas and said, "The husband is not the object of the longing."

"Then how can I answer? Isn't it true that an Egyptian does not take that which is not his?"

She raised her voice. "You know little of Egypt. An Egyptian knows when to close his ears and turn his eyes. And a counselor knows the difference between wise advice and foolish advice."

Cephas was trying to please her. "I'd like to find words to comfort you, lovely lady. I don't know Egyptian law or custom. I'm not even doing well with Hebrew learning. I search my mind and heart but can't find the answer you desire. I'd advise you to seek diversion by mixing with your children or talking with your friends. Beyond that, I see no exemption to the requirement of fidelity by the God of this universe."

Zelica shouted, "Then I reject the God of this universe! Why must I suffer? Isn't there a man capable of a little pleasant advice? You mock me, and I won't have it. I reject you, old man! I won't have you in my house another minute!" She ran from the room.

Joseph passed her in the hall. "Get rid of him, Joseph, or I will. I never want to see him again!"

Cephas and Joseph went immediately to the servants' chambers. "I'm sorry, Joseph. I didn't mean to make things harder for you."

"We must think of what to do for you, Cephas. For now, stay here. We'll find an answer."

Zelica had calmed down by the time Potiphar returned home that afternoon. She greeted him warmly and indulgently in her usual manner. She didn't mention Cephas, but praised the way Joseph had run things.

In his audience with Potiphar that evening, Joseph reported his progress in handling the affairs of the household, then carefully addressed the subject of Cephas. "I seek your indulgence, Master. It seems the counselor and your wife have trouble conversing because of differing views concerning deity. It grieves me that he must go, but we must have peace. The old man has been like a father to me. Is there some safe place we can send him?"

"I see no problem with this, Joseph. I'll send him as a gift to Pharaoh. I'll tell him of Cephas's learning, and he will probably let him stand with his other priests. He has priests to every known god in this kingdom, so why not a Hebrew priest? Pharaoh is Hyksos himself, so I think this will work. What do you think?"

Joseph fell on his knees and bowed. "An excellent solution. You're very kind."

"I'm not kind," Potiphar said, but he smiled. "I'm able to ease matters, that's all. Let it be done."

Joseph was summoned to the table of his master and mistress. "We want you to have dinner with us so we can discuss your position," Potiphar said as he motioned Joseph to sit down. "Zelica tells me you've charmed the entire household into submission and relative peace."

"Joseph is devoted to you," Zelica said. "He's not easily diverted from his duties and doesn't linger with the beautiful girl servants. I even hear he's a virgin."

Joseph blushed and kept his eyes on the table. Potiphar laughed. "I'm pleased with your work, Joseph. I'm even surprised at the change you have wrought in Jaeb. You may consider your position permanent."

"Thank you. I'll do my best to maintain your good opinion of me."

Joseph was moved into Jaeb's former quarters, a small room next to the servants' dormitory. It contained one bed and a small table. He was given clothing suitable for his new station, a crimson robe edged with gold and tied with a gold rope. His head was no longer shaved as a slave's.

Potiphar stayed home one more day, then left again.

Zelica smiled at Joseph each time they met or passed in the house. That evening, she sent Jaeb to bring Joseph to her in the dining room, where she sat at a small table near an open window. "It's my husband's request that you join me for the evening meal."

Joseph sat in a chair opposite her and rested one hand on the table.

"He has great confidence in your ability to look after me. I told him you filled the void left by my dead son."

Joseph put his eyes down.

Zelica moved her foot over by his, her perfume distracting. "Aren't you going to thank me for my words in your behalf?"

"Thank you."

"The way is clear, Joseph," she said quietly, leaning forward and placing her hand on his. "Now, even if my husband were to hear reports of anything between us, he wouldn't believe them."

Joseph moved his hand to his lap.

She continued. "You mustn't be afraid of me. I won't force our relationship. It will all come about quite naturally. Think of yourself as master of the house while Potiphar is gone—my lord and master. I'll be submissive to your every wish." She rubbed her foot along the side of his calf. "Think about it. When you're ready, I'll be here. I'll make it feel right."

Joseph stood and walked toward the door.

"Good night, my darling. Dream of me," she taunted as he left.

For several months Zelica was patient in her confidence that Joseph would eventually submit to her desires. She kept in good humor and smiled at everyone. It was assumed that the two would always have their dinner together. Sometimes when Potiphar was home, Joseph was able to eat with the servants.

The work in the household went well, and Potiphar was pleased with the reports. Joseph worked hard and relied on God to direct him. As a result, the house of Potiphar prospered. Everything that Joseph touched flourished and grew, and Joseph credited the Lord for blessing him.

The first week Potiphar left him in charge, Joseph's ideas for improving the cattle farm were under way. He and the steward worked well together and started by extending the growing area of grain raised to feed the cattle. They then purchased some cows and a bull of superior stock and breeding. Their plans proved fruitful, and the cattle multiplied abundantly. They kept the best of the stock and promised future auctions of superior calves.

Joseph directed the gardener in enhancing the courtyard in back of the house. It was now growing some new herbs and four new fruit trees that would supply shade for the children's play area. The gardener had come home from the marketplace several times, excited to plant a new seedling he had purchased. They even planned a large garden area near the cattle farm to supply more fresh food for the household.

Finally Zelica decided she must try a new plan. One evening at their meal she said, "I admire your strength of character, Joseph. You've been with us for over a year now, and I know you desire me. How can you be so strong?"

"I can do nothing by myself," Joseph said. "I draw strength from my God, Yahweh."

"My husband and I are Hyksos, you know. Our fathers believed in God, as you do, although such belief was given up long ago. We have taken on the customs of the Egyptians. But I want what you have. Will you teach me about your God?"

"Certainly," Joseph said. "When would you like to do this?"

"Why not tomorrow?"

"Very well then, tomorrow."

Determined to prove her point, Zelica was a model pupil. They met in the library once a week where Joseph taught her about forgiveness, repentance, obedience, and sacrifice. He taught that the purpose for being on the earth was to learn, experience, love, and give service. He told her of the final judgment and of a Messiah who would come to earth to redeem all men and women, and that through his love, they could return to live with Yahweh. Her husband was even pleased with her attitude of study. Lessons continued for several months. Zelica felt the time had come.

They entered the library to begin another lesson, but before they sat down, she questioned him. "I've been a good student, haven't I, Joseph?"

"Yes, you have."

"And I've kept my distance, and restrained my longing for you. Is it not so?"

Joseph's voice quieted. "I was hoping you had found peace with yourself."

"But you see? I've gone out of my way for you in every instance. Can't you appreciate the sacrifices I've made for you? I've even given up my idols!"

He searched her face. "Haven't you benefitted from your lessons?"

She threw her hands in the air. "Yes! And I see now that your God can love *both* of us. I see that he understands my heart. He knows I need you, Joseph. If He is to be my God too, then you must relieve this longing I have for you. Come to my bed. Let's be one and believe together." She put her arms around his neck and held on to him.

"You don't see!" Joseph cried. He pulled her arms off of his neck and held her away from him. "How can you twist things so much?" He walked out of the room, and she slowly crumpled to the floor and wept.

# Chapter Fourteen

# Mahta Given Away

The next day Zelica was in a foul mood and strode around the house looking for distractions.

As part of Joseph's routine, he stopped regularly at the nursery, looked over the children and the servants, and always spoke to Mahta and asked how she was doing. This day Joseph and Mahta were talking and laughing by the door when Zelica came by and saw him smiling down at the girl. She erupted into a fit of jealousy, then stalked off. Joseph followed her upstairs into the common room where she confronted him.

"I've given you every consideration. I've done everything I thought you wanted. Have you ever smiled at me? No. Have you ever laughed and talked with me? No. If that girl is what makes you happy, then you can't have her!"

"Mistress, she's a child I look after."

"No more," Zelica said, cold as marble. "She has to go."

"You must not hurt her. I'll agree to let her leave here, but I'd rather die than see her hurt."

Zelica raised an eyebrow. "She shall be sold to the pleasure house."

"No, absolutely not. If you even think such a thing, I'll leave too."

"And what do I get in your presence? Pain! Is that supposed to make me happy?" She looked at him for a moment as if to consider her options, then said, "All right. I'll send her to Pharaoh's nursery. But you must promise never to see her again."

Joseph's features softened. "You have my promise. And thank you."

Zelica shook her head. "Don't thank me. I hate her. But you must try to be a little nicer to me."

Joseph did try. With every encounter he tried to smile and act more considerate of Zelica. She enjoyed his attention, but it was far from the affection she craved. With the loss of hope in her conquest, she also began to lose her appetite.

One day Potiphar took her hands and held them out to her side. "What's happened to my bright-eyed beauty?" He pulled her close to him. "There are dark circles under your eyes and no color in your cheeks. You're getting too thin to be healthy. Do you need a physician?"

"I've been having pain here." She pointed to her heart. "It's caused me to lose sleep, but I'll be myself again soon. Don't worry about me, darling. You have enough to worry about, with all you do for Pharaoh."

"You're an exceptional woman, Zelica." He kissed her forehead. "You know I couldn't bear it if anything happened to you. Please take care of yourself."

---

It was Bazaar time again. Joseph sought out his old friend, Kumash, as he shopped for the needs of the master. The exotic booth was not too hard to find. Kumash was genuinely pleased to see him and gave him a strong embrace.

"Shalom, my dear Joseph. I see your curls have grown back. Let's see, it's been two summers since you left me. How are you doing? Is Potiphar treating you well?"

"Things are all right, especially now that I see you and this lively Bazaar."

Kumash, as perceptive as always, saw something in Joseph's answer. "Tell me about your situation."

"It's good," Joseph said. Looking around at Kumash's new goods, he felt a piece of silk. "I'm the overseer of the house of Potiphar and he treats me well."

"And what about Cephas and Mahta?"

Joseph looked at his old master. "They're serving in Pharaoh's palace. I don't see them anymore."

Kumash's voice softened. "Is that the source of pain I see behind your eyes, or is there more? Is this the destiny you saw for yourself, my friend?"

Joseph couldn't keep back a smile. "You're discerning as always, Kumash. But I'm where I should be—for now. The future will tell more. I'll be patient."

Kumash lifted both arms into the air. "Say the word, Joseph, and I'll buy you back. Even though I fear your father."

"Shhh," Joseph said, looking around to see if anyone was listening. "Please don't speak of that, but thank you. I feel better just seeing you again." He leaned closer and asked, "Do you have news of my father? Do you ever hear anything about my family?"

"Yes, my boy. I've kept my eyes and ears open. I listen and ask when I think it's safe to hear news of your home. Your brothers are respected and feared throughout all Canaan. There are those who have dared to encroach on your father's lands and wells. Your brothers, it is said, defend against the marauders. They are fierce in battle and never defeated. Your family grows in wealth and power. The wars your brothers win profit them more slaves and more servants."

"That's what I expected," Joseph said. "But please, Kumash, don't tell anyone else what you know about my family."

"I haven't and I won't. Your secret is safe with me. But there's something else." Kumash leaned forward and almost whispered. "They say that there was a sacred coat, torn and bloodied. It was presented to Father Israel when the son came up missing."

"That was my coat."

"I never tried to pry, but I always wondered how you came to be sold to me."

Joseph said, "My brothers sold me to Ahkmar. They were angry with me. I'm sure they have since regretted it and repented. I don't want to shame them. I told you that my God made it known to me that I was to come to Egypt. So here I am."

"You're brave, Joseph. I'll keep my eye on you. I'd like to see the end of this story."

"Please continue to listen for news. I miss them so much. I'll come look for you during Bazaar to find out what you've learned."

"Of course, Joseph. Of course."

"You said the coat was torn and soiled with blood?"

"Yes, but more. They also said that Israel tore the coat into twelve pieces. He gave a piece to each of his sons to wear next to their hearts. He wears one as well. He won't give up hoping. They're supposed to wear the cloth until the lost son is found."

Joseph looked at Kumash and sighed. "Thank you, and goodbye for now."

He couldn't bear going back to the house in his state of mind, and since he hadn't seen much of the city, he decided to take a closer look at Memphis. He walked up one street and down another, then went out through one of the ten city gates and covered the area around the entire city wall. When he found a straight course ahead, he stretched his legs and ran like he had as a boy. From outside the wall he could see the Great River and the beautiful white city glistening in the sunlight. From inside the wall, the palace blocked the view of the river since the temple and the palace were situated on its bank. Small streams were diverted from the river to run under the palace and down the side of each street, giving the city its fresh water supply.

As he walked, he tried to set his mind at peace. He wondered about his family and asked God to give him the faith and endurance he knew he was going to need.

# Chapter Fifteen

# Zelica's Friends

In another part of the pavilion, Jaeb followed Zelica with the horse and chariot while Zelica strolled about looking at the displays. She wandered aimlessly and couldn't settle her attention on anything. She was about to get on the chariot when she heard someone call her name.

"Zelica, darling, is that you?" She turned and saw two of her friends, Ayella and Ona, coming toward her. They were wives of counselors to Pharaoh.

"It's good to see you, Zelica," Ona said.

"It's been so long. Where have you been, my dear?" Ayella asked. "Aren't you well?"

"Do I look well?" Zelica said, scowling.

"You're beautiful, as always. Isn't she, Ona? But as I look closer, I sense that something is not quite right with you."

"You are so thin," Ona said.

"I don't want to talk about it now. But I do want to share my ordeal with someone." Her friends noticed a faint smile.

"Well, you certainly have my interest," Ayella said.

"Come to my house tomorrow for a midday meal," Zelica said, "and I'll show you."

Ona's eyebrows shot up. "Show us?"

"Yes, you'll see. I'll expect you both." She brushed each with a kiss on the cheek and left them looking expectant.

The next day Jaeb ushered Zelica's two friends into the dining room. They both had dark hair with similar blunt cuts, but Ayella's was longer. Ona wore a peach-colored opaque gown with a large opal necklace. Ayella wore a sheer white dress with layered skirt. Zelica lounged in a simple blue dress, already waiting for them. She smiled and motioned them to sit.

"Make yourselves comfortable, my dears. We shall eat good food, talk about old times, and forget our problems for a moment."

Zelica led the party through each delicious course. After the initial hot drink, flat bread with yogurt and cucumbers was served. The main dish of water fowl was baked to a golden brown and surrounded by green squash stuffed with nuts and goat cheese. The conversation was light with a bit of gossip. The last course of citrus fruit was served, each guest given a small sharp knife to peel their fruit. Then Zelica requested the overseer's presence.

She had her back to the door, but knew the exact moment Joseph came through the doorway by of the looks on her guests' faces. He came and stood inside the room waiting for Zelica's orders. She was telling a story, and when she finished, he said, "Mistress," to announce his presence. She asked him about the purchases of the day and he assured her they had been handled. She thanked and dismissed him.

Then she had to aid her friends, for they had both slipped with their knives and cut themselves when Joseph came in.

"He's exquisite," Ona muttered.

"Now you know why I'm sick."

"Where did you get him?" Ayella whispered.

"From the slave block. He stepped on that platform and I just had to have him. I only regret that he won't come to my bed."

"What?" Ayella cried. "Don't you own him?"

"Oh, believe me, I've tried," Zelica said. "He thinks it would be wrong. He's such an innocent; he believes his Hebrew God would punish him if he succumbed to me."

"That hasn't stopped any of the men I know." Ayella laughed. "Maybe you want him so badly because he keeps refusing you."

Ona added, "If he was yours on command, you'd probably get tired of him. Besides, he's a little too stiff for my taste. I like men a little less handsome and more wicked."

"Does he ever smile?" Ayella asked. "I like men with a sense of humor."

"You can make fun if you want to, but it doesn't make me feel any better," Zelica said. "How would you feel if he was in your sight day after day?"

"I couldn't bear it," Ayella said.

Ona shook her head. "Nor I. How long has he been here?"

"Over two years." Zelica went on to explain the history of her relationship with Joseph.

"We've got to get you back to your old self," Ona said. "I have a young servant from Punt you can borrow."

"Get rid of him—send him to me," Ayella joked.

"You're not helping me," Zelica said.

"Very well." Ayella gave a sly smile. "My husband, being a physician, employs a man knowledgeable in the use of herbs. I'll have him make you a love potion. You can sprinkle it on his food. It's sure to put him right where you want him."

"You know, I'm willing to try that," Zelica said, nodding her head. "I should have talked to you two sooner. Tonight I'll sleep. Thank you."

---

Joseph went to the evening meal with his usual reluctant submission. Zelica was smiling, happier than of late. The food was served, but as Joseph watched, it appeared in his mind that Jaeb had carried in demon food. Joseph jumped to his feet. "I won't eat tonight. It has been shown to me that my food is poisoned. Please excuse me." He turned and strode from the room.

For two weeks Joseph refused all of his evening meals until Potiphar returned.

"Is something wrong, Joseph?" Potiphar asked. "You don't look well."

"A disagreeable stomach, Master. I'll be all right."

"Zelica also worries me," Potiphar said. "I'm afraid she does too much for me. I'm going to send her to On where she can visit with family members for a while. Maybe she needs a good rest."

The following day Zelica found herself taken away in a chariot surrounded by her personal belongings. Her husband had given last minute orders to her servants, kissed her, and waved her goodbye. "Don't come back until you're strong," he called.

Inside the house, Joseph sighed with relief. Immediately his step was lighter, and he started to enjoy his work.

## Chapter Sixteen

# In Pharaoh's Service

Mahta had thought Potiphar's house was grand, but the splendor of the palace was unbelievable. "What am I doing here?" she often said to herself. She remembered how Zelica had shouted at Jaeb to remove her from her sight. Joseph had gone with Jaeb across the square to deliver her to the palace. He'd been quite clear in the urgency with which he admonished the servant. "Tell the chief steward that she's to work nowhere but the nursery. Tell him that Zelica, wife of Potiphar, sends her as a gift. We must be informed if any changes are made in her placement."

Mahta had tried to be brave. As long as she had been with Cephas and Joseph, she had tried to match their courage. She hadn't cried out loud in front of anybody during the whole ordeal of her slavery—not since Saku had beaten her friends. Her uncle had trained her not to cry. Maybe now her tears came because Joseph was so concerned, or because she might not see him again, or because of the unknown future. Hadn't Joseph and Cephas promised that the three of them would always be a family? What now? The tears would not stop.

Joseph had tried to comfort her. "It'll be all right, Mahta. Cephas will look in on you. This will be a fine place to work, and God will watch over you. Don't forget Him. I'll pray for you. Goodbye, dear little friend."

When Jaeb had presented her to the head butler, the man had been curt. "We don't need more servants. From Potiphar's nursery you say? She looks like she belongs in a nursery herself.

I don't see how I can refuse a gift from the captain of the king's guard, but..."

Jaeb persisted. "She's good with children. She was much loved in Potiphar's house."

"Then why isn't she still in Potiphar's house?"

"Just a matter of my mistress's temper. You know how that can be."

In the end, she had been received, placed in the nursery, and forgotten. She sought the strength to be brave and found solace in the fact that she would be with babies—she loved babies.

The nursery consisted of chambers that housed all of Pharaoh's children, twelve from his concubines. The queen, much younger than the king, had borne him one son, now four years old. Magron, who would one day replace his father as Pharaoh, was allowed to play with the other children only occasionally. Most of the time, he was with his tutor, who was beginning to groom the young prince for his future office.

The head of the nursery, Nuni, was a full-bodied, graying woman, kind but firm. She had come to the palace many years before as a slave girl. Most of her life had been spent caring for the king's children. Her skin was a beautiful bronze color, but no one knew of her origin.

Two other slave girls were already assigned to the children. One was about eighteen years old, a black girl from Punt named Mizrel. The other was a little larger than Mahta, fifteen years old and a Moabite. She was called Jain.

From the first moment the steward had thrust Mahta through the nursery door, Jain had befriended her, but Mizrel held back as if she resented the invasion into the lives of her and her friend. Nuni was warm, but all work. "Does the steward think we need four people to care for thirteen children? Come girl, do you know how to care for little ones?"

In spite of the number of caregivers, there was plenty to do. At night, when the children were asleep, the girls were allowed to go to their own bedchamber. The three shared the small quarters. Nuni had her own room. Food was brought in twice a day, and there was always a full fruit bowl on the table.

Being with children lifted Mahta's spirits, and suddenly her future bore a glimmer of hope. It didn't take long for her to gain the confidence of Nuni and settle into a routine that satisfied her. They all worked well together. The newcomer, they found, could work magic with the babes.

Sometimes at night the girls would lie in their beds and whisper to each other. "Tell us where you came from. What places have you been?" They happily absorbed all of Mahta's adventures and shared their own.

One night Mizrel asked, "Have you ever lain with a man?"

"No, of course not," Mahta said.

"Well, you might wish you had."

"What do you mean?"

Mizrel explained. "Why do you think Nuni lived to be such an old age? Why do you think I'm still here at age eighteen?"

"Why?" Mahta asked, wide-eyed.

"Because they take the virgins and offer them as sacrifices. I was violated at an early age. It was just a matter of luck, and my homely face, that I wasn't sent to the pleasure house. I'm fairly safe here. I may grow to be as old as Nuni."

Mahta was terrified. She asked, "How do they know who the virgins are?"

"They have ways of telling."

"Well," Jain said, "I'm just going to tell them I was violated too—if anyone asks."

Mizrel nodded. "The festival of the gods is coming soon. They'll probably be looking for a virgin."

Mahta hardly slept that night. For the next several days she was preoccupied with the things Mizrel had told her. Soon she convinced herself that it was only talk. Then just as she was beginning to relax, a messenger came to the nursery and announced, "The holy men require that we bring all virgin girls to the reception room. A place of honor awaits the one chosen for a special purpose."

Mahta found herself with Jain and several other young girls being hustled along into a large room where four men—the priests—awaited their arrival. A tall angular man stood up. "Line them up so we can see them."

The girls, each one paralyzed with fear, were pushed and shoved into compliance. Mahta could feel the bond of hopelessness they shared.

The men looked at every girl carefully. They talked among themselves. Then the tall priest spoke. "The girl we choose will be in a position of great respect. Only superior vessels are fit to be offered to the gods. If you are chosen, you must consider yourself in a place of glory and honor."

Mahta's mind raced back to all she had been taught by her mentors about the true and living God. He was a God of love and kindness. This couldn't be right. She closed her eyes and prayed for courage and understanding and protection, but she couldn't keep herself from trembling. When she opened her eyes, she heard one of the priests say, "This one won't do; she isn't comely enough." He motioned the girl on the end to move out of line.

"And you are too small," one of them said.

"Your body isn't adequate," they said of another.

"The one in the middle may be just what we need."

"Well, she's the right size, and not too ugly. Her hair's almost the color of the queen's."

One of the priests announced to the girls, "For the ultimate sacrifice, we would offer royalty, the queen herself. The gods look favorably on such a high vessel, but they would be placated by a proxy, one who closely resembles the queen in looks or rank."

"Yes, the one in the middle will do." It was Jain they had singled out.

Mahta had to cover her mouth to keep from screaming. The remaining girls were signaled to leave, but her feet wouldn't move. She held out her hands in supplication and tried to speak, to object, but no words would come, and she grew close to hysteria.

"Take that one away!" the tall priest said. "She doesn't appreciate the gravity of this holy offering."

Mahta, forced from the room, stumbled blindly back to the nursery. She spent the rest of the day vomiting and crying. Mizrel and Nuni kept quiet. They knew their place and the futility of talk, so they let Mahta experience her grief in solitude, knowing that such scars would never fully heal. They never saw Jain again.

The next time the festival came, for some reason there was no search in the palace for a virgin. In subsequent years, Pharaoh found excuses to postpone the offering. He didn't like the practice but he had to deal with the entrenched traditions of the long-standing priests. Each year at festival time, for the rest of her life, Mahta became ill.

---

The overseer's work went well in the house of Potiphar. There was less contention among the women. The staff tried hard to please Joseph, so the work was usually done well and on schedule. The master came to depend more and more on Joseph. He acted agreeable to the members of his staff, though his business for Pharaoh kept him gone most of the time. Over a year had passed since Zelica went away and he missed his wife. One evening Potiphar called all of his servants to him.

"Tomorrow your mistress will be returning home. I want you to do everything you can to make her homecoming a happy one. The house must be cleaned, her room made ready, her favorite food prepared. Obey her every wish. My wife must receive the honor and respect due her. Now, to your work, and I want all of you on the steps to greet her when she arrives."

---

The beautiful sorrel steeds whirled into view and the chariot came to a stop at the front door of the captain's grand house. The horses were lathered from the long trip, their large nostrils pulsating while drops of saliva dripped from their chafing bits. Zelica stepped from her chariot with the aid of the muscular driver. She was wrapped in a teal blue cloak to protect her from the dust and sun, her hair turbaned in a matching scarf. She removed the turban and shook her lovely red hair loose until it fell over her shoulders. Her cheeks held new color and her eyes were bright. She smiled as she looked around at the servants receiving her, but her eyes stopped when they met Joseph's. He quickly turned his attention to the chariot, and after reaching for her bundles, hurried inside to put them away. He had forgotten how beautiful she was.

For many days Zelica was the epitome of proper decorum, and Joseph relaxed. Potiphar was away, so Joseph was called to have dinner with her, which she ate in a polite and gracious manner, talking of general household subjects. Joseph said little, excused himself as quickly as possible and retired.

Later, Jaeb came to Joseph's room. "The mistress wants to see you."

*What did she want at this hour?* Apprehensive, Joseph tried to prepare himself. "Please, dear Lord, be with me."

He entered her private quarters, an area of the house that Joseph had little to do with. Only Jaeb, acting as Zelica's personal servant, was allowed here. Joseph had been here that first night, when she pretended to mother him, but now Jaeb was leading him through the bedroom into her bath area. Joseph felt uncomfortably warm. The room was of polished gray granite. Abundant jars of precious oils and perfumes stood on the floor. Lavish furs lay around the steps leading down to the sunken bath where Zelica was submerged.

Joseph focused on a vase across the room. "You sent for me?"

"Sit down, Joseph," she said.

"I'll stand, thank you."

"You're not still afraid of me, I hope." There was a smile in her voice.

"No, Mistress."

She lifted a leg out of the water. "Did you miss me?"

"I had much to do."

"Aren't you happy to see me?"

"I continue to serve you."

"Then come over here and hand me my sponge."

"I would prefer to stand here, please."

"Very well, I'll get it myself."

"No!" Joseph cried as she began to rise out of the water. He turned and hurried out of her room.

———◦◦◦◦———

The following evening at dinner Zelica said to Joseph, "While I was away I had a lot of time to think. Do you remember that I asked you once if you wanted to be my lord and master?"

Joseph looked at his plate and stopped chewing.

"You refused because I was already married. Well, I've decided to remedy that. I'm going to poison Potiphar."

Joseph, visibly shaken, swallowed hard, his countenance fallen in unbelief. "You can't. You..." He spoke just above a whisper. "I implore you not to even consider it."

"How will you stop me? Will you submit to me if I don't poison him?"

The muscles in his face and hands stiffened. "You force me to tell Potiphar your intent. I'll announce the deed if you carry out your threat. The servants will back me. You can't do such a foul and foolish thing."

"Don't be upset, Joseph," she said with a wry smile. "I merely wanted to see where you stand. I told you, you don't need to fear me."

No more was said. Zelica carried on as if nothing were wrong. For months she acted indifferently, but Joseph anxiously watched her as one watches a coiled serpent. He was sure that her pride was injured by his continual rebuff and that she might strike back at any moment. He agonized, fasted and prayed with singleness of mind.

One night Joseph was awakened by someone who had joined him in bed. Zelica lay next to him with nothing on and he bounded away. "Leave! Leave here this moment or I'll raise this entire household."

"Would you shame me? Would you shame your master?"

"I don't want to. Don't make me."

She slid from the bed slowly as if to taunt him, but he looked away. She wrapped herself in a silken shroud and crept away like a docile kitten.

Zelica continued to fawn over Potiphar while he was home, and he basked in her attention, unaware of her unscrupulous designs. But she was no average woman. She had won the love of the high-placed captain of the king's guard. No servant was going to reject her. She tried once again at the next opportunity.

"Joseph, lie with me or I'll kill myself," she said as she rushed into his room and pushed the door closed behind her.

Joseph was more calm, his resolve to refuse her unmoving. "You mustn't do that. It would be a waste of your great beauty. Think of your children. The concubines you despise would beat them. Your husband would bear inconsolable grief."

She moved toward him. "I see that you do care for me. It makes me so happy to hear you say such things, Joseph. I'll wait for you, my darling." She attempted to take hold of his hand and kiss it, but he abruptly drew it back. With a faint smirk, she turned and went back through the door.

Again Zelica went about the house smiling to herself, acting as if she held a cherished secret. Joseph was on his knees, appealing to a benevolent God at every opportunity, anxious that a crisis was inevitable.

———

High Bazaar day came again and Joseph looked for Kumash. Their conversations were always one of his enjoyable diversions, but Kumash didn't come this year. Joseph had walked the entire colonnade looking for his friend and didn't find him. *Where are you, Kumash? Why don't you come?* He walked in deep melancholy back to Potiphar's house.

Potiphar found him and said, "I have allowed the servants to go to Bazaar. Today my guard will march through the colonnade in review, and the entire household is free to watch. Do you mind staying with the house, Joseph?"

"I don't mind. I can watch from the terrace. Go and make us proud, Master."

"Thank you. I have much trust in you Joseph. Also, Zelica complains that the pain in her heart is bothering her again. If she stays home, see to her care as well."

# Chapter Seventeen

# The Accusation

Everyone was gone. Joseph returned to his room and fell to his knees, imploring God to give him strength and protection in his master's house. Then he arose and started for the terrace. Zelica stopped him in the common room, dressed in an elegant red gown. As she stood before him she suddenly dropped her gown. For the briefest moment he flushed at what he saw, but quickly moved back to avoid her.

"Now is our time, Joseph. No one will know. You don't need to feel shame. Come to the couch with me." As she talked she moved forward and pulled on Joseph's arm. He turned his head and wouldn't move.

"This is our chance, my dear. You can have me at last." She took hold of his robe and his mind raced, but he thought of nothing that could stop her—only that he must escape her grasp. He turned to run, but she still held on to his robe, so he twisted free and hurried out the door, leaving it in her outstretched hands.

"You leave me no choice!" she screamed.

When the servants and Potiphar returned, they found Zelica sitting on the couch, hugging Joseph's robe as she sobbed and rocked back and forth.

"Zelica!" Potiphar called as he rushed to her side. Jaeb picked up her garment and brought it to the couch where Potiphar covered her with it. "Why are you holding Joseph's robe? Zelica, speak to me!"

She slowly looked down at the robe, then at her husband's concerned face and seemed to come to herself. "Joseph tried to lie with me and ran in fear of being caught, but not until he had caused me much shame."

"You're distraught, Zelica." He put his arms around her. "Have some wine. When you are yourself, you can make your declaration."

"I am myself. I'll make my declaration now. With all my servants as witnesses and before my husband, I accuse Joseph of trying to violate me. You see—he left his robe."

Potiphar flushed with anger. "Bring Joseph," he shouted.

As Joseph stood before him, Zelica brazenly repeated her charge and Potiphar said, "What do you say, Joseph? How is it possible that you could violate my wife and break my total trust?"

Joseph stared intently at Potiphar. "I stand before you and all this household with a conscience void of guilt. Before my God I declare I am innocent."

There was a moment of uncomfortable silence. Potiphar was nervous; he almost believed his trusted servant.

"No! No!" Zelica shouted. "He did it! He's a liar! He tried to lie with me." Confronting her husband she said, "If you love me, you'll do away with him. He can't stay in this house any longer."

Potiphar was caught. He couldn't compromise. His jaw tightened and he looked from one to the other. In a low voice he said, "Put him in the cell."

Zelica flared. "Won't you have your Nubian whip him?"

"In time I'll deal with him to the utmost of the law. For now, my concern is for you." He ordered her servants to prepare her things. "I'm going to send you to your family again for a brief visit so you may be spared the ugliness ahead."

Soon the chariot was ready and Zelica was reluctantly bundled off on another trip.

Potiphar watched his disconsolate wife until the chariot disappeared, then went to the prison cell. The cell door was unlocked, and the captain stood back so Joseph could exit. "Follow me," he said, as he made his way to the library.

"I'll speak so no one can hear," Potiphar said. "I know you don't lie. I respect your integrity and your faith in your Hebrew

God. You know our culture and understand that in a position like mine, one usually chooses to play deaf and blind." He paused and looked down at the floor, then continued. "With the open declaration my wife made against you, I have to act. I'm the captain of the king's guard, the enforcer of the law, and I must uphold it. In this case the law requires that I believe either you or my wife. If I choose publicly to believe you, I would have to put my wife away. I'm sorry, but I cannot do that. In choosing to allow her story, I must put you away."

Joseph hesitated, then said, "I understand. In a way, I'm relieved. Do what you must."

Potiphar was moved, but continued. "The severest penalty of this law requires you to be put to death. But since you're accused of only trying to violate, I'll send you to prison so your life can be spared."

"So be it," Joseph said.

"It's within my power to bestow whatever favor I choose. Is there anything at all I can do for you, Joseph?"

"Yes. As you know, I came here with two others. I promised to look after them and I worry about the safety of the girl. She's so young and helpless. Your wife sent her to Pharaoh's nursery and she's probably still there. I worry that if she's ever in trouble she might be sent to a pleasure house."

"What do you want me to do?"

"Would it make her more secure if she were a married woman?"

"The law supposes that a married woman is out of reach of another man. In reality, it is not unusual for the husband of a beautiful woman to be found dead so that his wife can be made available."

"It would be difficult to kill me if I were in prison. Besides, I don't think this child would stir up that kind of ardor."

"Yes, that is in your favor."

"Then if there is no better way, I'll ask you to bring the girl here so I can give her my name."

"I'll do it. I'll even supply a priest and you'll have a proper Egyptian wedding ceremony."

Joseph stayed secreted in the library, and Potiphar left with no further discussion, returning in the darkness of night with his friends.

"Joseph, this is Ramieth, and his wife, Rena. Ramieth is a priest in Pharaoh's temple. Tomorrow he leaves for his new assignment as head priest of the temple in the city of On; his absence tonight won't be noticed."

"Thank you for coming," Joseph said as he bowed to the couple.

"You will be pleased with these people, Joseph. They can be trusted and they're sincerely good. Now I'll get the girl. Stay here and keep quiet."

Potiphar had told his friends why the young slave wanted to be married and of the difficult duty he faced in putting Joseph away. After the captain left there was a moment of awkward silence before Joseph said, "What does your role as a priest involve?"

The man said, "I'm in charge of the physical care of the temple, not the ceremonies—although I have authority and training in all aspects of temple work. Potiphar tells me you're a Hebrew."

"Yes. I come from the land of Canaan."

The priest looked thoughtful. "Many years ago a Hebrew came here. The pharaoh respected his wisdom and they were on friendly terms. When I was a young student priest I was called to a gathering to be taught by one who had studied with the learned man. He taught us many things: the study of numbers and of the earth and stars. His words made a great impression on my mind. Later, the older priests told me to disregard the lessons, but I have never forgotten them. Many here revered him and kept his teachings in their hearts. His name was Abraham."

Joseph was about to respond when they heard Potiphar at the door and stood up. Joseph smiled as his master entered the room, but then his eyes widened and his mouth dropped. Before him stood the most beautiful woman he had ever seen. The light from the lantern brightened the highlights of her honey-colored hair. Drawn back near the crown of her head, it fell from there in soft natural curls down her back and over her shoulders. Her simple blue gown flowed gently as she walked with grace and dignity toward him. Her soft skin, flushed pink from excitement, matched her golden hair. Her brown eyes smiled warmly at him.

"Shalom, Joseph."

He couldn't say anything.

She chuckled and said, "It's been a long time."

"Mahta?" he murmured, then bowed briefly. "Please forgive me. I sent for a child, and a woman comes. I had thought to...I'm sorry...it's obvious..." He stood abashed, unable to collect his thoughts at her beauty that so far surpassed his memory of her. Finally he said, "You could have any man you choose."

She smiled as though she held a secret. Then her expression turned more serious. "If that's true, then my decision is simple, but first I must know why you sent for me."

"It was presumptuous. I thought to save you from an uncertain future, to offer you my name to protect you, but I can see you're well. I always cared—I didn't know how much. But now..." He paused, then said softly, "I would be honored to have you as my wife."

She held her expression, and Joseph quickly offered, "Maybe you need some time to think. Forgive me for asking so much of you."

She stepped toward him. "I don't need any time to think, Joseph. I chose you the moment I met you, many years ago in Ahkmar's caravan." She then whispered, "How did you not know that there could be no one for me but you?"

Joseph was happy, but concerned. "I have nothing to offer you but my name. Did Potiphar tell you of my situation?"

"Yes, but it doesn't matter. You taught me to have faith. I'll trust in God to help me endure our separation."

Ramieth smiled and Rena wiped her eyes, touched by the scene they witnessed. She couldn't help thinking how much they belonged together.

The ceremony was short with no need to impress a crowd. Afterwards everyone hugged quietly and smiled broadly. "Thank you very much," Joseph said to the priest.

"What will you do now, Mahta?" Rena asked.

"I suppose I'll go back to the palace and work in the nursery."

Rena, wanting to help ease their future life apart, turned to Ramieth and Potiphar. "What would it take to have her released to our care? I'd like to take her with us to our new home."

"The document is within my power to secure," Potiphar said.

"Just to be sure, why don't we adopt her as our legal child?" Ramieth said. "That way she would be assured of safety." After thorough discussion they all agreed.

"Joseph, take Mahta to my private chamber for the night," Potiphar said. "It's quiet, and no one will disturb you. Tomorrow you must go to prison."

---

Alone in the private quarters, the couple stood facing each other, self-conscious yet joyful in their marriage. Joseph took Mahta's hand and said, "It might be well for us to go through a ceremony of the Hebrew custom to satisfy the covenants of God. I have the right to minister the oaths."

"Yes, of course," she said. Then, as if feeling a need to reassure him, she added, "I haven't changed my mind, Joseph. You need not be shy. I'll be your wife in any country, custom, or oath."

So the young people performed their vows according to Hebrew tradition, their awkwardness slipping away. When the words were finished, they stood still, holding right hands as Joseph gently lifted the golden lock of hair that fell over Mahta's shoulder.

She closed her eyes at his touch and drew closer to him, living her dream of years. She now had her first love, her only love, and Joseph, who had resisted the worthless imitation, found a real love beyond imagining. Soon the two were entwined in an embrace so natural that there was no fear of how to proceed. They belonged together, and their union found completeness in their expressions of physical and emotional intimacy.

Through the night the young couple clung to each other with deep emotion. Neither slept. There would be time for such things as sleep in the empty years ahead.

# Chapter Eighteen

# Prison

Ramieth and Rena came by morning light, eager to collect their prospective daughter, take the necessary legal steps and be on their way. Potiphar came also with two of his men to take Joseph. No one spoke more than required, for what lay ahead was impossible to view with optimism.

Joseph and Mahta embraced one last time, unable to say goodbye. Finally Joseph pulled away, joined his escorts and didn't look back. Mahta wept quietly as he moved out of sight.

Joseph and the guards crossed the deserted pavilion to the far corner of the palace compound where Pharaoh's prison was located. As they entered a small receiving room, two prison guards took him by the arms and led him through an outer chamber and past a few benches where more officers sat in a relaxed attitude of duty.

The guard room was only partially roofed, the open area enclosed by a high wall with a gate that opened to a large dirt yard. The largest part of the yard served as the prison cemetery and was also surrounded by a high wall with a gate on the far side.

Finally the keeper of the prison unlocked the cell door, shoved Joseph into the inner chamber, then closed the door with a clang.

The smell overtook him and he began to retch, unprepared for the conditions facing him. The stench was a mixture of human waste, unwashed bodies, vomit, mold, and rot. Being in the hottest time of year, the heat was bearable in the fresh air, but smothering in the cell.

He struggled to compose himself and began to study his surroundings. As his eyes adjusted to the dimness, he could tell there were others in the room, but could not distinguish how many. The prison consisted of one large room, the floor and walls laid with oversized bricks. The only light came from two small windows next to the ceiling. Thick layers of straw were piled here and there.

The room seemed filled to capacity. Groups of men huddled together. Some of the prisoners, avoided by the rest, lay very still, apparently ill. Others sat by themselves, obviously shunned.

There were no benches, and the space along the wall where one could sit to rest his back was entirely occupied. The eyes of the men watched Joseph as if to challenge him. He stood for a long time until he felt oriented enough to sit in an empty spot in the middle of the chamber.

As he sat down, he closed his eyes and fought the consuming need to cry. "Please, Father, help me be strong," he prayed. "Bear me up; hold on to me. I thank thee for releasing me from Zelica's torment, but help me deal with the injustice of her accusation." His mind turned to Mahta—beautiful, loving Mahta, who had suddenly added a new dimension to his life. "Lord, please watch over her." He felt a brief wave of sorrow for chaining her to an unknown future, but he quickly put it from his mind. *I must be sure of God and of myself.*

When he opened his eyes he saw a variety of looks coming from his cellmates. But he closed his eyes again and asked for help in understanding each soul he would come to know.

For the first couple of days, Joseph studied each prisoner intently. As he grew familiar with their faces, he remembered his first day in Memphis, for here was every kind of man. One of the tall, dignified black men he had seen on the common now sat emaciated and gaunt, staring out of vacuous eyes. Some were Hyksos, some obviously Egyptian—the king's own servants, no doubt. A few came from the North, perhaps even Canaan. Those who appeared to be peasant farmers huddled together in one sector—probably unable to pay their taxes, Joseph thought. All were dispirited and without hope. The Egyptians clustered together and had their way with where they sat, ate, or slept. Joseph learned that the boldest was named Zeeroth. In the shadows against the wall, a man mumbled and growled, his face grotesquely swollen as if he had been beaten. Each man's country was easily identified because each still wore the clothing he was wearing when arrested. But some outfits were so ragged that one could hardly recognize the original. In some cases all that remained was the loin cloth. The length of internment could be calculated by the condition of the clothing.

At mealtime the door creaked open and a couple of buckets with wooden ladles were shoved inside and picked up by a swarthy prisoner who uttered profane grunts and kicked anyone in his way as he carried them to the middle of the room. The strongest and most vicious were the first to slurp the food into their mouths. When they were satisfied, they moved back and allowed the others to each have a turn. Those too weak to go to the buckets did not eat. This happened twice a day, and the containers were put back by the door after they were emptied. Water came in the same way. Sometimes fresh straw was thrown through the door.

Once in a while a pail containing an acrid solution was pushed inside. It was meant to kill the lice and mites. On the second day, the men moved away from a still figure lying at the end of the room and one of the prisoners spoke to the guard. Two guards then entered, each with a pail of solution. One sloshed the contents of his bucket on the floor as they walked— to protect their feet, Joseph thought. The second bucket was then splashed on the stiff body, and it was carried out to the burial yard.

Death was common and disease easily transmitted. Men were coughing and wheezing from every corner. Human waste lay in a gutter that sloped through the middle of the floor to a small opening in the outer wall. The waste could be washed away by pouring water in the trough, but no one bothered to do so. The sick ones who were too weak to move soiled the straw on which they slept. More straw would be piled on top to cover it.

The sight and stench was so bad that Joseph didn't eat or talk for three days. Instead, he fasted and prayed for the strength to endure his confinement. He reviewed his life and wondered what his father would say, wondered if this was truly God's plan and if he could do it. Then he repeated to himself, "When you begin to feel sorry for yourself, find someone in greater need and go to their aid."

On the fourth day he saw several fat rats eating some straw dried with vomit next to the face of a motionless man. He made his way to the man, kicked at the bold rodents, then filled the water ladle and brought it to him. Holding up the man's head, he put the ladle to his cracked lips and let the water trickle onto his swollen tongue, some running down the sides of his face. Then he remained close to the ailing man.

At the next mealtime, as the food bucket was set down, Joseph quickly moved to the center of the cell, grabbed the ladle and brought food to his sick friend.

"What are you trying to do?" Zeeroth snarled.

"You'll ruin it for the rest of us," another Egyptian said.

"They're better off dead; it's the only way out for these unfortunate beggars," one of the peasants said.

Joseph approached him and asked, "What is your name?"

"Heth."

"Well, Heth, what do you mean, it is the only way out?"

"Don't you know? This is where the guards throw those they don't know what else to do with. Bazaar just ended. It's always full in here after Bazaar. Then as they die off, we get more room."

Joseph looked puzzled. "Do you mean that many of these men have committed no crime?"

"Not by the laws I know," Zeeroth said. "Some were just drunk, or sick." Pointing to the thin black man he added, "That one over there had his money stolen, and couldn't speak Egyptian."

Heth broke in. "The guards' duty is to keep order and keep the city streets clean of human trash. They clean up by throwing the garbage—these wretches—in prison."

"You mean no one gets out of this filthy place alive?" Joseph asked.

Zeeroth explained. "Half of those here are from the palace. This rat's nest is Pharaoh's prison. The overseer of the palace guard keeps track of the ones Pharaoh sends in. He can throw anyone in, anytime he feels like it. Most of the time, after he calms down, he sends his steward to bring them back. The law states that only Pharaoh can get a prisoner out. If a family has one of its members here, they can go to the officers of the guard, who can petition Pharaoh. If he has time or inclination, he orders a release. He doesn't even know about the other half who are here. Probably wouldn't care anyway."

"So if a man is sick with no one to care for him, he is sent here to die?"

"If they find him lying in the street, yes." It was Heth who spoke.

"Has it always been this way?"

"Things have been difficult since the shepherd kings, these Hyksos, took over," Zeeroth said. "When the true race of Egypt ruled, the law ran more smoothly; troublemakers were usually banished. Now that we have a shepherd king as Pharaoh, he fills the main positions, especially his force, with his own kind. They think this is the way to keep order."

"So do you resent all those in here who are not Egyptian?"

"If Egyptians only were in this prison, we could at least communicate. We could establish some routine. Those who have tried have given it up as hopeless. The keeper never even looks inside anymore. The guards come in only to pick up the dead or call out an order. And yes, I do resent the others. Outside of prison we Egyptians would not even eat in the same room with the inferior races. In here, we are forced to eat slop from the same ladle. If we don't get to the buckets first, we have to eat contaminated food. That man you just fed is Hyksos, and I guess that you are a Hebrew. You have defiled the meal. We Egyptians may not eat now. Look around you. Do you wonder why there's hate in here?"

"I don't believe in a superiority of races," Joseph said. "But from now on, I won't come to the buckets before you." He returned to nurse the Hyksos man, who thanked him in a weak voice.

"I'm glad you can speak. What's your name?"

"Moesha."

"My name is Joseph. Rest now. We'll talk when you're stronger".

At the next meal, Joseph ate a little of the pottage, then fed his friend. The food seemed to be all the leftovers from the king's kitchen, thrown together to make swill. Nevertheless, it contained nutriments, and Moesha responded to Joseph's care. After a few meals, he could sit up and he finally spoke. "I heard what the others told you about the conditions here. It's true. I'm Hyksos, but I didn't make my home in Memphis. I have no family and I made my way in life by traveling about selling my goods. I dealt in star charts, fortunes, charms, and written prayers. I came every season to Bazaar and I did well."

He continued. "This year, at the beginning of the festivities, things went wrong. I was tending my shop when a ruffian, chased by a guard, ran by and, unseen by me, threw a gold bracelet among my wares. Later, the owner of the bracelet found it lying there and accused me of stealing. I was whipped and thrown in here. I have no one on the outside, so like many others, when I got sick I gave up hope and waited to die."

"You're a good man, Moesha," Joseph said. "You must take hope and help me make it better in here. Let's see to the needs of the others."

Together Moesha and Joseph ministered to the ailing black man who was pushed into a corner and forgotten. The large man was lethargic, and no one could speak his tongue. Joseph, by signs, let him know that they were his friends. They fed him and cleaned his straw.

Eventually a few words became common between them, and soon he began to cooperate. His name, they decided, was Uahma, which quickly became Wama. He had an innocence about him and he became almost cheerful as they learned more of each other's language.

Wama made known to Joseph that he had stolen some bread, having been parted from his group and from his money by trickery.

Against the wall, not far from Wama, sat the burly man whose face was swollen and misshapen. He could move to the food and water, but always returned to his spot, never speaking. If Joseph went near or even looked at him, he growled.

"If I only had some oil or salve, I could relieve the pain on his head," Joseph said to Moesha.

And so it went. One by one, little by little the two men went about doing what little good they could and gaining friends in their success. Three weeks had passed since Joseph's imprisonment and conditions were still deplorable, but the attitudes of some were improving.

# Chapter Nineteen

# Prison Reforms

One day the prison door was thrown open and a guard shouted, "The Hebrew, Joseph, has a visitor!" A murmur ran through the room as Joseph stepped blinking into the guard room, all the guards standing attentively still. He had to shield his eyes until they became accustomed to the light.

"Hello, Joseph." It was Potiphar who spoke, and whose presence caused the guards' stiff behavior.

"Master," Joseph said, "how good it is to see you."

"You don't look well, Joseph."

"My needs are not my concern when so much is lacking for the others here. May I speak freely to you, Master?"

Potiphar laughed. "Since when didn't you speak your mind to me?" He motioned Joseph to a bench where they sat down.

Joseph spoke earnestly until Potiphar stood up. "Wait here." He stepped in to see the keeper of the prison. When he returned he motioned Joseph to join him in the reception room.

The keeper was flushed and nervous. "Make a list," Potiphar said to him. Turning to Joseph, he said, "I feel remiss in allowing conditions to deteriorate to this level. This prison is under my authority and I'm responsible for its management. I haven't been inside here for a long time and I was unaware that the keeper and his aides were so lazy. It seems the meager supplies meant for this prison have been confiscated. I'll find out who is responsible for this. In the meantime I'm signing a blank order. Anything within reason that you need will be furnished to you, Joseph. I have talked with the keeper here and he agrees that you should have full responsibility inside the prison. The guards are to assist you as you have need. They will answer to me if there is any trouble."

Joseph said a silent prayer of thanks to God, then began naming the desperately needed supplies. When he finished he turned to Potiphar and thanked him.

"No, I thank you. I hope these things will make it better for you. I can do nothing about releases, but at least I can make you comfortable. I will check back with you in about a month."

Potiphar left, and Joseph spoke to the keeper. "Before the new supplies arrive, we must clear the floor of filth and burn the soiled straw. The cell door must be left open to the yard out there. I'll promise good behavior from the prisoners, but you'll need your guards stationed and alert.

"I understand why we cannot use shovels or other tools, but we will need brooms and many buckets of water. Fresh straw will be needed by evening. We'll need clean fabric for new loin cloths, and later, when the other cloth goods come, we'll make tunics.

The surprised keeper barked out orders for brooms and sent a man to get the cloth. He made sure the straw was available, then dropped into his chair, tired and bewildered. In all his years in charge, he had never seen such an unbelievable sight.

Joseph stepped back into the foul-smelling darkness, moved to the center of the room and raised his voice to get all the prisoners' attention. "The captain of the king's guard has taken an interest in our welfare. We're to have proper supplies for our prison."

"He thinks he's important," one of the Egyptians said, and the man with the grotesque face growled, but most of the prisoners expressed enthusiastic approval.

"They are bringing brooms," Joseph continued. "We'll carry this foul straw out to the yard, and after we sweep, we'll wash the bricks and rinse the residue through the gutter. Tonight we'll sleep in a clean room on fresh straw."

When the brooms arrived, Moesha and Wama jumped to the task of gathering straw and scooping up the human refuse. Most of the others soon joined the effort. Joseph pushed on the cell door and propped it wide open, letting in light and fresh air. At first the prisoners viewed the scene with a feeling of wonder. *Could this be happening?* The light and air alone gave them a new sense of life and strength.

Joseph picked up a bundle of straw and said, "Follow me." The straw was deposited in the dirt outside, and when the pile was heaped high, the keeper set it on fire. Joseph took off his ragged clothing and threw it on the fire, then made a loin cloth from the clean linen provided. The prisoners followed his lead, throwing onto the fire the last vestige of distinction each man claimed that symbolized his homeland. As the flames rose, however, so did the hope of many who watched.

Back inside, the scrubbing took place. Soon the fresh straw arrived by carts through the outside gates. If any prisoner contemplated an escape, not one made such a move, though the guards were watchful.

The atmosphere in the prison that night was one of good cheer. For the next several days supplies continued to arrive. Shelves were placed against a wall. A table was set in the middle of the room. A wooden bowl for each man was provided and placed on the shelves.

The benches the guards sat on in the outer chamber were originally intended for the prisoners. Now new benches arrived and were placed around the outside walls.

One day a barber arrived and Joseph announced, "We're to be shaved to get rid of lice and mites, but after that, we can have moderate haircuts to our liking. We'll go one at a time into the yard where our hands must be bound behind our backs. I'll go first. Please line up and be ready when I return."

Even the ones who hated Joseph submitted to the shave. One could assume who had been imprisoned the longest by the length of his hair and beard, but everyone's was dirty and matted. The head shaving brought a welcome relief to the itching and irritation they had endured.

The cloth for their garments came already cut the proper length, each piece with an opening for the head. A sash was provided to tie around the waist and hold the garment together.

Everyone was grateful when the medicine and balms arrived. There was aloe for wounds and for washing; bitter root for running bowels; siapa leaves to make poultices for infections; medicinal leaves for cramps and stomach ache. There was also a little healing oil, salve, and cloth for bandages. No prison had ever been supplied like this. Potiphar had responded out of his great respect for his former servant.

One of the prisoners who had seemed hostile yet quiet came forward. "I'm ashamed to tell you this, but I'm a physician. My name is Pleoris. I was sent here after I could not save the ailing son of a magician in the king's court. I have been here many years. When I first came I tried to help, but when it appeared hopeless I gave up. Now I am renewed in hope. If you agree, I'll do what I can for the sick."

"Thank you. You're needed over here." Joseph led the physician to the wall where sat the battered man who growled. Together they cleaned, salved, and bandaged the man's head.

The man allowed their service, but when they had finished, he drew back and stared viciously at them. "Don't think I'm going to thank you, Joseph," he said almost inaudibly.

Joseph, with furrowed brow, looked hard into the man's face and said, "Saku, I didn't recognize you."

---

The reform brought several changes. The quality of the food was somewhat improved and the portions increased. Water was plentiful enough for drinking and bathing. Fresh straw came and the old was burned monthly. The prisoners tried to keep a cleaner chamber, rinsing the gutter as needed.

Joseph saw to it that each morning everyone walked around the dirt yard in the sunshine. The door to the inner chamber was left open to let in fresh air.

To placate the Egyptians, Joseph portioned off a section of the room with small straw bundles. They were allowed to dish up their food first, then go into their private sector to eat. They seemed satisfied with this arrangement, and as the reforms proceeded, Joseph convinced the guards to bring three buckets instead of one. That way the Egyptians had their own bucket, and the others received better portions.

On Potiphar's next visit he noticed the improvement, pleased to have ordered such a change. At Joseph's apprisal, he made a new requisition, and after he left, a few more items were procured. The keeper of the prison himself stepped inside the large room one day and ceremoniously lit the sandalwood incense. The response was positive and dramatic among the prisoners. As the smoke rose, so did their spirits. They all agreed to ration the remaining incense for special occasions.

A few days later, a large basketful of purple grapes came. Moesha went among the men, carefully placing a cluster in each of their hands. Some ate greedily, but others ate the grapes one at a time, relishing each ripe fruit as the sweet juice burst into their deprived mouths. Later, pomegranates and then citrus brightened their drab existence.

The improvement did not take care of all the problems. Sickness and death still plagued them—even with the physician's care. In some cases the improvement gave strength to the opposition. Those with hardened hearts who refused to change became more bitter. While all the prisoners seemed to talk more, the antagonists now made frequent complaints. Lethargy turned to revolt, and fighting took place. The guards, who had previously entered the room only to dispose of the dead, were often needed to break up fights. Joseph tried to divide the room to isolate the sick and provide others a refuge from the aggressive. He was often cursed, spat upon, and threatened for his efforts.

Almost daily Joseph tried to attend to Saku's needs, or to do something kind for him. All he got in return was the usual snarl. Pleoris had seen him repeatedly minister to the growling man, and one day he asked, "Why do you bother with him, Joseph?"

Joseph contemplated and answered, "Sometimes the person acting the sourest is the one who needs love the most. Anyway, I cannot let someone else's bad behavior determine my mood."

Rather than give in to defeat, Joseph drew closer to God, his heart and mind intent on doing His will. The more difficult the situation, the more submissive to God he became.

Several months had passed until the time came for another visit from Potiphar. When Joseph went to meet the visitor, he was expecting to see his master. But it was not the captain of the guard who waited for him; it was his wife.

Zelica held a rose out to Joseph as he was presented to her. She wore a flowing gown gathered under the bust by a long gold braid. The dress was a green shade that matched her eyes and accentuated her red hair. But despite her apparent cosmetic effort, she looked drawn and pale.

"Hello, Joseph. I'm back from my trip."

He didn't answer.

"Aren't you happy to see me?"

"You shouldn't have come here."

"I came on your behalf."

"How so?"

"It's not too late, my darling. I can have you released. Just say the word and I'll see you're freed."

"What word would that be?"

"That you admit your love for me. That we can be together."

"I have nothing to say to you." Joseph turned, stepped back into the cell and shut the door.

"He forgot his rose," Zelica said as she handed it to a guard and left the prison.

The guard sent the rose inside. But as it passed from one prisoner to the next, it was handled and sniffed and caressed until it withered and fell apart.

# Chapter Twenty

# Unlooked-for Visitor

The men Joseph cared for either loved him or hated him. The keeper sensed that the man he had put in charge was someone of importance. Potiphar had left no doubt of that. So when the next visitors arrived, the keeper came in person to Joseph and announced, "The priest of On and his family have come to see you."

Joseph greeted Ramieth and Rena with affection, then gazed at Mahta, his eyes never leaving her face, as Ramieth spoke.

"We had business with Pharaoh, so we brought your bride. She sorely misses you, but we can stay only briefly. Rena and I will wait outside so you can be alone." The keeper followed them into the guard room.

Joseph and Mahta held each other close with tears in their eyes, not wanting to let go. Joseph spoke first. "I grieve for you to see me like this."

"We have seen each other in difficult circumstances before."

"How are you, my beautiful precious wife? Are you happy? Do your new parents take good care of you? There's so much to talk about." Joseph spoke as he kissed Mahta over and over. "You smell so sweet, so delicious. My heart could burst for love of you."

She smiled at the wonder of being with him again and feeling his love. "I'm well taken care of, Joseph. My new parents are good and kind. I live to be with you again. I pray daily for our reunion." She paused, then smiled broadly. "I have news for you that I have waited to share."

Joseph, hearing the smile in her voice, held her at arm's length and looked into her eyes.

"We are to be parents," she said.

He drew her close and held her tenderly as they wept softly. Then they talked together, never pausing for a breath, until Ramieth and Rena reappeared an hour later.

"I'm sorry we don't have more time," Ramieth said. "We don't even know when we'll be back in this city. We'll come when we can."

"Thank you for your care," Joseph said. "You've done so much, and I ask that you continue to look after my wife. She's with child."

Delighted, Rena clapped her hands, and Ramieth beamed.

Joseph said, "Please let me know when it comes."

Yes, of course! We'll send word. What wonderful news. Did she tell you we gave her an Egyptian name? Now that she is legally an Egyptian, she is called Aseneth."

"Aseneth," Joseph whispered. "I like it."

They were at the door now and had to go. Rena said, "I'm sorry that we have to rush."

Joseph wished them well, then embraced his wife once more. "Goodbye...Aseneth."

It was seven months before they returned. When Joseph came in, the priest's family stood in the reception room. The keeper had absented himself again. Ramieth and Rena beamed over their three-month-old grandson. Joseph looked from Mahta to his son and back again, unable to take in enough of them.

Ramieth said, "We'll leave Aseneth and the baby with you while we attend to our business. The keeper has given permission for this visit to exceed the normal time allotment. This may be our last trip to Memphis for a long time. We'll be back later in the afternoon."

Joseph took the infant in his arms, in awe at the miracle of life he beheld. "The boy is large and well-formed—a credit to Israel!"

"You'll be pleased to know that in keeping with the covenant of Abraham, he has been circumcised."

"You had it done to fulfill the covenant?"

"No, the Egyptians practice circumcision for a different reason; they do it as a matter of course. I just went along with it knowing you would have approved."

"I do approve. I'm pleased, in fact." He looked fondly at his son, instinctively rocking back and forth as he cradled the little bundle. He kissed his temple, smelled the sweetness of his soft skin, trying to commit it to memory. He began to sing softly the lullaby he had heard Mahta sing in Ahkmar's caravan years before. The baby smiled and cooed. "How can a slave in prison have this kind of joy?" Joseph said in wonder.

Mahta shook her head. "You shouldn't be in prison. Each night that I pray, I pour out my heart to God and ask that I might have understanding. But Joseph, I don't understand."

"I know this is difficult—perhaps the most difficult challenge we will ever face—but we must wait patiently on the Lord. This trial will end. I just don't know when. But I believe I'm of some use here—giving help where I can. Many here have awakened their own compassion and much good is being done."

"I didn't mean to complain. I, too, feel blessed. I can't believe the joy such a small soul can bring. I really am happy, Joseph. I just need you."

"And I love you. There is much that we need to talk about, but first I would like to give a father's blessing to my son." Joseph held the baby close and gave him a name and an inspired blessing of promise. The name he chose was Manasseh.

"Wait here a moment," Joseph said. He handed the baby to Mahta and left the room. A few minutes later he came back and said. "I want to show my friends." He had gathered Moesha, Wama, the physician, the keeper, and some others to the guardroom. Then he took the infant and stepped through the door. "My friends, meet my son." The men were visibly touched as they gathered around and made all the usual sounds grown men can make when admiring such a tiny child.

"I must take him back," Joseph finally said.

"But Joseph, may we see your wife?"

Joseph agreed, opened the door and held out his hand to Mahta as she stepped to the doorway. Their eyes opened wide and there was an audible gasp as the men beheld her beauty. He then enfolded his loved ones with his arms and moved them gently back into the entry room as the door closed on the men who still stood looking.

Joseph and Mahta talked long to try to cover all the time that had been lost to them.

"Joseph, do you remember how we used to talk about forgiveness? Since the baby was born, I've felt the need to set my life in order, to be the best person I can be. I've been trying to forgive those who have wronged me, but it's not easy. Some I can easily dismiss from my mind. Others may go with me to my grave."

"Who are you having difficulty with?"

"I had trouble at first with Potiphar's wife, but I think she is a disturbed woman. I no longer feel any animosity toward her."

"And your uncle?"

"If he had not sold me, I might have suffered real torture living with him and I would not have met you or my new parents. No, I am grateful to my uncle. He is forgiven." She paused, then shook her head. "I can't erase from my mind the picture of Saku whipping you and Cephas. I still see him taunting and spitting at you. He was responsible for your detainment at Potiphar's house. How can I forgive him?"

"Perhaps you could if you could see him now. He's here."

Mahta jumped to her feet. "He's here? In this prison?"

Joseph nodded.

"And you see him every day? How do you deal with him? Does he try to harm you?"

Joseph pulled her close. "As far as I can tell, he has been robbed and clubbed by his companions and has had many fights with other prisoners. His face is grotesque; it's hard to recognize him. He has been here for many years. Just before I came, he was in a violent fight with a prisoner, which opened up some of his head wounds. He doesn't talk—he growls. And he sits in one place all the time. He is to be pitied. It would waste time to hate a creature such as he. I no longer bear him ill will. I don't know how well I'm doing at pardoning some of the others who have hurt me, however."

"Well, if you can give up hating Saku, so can I. I free him. He shall no longer haunt me. Will you tell him for me?"

I don't think he'd comprehend our forgiveness at this point in his life. But when the time is right, I'll certainly tell him—for both of us."

"I love you, Joseph."

# Chapter Twenty-one

# Adjusting to Prison

"It's almost Bazaar time," an Egyptian said to Joseph. "You have no idea what awaits you. If the usual numbers arrive, we won't have room. You and your healer have kept too many alive."

"You may be right," Joseph said. "We must prepare the best we can." He set about getting the help of as many as would cooperate.

After the first week, they had many new prisoners whose difficult adjustment drew empathy from some of the more seasoned prisoners. In the weeks that followed, a pattern was established as the old had to make room for the new.

On one occasion someone sat down in Saku's spot while he was gone for food. It almost caused a riot. After that, part of the prisoners' orientation included where not to sit.

Some tried to be decent, but others hated everything, including Joseph. One day Moesha told him, "I think if you did not speak out loud about your God so much, you would be more accepted."

"That may be," Joseph said, "but that is who I am. My father blessed me to be a prophet of God and so it is my duty to talk about Him and to Him. I cannot do otherwise."

The expected number of fights broke out, but also, a great deal of kindness was shown. Adjustments were made and activities were settling to a normal routine. Joseph tried to acquaint himself with every man who came in. He was becoming good with languages. As a challenge, he tried to learn every varied tongue he encountered. In the year he had been confined, he had already mastered several. With this new season he found a few more opportunities.

Each prisoner eventually found his place. The Egyptians took in their own kind. The usual groups came about, but Joseph was most concerned about the loners.

One day he tried to comfort a young man he found sobbing. "It's hard to get used to a place like this," Joseph said.

"I don't belong here," the man said.

"A lot of these men don't belong here."

"It's one thing to be innocent. It's another to be despised and persecuted."

"Why do you feel you're despised?"

"Because I'm different."

"Yes, I see you are more delicate than most."

"I am a man whom other men find attractive. I worked in the pleasure house. There was a special need for people like me. I belonged."

"So what happened?"

"I made the mistake of strolling on the pavilion in the midst of Bazaar. I saw a former patron and tried to speak to him, but his partner was jealous. I usually avoid any kind of trouble, but his man hated me and wouldn't let it die. He harassed me until I hit him with a pair of shoes I was carrying. A guard was there and I was arrested."

Joseph tried to suppress a smile. "What is your name?"

"Lym."

"How can I help you, Lym?"

"The men in here hate me. They not only shun me, but they make rude faces at me and say crude things."

"Do you provoke them?"

"Not on purpose—I cannot stop being what I am."

"Do you think you can win their respect?"

"I can try, but abstinence is difficult for me. How can I change?"

"You are not alone. Almost every person in here must give up some kind of habit in confinement. It isn't easy for any of us. I would like to share an experience from my childhood with you. I had older brothers whom I idolized. I wanted their approval, but they treated me meanly and ignored me. I went to my mother, crying. She said, 'You must not care what others think of you. Only what God thinks.'"

"How do you do it?"

"There are hidden resources in all of us that we can call upon in need. I fast and pray to my God."

"I don't have a God, but I would fast if I thought it would help."

"I'll pray for you, if you like. Maybe you'll find a way to get the strength you need."

"Thank you. You give me some hope."

After three weeks, Joseph had noticed no change. Lym still sat alone and cried often.

"Lym, I'm sorry you're still distressed."

"Have you been praying for me?"

"Yes."

"Well, it hasn't helped. I still have insatiable desires and I can't be something I'm not. They all sense my frustration and they still hate me, so I've decided on a plan. When my people find out I'm here and come after me—and they will—as soon as I'm out, I'm going to be castrated."

"That is a drastic remedy, Lym."

"Yes, but I'd rather be a eunuch in a position of respect than one who is a victim of his own or others' appetites. Being in here has made me see how vulnerable I am in my present state."

"I wish I could have helped you find peace."

"In a way, I am at peace—in contemplating my decision."

Joseph nodded. "Let me know how things work out for you."

Lym was released from prison one month after he was arrested.

———◦∞◦———

Storytelling began with Joseph and Moesha sharing tales of their lives with each other. Joseph also told of miracles and of past events such as those concerning the city of Enoch, the tower of Babel, the garden of Eden, and the great flood. Soon others joined the group and began to share. Stories poured from each man's life until barriers and prejudices fell away.

Music was an unexpected pleasure inside the prison. It came through a lively Lebanese man named Hamafi, an innate entertainer who did everything in a dramatic way. The way he talked and moved about brought smiles to the prisoners' faces. He was allowed to bring his flute and a small, four-stringed harp, which he always carried on his back. Hamafi had enough language skill to translate most of his songs into a common voicing.

It didn't take long for many of the men to learn to sing along. Another cellmate could play the flute. So on a typical afternoon, many would gather to sing, clap, or listen. Sometimes Hamafi would dance his stories as well as sing and play. This was the happiest time Joseph had witnessed in the prison.

One afternoon as Hamafi and his friend played, Joseph began to dance as he was taught in his youth. He motioned Moesha to join him and they placed their hands on each others shoulders and stepped the patterns of tradition. Soon others came to the circle while those who watched moved back to make more room. There was clapping and laughter as Hamafi stepped into the center of the circle and cavorted appropriately as he played.

Suddenly above the music a terrifying yell was heard as Saku came crashing through the group. Before anyone knew what was happening, he was on top of Hamafi with his hands around his throat.

Several of the men grabbed Saku, but his grip was tenacious, his hatred summoning a superhuman strength. He fought off his attackers, yet continued to choke Hamafi at the same time. Joseph was also trying to separate Saku from his victim.

One of the stronger men picked up a heavy bench from against the wall, stumbled through the men and struck Saku on the head. Saku released Hamafi and fell to the floor, his head bleeding profusely.

The physician began working on Hamafi as Joseph bent over Saku and gently gathered him in his arms. Saku opened his eyes just long enough to look up. He hoarsely whispered, "Joseph," and was gone.

Joseph wept, not because Saku was a loss to anyone, but because of the futility and loneliness of the departed life he held in his arms.

"I'm sorry, Saku. I never had the chance to tell you we forgave you. I hope you are finally without pain."

No one stood with Joseph as he watched Saku placed in the ground.

It took a long time for Hamafi to regain his strength, but slowly, he began stepping about. He tried to put forth a picture of gaiety, but it was never again as it had been before. His voice could not function with clarity. He was happy to play, however, while others sang.

"You are a blessing just by your presence," Joseph told Hamafi when he apologized for his inadequacy. "Your music will fill my heart long after we are parted, as it will for the others as well. If you desire it, I'll give you a blessing for your health." Hamafi knelt before Joseph and, with Joseph's hands on his head, received the evocation of healing from heaven.

For that entire year, the incident with Saku hung solemn in the air. The men seemed to have a better appreciation for life as a result of it. Even some hardened lawbreakers came into the circle of music.

The next Bazaar brought the same inevitable crowding and problems into the prison. One day Potiphar appeared, not to visit with Joseph, but to address the prisoners. "Egypt is being threatened by Syria and we are on the verge of a serious war. Our borders are being watched day and night. Any of you men who will volunteer to come with me will be made soldiers of the king's guard. If you survive battle, you'll have your freedom."

"Will we receive pay?" a prisoner asked.

"No, but you'll be fed a soldier's rations and receive a uniform. You'll regain some of the respect you lost upon imprisonment, and perhaps, if we are victorious, win some honor."

Eagerness brightened the eyes of some of the forgotten men who had lost all hope of ever leaving the prison. The Egyptians were hesitant; some had hoped for a release, but others, out of loyalty to Pharaoh, stepped forward. "Do you know where we'll be sent, Captain?"

"Probably to the borders. We're taking all the guards we can gather to reinforce the battlefront." To Joseph he said, "The prison will be left with only a few guards, as will the palace."

Moesha and Wama were among those with no hope of pardon and wanted to enlist. Joseph pulled them aside.

"I can't stop you from going if you want to. I know the outlook in here seems hopeless to you, but if you'll trust me and my God, I'll promise you that someday you may accompany me out of this den."

"I'll stay if you want me to," Moesha said.

"I do need your help here."

"Then I stay," Wama said, smiling.

Joseph agreed with the physician that he was needed behind also.

When Potiphar marched off with his guards and seventy of his new recruits, only about fifteen men remained in prison. Hamafi was among those who left.

The keeper of the prison looked a little dejected as if his importance depended on the number in his prison. When it was full, he considered himself a good steward.

A new routine was established. Joseph used the extra time and quiet to study. Moesha, who had obtained a flute of his own, spent a lot of time practicing. When he could, Wama sang along with Moesha, having picked up bits of the different languages. He was generally useful and attentive to anyone's needs, and the men were amused to hear him attempt new words.

Joseph and Pleoris, the physician, had many discussions about medicine, worship, and philosophy in general. "I have been interested to observe your use of herbs," the physician said. "I have learned a lot from you. I was taught much about the body, but there is still more to learn. We don't know the mysteries of the inner workings of a man."

"I have watched you put bones back in place."

"Oh, yes. I know about bones, and I know about the conduits that carry the blood to and from the heart. Yet as I practice I become aware that the more I learn, the less I know."

Joseph laughed. "And isn't that the beginning of wisdom?"

"I suppose."

"But I wonder," Joseph said, "why you lay dried bones before a patient and proceed to do incantations and magic."

"That's what I mean," the physician said. "When we don't know what to do, we turn to magic for cures. The incantations are supposed to reach inside a person's body and awaken his soul. It is believed that the soul has the knowledge necessary to heal its own body. Therefore, by chanting and rhythms the spirit of a man is called upon to overcome inadequacies and fulfill its own wholeness."

"Does it work?"

"I don't know. How can we tell?"

"Well, we don't differ greatly in the essential nature of our beliefs. I was taught that we can call upon God to heal a man. Where our own ministering might fail, God's power can surely work if he wills it and we have enough faith. The difference is that your incantations and my prayers call upon disparate deities for the resolutions."

"I've seen you work some miracles by your blessings."

"God's blessings. The healings work only by his grace and our faith. A determined faithful person can accomplish for himself what none of our methods can."

Joseph's peace was jarred as the keeper suddenly appeared and said, "That woman is here."

Joseph went reluctantly. When he approached Zelica in the reception room, he could see that something was terribly wrong.

"Leave us," Zelica said to the keeper. Her eyes were blank and hollow, her face lined and marred by the remains of too much makeup. She would have appeared comical if it weren't for the way she trembled.

"What is it, Mistress?"

"He's dead," she said, her voice without emotion. "Your master, my husband—the man who adored me is dead." She swayed as she spoke, and Joseph, stunned himself, helped her sink into a chair.

"How?" he asked.

"The captain of the king's guard gave his life in battle."

"And the war?"

"Oh, the Syrians were pushed back, but there were many casualties. As far as they can tell, the entire company Potiphar led was all killed. They were the initial line of defense, but Egypt remains inviolable."

Joseph thought about the seventy from prison and wondered if any had survived. "It grieves me to hear such news. I'm sorry, Mistress."

"Don't ever again call me Mistress. I've never acted superior to you. Just once, let me hear you say my name. Say it!"

"Zelica," Joseph said guardedly.

"There, that wasn't so difficult, was it?" She relaxed a little. "I'll miss him immensely."

"Yes, I'll miss him, too."

"How can you miss him?"

"You didn't know? He came often to the prison. It was part of his custody. He was responsible for having the keeper of the prison put me in charge. He was good to us. We may not fare as well without him."

"Not many people saw his good side." Zelica softened as she spoke, then remembered. "But Joseph, you must hate him; after all, he had you imprisoned."

"He did his duty. I hold no ill will."

"See how wonderful you are, my dear. Do you have any ill will toward me?"

"No."

"I knew it. You do love me. You have always loved me."

Joseph stood up. "No, don't do this, Zelica."

"You see, even the way you say my name is full of feeling." She put her arms around his neck and leaned her body against his.

"Stop," Joseph said as he tried to restrain her. "I'm sorry for you. I want to help, but I don't love you."

Her old fury returned. "I don't want your pity. How dare you feel sorry for me."

"What would you have me do?"

She mellowed. "Marry me. Isn't that what you have always wanted? I'm free. You can have me now by your own standards."

"There is no way I can marry you."

"Why? Tell me why?"

"I'm married, Zelica. I married Mahta. We have a child."

"No!" she screamed. "How could you? When did you have the chance? I'll kill her!" She began beating on his chest. "I hate you! I hate you!"

The keeper hurried into the room. "What's the matter here? What's going on?"

"The captain's wife comes to report her husband's death. He died heroically on the field of battle, but she is distraught. Perhaps you should summon help. See that she is escorted home and given aid."

Zelica didn't look back as she was moved woodenly through the door.

Upon returning to his place inside, Joseph sought communion with his Lord. "Whatever I have had to bear, I have borne with Thy help. Thou hast comforted me in the depths of this hole. Give now Thy succor to the woman. She is lost and without relief. And help me to learn, to give what I can without harm and without rancor."

After his prayer he sought out his friends and told them about Potiphar and his company. Then, saddened and spent, he lost himself in sleep.

About midnight the keeper awakened Joseph. "I just thought you would want to know," he said.

Joseph sat up. "What is it?"

"The wife of the captain is dead. She took poison."

# Chapter Twenty-two

# Happiness from a Son

Somehow, Zelica's passing made Joseph more lonely for Mahta. He carried on the daily routine of the prison with optimism and good cheer, but at night, alone with his thoughts, he agonized in his loneliness and pled for release. He worried that he would forget Mahta and he constantly sought to call up the memory of her beauty, her voice, her walk, and her fragrance. "And how, oh, Lord, can I be a proper father to a son I have not seen these many years?"

By the time Mahta and her parents were able to visit Joseph again, Manasseh was four and a half years old.

"I can't take it all in," Joseph said. "He's so intelligent, and he speaks Egyptian better than I do."

"Yes, but don't fear; I've taught him Hebrew and he speaks that equally well."

"See how capable he is? He reminds me of his uncles Simeon and Judah. He is so physically skilled."

"And you sound just like a father."

"But you must admit he is extraordinary."

"You'll get no argument from me," Mahta said.

"Or from his grandparents." Ramieth and Rena were smiling broadly.

"He gets beauty from his mother," Joseph said as he kissed Mahta again.

"There is beauty enough, as I perceive it," Rena said. The priest and his wife took the boy and left the couple alone.

"I miss you so," Joseph whispered.

Mahta snuggled against his shoulder. "I promised myself before we came here that I wouldn't say anything contrary, that I wouldn't mourn the time you lost not seeing your son grow."

Joseph sensed a resistance in his wife, an edge to her voice. *Has she been having doubts?* "Mahta, I have yearned to watch his first steps, to hear his first words. Yet why would the Lord require this sacrifice of me unless it is preparing me for something magnificent?"

"Joseph, do you know of any imminent release? I know I shouldn't ask, but..."

"No, I'm sorry. Without Potiphar, I don't know what is happening outside. Zelica could have retracted her charges, but she didn't. Now she, too, is dead. Faith in God is all I have."

Mahta sat back. "Can't you ask God to get you out of here? It seems to me that one who is so favored by God could at least get an idea of His intentions." There were tears in her eyes.

Joseph bowed his head and fought to control his emotions. "Yes, I do ask, and yet I don't know His intentions. I only know that I must believe and be patient. He's aware of us and continues to watch over us. In His time He will reveal His will."

Mahta looked down and contritely said, "It is difficult, but deep inside I feel that what you say is true. I will say no more of it now." She sighed. "I was sorry to hear about the deaths of our former owners. I liked the master. I never did understand our mistress, but I know she was in love with you. Did you find her attractive? I didn't believe her charges—"

"Mahta..." Joseph held her firmly with two hands and looked deep into her eyes. "There was nothing but misery in my dealings with Zelica. I have never loved any woman but you."

Mahta released an audible sigh. "Thank you, Joseph. I needed to hear that. That woman flaunted her beauty around me and inferred a relationship with you. I know I was such an uncomely child, but I always hoped, and I always loved you."

"And I always loved you, even though I was unaware of it."

They talked for two more hours, trying to cover all the significant happenings in their lives during their separation. After the grandparents and boy returned, they all joyfully watched as Manasseh sang a few songs and showed Joseph his muscles. Manasseh had won Joseph from the first moment they saw each other.

Parting was more painful this time than ever before. Mahta said, "I don't know when we can come again, Joseph. It seems to become more difficult to get away. Ramieth has almost total responsibility in the temple at On. He can't leave anyone to fill his position. I, too, must exercise faith and patience, but just thinking of you and knowing you are mine fills my empty hours with warmth."

"I must try to be as patient as you are, Mahta. I know we'll be together one day."

Manasseh kissed his father and said he would try not to grow too much before he saw him again. Joseph waited until the family was well away before he shed his tears.

———◆◆◆———

Potiphar's replacement was a young man named Zarill who had proven himself in service under the captain. Fortunately Potiphar had often spoken to Zarill about conditions of the prison and the need for reform and supplies. Zarill made it a point to methodically study all stations within his stewardship. So on this day he had come to assess the prison and its workers.

He presented himself to the nervous prison keeper and was led into the cell as the keeper tried to explain the daily routine. Joseph was summoned and Zarill introduced himself and said, "The man I replaced spoke highly of you and of your efforts to improve this prison. I intend to carry out the same reforms the captain began. You may continue to be the voice from inside. I'll respect your judgment as I was told I could."

"Thank you," Joseph said. "I'm pleased to meet with you, and to hear what you have to say."

The young captain made a face. "This room is stifling and smelly. Can we do something about it?"

Joseph nodded. "It smells pleasant compared to when I first came. We do what we can to keep it clean. At least now we are allowed to keep the door open."

"I'll add a bag of lime to the acquisition. You can keep it by the gutter and sprinkle a hand-full as needed. That will cut down on the odor and the flies."

"You are very discerning. Thank you."

"Are your eating vessels adequate?"

"Yes. Each man has a bowl assigned to him. After eating, he washes it and puts it in its place on the shelf."

"Do you need anything else?"

"I think we have what we need, given our conditions. We do need replacements of medicines and the other necessities from time to time. But perhaps I might request an animal."

"An animal? I don't understand."

"Some of these men have been imprisoned for many years. After a time, one forgets what the outside world is like. I remember how it felt to care for animals and I think the men could forget themselves a little if they were responsible for an animal. Any kind will do."

"Well, that is one request I never expected to hear. Is this a test to see how far you can get me to go?"

"No, sir. I'm serious about this and have given it a great deal of thought. I'm convinced it would raise the spirits of the men."

"Then I'll do my best, but I can promise nothing."

Two days later a wooden cage was delivered to the prison. It contained a timid, smoke-colored cat that had obviously been neglected. A couple of weeks later she bore a litter of four kittens.

———

When the servants of Pharaoh fell into disfavor with their master, he often ordered them imprisoned. He was unaware of the conditions there, for he hadn't visited the prison for many years. Though the prison had originally been built for housing lawbreakers, imprisonment was, to him, simply a way of ridding himself of a temporary annoyance.

Whatever Pharaoh of Egypt did must be superior to that of anyone else. So when two kings from neighboring countries came to pay tribute to Pharaoh, he ordered a fine dinner, and the visiting kings were impressed by the lavish output of food. The entertainment was excellent to match the banquet.

As Pharaoh was about to drink his second cup of wine, he saw a fly in it, yet stifled his anger in deference to his guests. But when he bit into a sweet bread and felt grit in his mouth, he was furious and called his chief steward to him. "Who is responsible for baking these buns? And who poured this cup of wine?"

"I myself poured the wine, but the bread was made by the head baker in your kitchen."

Pharaoh stood up and motioned to his palace guard. "You will escort this butler, who serves flies to his king, and the baker, who puts rocks in his bread, to the prison at once."

The two servants quickly found themselves in the royal prison, their frustration evident, for they felt they had done no wrong. But they knew they could not dispute the word of the king of Egypt.

Joseph tried to ease them into their surroundings and put them in the group of offenders from the palace. They had been confined for only a few days when, one morning, Joseph noticed a small stirring in their section.

As he approached he heard the baker say, "But that's strange. It was similar to mine. That's just the way I feel."

Joseph asked, "Is there anything I can do for the servants of Pharaoh?"

A prisoner said, "Not unless you can reassure these two men, who are disturbed by their dreams."

"God can tell you the meaning of them," Joseph said.

"Well, God is not here," one said. The others laughed.

"No, but his servant is, one who has the gift to interpret dreams."

"That would be you, I suppose?" an Egyptian said.

"You have been of no help," the butler said, as he pushed the others aside and faced Joseph. "I'm willing to lay it before you if you can enlighten me."

"Come," Joseph said, and he led the man to a bench in a somewhat quiet corner of the room. The baker came with them also. All three sat down and the butler unburdened himself.

"In my dream a large vine grew up in front of me. It divided into three branches. It grew with great speed, became tall, and soon blossomed. The blossoms became grapes that ripened on the vine. I picked the grapes, pressed them into wine and served it to Pharaoh. He drank from the cup I gave him." He paused, then said, "It's not that the dream is so unusual, but it left me feeling disturbed. I can't shake it from my mind."

"That's because it is a significant dream," Joseph said. "The three branches of the vine represent three days. In three days Pharaoh will send for you. You'll be restored to your previous position and again serve the wine cup to your master as you did before."

The butler gave a relieved smile. "I have the feeling you're right. I'm at peace from hearing your words. Truly you do know the meaning of dreams."

Joseph implored the chief steward. "When you return to your position, please remember what God has done for you and petition Pharaoh on my behalf. I am here for no reason. I've committed no crime. Pharaoh's favor is my only hope of a release. Could you help me in this way?"

"Yes, if you're right, I'll ask the king to release you."

"Would you hear my dream?" the baker asked.

"Of course," Joseph said.

"There were three white baskets on my head. The largest basket held an assortment of buns I had baked. Many birds came and ate the buns from the basket."

Joseph translated. "The three baskets are also three days. In three days you'll be taken from this prison, but the rest will not be to your liking. It represents birds eating the flesh of a dead man. The birds eating bread means that you'll be put to death."

The baker was silent. He chose to believe that Joseph was wrong and didn't want to talk about it.

Three days later the palace guard came to retrieve the two. Because of subsequent queries the king had made about the affairs of the kitchen, the chief baker was beheaded. The chief steward was forgiven. He was needed at the celebration Pharaoh was organizing. Pharaoh's wife had just delivered him a son and much was to be made of it. The butler resumed his station, and the festivities lasted for eight days. In the distraction of merriment, the chief butler forgot the promise he had made to Joseph.

# Chapter Twenty-three

# Evil Priests and Cephas

Three years had passed since Joseph had last seen Mahta and Manasseh. He struggled daily to maintain optimism. The Lord gave him many answers to prayers, which kept him humble and submissive. Still, at times he nearly succumbed to despair, and many nights his straw bed absorbed his tears. He tried not to dwell on the fact that he was deprived of his loved ones. His boy would be almost seven years old now. Mahta had grown more beautiful each time he had seen her; by now she must be more exquisite than ever.

He still prayed daily for his father and brothers, and ached for news of them. On occasion a Hebrew would be cast into the cell and Joseph would try to find out if they knew the family of Israel.

He was in such an attitude when the keeper brought in an old man and announced, "Here's a Hebrew for you, Joseph."

Joseph went immediately to the slumped figure on the floor. Lifting him up to assist him, he cried out, "Cephas, oh, not you! How is it you are in this hole? I'm happy to see you, but sad that you must be here."

"Joseph, is that you?" Cephas sounded weak and shaky.

"Yes, good friend, and I'm glad that I'm here to receive you."

"We need to talk, but not now—after I rest. I'm tired and sick. Can you help me? Joseph...of all people."

Joseph made him a bed of straw and helped him sip some water. Then he sat by his side and rubbed his head. Cephas was soon asleep, but Joseph wouldn't leave his side. Night came and the patient didn't awaken, so Joseph lay down beside him and slept. The next morning, some time after Joseph had risen, Cephas finally stirred.

"How are you feeling, friend?"

"Somewhat better, thank you."

"Yes, you sound better. I'll get you some food, but I can't say how it will taste. Then we'll see if you can talk."

Cephas ate willingly and after a time seemed more like himself. When they were both comfortably secured in their quiet corner of the room, Cephas asked, "Why are you here, my prince?"

Joseph told his old mentor the details of his service with Potiphar. He explained his eventual imprisonment and his long endurance to the present.

The old man shook his head. "How you could be required to put up with that mad woman is beyond my knowing. I'm sorry to hear of Potiphar's death, but I'm delighted to hear about Mahta and the child. I saw her in the palace, you know, whenever I could. I watched her grow from timid child to elegant woman, as an unsightly cocoon relinquishes its beautiful secret. So you thought you would rescue her, did you?"

"Yes, but it was she who rescued me. Although I must tell you—and I can tell no one else—I wonder if she'll wait for me. She's so beautiful and it's been such a long time. She may not endure."

Cephas shook his head. "Don't let those doubts invade your thinking. She'll wait."

Joseph smiled and said, "I don't need to tell you, do I, how much I ache to be with her and my son?"

"I can imagine and I would surely love to see that boy. Does he look like you?"

"He does, or I should say he looks like an Israelite. But Cephas, are you strong enough now to tell me your story?"

"You know me, Joseph. My mouth works when little else does."

———◦◦◦◦———

Cephas said, "You remember, don't you, that Potiphar gave me as a gift to Pharaoh? He took me to the palace and delivered me in person. I must say he made quite a great matter of it as he presented me to the court. My skills took on a new light to hear the captain extol them. But all the words mean nothing if one cannot ascend the steps.

"By Egyptian standards, a person can be worthy to be in Pharaoh's presence only if he can pass the test. There are forty-nine steps leading from the floor to the throne where the king sits. Each step represents one of the languages spoken in the countries or provinces in this part of the world—forty-nine languages, forty-nine steps. The fiftieth is the platform which only Pharaoh himself has knowledge enough to attain.

"Certain steps are made wider to seat the wise men: the tenth holds the man of medicine; the twentieth holds the architects and men of numbers; the thirtieth holds the stargazer; and the fortieth holds the priests who represent all the gods of Egypt. The other steps hold magicians, entertainers, and counselors.

"In my first audience, I was able to achieve the fifteenth step, which pleased Pharaoh enough to let me remain there as a counselor. When he needs advice, however, he usually asks those closest to the throne. I seldom had any influence in the affairs of the court. Once in a while, when a political or military move was to be decided, all the advisors would be asked to concur. Only then did I exercise my authority. This year in the season of the festivals I finally had a chance to express an opinion."

Cephas gave a regretful smile and continued. "Every day the priests go into the temple to care for the wooden and stone gods. Only the priests and Pharaoh are allowed in the temple. They put food before the gods and dress and undress them. During the festival time, additional ceremonies take place. The statues are borne into the streets where the common people may see them. Other rituals involve sacrifices made to the gods. The old priest, Kenah, is obsessed with the offering of human sacrifices.

He came here many years ago from the land between the rivers and convinced the previous Pharaoh that they needed the sacrifices.

"On this festival occasion the priest Kenah and the priest Korash argued about whether the sacrifices should be a grown male or a virgin female. Korash argued that the season of grain had been meager and therefore needed a masculine symbol to make it more abundant. Kenah believed that all the gods preferred virgins for productivity.

"Pharaoh listened to both views, then said, 'I would like an opinion of a different sort.' He walked down the steps, stood before me and said, 'Are you not a Hebrew priest?'

"'I am,' I said.

"The priests on the upper steps were visibly upset by the king's actions. They whispered among themselves as Pharaoh then asked, 'And what kind of sacrifice does the Hebrew priest suggest?'

"I said, 'The Hebrew God accepts animal sacrifices only on occasion for specific meanings. He does not require a sacrifice to make the grain grow. Prayer and a sincere heart, knowledge and hard work will suffice for that. And He never requires the sacrifice of human life. He asks only that they live their lives for Him.'

"I stirred a hornet's nest with my words. I could tell by the look on Pharaoh's face that he was half-amused, and he may have agreed with me. He maintains a delicate balance in his position. He must placate the Egyptians and, at the same time, try to insert some Hyksos reforms.

"He walked back up the steps and announced, 'For now, we'll suspend human sacrifice until a solution may be reached.'

"The priest Kenah was hungry for blood. He had never been treated in this manner and was determined to have his way. When next we met for our meal, the priest came to my table, which was separated from the others since I'm Hebrew, and he threatened me, saying, 'You're meddling in powers over your head, Hebrew. You will, in future, keep your mouth quiet. It's dangerous to stand in the way of the gods of Egypt.'

"When the next council was held, everyone in position on the steps, Pharaoh motioned to me. 'I'd like the Hebrew to come up to the twenty-fifth step so that I might inquire of him when I desire.'

"I didn't look at the others, but I could feel their hatred as I took my place on the twenty-fifth level. Then the priest Korash spoke. 'Does Pharaoh do wisely in exalting a man who doesn't know the required languages?'

"'Pharaoh can promote whom he will,' the king replied. 'The man is bright; he can learn.'

"The court was excused for three days. On the third day when we were supposed to convene, I went to my meal first, as usual. Soon after eating I had severe cramps in my stomach and I knew I had been poisoned by Kenah. I hurried to the table where he was seated and said, 'You have chosen poorly to be my enemy. I'm an ominous foe.' I then cracked him on the jaw, but as I did so, blackness overcame me. I remember vomiting and sinking between bouts of darkness. The next thing I knew, I was here with you."

Cephas appeared pale and unwell, and Joseph was concerned for his welfare. "I'm glad we're together again, old friend, even though this place is not to our liking. I'll nurse you back to health, and we'll have many good visits."

"We must talk while we can," Cephas said. "I know something of the poison my enemy used on me. It didn't kill me immediately because I vomited so much. It gets into the system, however, and in time, it will work completely. I'm old. My body can't fight back. No, dear son, I'm afraid it's just a matter of days before I join my family on the other side."

"Then we'll cherish every moment we have together, and yes, we will talk. How often I've yearned to have your company and your wisdom when I've felt quite alone. You're exhausted now, I see. Rest, and I'll attend to some tasks. When you awaken, I'll be here."

Joseph ministered to his sick friend unceasingly, and Cephas tried to rally. There were brief times when he felt well enough to talk. On one of those occasions he told Joseph, "I have been thinking of your conversation with Mahta, the one when you talked about forgiveness. It occurs to me that I must search my soul. I must purge the bitterness from my heart in order to be fit to meet my Lord. I have treasured a desire to revenge my family's murders for a long time."

"You've been dealt more than your share of wrongs. How do you see yourself letting them go?" Joseph asked.

"The offenders have been coming to me. As I lie here and weave in and out of consciousness, I see a different place. Sometimes I visualize my past. It takes the form of those wrongdoers walking down a road toward me, dressed as beggars. They stop in front of me and without speaking, make known to me that they cannot continue on the road without my forgiveness."

"What do you do?"

"Nothing. They're still there—fixed on the road."

"What are you going to do?"

"I'll face them one by one and send them on their way."

"Can you release even the priest Kenah?"

"Yes. As I see him, he is a pathetic, small-minded man. His shriveled soul needs much compassion. I'll not jeopardize my own progress by hating him."

Cephas sank back down on his bed of straw and slept again. When he awakened, he spoke. "They're gone, Joseph. The road is clear. Now I can make my way home." He closed his eyes for the last time.

"Goodbye dear friend. I'll look forward to our meeting in the better world."

Moesha, Wama, and the physician helped Joseph bury Cephas in the prison graveyard.

"I'll be back to get you and give you a proper burial," Joseph promised.

# Chapter Twenty-four

# Pharaoh's Dream

Two years had passed since the baker and the butler had dreamed their dreams. Joseph had waited impatiently at first, certain that the butler would petition his case to the king. When time passed with no word, he abandoned his hope.

Suddenly the palace was astir with talk of dreams—Pharaoh's dreams. While dreams had been a regular part of the king's sleeping pattern, this time they exasperated him. He couldn't understand why two dreams would cause him to feel so disturbed and he demanded to know their meaning.

He laid them out before his wise men and priests, his counselors and magicians, but no one could offer a pleasing explanation, and the height of his frustration moved his whole court with an urgency to find a meaning. Word of the dreams had even reached the prison.

In the course of the daily discussion throughout the palace, the butler suddenly remembered his own dream and the man in prison who had accurately unveiled its meaning. The butler went before his master.

"Oh, King, I beg for this servant's pardon. I'm slow to remember, but there is a man in the prison who sees the hidden truths in dreams. He interpreted my own dream when I was housed there with him, and all that he said came to be. Perhaps this Hebrew prisoner may be able to enlighten the king."

Pharaoh immediately summoned Zarill, who had been called back from his duty on the border and assigned to the palace. "Go to the prison and bring this Hebrew who can interpret dreams. He shall hear me."

Zarill hurried to Joseph's cell. "Come, Joseph! The king wishes to see you. He is puzzled by a dream."

Quietly Joseph thanked God and pleaded for utterance to speak words of truth.

Zarill scrutinized his prisoner. "You won't do in your present condition, unfit to be presented at court. Pharaoh will permit no one to enter his presence unless he's been prepared."

He quickly sent a runner to obtain a tunic from the palace wardrobe, had the prison keeper summon the barber, and a guard fetch supplies for a proper bath. Joseph's head was again shaved to insure the cleanliness of Pharaoh's court. His body was scrubbed, sweet smelling oil applied and a fresh loin cloth provided, followed by a soft tunic that felt luxurious next to his clean skin. He was now presentable.

Zarill hustled his ward from the prison, but Joseph halted as they stepped onto the pavilion floor. "I must have just a moment to breath this delicious air." He took a few deep breaths, composed himself, then went on.

A pink alabaster lion stood before the palace doors, guarding the entrance through the garden. Joseph had seen it before, but it had not impacted him then as it did now. Everything looked so beautiful. Entering the palace doors, he noticed huge urns filled with colorful flowers. He couldn't remember seeing such a variety of vivid colors before, and he thanked God for sending such beauty to the earth. Their scent lifted his spirits even more.

Upon entering the palace, Joseph was struck by the coolness of the hallways in contrast to the heat outside and that of the prison cell. He couldn't resist touching the cool marble walls and placing his cheek against its smoothness.

The halls were carefully guarded, for they were furnished with all manner of gifts for the king of Egypt—ornately carved tables displaying vases of the finest workmanship, some porcelain, others gold or silver. On the pillars and walls were carved colorful pictures depicting Pharaoh and his land as well as far-away lands and places. The rugs on which they trod were also detailed in design and rich in color.

From the moment they entered the palace, Joseph sensed the stares of the workers who cleared their passage. They were expected. Soon Joseph found himself in the large throne room at the bottom of the many stairs. The counselors were not present. Only Zarill stood with him, the steward in attendance above.

Pharaoh didn't wait for the usual protocol. As soon as he saw his visitor, he left his seat and walked down to the third step. His condescension implied his willingness to talk with a commoner, for commoners were heard from the third step.

Joseph didn't know the procedure. He bowed awkwardly, then looked into the eyes of his host.

"Do you know why I have summoned you here?" Pharaoh sounded impatient.

"You are troubled by a dream?"

"Two dreams—each on separate nights. I've had no respite since they came to me."

"God will give you an answer to your dreams."

"God will not be held accountable. If I don't get satisfaction, *you* shall suffer the consequences."

"So be it. Tell me what you saw."

Pharaoh began. "I found myself standing on the bank of a river, looking out at the stream, when cattle began rising out of the water—large, fat, healthy cattle, seven in all. After each one surfaced, it made its way to shore and into the meadow on the other side. All seven went into the meadow and began to graze.

"As they ate, seven more cattle came forth, the same kind, but sickly, thin, and wasted. The thin cattle followed into the meadow, but instead of eating the grass, they turned on the healthy cattle and devoured them, yet remained as gaunt as before. Then I awakened. It haunts me still."

Joseph asked, "Didn't you say that you had two dreams?"

"Yes. In the second, a stalk of corn grew. In the beginning, the stalk bore plump, beautiful ears, seven in all. Then, after the stalk was full, seven more ears appeared, but the new fruit was withered, dry, and thin. The seven thin ears consumed the seven plump ears. I awoke and felt the same restlessness. I consulted my wise men and magicians, who gave me all manner of useless explanations, but no one could quell my frustration."

Joseph said, "Both dreams have the same meaning. God has given you a message in two different ways. He has shown you what is soon to happen. The seven good cattle and seven plump ears represent seven plentiful years. The seven sickly cattle and seven withered ears are seven years of famine. He has sent the second dream to confirm the first. The warning came to allow you time to plan. You must appoint an overseer who understands what must be done.

"During the plentiful years, grain must be gathered and stored, that Egypt and her neighbors not perish in the famine."

Pharaoh nodded. "Yes, yes! You tell it rightly, for my frustration is gone. Now I must think on the problem." Without offering thanks, the ruler turned and started up the steps, waving his hand to dismiss them.

Zarill led Joseph out of the palace. "Now what am I to do with you? The king made no mention of a pardon or release."

"No, he didn't," Joseph said. "I think he was too concerned with the seriousness of the task he faces. Perhaps when he realizes what has happened, he'll grant my freedom."

Walking back down to the place of his long tribulation was difficult for Joseph. Even Zarill appeared subdued in spirit to realize his companion must again be imprisoned. "I'll keep the palace robe at hand in case we need it again," he said.

Upon seeing his cellmates, Joseph gave a half-hearted explanation for his return. His friends didn't press for more.

All those who had shared in the joy of Joseph's summons now kept to themselves and avoided Joseph's eyes. When all the tasks were done, some a second or third time, each prisoner took his place in the straw where he slept. No one in Joseph's section spoke. Moesha watched Joseph as he walked one more time to his place in the dismal cell. He watched as Joseph closed his eyes and said his nightly prayers. Then he said, shaking his head, "How can you? How can you pray to a God who abandons you?"

"I don't know that I've been abandoned. It's Pharaoh, not God, who has forgotten me for the moment."

"I don't see how you can endure in patience any longer."

"Today, Moesha, God revealed Pharaoh's dreams through me. Surely my pardon is imminent. I have endured long, it's true, but endurance is a mighty teacher, and a patient heart is given much."

"And what if Pharaoh doesn't act on his dreams? What if he ignores God's revelation?"

"God's purposes are not frustrated by man."

"I'd like to believe you."

"I speak the truth. You'll see in time."

They said good night, and Joseph lost himself in a deep, compensating sleep.

In the king's chamber there would be no sleep. This night he spent pacing.

*Who could fill the requirement for such an enormous task? Where can I find a man equal to saving Egypt? Can I, by myself, implement a plan of preparation?* These questions and more troubled him as he walked to and fro. His faithful steward kept constant vigil with him.

In his mind Pharaoh called up his wise men and posed his questions to each of them in turn, but he couldn't imagine that they would find an adequate solution. He still smoldered from the inane answers they had given in response to his dreams.

*No, I'll not seek counsel on this matter.*

By morning light he was spent, yet left with no ideas to satisfy his mental quest. "Is there such a man in the whole world?" he said aloud in front of his butler as he received his change of clothes.

"I don't know, Master, but if you will pardon my suggestion, perhaps the man who saw your dreams might also see the remedy to your dreams. If his God can solve your riddle, might he not also send a rescuer?"

Pharaoh stopped short. "You may be right. Why didn't I question the dreamsolver? His God indeed may reveal the solution to me." Orders were shouted as the king stepped from his chamber, and soon the palace was astir with compliance.

# BOOK TWO

# ASCENSION

# Chapter Twenty-five

# The Stairs

Joseph was stretching as he awakened to his usual surroundings. His friend was nearby. "Moesha, I had a fitful night. I started dreaming as soon as I closed my eyes and continued until the moment I woke up.

"A dream, Joseph?"

"Yes, and instead of feeling rested from sleeping, I'm worn out from mental exertion."

"Tell me about it."

Joseph gazed absently across the cell. "I was in a large classroom. It seemed to be like my father's house, where I studied as a child, but I was the only student. I had one instructor after another, the first like my father, but they changed as the lessons changed. I dimly remember being visited by my grandfather, Isaac, and his father, Abraham. All night long a steady stream of teachers confronted me. Each one taught his own topic. And I believe it was Cephas who coached me on the subject of the heavens."

"Why do you suppose you would have such a dream?"

"I don't know, but my head feels heavy as if filled to overflowing."

"But if it was just a dream..."

"That's just it—it must be of great significance. I wonder why."

Joseph had washed his face and was thinking of going back to sleep when the door burst open. Zarill was back.

"Didn't I tell you, Joseph?" he fairly shouted. "The king sends for you. He's convening his committee. You're to come at once!"

---

This audience differed greatly from the one the day before. The room was full. The king sat on the throne, regal in his finery and attended by many servants. The steps held the wise men and counselors of the court, just as Cephas had described it. The only vacant spot was the empty second throne next to Pharaoh.

All eyes were on Joseph. The appraisal seemed long to him, and he was uncomfortable. Finally a spokesman announced, "Pharaoh, god of Egypt, condescends to receive the Hebrew prisoner. Does the Hebrew know the language of Egypt?"

Zarill, still standing at Joseph's side, quickly whispered, "When they ask if you know a language, reply to them in that particular tongue and speak loudly so Pharaoh can hear."

"I conversed with the king in his language only yesterday," Joseph said loudly.

"That will do. You may ascend the first step. Do you have facility in Chaldean?" the inquisitor asked.

"Chaldean was what I first spoke," Joseph said in Chaldean.

"Take the second step. And what of Syrian?"

"In Syrian, I have no trouble, for it is similar to Chaldean."

"That will do—rise again. Speak now as in Canaan."

"I was brought here from Canaan."

Ascend to the fourth step and use the language of Lebanon."

"Lebanese is not a difficult challenge."

"Step up again. How well do you know the language of Punt?"

"I learned in prison to converse in that language."

There was an audible stirring from the men on the steps above. The idea of a prisoner even being on the king's steps was inconceivable, but even more so that he could ascend to the fifth level.

Joseph continued in the same manner until the tenth level. There, Pharaoh interrupted. "The subject is now standing by the man of medicine. He must show that he is knowledgeable in this area. The man of medicine will now question him."

The physician thought a moment, then said to Joseph, "You come to us from the prison where you have been enclosed for some time. Isn't that right?"

"Yes, I have been unjustly confined."

"Justice is not my concern. I must extract your knowledge of medicine. Since the greatest problem we face in our prisons is a running of the bowels, I should address that as our question. What then, is the proper incantation to cure this ailment?"

Joseph faced the physician. "An incantation will not cure it. The scourge is not in the patient's ear, but in the belly. God has provided us with all the proper remedies if we will but use them. Growing in your very gardens are the bitter herbs required. These herbs, when ingested, will bind the contents of the bowels and end the loss of fluids from the body. We saved many lives by this method in the king's prison."

The court physician raised a brow and turned to Pharaoh as if sure he would condemn Joseph.

Pharaoh simply looked from the physician to Joseph and back again. Finally he said, "I find nothing to censure in that answer. We must test this method to see if it works. If so, we are indebted to this man for his knowledge. If not, we may return him to the prison. Proceed with the hearing."

Joseph's facility with foreign words was satisfactory up to level twenty. There, Pharaoh again interjected. "The architects will now question the young man."

Their spokesman turned to Joseph. "The great pyramids, known even in distant lands, stand as monuments to the glory of Egypt, their magnificence unsurpassed. The lost skills of those architects were renewed to us through a wise man who once dwelt among our fathers. We wish to build such monuments, that we may honor our kings in burial and proclaim to the world that their greatness exceeds that of past kings. What are the measurements of the greatest structure, that we may surpass it in size?"

Joseph answered without hesitation. "The length of each side measures 440 royal cubits at the base. The height stands at 280 royal cubits."

The spokesman stared in silence until Pharaoh addressed him. "Do you accept this response?"

The architect turned to Pharaoh. "He answers correctly, but..." He paused, as if hesitant to allow Joseph to proceed. Finally he said, "I wish to ask another question." He turned back to Joseph. "What is the inclination that accords with such proportions?"

Joseph gazed into the eyes of the spokesman. "The great pyramid bears a seked of five palms and a half." He then bowed his head and added, "I might suggest that such a proportion offers the most pleasing aspect since it relates to that of the circle."

A rustle of murmurs moved through the court, and the architect stood open-mouthed, his head nodding slightly.

Joseph's head remained bowed until Pharaoh again spoke to the architect. "What say you to this?"

The architect simply stepped back and spread his arms as he turned toward Pharaoh. The king motioned the architect to his seat, then looked directly at Joseph. "You may proceed."

Joseph demonstrated the languages through the next ten steps. At the thirtieth level, the stargazers stood. One said, "When the sun god, Amon-Re, comes from his hiding place and greets us every morning, he gives us light and life. He enables us to borrow his energy and perform our daily labors. When he hides again, darkness overtakes us. The question is two-fold: how can we function without his light, and where does he go to hide"?

Joseph faced his challengers. "The answer you expect is that by night we receive light from the moon god Khonsu—but that is not true. Nor is it true that Re goes to the underworld to hide."

Some of the priests on the higher level looked to each other as if to revile Joseph, but Pharaoh again held up his hand as Joseph continued.

"For life, man is not dependent on the light of Shinehah by day, or that of Olea by night. Man is dependent on the True and

Living God, who gives His light to Shinehah and Olea. From God, man receives light as well as life and love.

"In the heavens, the Kokaubeam, the great lights of the firmament, are set in their order of reckoning, even as Olea and Shinehah are set in their order. And just as one is greater than the next, still others are greater than they. Kolob, the first governing creation, is greatest of all Kokaubeam because it is nearest the throne of God. Oliblish stands as the next grand governing creation.

"One revolution of these great governing bodies, being one thousand years of man's reckoning, is but one day to God. Our world moves in obeisance to Kolob, even as Shinehah and Olea move according to their order. Shinehah does not flee to hide in the underworld, but moves in the pattern of harmony and motion that God designed."

The stargazers conferred one with another. One finally said to Pharaoh, "We are not unfamiliar with this reasoning. This teaching reached us many years ago, but we cannot prove one belief over another. We recognize the knowledge with which he speaks, but we do not concur with his doctrine. Nevertheless, we agree that he may ascend by merit of his learning." Joseph stepped onto the thirty-first step.

The next ten steps included languages derived from Akkadian, including that of Assyria and Babylonia, all of which Joseph demonstrated with fluency.

The priests of the gods of Egypt stood ominously on the fortieth step, some clearly displeased that Joseph had ascended so far. He said a silent prayer. "Father, be with me still. Let Thy truth be my voice. Help me to withstand the evil I feel emanating from these men."

He studied his opponents thoughtfully as they scrutinized him. It was obvious who the chief high priest was by the leopard skin he wore. Finally a tall, angular man stepped forward, but it was not the chief high priest. Remembering Cephas's description, Joseph discerned that this man who was to be the questioner was Kenah.

The priest spoke. "We hold no league with Hebrew doctrine. You may have impressed some of this court with your clever words, but we, the priests of Pharaoh's house, are not swayed by them."

Joseph replied, "It's true that many tenets of faith abound in our world, but one must show allegiance to that verity which bears him sweet fruit."

Pharaoh interrupted. "Ask your questions and get on with this proceeding. Your king is weary and desires answers, not debate."

"Very well," the priest said. "Let our query be this: What is the Supreme Sacrifice?"

Joseph closed his eyes a moment, then began. "You won't comprehend or agree with what I'm about to say. I say it nevertheless as a matter of declaration.

"The time will come when God, the Father, will send His Only Begotten son to dwell on earth. The Son will come to redeem mankind. He will establish a gospel of peace and love. All this will be done to benefit mankind, but He will be reviled, persecuted, and hated. God, allowing the greatest suffering of all to happen to his Son—this Son offering himself to suffer it—constitutes the Supreme Sacrifice.

"In similitude of this great sacrifice, it has been established as a covenant between God and man that we symbolically offer up sacrifices. We confirm God's sacrifice by offering up the first fruits of the field and the firstlings of our flocks. It has not and never will be required for man to sacrifice another man's life."

Joseph reached back in his mind at this point. He wanted to duplicate as nearly as possible the exact words Cephas had spoken. He turned toward the priest of Kenah and with deliberate delivery said, "God does not require a sacrifice to make the grain grow. Prayer and a sincere heart, knowledge and hard work will suffice for that. He never asks humans to give their lives for Him. He asks only that they live their lives for Him."

The priest Kenah burst out in anger. "That is the most dissentious doctrine of nonsense I have ever heard. This man should be condemned at once for his effrontery."

Pharaoh held up his hand and said to the priest, "Did your god provide an answer to the king's dreams? Did he show what needed to be done to save our present lives?"

The priest cried, "Egypt's gods give a different answer than that of the Hebrew God."

"Yes, indeed," Joseph said. "The Hebrew God has shown Pharaoh how to save Egypt and her neighbors. The Hebrew God is the One True God." As he spoke, murmurings broke out on all sides, but the king raised his scepter and struck it on the floor. Advance!" he commanded.

The room fell silent as Joseph took the forty-first step.

The next nine steps represented the most distant and obscure dialects with no local means of learning them. Only Pharaoh held knowledge of them. If a way were found, the priests would have eagerly mastered the unique tongues for that would have placed them closer to the throne. Now, they watched apprehensively as the dialects were presented.

Joseph searched his mind. Into his remembrance came the scene in the classroom from the dream the night before and he responded appropriately on each of the next eight steps. His opponents were clearly disturbed since Pharaoh was the only one conversant in any of the dialects. The proceedings depended on his nod of approbation before each ascension, and the holy men watched and listened, straining to know if Pharaoh and Joseph truly shared communal knowledge.

On the final step, the last obscure language was demanded. Joseph closed his eyes, but he couldn't call up the memory of it from his night vision. Silence filled the room, and he quickly said a prayer. Then something tugged at the back of his mind and into his head came a picture of his friend, Wama, smiling his broad smile. "Of course, thank you," he said to himself. Aloud, he spoke accurately and with ease the language he had learned from his black friend in prison.

The spokesman looked at Pharaoh, who nodded, and with one final step, Joseph took his place on the dais and stood next to the king of Egypt.

# Chapter Twenty-six

# Apophis

Extending across the room behind the royal chairs hung a double row of curtains that divided the throne room from the king's private residence—a delicate veil in front of a heavier, elegant fabric that functioned well as a barrier to sound.

Joseph had no sooner stepped on the high plane than Pharaoh motioned to him and said, "Come with me." He held back the drape and the two of them passed from the platform down a few steps into large, comfortable living quarters. The courtiers on the stairs were stunned, some shaking their heads at such incredulous events. They had never seen anyone invited into the king's private room from the court steps. A natural hatred erupted in some of the wise men. This man was much too learned, too smooth, and too threatening. He must be distrusted.

Inside the curtain, Pharaoh signaled his servants to leave them, and as soon as they all departed, he settled himself in a comfortable cushion and removed his crown. The king suddenly transformed from ruler to man in Joseph's sight, the look on his face one of weariness. He was handsome, but his jaw was set, his cheeks lined, and his face showed the tension of frequently clenched teeth. His eyes were dark blue and deep-set, and his head was shaved but for a traditional side lock.

He sounded for a servant and requested food, then motioned to his guest. "Please, be seated." He searched Joseph's face and said, "My name is Apophis. Tell me who you are."

"My name is Joseph. I'm a slave, but I have been wrongfully imprisoned for eight and a half years."

"I can rescind your prison sentence. Who was your master?"

"Potiphar, captain of the guard, who died in battle."

"Potiphar... Yes, I remember. I heard that Potiphar's wife had suffered at the hand of a young slave—that the slave was imprisoned by her accusations. You are that slave?"

"I am, but I was innocent."

"I believe you—I knew Zelica. But how did you come to be a slave in the first place? This is all very unlikely, you know. No one has been able to ascend the steps since I myself did so thirty years ago. But I was groomed for it all my life. Now you, a slave from prison, not only ascend the steps, but answer the dreams that concern the fate of our lands. How can I help but be intrigued by you? Do you plot to overthrow the king? Am I taking chances being alone with you?"

"You wouldn't have invited me into your private chamber if you believed me to be a threat."

"Yes, you're right. I feel nothing but a sense of peace in your presence. But that doesn't mean I trust that feeling—or you. For years you could have planned and prepared to come to this moment."

At this point food was brought, and Joseph's eyes surveyed the fowl, fruit, bread, and honeycomb set before them. Pharaoh nodded and gestured Joseph to eat, but kept his watchful eyes upon him. Joseph ignored the gaze; the food was too inviting. He selected a meager portion and took his first bite. The tender meat was succulent and delicious. Joseph closed his eyes. He couldn't remember ever having tasted anything so good. He sampled a little of everything with obvious delight.

Pharaoh concentrated on Joseph as he ate, his thoughts questioning. *Has the Hebrew God sent this man? Is this the man my dreams indicate is needed?*

When Joseph had his fill of food, Pharaoh spoke, "Come now. Tell me your story."

Joseph thought for a moment, decided it was the right thing to do, and told the ruler of Egypt his account from the beginning. He told of his family and childhood, of being sold into slavery, of Potiphar's house and prison.

The king listened intently, nodding from time to time. Sometimes he searched Joseph's face carefully, but he didn't interrupt. When the tale was finished, Pharaoh nodded. "How did you know the answers on the stairs?"

Now Joseph told of his long acquisition of languages and of his instructive dream only the night before.

The king smiled, reassured. "I see more in your story than you might think. I know of the Hebrew prophets and the true line of authority. You and I are not so different as you might think. My forebears once believed as you do. But I now hold to the ways of Egypt. You may not want my crown, but it's obvious that your God in his wisdom has put you in the only position in the world where you can do some good. I see that, and yet I'm not threatened. The people believe that Pharaoh is a god. I'll remain Pharaoh, god of Egypt, for the sake of the people, but you, Joseph, shall be the one who governs. What have you to say?"

"I will happily assist in any way that I can."

"Not assist—govern. I want you to be the overseer you spoke of in your summary of my dreams."

Joseph bowed his head. "With respect to you, I have been taught that to have ambitions regarding a kingship is wrong. I desire to do only the will of God."

"Then if it is His will, you must comply. You said yourself that we need someone who can see the problem and accomplish its solutions. Your God has sent you here, hasn't He?"

"Yes, I'm sure He has led me to this moment."

"Then you must sit with me in government."

"Yes, I submit to Pharaoh's request."

"Good. I'm glad your God is mindful of us. Now, you must have sensed that some of my advisors are displeased with me. They plot and strive to regain their previous position—especially the priests. They are of the old dynasty. I dared not change the traditions and rites, but where possible, I installed Hyksos to positions. The holy men will be upset at these events, for it is by their own law that I—and now you—have been able to come to power. When they required that a ruler master the steps, I'm sure they never believed anyone but an Egyptian could do it. So while we are able, we'll use the power to do what good we can. I fear that our greatest threat is the priest Kenah."

"Perhaps I can help. Is murder reason enough to displace a priest?" Joseph asked.

"Kenah enjoys putting people to death with his human sacrificial rites," Pharaoh said.

"But I'm not speaking of rites. If it could be proven that he took another priest's life, wouldn't that warrant censure?"

"What are you saying?"

"The priest Kenah poisoned my friend Cephas. He was the Hebrew counselor you had in your court."

"Can you prove it?"

"I don't know."

"Let's pursue this further but keep it to ourselves. I have great hope in things to come with you in charge. I've kept my court waiting long enough. I purposely didn't dismiss them because I'm displeased with them of late. They must remain in place until I excuse them and they'll be angry by now—even more so when they hear what I have to say."

As Apophis replaced the crown on his head, he again became Pharaoh and led Joseph back through the curtain. The men on the steps straightened and looked toward the throne. The ruler raised his scepter and, gesturing to Joseph, announced in a loud voice, "I, Pharaoh, god of Egypt, declare this man to be overseer of all Egypt. He will be called Zana-panea—one through whom God speaks. His words will be obeyed."

He took the gold necklace of authority from his own neck and placed it on Joseph, then did the same with the gold ring from his finger. He summoned his servants to bring a royal robe and crown. He placed the robe over Joseph's shoulders, but as he lifted the crown, Joseph shrunk back. "Joseph," Pharaoh whispered, "your God sent you to save Egypt. He won't mind if you do it wearing a crown." He firmly laid the symbol of authority on Joseph's head as the stunned men of the court observed in unbelief.

"Send for the chariots and the runners," he shouted. "They shall lead our young ruler through the streets of the city, announcing what has happened." To Joseph, he said, "You will ride in the second chariot, not Pharaoh's. The people know my chariot and they'll know what it means." He turned. "I haven't slept. I'm going to rest now, and when you have been properly paraded throughout the city, come back to my chambers. I want to talk more about pending matters."

Runners went ahead of Pharaoh's empty chariot, sounding trumpets and proclaiming, "Pharaoh, god of Egypt, declares Zana-panea the new governor, whom God has sent to save the land."

Joseph, riding in the second chariot and uncomfortable in his sudden office, noticed the curious expressions of the onlookers who filled the streets. Zarill, captain of the king's guard, followed in a third chariot, his guard trotting in step behind as they went slowly up one road and down another.

At last, they traveled by the prison where the prisoners stood alert at the sound of the trumpets. The keeper of the prison ran out to see the procession pass by, his eyes briefly meeting those of the honored man. "It can't be," the keeper said to himself, and soon the procession moved out of sight. He hurried back inside, out of breath. "My eyes play tricks on me," he said to his guards.

Moesha, who stood near the open cell door, leaned closer as the keeper continued. "If he were not so much on my mind, I would say that the young ruler riding in the second chariot was Joseph—Zana-panea, they called him."

"One who speaks for God," Moesha said to himself. "What is happening to you, Joseph?"

# Chapter Twenty-seven

# Orientation

As Joseph and Zarill walked back into the palace, Zarill said, "I don't know quite what to think or how to treat you." He seemed nervous. "This morning you were my prisoner. As the day ends, you're my superior."

Joseph laughed. "I don't know myself. Bear with me, my friend, and we'll grow in understanding together. But for now, be my guide and guardian awhile longer—I don't even know where to go, or where to lay my head tonight"

"Where do you wish to go?"

"Pharaoh bid me return to him on completion of our tour."

"Very well, but he doesn't like to be disturbed. We'll see how far his shared power will take you."

The steward opened Pharaoh's private door and let the two enter. "He's expecting you." Zarill and Joseph looked at each other and smiled.

Inside, Pharaoh walked from his bed and motioned for Joseph to sit. Zarill stood by the door. Food had been set on the table by previous order. "Help yourself," Pharaoh said. The scent of meat and fresh bread filled Joseph's nostrils. He was hungry. He placed some meat on a piece of flatbread and ate gratefully while Pharaoh spoke. "Send for a scribe," he said to his steward. "He shall write the words that shall be obeyed." He turned to Joseph. "First of all, you will need a place to live. I shall order an addition built next to the palace. For now, you will be given quarters in the palace.

"Next, you must pick your staff of servants, counselors, or whatever you choose. You must have your own scribes, for your word will also be law. You'll need personal guards for security. Do you want me to assign these for you?"

"Everything is a bit overwhelming. I'm sure I'll need your help, but I do have some ideas about assignments. Am I free to choose whomever I like?"

"You are."

"May I have Zarill as my chief captain?"

"I see," Pharaoh said. "You catch on quickly. But yes. There are sufficient good men in the ranks to handle the shuffle. How say you, Zarill?"

The young captain felt honored by the promotion. In Pharaoh's service he was third in rank, but in Joseph's court he would be his right hand—his first in rank. "I accept your appointment with gratitude for your esteem."

"I already need you to accomplish many things, Zarill," Joseph said. "We'll think on it tonight and begin our plans in the morning." Turning back to Pharaoh, he said, "Many men were wrongfully imprisoned with me. I should like to appoint some of them to my staff. I would also like to bring about a new system for the prison, with your approval."

"Yes, all in good time. When you become accustomed to your authority, you can make changes at your own will. For now, we'll discuss each change. You must be weary. It may serve our efforts better if you and your captain begin fresh in the morning."

"Thank you, I am indeed tired."

"Wait, Joseph, before we retire. I have told you what I want. Is there anything you, yourself, desire at my hand?"

"There is, my king. I married a slave girl who was given to you by Zelica as a gift and is now living as an adopted daughter with the priest of On. I would ask that you give her to me. Her Egyptian name is Aseneth."

"Let it be done. Is there anything else?"

"Yes," Joseph said. "A great man lies buried in the prison graveyard. I'd like him to have a burial place of honor, befitting his greatness."

"Let it also be done." Pharaoh looked at the scribe to make sure it was all recorded. "Tomorrow begins a new era in the world of Egypt. Now, go to your beds and sleep well."

Joseph was shown to his quarters, and the steward left a servant outside the door to do his bidding. The chamber consisted of one large room divided into three smaller sections. The bed was large and inviting with clean linen. Fruit lay on a bedside table. He chose some purple grapes, smelled them, then ate them slowly, enjoying their sweetness as they burst in his mouth. He walked around the room, touching the furnishings and the luxurious fabrics, and laughed softly in wonder and delight. Then he stepped to the middle of the room and raised his arms and face toward heaven. "Thy servant is here to do thy bidding, Father." Then, he sank to his knees, bowed his head, and spoke through his tears as he continued.

"Thou hast preserved me from those who would slay me. Thou hast lifted me up from the pit. Thou gavest me strength against the designing woman. Thou didst show me great and wonderful works in the den of iniquity. Thy care hast exalted me from prison to a throne." Joseph allowed the tears to flow freely as he praised his beloved God.

"I marvel at Thy greatness and goodness. Now I must ask more of Thee." He broke off sobbing for a time, then went on. "Help me to know and do Thy will. Keep me close to Thee. Watch over me day and night. I tremble at the task Thou hast set for me, but I know that with Thy help it can be done. I would be but a vessel through whom Thou canst work. Bless my loved ones, Lord. Keep watch over my father and brothers. Tender their hearts toward me. Bring my beloved wife and son in safety to be with me."

He ended his prayer with expressions of gratitude, then went to the great soft bed and let it envelop him. *I wonder what Mahta will think.* Then he gave up his thoughts to oblivious sleep.

When Joseph awakened early the next morning, he saw his crown sitting on the table. "It really is true," he said to himself.

Suddenly he heard activity outside the door, and the posted servant knocked and called out, "The groomers are here, sir."

"Thank you," Joseph said, not knowing what to expect.

Through the door came an entire flock of people, and before he knew what was happening, he was sponged and oiled, powdered and perfumed, then outfitted in royal garments.

Pharaoh's steward appeared. "The king requests you to join him in his chambers."

"Thank you, but wait. Are you the same butler whom I met in prison?"

The words had a dramatic effect upon the steward, and he suddenly collapsed at Joseph's feet. "Please, sir, I didn't mean to forget you. It wasn't until my master was troubled by his dream that my poor mind was set to remembering. It was I, however, who finally told Pharaoh to send for you. Please don't punish me."

Joseph bid the man to stand. "I have already forgiven you. I see that you're an excellent servant. I'm happy that the king has one so faithful in his service. Thank you for recommending me to him."

"You are a great man; I knew that even in prison. I shall do all I can to make it right for you."

"I see that already. Come, take me to our master." Joseph's servant followed, carrying the crown.

Pharaoh was smiling as Joseph came in. He appeared refreshed, as one whose burden had been lightened considerably. "Come, my scholar," he said. "I want you to meet my family."

Sitting in the center of the room with her children around her was a beautiful woman dressed in a gold and white gown, her dark auburn hair falling softly over her shoulders. Her brown eyes held a look of wisdom and kindness, her delicate features enhanced by a soft, natural blush on her cheeks. She smiled as they came near.

"Here is my one source of joy," the king said, "my wife, Yrameesa, and my children. My oldest son, Magron, is twelve years old; my daughter, Rona, is six; and, our little Tephnaro is two."

"You are a blessed man to have such a family," Joseph said.

Yrameesa spoke. "I understand they have gone to bring your wife. You must be happy about that."

"Indeed, I am. I also have a son, Manasseh, who is seven years old."

Both Pharaoh and his wife looked surprised. "But you are too young," Yrameesa said.

"Yes, my marriage was a hasty decision because of my impending imprisonment. But I don't regret it even though I have been separated from my loved ones for eight and a half years. The hope of being with them again makes me glad we went through with it."

Yrameesa spoke. "I wish to hear about your experiences. I also look forward to knowing your wife. Your coming is of great benefit to us. My husband is tired and needs to share the burdens he has been shouldering so long. He also needs someone besides me with whom he can talk. Being a king is a lonely concern."

"Never mind that," Pharaoh said. "Come, Joseph. We must go to the throne room. I have convened the court for our first declarations of business. You will sit in Yrameesa's chair. She doesn't attend much anymore; she would rather be with her children."

They hurried to face the advisors and begin a new era.

# Chapter Twenty-eight

# Playing the Role

Joseph had little to do but watch and listen. He learned much, his attention largely on the old priest so that he might study his foe as much as possible. By listening to the proceedings, he was able to formulate ideas for his future plans. The session was short, but worthwhile.

Zarill stood by his new master's throne, and as soon as the meeting ended, Joseph asked him to come to his quarters for some planning. "I want you to gather some men on whom you can depend. I have much for you to do. First, I will choose my guards. One, I'll take from the prison. The other is the Nubian that was attached to Potiphar. Do you know where he is? Did he die in battle with his master?"

"No. He was with Potiphar, but he was not a soldier. As far as I know, he remained in camp when the battles took place. Maybe Potiphar wanted it that way so his Nubian would be preserved."

"I hope so, for I want you to find him. I think he would agree to stand with me, and I would be good to him."

"Consider it done."

"Second, I want you to go to the prison. I'll sign releases for all of the innocent, but some of them are to be brought here." He then gave Zarill the list of names and signed his first order as ruler.

Zarill said, "These releases have long been needed, but the prison must still be reformed to avoid imprisonment of the sick and innocent."

"I agree. We'll implement those changes soon. Be thinking of a just man who could evaluate the offenders; but right now, the releases will suffice. Tell the prison keeper I'll bid him to an audience soon."

Zarill looked pleased, and Joseph smiled as he continued. "Now, I have a special assignment for you, but I think I'll wait a few days. Let's get our staff, and you get your trusted men. Then we'll go forward. By the way, Zarill, how long is the trip to On and back?"

"A swift courier could accomplish the trip in one day."

"That means my wife and son will probably be here by tomorrow. Let me know as soon as we have word of them."

Talk of the recent events in the palace still filled the prison. The keeper tried to remember the face he had seen in the royal chariot, and Moesha kept thinking about Joseph. But the routine went on until Zarill appeared and engaged the keeper in animated conversation. Soon they both stepped inside the cell, the keeper flushed and excited as Zarill said loudly, "Those whose names I read will please come with me!" He then read over a dozen names.

Moesha, Wama, and Pleoris stepped up immediately, each hoping that Joseph would keep his promise to take them with him when he left. Others moved forward hesitantly, those with broken spirits being led by the hand. They were all taken into the small reception room where Zarill told them, "Our new ruler has signed a release giving each of you your freedom. You may leave here now and go wherever you like. Those who have no place to go can come with me and find work in my master's service. Some of you he has asked for specifically."

The keeper could stand it no longer. "It's Joseph! I was right!" he cried, and the prisoners looked from the keeper back to Zarill, who smiled.

"That's true. It is Joseph. He ascended all forty-nine stairs, and Pharaoh has made him second in power to himself."

The men began exclaiming among themselves as Moesha and Wama smiled. A few stood open-mouthed.

"Who will go out on his own and who will come with us?"

"I stay right here," a spiritless old man said.

"I will also stay," another said. "I hated Joseph. I have no one and no place to go. Here I have food and a place to sleep. I will stay."

Three men went back to their families. The remaining eleven followed Zarill across the pavilion into the servants' quarters where they received baths and clean clothing.

Some time later, inside Joseph's chamber, the group knelt before their new master.

"Hello, Moesha, Wama. Hello, my friends. How are you all? I welcome you to make your homes with me.

One found his voice. "What do we call you?"

"My Egyptian name is Zana-panea. When we're in public, you will address me thus. In my private chambers, my friends, you may call me Joseph."

"What are we to do?" another asked.

"Moesha will be my head steward, Wama my personal guard. I'll need messengers, attendants, and a physician. I'll find something for all of you to do. Zarill will take you now and show you your room in the servants quarters. You may return when you are ready."

They left, eager yet humbled at the prospect of their new lives in the palace.

———❖———

His first full day under the mantel of office had been a long and tiring one. When Joseph finally gave himself up to the bed, he fell immediately to sleep. He didn't know how long he had been immersed in dream when he was called back to the edge of reality. As he came to full awareness, he realized Apophis sat on the edge of his bed.

"I'm sorry to rouse you, Joseph, but I want to show you something."

Joseph put on a robe and followed his friend out of the palace to the temple complex where they passed through a gate and crossed the outer enclosure, stopping before the massive pylon, the gateway to the temple proper. Pharaoh turned to Joseph and explained.

"The priest on watch is my trusted friend. He can keep a confidence. I have told him that I'm bringing you here. He doesn't know why, but that doesn't matter. I want you to see what the temple involves so you'll better understand the soul of Egypt. If you were not who you are, you might even want to take part."

They passed through the portal of the great pylon into the outer court where stood a large statue of the twin gods ma'at, crowned with the appropriate ma'at feathers. With extended winged arms they guarded the way, one hand holding an ankh, a symbol of life. Pharaoh and Joseph crossed the courtyard and stopped once more before a door plated with copper. Pharaoh spoke again. "No one is allowed beyond this point. Only the pharaoh and his family have use of the temple."

He opened the door to a great hall where two rows of large columns extended the length of the chamber. Dishes of fire stood burning in its four quarters. In the center of the room stood a golden pedestal supporting a basin filled with water.

"It's beautiful," Joseph whispered, as they stepped onto the polished floor of pink marble. "I'm in awe." Before them on the floor was an inlaid pattern of a lotus flower.

Apophis led him to the center of the room. "This basin holds the sacred water that is used to cleanse me before I enter the inner sanctuary. Here I'm prepared and clothed for my passage through the rituals."

The sound of speaking brought the night priest into the room. Seeing that it was Pharaoh and Joseph, he backed into the doorway and did not reappear.

"Come," the king said, and he took him into the second room.

"This is the Hall of Two Rights. Here I am anointed and given a secret name." There was nothing in this room but a small vessel containing oil. On the walls, however, a series of paintings depicted the steps one must go through.

"All of these ceremonies are to prepare me to get from this life to the next. These pictures portray some of the pitfalls of being mortal. You see how the gods of various kinds offer assistance as needed."

They stepped into the next section.

"This is where the purification takes place." Joseph saw that the panels still continued in bright detail. Standing on the floor were eight large golden jars. Their use was not explained.

In the next section, Apophis told him, "This is the area for initiation and teaching. Here I am coached in the right things to say to the gods. You see the pictures in all the rooms that illustrate the rituals."

They moved again.

"And finally, this is the Hall of Shu, where, if I pass all the tests, I am embraced by the gods and my progress is secure."

They returned into the great hall. To their right at the north end hung a curtain through which they passed into another area, also with rows of columns, but only partially roofed and without walls or pictures. Joseph counted five alabaster lion couches, each edged with a trough and a hole that funneled to a gutter below. Two were very large, three the size that would accommodate a human. A diverted rivulet of water from the Great River ran through the room.

"This extension of the temple represents the preparation of the dead for heaven. As you see, the pillars and stones are set for study of the stars. Here, also, the embalmers work. The oversized beds are for the mummification of the sacred bulls. The god Ptah, patron of our city, is represented by a bull. Therefore this certain species of bull is carefully preserved and given a special place of burial."

"I didn't know this," Joseph said. "What are the smaller couches for?"

"The embalming of the royal family, or other hierarchy, as is seen fit."

"And those rooms?" Joseph asked, pointing to three open doorways.

"They house the gods of stone and wood, and are workrooms for the priests." As they talked, Apophis led him to a stone couch and motioned Joseph to sit. The crescent moon shone through the columns.

"There are many priests. I hope to learn them all. It seems you have gods of every kind of symbol in nature—the gods of the sun, moon, stars, wind, and rivers."

"Yes, I know, and they increase. With the smallest justification, a new reason can be found to deify something and a new priest appears. If they aren't stopped, there will be as many gods as there are trees and flowers, and a priest for each one. I'm trying to minimize that, but it's difficult. The pharaoh before me was lax. Many changes took place under his rule, and the priests were the ones in control. Some priests are sincere, and believe they are doing right."

"Who are the others?"

"You mentioned it yourself. The priests Kenah, Libnah, Korash, and others came about when their stone gods—of the land between the rivers—were introduced here. They brought their religions with them—and their evil ways. I don't believe in their stone gods, but they are not easily deterred. The past pharaoh let them get too strong an influence."

"I'm relieved to hear what you say. It clears my thinking. I was confused about much of what went on here."

"Yes. I believe that in the beginning, the righteous pharaohs built the temples and allowed the ceremonies in a sincere effort to emulate the religion of their fathers before Noah. But truth has been lost, and the difference between what your people believe and what has evolved here has become irreconcilable."

"I can see similarities in what the Hebrews and Egyptians believe, but when one loses communication with the true source, strange things happen. I have observed that man with his inadequate mortal mind cannot find out about God by himself. Only God can reveal himself to man."

"It must take a great deal of humility."

Joseph nodded, "God can't reach a prideful heart."

"Do you believe in ceremony in your religion, Joseph?"

"Yes. We have a ceremony of sacrifice and of marriage and some other sacred ordinances. We don't make rituals from our love of nature, but I cherish all of God's creations in my heart."

"That's why I wanted to talk with you, Joseph. I realize that I don't know the answers. I was impressed by your ability to answer my dreams and see so clearly their solution."

"I haven't seen all of the solutions yet."

"But you will. I don't even understand my own yielding to you, yet I feel a strong witness of confidence in you and your God. I have no doubts."

"To return the compliment, I admire your desire to serve righteously. I sense you really do care about Egypt and its people."

"That's true, but it exacts a great deal. I have lived but fifty-five years, yet the weight of the office has made me feel like an old man."

"Tell me how you came to be on the throne of Egypt."

# Chapter Twenty-nine

# Apophis's Story

"It was my grandfather who conceived the idea and the plan. He was a mighty chieftain of the Hyksos, a nomadic Shemite tribe that roamed the large deserts of the Sinar Valley. He held the status of a king, and was invited from time to time to the palace in Memphis to pay tribute to Pharaoh.

"Egypt for many years had held power over its surrounding territories. The tributes and taxes had been exacted as a matter of course. My grandfather resented the tolls, but didn't know what to do about it.

"On one of his trips to Memphis, he was invited to observe a day at court, an occasion when some new advisors were being installed. Intrigued by the ceremony of the ascension, he listened carefully to the questions and to the language probe. For months afterwards he couldn't forget it.

"One night as he lay on his bed thinking about it, he asked himself, 'Why can't I learn the answers to the questions and become an officer of the king's court?' As time went on, he even thought to attain the throne.

"The next time he was invited to the king's court, he took careful note. It was a plan that would take many years of study and preparation. He began a quest in search of every known language. It took a long time to visit every area of the province. He infiltrated the Egyptian hierarchy and through careful training managed to get some of his own men installed in key positions in the government. As he did this, he trained his army and allied himself with smaller nomadic tribes who would assist him.

"When he was finally ready, he was very old, but still determined to see it through. His only son, my father, didn't share his dream, so rather than force his son, he turned his attention on me. I was five years old when he began my lessons. I was twenty-five when his plan came to fruition.

"With a carefully laid plan of attack, he invaded Egypt and his troops swept everything in their path. They came upon Memphis from the main roads, from the deserts, and even on boats from the Great River.

"Then when he had the pharaoh on his knees, he demanded the court to convene. The spokesman was ordered to recite all the questions of the ascension. With me as the candidate, the old man stood and watched as I made my way up each step and came at last to the royal chair.

The old pharaoh, who had no sons, was banished to a room in the palace, where he died a few months later. My grandfather saw me through three years on the throne, then he died.

"The transition was so easy it was frightening. You'll notice that my borders are well-guarded and my staff is hand-picked. The same kind of take-over will not happen in my time. I have devoted my life to the glory of Egypt. I didn't even marry until I was forty years old. Oh, I had concubines, but Egypt was my first love, until Yrameesa."

Joseph asked, "So now you want me, a Hebrew prophet, to share the crown with you?"

"I would not have thought so a week ago. Your God humbled me completely with my dreams and your answers. It's still for the good of Egypt that I act."

"Yes, I feel it too. I have fallen in love with Egypt myself."

They were listening to the water of the river running its course beside the temple and lapping at the steps that led down to the stream. The light from the fire dish sent a sober reddish shadow over them. Apophis glanced at Joseph with a slight smile on his face, leaned back and said, "It all started with a robe, you know."

"What?" Joseph asked, a little startled. "What are you talking about?"

"Egypt." He gestured. "All of this—all of the glory that is Egypt couldn't have been were it not for the robe."

"What do you mean?"

"I have been searching the archives. Of course I studied the history of Egypt before, and even after I obtained the throne, but my study has uncovered something I didn't suspect."

"Something about a robe?"

"Yes. Do you remember the story of Noah drinking wine and falling asleep and how his son, Ham, saw his father's nakedness?"

"Yes. Shem and Japeth crept into the tent backwards to cover him. I remember."

"Well," Pharaoh said, "I found a more detailed account—in an old dusty sealed scroll."

Joseph raised an eyebrow. "What did you learn?"

"That the reason Noah was naked was because Ham had stolen the robe from off his father. He took it because of what it represented. Ham saw Noah naked because he, himself, had removed the vestment of the priesthood.

"Shem, the more righteous son, had either already received, or was promised that he would receive, the birthright. When Noah bequeathed the blessing, the coat was to go with it. Ham was jealous. He wanted the birthright for himself, and since he couldn't have it, he stole the symbol of its authority.

"Later, Ham led his followers south, and they multiplied greatly. They believed he had the power of prophet, patriarch, and king by virtue of the coat he flaunted. He made much of the glory of the robe. It was ceremoniously handed down from one ruler to the next, each king thereafter being called Pharaoh after the name of Ham's son. The people, believing implicitly in the power of the garment, gave total obeisance to its wearer." Apophis paused.

Joseph picked up the story. "In the meantime, Shem, who had the real authority, settled the middle countries and quietly taught his people to serve God."

Pharaoh smiled and added, "While Egypt became mighty and built great cities and colossal edifices. Then the interest became obscure and the original coat was forgotten. Now, all of the royal clothing is patterned after the style of the first garment. The office itself has simply replaced the need for the true symbol."

"Do you know where the original robe is?" Joseph asked.

"There is a questionable story about one of the pharaoh's descendants—a king in an outlying settlement—wearing it out to hunt. His name was Nimrod. He was a wicked man who loved power and believed the animals would be subdued by the power of the coat. While on the hunt, the king was set upon by enemies and killed. The robe never came back."

"Maybe I know the rest of the story," Joseph said.

"How is that?" Apophis leaned closer.

"As a child I heard the story of my uncle, Esau, going out to hunt. He supposedly confronted Nimrod and slew him, then removed his robe and brought it home. Upon returning, he showed the spoils of his hunt to his brother, Jacob, who is my father. Esau then traded the robe to Jacob for a mess of pottage, because he was so tired and hungry."

"Do you think it was the very coat?"

"I don't know, but my father must have recognized it as something special because when he blessed me with the birthright, he gave me the garment."

"The same one?"

"Yes. I'm certain it was the one he bought from Esau."

"I've wondered," Pharaoh said, "if Noah had the coat handed down to him, could it be the same garment Adam was given by God in the Garden of Eden?"

"Do you wonder how the original skins could have lasted that long?"

"Yes, I have wondered."

"I've thought of that also. But even if it were replaced at some time, wouldn't it still carry the same virtue?"

"Yes, I suppose—or maybe God's clothing doesn't wear out." They laughed.

"But Joseph, what happened to your coat of authority? Where is it now?"

"I heard that my brothers took it to my father with lamb's blood spilled on it. They told him they had found it thus. He refused to believe me dead, so he tore it into twelve pieces. He and my brothers were to wear a piece of it next to their hearts until I'm found."

They were both quiet for a time. At last Pharaoh asked, "Doesn't it seem meaningful to you that we sit here together, you and I?"

"You mean that after all these years the descendent of Shem, with the real authority, sits with the one who represents Ham and his usurped authority?"

"Yes."

"It would, but as you yourself said, aren't we glad that God is mindful of us?"

"I *am* glad, and I eagerly wait to see what next our road will reveal." The sky was raising its colors of dawn, and Pharaoh added, "We have talked the entire night away. We must be off to our beds. Yrameesa was right—it is good to have someone I can talk with."

# Chapter Thirty

# Mahta's Quandry

Mahta and Rena were in the garden courtyard watching Manasseh at play. "He's so strong," Rena said. "See how he pulls himself up? And so big for his age."

Mahta laughed. "And of course Joseph would say it is because of his blood of Israel."

"He amazes me," Rena said. "This is the first time I have had a child to observe, but for almost eight years now, it's been nothing but joy. How grateful I am to have found you, dear Aseneth, and to have shared your son."

"It is I who am grateful. You are the mother I never had but always dreamed of. How blessed I am to have been brought to your home and to be loved by you. When I think where I might have been..."

"Well, don't think about that. Think of what we're going to do with your boy if he doesn't stop climbing on the garden wall. Come, Manasseh, it's time for our meal."

A servant approached. "There's a chariot outside—and a messenger. He has come for Aseneth."

Mahta stood, clutching her heart, eyes wide. Could this be the moment she had waited for these many years?

"Show him in," Rena said. "We'll see him inside."

When the palace messenger faced them he said, "Pharaoh commands me to come to you. Are you Aseneth?"

"Yes."

"There have been many changes at the palace in Memphis. I am to bring you there with me."

Rena and Mahta looked at each other. "What does Pharaoh want with her?" Rena asked.

"I don't know. I'm sent only to bring the woman, Aseneth."

"What do you think it means?" Mahta asked her mother.

"Let's not expect the worst," Rena said, then turned to the messenger. "You must be tired and hungry. We'll eat, and you will sleep here tonight. Tomorrow the priest of On and his entire family will journey to visit Pharaoh in Memphis." To a house servant she said, "Go to the temple. Tell the priest we bid him come immediately."

At their meal Rena asked the messenger, "What are the changes you spoke of earlier?"

"Another ruler—one second in command—has been instated by Pharaoh himself."

After the evening meal, when the king's courier was asleep in his room, the three quietly conversed. Mahta wondered aloud, "If it were anything to do with Joseph, they would have asked for the name *Mahta*, not the Egyptian name *Aseneth*. No one even knows my previous name. Do you suppose something has happened to my husband?"

"No, child. Don't even think that way."

"But why does Pharaoh send for people?"

"Any number of reasons," Ramieth said. "He is hasty at times and always unpredictable. But legally, you do still belong to him. They may have reviewed our adoption of you and decided to question it."

"Maybe he wants you back in his nursery," Rena said. "You were well-liked there."

"But what if it is one of those priests who looked at me when they wanted to choose a virgin for a sacrifice."

"We really shouldn't be guessing. I'm sure it is nothing serious. Aseneth, go to your bed and try to sleep. We'll know soon enough."

When Mahta had gone to her room, Rena asked her husband, "What's the worst thing that might happen?"

"I wonder if Pharaoh seeks a bride for this new ruler. He may recall how beautiful our daughter is. Remember, she was married in secret."

"But if they searched the records to find her adoption, and traced her here to us, they would also have found her marriage entry."

"I don't know. But worse still may be what she herself said—to be chosen for a sacrifice."

"But hasn't the sacrifice of humans been suspended? We're both guessing now. Let's put it out of our minds and go to sleep. Tomorrow we shall go to Pharaoh."

"Yes. I still have some influence in the court. They'll not put me off too easily."

The morning saw three apprehensive people preparing for the trip. They were late setting out. No one spoke much during the journey. Mahta rode with Manasseh in Pharaoh's chariot. Ramieth and Rena followed with their driver in a wagon of their own.

Mahta was glad for the delay when the chariots had to be put on the first boats to cross the Great River. She knew, however, that once on the other side, it was only a short time until their encounter with those in the palace.

Posing a commanding presence, Ramieth said loudly, "The priest of On is here to present his daughter, Aseneth, to Pharaoh."

"Wait here," they were told.

---

Joseph was reviewing with Zarill the positions he needed to fill. It was Pharaoh himself who came to Joseph. "My servants inform me that the priest of On is here with his daughter, Aseneth. Could that be the same Aseneth we sent for as Pharaoh's gift to his new governor?"

Joseph jumped to his feet. "How should I do this? I prefer not to meet them in the throne room. Could we have them brought here?"

"As you wish," Pharaoh said. "I shall order rooms to be prepared for her parents and the child. This is one reunion with which I want no interference."

When he was alone, Joseph paced. *Does she still want me? Maybe she's wearied of waiting. How should I present myself? What do I say to my son?*

It was Moesha's first duty as head steward to fetch the waiting party. He went the long way around and approached the family from the outside door. "You will please come with me."

Moesha had seen Mahta once in the prison. Now he was struck by her beauty, but she did not recognize him.

"Aren't we supposed to see Pharaoh?" Ramieth asked.

"You are summoned by the new ruler, Zana-panea," the servant told them.

*One who speaks for God*, the priest thought. Then he said aloud, "May we know the nature of the summons?"

Moesha stopped and looked at Mahta. "The new ruler wants to observe Aseneth."

Mahta paled and hung back, but Moesha moved on, and she felt as though the long hallway stretched on forever. Yet sooner than she had hoped, they arrived at the private quarters. *If only Joseph could be with me now.* The steward opened the door, and as they entered, they saw the ruler, sitting with his back to them, wearing his crown and finery.

"The family of the priest of On awaits you," Moesha said in his most authoritative voice.

"Leave us alone," the ruler said, and the servants departed.

The family from On stood fearfully, wondering what was about to happen. Mahta's face was hot, but her hands were cold. She tried not to shake.

Ramieth stepped forward and said, "We are at your service, Majesty." He walked around and bowed himself down before the ruler. When he looked up into his face, he smiled as recognition dawned. "Mahta dear, come." He held out his hand. "Come see your husband."

"No, please." She stepped back as the figure arose. He turned, and she felt as if her heart stopped beating as he came and stood before them. Rena dropped to her knees, but Mahta stood unsure, her eyes on the ruler. Then his solemn face broke into a smile and he lifted the crown from his head. She gasped and covered her mouth with her hands.

"How—what are you doing here, Joseph?" Rena asked, and Manasseh gazed at the man who stood smiling at his family.

"It is I," Joseph said, "and all is well."

Mahta's forehead was still furrowed. She didn't know whether to be happy or angry. "Why did you do this to us?" she demanded.

Joseph began to explain, reaching out his arms to Manasseh, who adjusted quickly to the strange circumstance. He had been schooled for seven years regarding his remarkable father, and he embraced him willingly and happily. Rena and Ramieth embraced him as well. Finally, with his arm around his son, Joseph turned to Mahta, who stood back fighting tears, afraid to believe what was happening. Finally Joseph reached out, and she ran into his arms, sobbing. They both wept as they kissed each other again and again. Manasseh stood between them, smiling as they squeezed him in their embraces.

"Come, my loved ones. Let me tell you my strange, wonderful story." And he did so as they listened in astonishment.

They, in turn, told him of their frustrating summons, and he said, "I'm sorry. I didn't know it would be handled in such a manner. But you're here and I'm glad. There is much to do, but right now, by command of my office, I will order that we be allowed all the time we need for a proper reunion."

Rena spoke. "In due time. Right now, by your allowance, we will depart and leave you to your wife and son."

"Rooms have been prepared," Joseph said as he sounded for his servant and smiled at their expressions of awe towards him as a ruler.

When Moesha came, Joseph introduced him and told his family about him. "Moesha, my wife's parents will go to their chambers now. In a little while I'll send for you to take my son to them for his bedtime. What do you think of my son?"

"I saw him as an infant, you know. I also had a glimpse of his mother, whose beauty now exceeds my memory of her. The boy is a credit to Israel and appears born to be a prince."

When Joseph and Mahta were finally alone, they faced each other and all the doubts that had gnawed at their souls from years of separation seemed to vanish.

"You are more beautiful than I remembered," Joseph said. "I have never had you out of my thoughts and I have so much to share with you."

She took his hands and kissed them, weeping. "Oh, Joseph, you were right. Your God did have great plans for you."

"Our God. And the plans included you. Are you ready to be a queen?"

"Oh!" She straightened. "I didn't think about that."

"Yes, my queen—you were always my queen. Now all of Egypt shall bow to you. But for tonight, you are mine alone."

They fell into each other's arms, and the long years of waiting, doubting, and yearning became a part of the past.

When Ramieth awakened the next morning, Rena was sitting on the edge of the bed, crying.

"What is it, my dear? Aren't you happy about these events?"

"Yes, very happy. I cry because I don't know what will become of us. Have I found a daughter and a grandson just to have them taken from me?"

"But they're still ours."

Just then they were interrupted by Joseph and Mahta entering their chambers. "What's the matter?" Mahta asked as she ran to her mother's side.

Ramieth said, "She's upset because she's afraid she'll lose her children."

"Joseph and I were discussing that very matter," Mahta said. "I don't want to be separated from you two either."

Joseph added, "I suggested that you be able to keep these chambers and stay here with us. A grand house is to be built for me next to the palace. I will provide chambers in it for you."

"But what about my duties at the temple?" Ramieth asked.

"You forget, Ramieth, I am governor. I can make appointments and releases as I see fit. Of course, you may keep your position if you so choose. On is not so far away that we cannot visit at will."

"Of course," Rena said, wiping her eyes. "I am being silly. We can certainly work something out. Thank you, Joseph."

"You will stay then?"

Rena and her husband looked at each other. "No," Ramieth said. "For now, we will return to our home. Rena loves our house and her garden, but I am getting weary of my burdens. I would not mind being replaced before long."

Rena smiled. "I would be comforted if we could have Manasseh visit us often. And we could come here."

"Anytime," Joseph said. "The royal chariots are for your use." He laughed. "I may come to enjoy the privileges of royalty."

Manasseh awakened and came in rubbing his eyes. One by one he hugged everyone, then asked his mother, "Do I get to sleep in here all the time with Grandmother and Grandfather?"

"When they are visiting with us, you may stay with them. When they go back to their house, you may stay in our chambers. If we must be away, you will stay with the other children."

"The other children who live in the palace stay together in the nursery, where your mother used to work," Joseph said.

"May I meet them?"

"Yes," Mahta said. "I will take you there later. I want you to see my old friends."

One of Pharaoh's servants appeared and announced, "The king sends word that he wishes to visit the new family.

"Does he want us to come with you?" Joseph asked.

"Pharaoh will soon visit the chambers of Zana-panea."

"Very well. Come my loved ones. Let us be found in my quarters when Apophis arrives."

# Chapter Thirty-one

# Royal Families Meet

They had been inside the chambers only a few moments when Pharaoh came with his wife and children.

"Welcome to you," Joseph said.

"I would like to meet your family," Apophis said, "and have them meet mine. Please, there is no need to bow."

All in the room except Joseph were on their knees. Mahta had even pulled Manasseh to the floor. They all hesitantly arose at the king's bidding.

"You must become accustomed to being royalty yourselves. You of the family of Zana-panea need not bow to anyone."

Joseph led Mahta and Manasseh forward. "This is my wife, Mahta, known by the Egyptian name Aseneth, and my son, Manasseh. You already know Ramieth and Rena."

"The priest of On is well-known, and all his good work. Rena, it is a pleasure to see you again. Inside these walls we may use our common names. Joseph has told me of the adoption. It is hard to say who would benefit most from such an arrangement.

"I was the one who was blessed," Mahta said, but at the same time Rena and Ramieth both said, "We have benefitted most."

Everyone laughed, and Apophis continued. "But the loss is mine. I didn't know I was relinquishing ownership of such a rare and beautiful woman."

"Thank you." Mahta blushed.

"What a fine young man your son is, Joseph. Didn't you tell me he is not yet eight years old? He stands more the size of a twelve-year-old." He motioned to his own son. "Come over here, Magron. My son is twelve and he is not small. Yet you can see how near in size they are."

The boys met eye to eye and exchanged some kind of undeciphered communication.

"These are my two other children, Rona and Tephnaro, and this is my queen, Yrameesa."

Yrameesa said, "This lovely bride of Joseph's was attendant to my child in the nursery nine years ago. Isn't that true?"

Mahta was surprised. "And you remember me?"

"Now that I see you, I do. But I must confess, Joseph told me of your situation before you came. Now I see that you are the perfect partner for Joseph. I couldn't have found one so well-matched as are you. It seems that higher powers than ours have a hand in these affairs."

"Thank you again," Mahta said. She smiled and sent a look of adoration at her husband.

Apophis spoke. "We want you to feel welcome. We'll try to give you every assistance in adjusting to your new world here. You are free to ask for anything you need. I have summoned a gathering in the throne room to present the new queen to the court. If you would all please come as soon as you are able, we will introduce the new ruling family befittingly."

---

Mahta soon learned the difference between the informality in the private quarters and the pomp and ceremony of the court. She was not at all comfortable in her new role.

Pharaoh and Yrameesa sat in all their regalia, looking serious. Two more chairs had been placed on the dais.

The spokesman of Pharaoh announced in a loud voice, "For the people of Egypt, we present the ruler Zana-panea, his wife, Aseneth, and the rest of the honorable family—Ramieth, the priest of On, and his wife, Rena."

They stepped through the curtain and stood behind the thrones. "And Manasseh, son of Zana-panea." Manasseh stepped out and took Rena's hand.

Joseph wondered what the men gathered on the steps were thinking of these new developments. *In time. I will get to know them each as time allows.*

As Mahta's eyes searched the room and studied each counselor, her gaze stopped on the enclave of the priests as a cold shiver ran through her. The object of her worst memory stood gazing up at her—the old priest who took her best friend, Jain, to the sacrificial table. With difficulty, she composed herself and avoided his eyes.

"I'm glad that is over," she said as they returned to their rooms. "Will I be required to be in that position often?"

"I don't think so, unless you desire it. On some occasions it may be proper for you to be there. As far as I know, Yrameesa seldom attends court."

<hr />

Joseph sprawled across the bed and watched Mahta as she spoke. A contemplative smile accompanied his steady gaze, and she abruptly asked, "What? Why do you study me?"

"You put me in awe," he said. "You were a quiet, unschooled child when I left you at Pharaoh's palace, and I thought I knew you. So I ask myself, 'Who is this well-spoken, knowledgeable woman I am coming to know more each day? This woman who has the bearing and grace of a queen, the words of a scholar, and the facility of a diplomat?'"

"You exaggerate my qualities, but it's true that you don't know much about me." She sat down on the bed next to her husband, gathered her knees in her arms and explained. "It was you and Cephas who taught me so much—all those late evenings when you discussed the things of God and of the world. When Cephas taught you under the stars, I was there. Remember? I was like the thirsty desert drinking in every word.

"In the palace nursery, I was often with the royal children when their tutors were called in, and I learned all I could. Then, in my eight years with Rena, she taught me the protocol and manners of a dignitary's family."

Joseph sat up. "You learned well, but I insist that many God-given qualities make you who you are and I will never tire of the study."

"I would rather be inconspicuous."

Joseph smiled. "It's difficult for one with your beauty to be inconspicuous."

"Thank you, Joseph. I love you. And Joseph— Oh, never mind. We will talk later."

"Is something bothering you?"

"It's just that there is so much to share, so many questions. Later, my darling. Here is your commander to meet with you. I will see you this evening."

---

That afternoon Mahta and Manasseh stepped into the nursery. Mahta smiled to see Nuni and Mizrel. "Hello, she called.

Nuni looked up in wonder. "Mahta, can it really be you? And who is this becoming child beside you? I have wondered about you ever since you were taken away that night. I didn't think I would ever see you again."

Mizrel came and embraced her former workmate. "It is so good to see you, Mahta." They were led to the table and chairs in the middle of the room.

"This is my son, Manasseh," Mahta said. "I want him to meet the children. Then I'll tell you everything."

Nuni and Mizrel looked at each other. "We cannot allow your son to play with the palace children," Nuni said. "The servant offspring are kept separate from royalty—you must remember that, don't you?"

Mahta persisted with her radiant smile. "Of course. I'll keep him by my side for now. Are there still some children here I might remember?"

"A few, but right now we are waiting for the new prince, the son of Zana-panea, who is coming to live in the palace. They say his parents want to keep him with them, so we may not often have him to care for. I do wish someone would tell us what to expect."

"Maybe I can help," Mahta said.

"But what do you know?" Mizrel asked.

"Do you remember how I used to speak of Joseph? The one who came with me and Cephas from Canaan?"

"Yes, I remember," Mizrel said.

"You probably heard that Zana-panea was brought from the prison to answer the king's dream, and that he was a Hebrew slave."

Nuni gasped. "You don't mean that your Joseph, is—"

"Yes, I do," Mahta said, laughing.

"And is he the one you married?"

"He is. My Egyptian name is Aseneth."

Nuni grabbed Mizrel and pulled her down in front of Mahta. "This is our new queen," she said.

Mizrel's mouth dropped, "You mean the new ruler is the same Joseph you told us about? How can a slave possibly rise to the throne?"

Mahta chose her words carefully. "I believe he is favored of God—the One True God. And slave or free, he is a powerful man himself. You will see when you meet him. But now, you must get up, for we must always be good friends, and I hope we'll have many happy days ahead of us. I'll send Manasseh here to play as often as possible."

At her friends' request, Mahta told her story, and when she left, the nursery women were more devoted to her than ever before.

# Chapter Thirty-two

# Conspiracies and Plans

The court was dismissed, and the old priest trembled with anger. He pulled aside his trusted ally. "How can we handle this new governor and his bride? We do not want a Hebrew on the throne. The gods of Egypt will become restless and angry, the consequences grave."

"What do you propose we do?"

"I have no plan at present, but we must please the gods. We must think of a way to balance the affairs at hand."

"She is beautiful—the new queen."

"Yes. She'd make a pleasing offering."

"You mean—"

"Nothing. We'll bide our time. Perhaps the gods will show us a way."

---

Joseph and Zarill had been locked in intense conversation for most of the afternoon. There was much to discuss and plan. "Have you learned anything about the Nubian?" Joseph asked.

"No. I have asked everyone who might have associated with Potiphar, but no one knows what became of his slave. Do you suppose he might have run away? Or tried to get back to his own country?"

"He would have had a difficult time if he did. He had no voice, you know. Of course, it would be difficult for him wherever he might be."

"I'll continue to seek him, assign my best man to search for him."

"Speaking of your best men, there is something special I want you to do for me."

"You mentioned that there might be."

He nodded. "You know the old priest—the priest Kenah?"

"I do, although I cannot say I respect him."

"Nor do I. I suspect him of causing the death of my friend, Cephas, the Hebrew priest who stood for a time on the steps. He offended the priests of Egypt with his forthright speaking and was poisoned the next day."

"Isn't the priest's role to sacrifice life?"

"Only as an offering to a god, but such rituals have been suspended by decree of Pharaoh. Either way, he is not free to kill another priest—or any other person."

"So what do you want me to do?"

"Make a quiet yet thorough search for proof that he did it. Do you have some men you can trust to be discreet?"

"Yes, and I will do some of the work myself. I know a woman who has knowledge of poisons."

"That may be a good place to start. I don't think our own court physician would be in league with the priests. Anyway, do your best."

---

The first week in office set a demanding pace for Joseph. He wanted to do his best to represent his new title. The appointments alone required more than he had thought. The depth and breadth of his responsibilities were overwhelming. Yet all he really wanted to do was get to know his family and be what he should be to them.

"I don't see why you can't just take your time," Mahta said. "Pharaoh has had the responsibility for years. You can't take it all on in days."

"That would be true if there were time. The problem is that we have only four or five months before the next planting season begins and I must have the entire country prepared to bring about the greatest harvest the world has ever seen. Getting the palace and the staff organized is only a prelude to the real task."

"Do you know what to do?"

"No, but God does. And if I can remain humble and submissive, He will show me."

"But—granaries to hold and preserve food for fourteen years?"

"I know. But it can and will be done."

"Well, for tonight you must relax. Pharaoh is giving a large banquet in our behalf to honor my parents before they leave."

"Yes, I have seen the bustling preparations going on for two days. Is Manasseh expected to attend?"

"Yes, it was specified that he be there."

They entered the banquet room and were shown to their places next to Pharaoh and the queen. Around the room, members of the council and their wives and other guests were seated. Joseph noticed Zarill with a lovely young woman. He smiled and nodded at him. Mahta paled as the priests Kenah and Korash walked deliberately in front of the king's table and stopped and looked at her. She pretended not to notice.

The banquet met the usual standard of excellence that Apophis demanded. Course after course of food was presented. It began with fruits and breads followed by a custard and then various fowl done in exquisite fashion—boiled hen, baked pheasant, roasted duck garnished with nuts and herbs. There were fancy squash dishes and other vegetables to accent the main dishes. Finally a seed cake soaked in honey was served, and all of it was accompanied by abundant wine of the grape, both fresh and fermented, as well as plenty of the barley beverage Egypt was known for.

The servants presented the food as artfully as the cooks prepared it in king's kitchens. It was a delight just to watch the skill with which the dinner was served.

From the arrival of the first guest, music began to play. There were instruments of wind and various strings. Skilled musicians were a regular part of the king's staff.

There were also dancers. Not just the Egyptian type, but several other troupes from various countries were represented. The drum beat that accompanied the dancers from Punt was particularly hypnotic.

There were even wrestlers. Mahta was not entertained by the wrestling, but Joseph was. It reminded him of his youth and home. He could not help but compare what these fighters did with what he thought Simeon might have done. No one could take down Simeon.

Joseph was not the only one who was entranced. Manasseh was up on his chair, then down on the edge of the floor, watching the men on the mats who glistened with sweat as they groaned and grunted or even roared. Soon Magron joined Manasseh, and the two youngsters reveled in the contest before them.

Joseph and Mahta commented about the incredible lengths to which Apophis would go to have such a banquet. But throughout the evening, Mahta felt the priests looking at her. She pretended not to notice, but she planned to mention it to Joseph when they went back to their chambers. After the exciting activities, Manasseh went directly to bed and the two were alone. "Did you enjoy yourself tonight, Joseph?" she asked.

"I did—very much. It took my mind off my work for a little while. Did you like it?"

"The food was superior to any I have ever experienced."

"And the entertainment?"

"I loved the dancing and music."

"But not the wrestlers. Did you watch your son's face?"

"I'm afraid I did."

"I wish you could have met my brothers. But there is something I have to tell you. I spoke with Apophis and we feel that I must take a tour of all Egypt to inspect the land and ascertain its productivity potential. I leave in about a week. Would you like to accompany me?"

"Oh, Joseph." Mahta sank into a chair. "I just got you back."

"That is why I ask you to join me. I don't want to be separated from you."

"What about Manasseh?"

"He could stay with Ramieth and Rena."

"I suppose he could, but—"

"I'm sorry I have made your life so difficult. But I can't bear to be away from you."

"We must do what we must. Being married to a servant of God—and to Egypt—has its price."

"Then you will come?"

"Yes, and I will try to behave as I should."

"We will have much to do to prepare in only one week."

<hr>

The next day the architects and builders were in conference with Joseph for several hours. He sent for Mahta.

"Now is the time to tell them what we want. They will begin soon to build our house next to Pharaoh's."

The group discussed plans and finally parted with a few decisions resolved. The planners had pointed out that Zana-panea should surely have a throne room, not with as many steps as Pharaoh's, but a reception room nonetheless. They also argued the need of a prison cell. Every home of great standing had a room for confinement. "What if the servants broke the law?" they said. In the end they had their way. Joseph did not like being reminded of a prison, but it brought to mind another matter that needed to be rectified.

After meeting with Pharaoh the following day, he called the architects back. He sent for Zarill, and for his old friend, the keeper of the prison. He also summoned Pleoris, the physician. When they were all met, he told them, "We must reform the prison and the care of the sick. I have been giving it some thought. As a matter of fact, I had eight years to think about it and I have come up with a plan."

He turned to the builders and said, "Above the flat roof of the prison there is adequate space to build another large room— an infirmary. I want this capable physician to work with you in deciding what will be needed. People will no longer be thrown into prison merely because they are sick. The common people who do not have their own private house physician will not be denied care. We will get staff and train them.

"As for the prison, Pharaoh agrees that we must find a fair-minded man who will be able to discern between the truly criminal and the lesser lawbreakers. A system of justice shall be established that fits the punishment to the crime. In some cases the guilty may be reprimanded or required to make reparation to the victim. In harder crimes the penalty may demand imprisonment in terms of months or years.

"I would like the builders to separate the prison into several separate cells. The lesser offenders need not be subject to abuse by the inveterate criminals. Now that you know what I want, I leave it to you. Do your best and then report back to me next month."

The old keeper shook his head. "You astound me, Joseph, or should I say Zana-panea? I knew it was you, you know. What am I to make of all this?"

"Are you happy with these plans? Can you fit yourself to the changes?"

"Of course. I can change as well as any man, and I see the need. Why, there's a man in there right now who doesn't belong. He came in a few days ago. They didn't know what else to do with him because he can't talk."

Zarill jumped to his feet. "Do you suppose...tell me what he looks like?"

Zarill was right, and in a short time the Nubian was presented to Joseph. He looked terrible, having seen some difficult times.

"Hello," Joseph said. "Do you remember me?"

The mute nodded slowly but did not respond to Joseph's smile.

"I realize life has been difficult for you since you lost your master. I can't imagine what you must have been through. I was saddened also by Potiphar's death." He paused, then said, "I have been looking for you." Joseph then told him briefly about his own imprisonment and ascension. The slave looked at him with cold, if not unbelieving eyes.

"I want you to attend me as you did Potiphar."

The Nubian began looking around the room, searching for something. Finally he found a cord used to tie a robe together and motioned the use of a whip.

"No, I will not require a whip. I do not believe in beatings. What I want you to do is protect me, be my personal guard." He motioned Wama to come over from where he usually stood by the door. "This is Wama. He is my personal guard and I want you to be one also. I will have two. Wama and—I never heard Potiphar call you anything but 'the Nubian'. May I call you Punt? That is where the captain said he found you, in the city of Punt."

The nod was more sure this time

"Very well. I shall have two protectors, Wama and Punt. Moesha will take you to the servants' quarters for a bath, a meal, and some clothing. Get a good night's sleep and I will see you in the morning."

The contrast between the personal guards was almost humorous—Wama, who always smiled, and Punt, who never smiled. But they were both magnificent examples of the male body.

# Chapter Thirty-three

# Integrating and Staffing

A runner came to their quarters while Joseph was busy. He motioned Mahta to come. Later, she was waiting for Joseph when he entered their private bedchamber. She stood with arms folded, her face strained.

Joseph smiled. "What is troubling my lovely bride?"

"You will probably think it is funny. I do not. I let Manasseh go to the nursery to play with Magron, but then they had to send for me."

"Where is he now?"

"With Rena, getting ready to go to On."

"Well?"

"It seems the two boys could not wait to act out the wrestling moves they saw the other night."

Joseph only laughed.

Mahta ignored the laugh and continued. "They both ended up crying, but neither one would quit. They hung on to one another until Yrameesa and I ordered them to stop."

"He comes by it naturally, you know. Did he win?"

"Joseph! He isn't even eight years old, and Magron is twelve. No one won." She suppressed a smile.

"I must see to his instruction some day."

———

The morning of the farewell was difficult for everyone. Joseph needed more time with his son, and Mahta had never before been separated from him. The older parents were sad to leave their daughter. Before leaving their quarters, the family gathered in a circle to have prayer. Ramieth and Rena never objected to joining in, even though they were of a different faith. Joseph asked God to bless all the family's travels.

After watching the barges cross the river and the chariot move out of sight, the couple walked slowly back to the gate. "When do you want to leave for your inspection tour?" Mahta asked.

"Can you be ready by tomorrow?"

"I had hoped you would say that. I can keep busy today getting ready so I won't have time to think about being lonely."

"And I have a few matters to secure. I will see you this evening."

After their parting kiss, Mahta marveled that anything could be so pleasing. She often prayed that their lives would never be interrupted again.

Joseph had told Apophis the day before that he needed a few more people to fill his staff. Now, as he entered the palace, a runner met him and said, "Many people await your arrival in the throne room."

The floor level of the reception hall was alive with hopefuls. "Why are all these people here?" Joseph asked.

"They have come in response to your request for workers."

"Not this many. Very well. Send for Zarill to keep order, then separate them into groups according to needful positions."

Joseph addressed the first group, who sought a political appointment. "I need a magistrate knowledgeable in the law, a fair-minded man who knows the difference between a nuisance and a lawbreaker." He then interviewed each of five men seeking the position. The fifth man seemed vaguely familiar to Joseph. "Do I know you?" he asked.

"I was afraid you would recognize me. Now I know I won't get a position."

"How is that?"

"We were in prison together."

Joseph searched his face and said, "Oh yes, the Egyptian Zeeroth. I didn't recognize you without your long hair. What abilities do you suppose are needed to fill this position?"

"Oh, I have qualifications. I just thought—"

"Wasn't I in prison as well?" Joseph said. "What qualifications do you have?"

"Before Pharaoh condemned me, I worked in his library organizing the scrolls of papyrus that held Pharaoh's words of law. Before that, I was a runner for the court."

"Then you know Egyptian law?"

"I do," Zeeroth said. "Do you recall I recited the inequities of justice in the cell we shared?"

"Yes, and I believe a man who has been confined knows best the inclinations of a man's heart. You were released by Pharaoh, weren't you?"

"He released me after his anger diminished. I was imprisoned for about five months."

"Enough to have empathy and hopefully mercy. The law you know. I can only hope you know humility also. The position is yours. Later we'll discuss in detail your duties. It will be necessary to school more young scholars in knowledge of law."

Zeeroth stood gaping at him as Joseph smiled with a nod of approval. He sent him out, then walked with Zarill across the room. "What are these other groups?" he asked.

"This group said you needed a scribe. These hope to be runners. These women seek to become hand-maidens."

"Send for my wife. She must choose her own women servants. I'll talk with the runners first."

About twenty young men stood in the group hoping to be messengers. "I won't ask whether you are swift in a race; I assume you can run. What I want to know is how well you're able to carry a message in your head, and with what proficiency you can present it."

Each aspirant was tested on his ability to speak. Joseph ended up choosing five of the twenty—three for daytime errands, two for night. "We may need more as time progresses," Joseph told Zarill.

Everyone turned as Mahta came into the room, but she didn't like them looking at her. Joseph did, however. He smiled with pride, held out his hand to her and said, "Pharaoh gathered these women who are willing to be your maid-servants."

"But I don't need any," she whispered to her husband.

"It's expected that a queen have an attendant," he whispered back.

"Very well, I'll take one. One only."

She looked at the group of women. They ranged in age from about fifteen to fifty. Right away, one of the faces caught her eye, and for a brief moment she was reminded of herself in a similar situation. "I'll have that one," she said, pointing to one, then starting out of the room.

"Very well. Come forward," Joseph said to the girl. "What is your name?"

"Hegis."

"How old are you?"

"I am eighteen years old."

"What is your experience?"

"I am an orphan. I was sent to the palace when my parents died. I have worked in the kitchen and in the nursery. I have since been a dresser for some of Pharaoh's people."

"Are you trustworthy and honest?"

"Yes."

"Good. Zarill, have your runner show Hegis to her new mistress's chambers."

Joseph then looked at the group waiting for the scribe position and saw a familiar face smiling at him. "Jaeb! How is it that my old friend is here?"

"After my master and mistress died, I went to work in the palace as a housekeeper. I heard about your position and desire to be with you."

"You may come to my household to assist my steward, Moesha, in any way we can devise. But for scribe, I must choose one who has experience." He ended up choosing a man named Sagorth.

All the entourage followed their new master to the now seemingly small chambers. "As soon as my house is built," Joseph said, "you shall have more room as well as more responsibilities." They were oriented to their current duties and dismissed to the servants' quarters.

After they left, Mahta asked, "What are we supposed to do with all these servants?"

Joseph laughed. "I don't know. In time we will need them. For now, we will just stumble over them."

They both laughed as Joseph pulled Mahta onto the bed.

# Chapter Thirty-four

# Overseeing and Seeding

The sky was just beginning to lighten as the travelers went into the yard to meet their traveling company. "Who will accompany us?" Mahta asked.

"We'll have a group of about twenty," Joseph said. "The driver and the guard will ride forward in our chariot. Some of the others will trade off as the drivers tire. Wama and Punt will take turns standing with us. Moesha will stay behind to watch after the household."

Their chariots were like the one Joseph had used on his procession through Memphis, with room for two to sit on the seats and two to stand. Their guide knew well the layout and routes of Egypt, and was more skilled in growing crops than any other in the country. Their steward would also serve as cook for when their travels covered uninhabited territories. The guide and steward shared one vehicle, and the drivers and soldiers shared three others, making five chariots in all. A large square wagon carried supplies and water, and another contained nothing but seed. All the horses and equipment were loaded onto two barges.

"We'll travel the river as much as we can," the guide said. "When we dock at each point, we'll travel outward to the settlements and back."

The first two hours of the trip seemed endless, but after they became accustomed to the pace, they relaxed and enjoyed the remarkable scenery and how the Great River nurtured life from the soil.

Their visit to the first city set a pattern for their work. The people recognized the royal chariots and had heard of the new ruler. Most of them were curious and friendly, but hesitant to receive new directives.

Joseph called local leaders together to reassure them of his help and to question them about their resources. Sometimes he needed to replace a territorial or city leader, doing so with guidance from God.

He looked over their fields and lands and often saw how water could be channeled from the river to make more areas productive. "We won't wait for the river to overflow and inundate the land. With water wheels and water oxen, we'll bring the water to our fields to make the thirsty soil fertile." They spent much time to extend the needed flow in a canal project in the Fayoum Valley.

He and his expert exhausted the subject of when and how to plant. Where certain crops flourished, those were encouraged. In some places, new grains were introduced. Wheat, rye, and barley were the prominent grains to be planted. Lentils of every sort were assigned in the proper areas. If more seed was needed, it was promised to be delivered.

The leaders, though hesitant at first, ended up loving Joseph and Mahta by the time they left. Most of the small settlements were happy to see them come and made a festival of it. The guests were shown great hospitality and given excellent meals.

Joseph couldn't tell whether the people really believed that there would be seven years of plenty and seven years of famine, but all eventually went along with the planning. Most didn't even object when Joseph told them they would be required to donate one fifth part of all they produced to a central store house. The granaries were explained, but Joseph had to tell his growers that the plans for building them were yet to come.

"But we already have silos," some said.

"Yes, adequate for one or two years, but we must build better ones to accommodate enough grain for fourteen years."

Joseph had tried to conceive a plan, but it had not yet come. "When we return to Memphis, I'll sit down and concentrate," he said to Mahta. "Maybe by then God will have shown me how they are to be built."

The trip took a little over two months to complete. Although they were well received and treated with respect, it was still a difficult journey. "Every time I feel like complaining about being tired and dirty," Mahta said to her husband, "I think of the caravan of Kumash when we walked as slaves."

"I often think about that. This may seem difficult, but when we pass a nomad group with their camels and donkeys, I pray for them and express gratitude for our ease and our chariots."

Often the vehicles became stuck in the sand and everyone had to help free them. Several times they had to hurriedly raise a shelter to withstand a dust storm. Usually it was intolerably hot and dry, and to weather the unmerciful lands, they had to dress in the clothing of the desert dwellers and use shrouds to protect their heads. Mahta began to wonder why she had come. She missed Manasseh and felt burdensome to the company. But one day Joseph said, "Thank you for being with me. It would be unbearable without you. You make all the men behave at their finest, and the people adore you. You lend honor to the position of queen." The journey was easier for her after that.

The last segment of their tour took them to the mouth of the Great River whose lush territory needed little help from man. "We will get our best crops from here," Joseph said. It was delightful to bask under the great shade trees and eat the plentiful dates and figs.

Mahta was especially happy because each moment brought her closer to On and to her son. They stayed two days with Ramieth and Rena. But to Joseph's sorrow, On presented the most resistance. The powerful leader, Opeph, had ideas of his own and didn't want interference from an inexperienced ruler from Memphis. "We have granaries sufficient for our needs," Opeph said. "I will see that the people contribute their share, be it one fifth or one half. Leave it to me."

"Pay no attention to him," Ramieth said, "He's in love with his own importance."

"There are always some who think they have better ideas than God," Mahta said. "Never mind. We are almost home and our tour has been quite successful. You are a marvel and a wonder, Joseph."

"Let's turn to the most important matter at hand," Rena said, "Manasseh's eighth birthday. He has waited for you so we can celebrate."

"Has he behaved himself while we were away?"

"Well, you know his grandmother thinks he is perfect, but we won't mention his most recent activities."

"What activities?" Joseph and Mahta asked at once.

Ramieth answered, "It seems he has engaged every sizable youngster in the territory in a wrestling match."

"Oh, no," Mahta said. Joseph said nothing, but could not hide his smile.

That evening Joseph took Mahta and Manasseh on a walk along the banks of the river by the temple. The smell of the night-blooming jasmine permeated the air. Joseph's heart was full as he held the hand of his son. They talked of many things. Mahta had taught Manasseh well about God. It was a special occasion for all of them as they sat by a quiet pool near the temple of On.

# Chapter Thirty-five

# Detecting Murder

When Zarill had watched the chariots and wagons loading onto the boat, he made note of the things he would accomplish while Joseph was away. He had already drawn some of his elite guard into this confidence. As soon as his master was out of sight, he had sent runners to gather the small secret group.

"I hope you all understand the need for secrecy. The duties you must perform will not be like any you've experienced before."

He explained the enmity between Kenah and Pharaoh and told them of the conflicts between the priests and Zana-panea. "It's almost impossible to unseat a priest, especially this one. He's very powerful."

The young group swore their allegiance to Zarill and the king.

"You must watch the old priest and his cohort, trading off duties so you can account for their actions in daylight and dark. You will report your findings to me daily."

Three weeks later his vigil bore fruit. Bazaar was beginning again. A young captain reported to Zarill. "As the people come into the city, the old priest goes among them and gathers groups to himself. He begins to extol the greatness of Egypt but gradually expresses his disappointment in the present conditions. He then cleverly alludes to the new ruler as power-hungry, saying, 'Even now he is covering the whole of Egypt to see how much territory he can take to himself.' In this manner, Kenah disquiets the people."

Zarill went about his own search. A woman he knew was an apothecary's assistant whose duties included crushing the herbs or seeds with mortar and pestle. By Zarill's prompting, she took note of the various physicians and their purchases. She also noted the potions the apothecaries themselves carried out of the shop.

"Many people come and go," she told Zarill. "Even the priests stop by to get the balms and essences they set before their gods. It would be impossible to track the course of a poisonous plant from its source to its final destination.

"Sometimes the apothecaries forage themselves, and sometimes they send gatherers to harvest the medicinal herbs. Often the peddlers at Bazaar sell bundles of dried leaves or berries, which find their way to the bedside of the ill. Of course, such plants as the deadly hemlock are easily available, some even grown among the flowers in the city's gardens."

Zarill looked disappointed. "So you think I've set myself an impossible task in trying to detect a murder by poison."

"Yes. Anyone who knows about herblore could easily obtain any deadly plant. But if I were of a murderous intent, I wouldn't go to the apothecaries. I would simply gather poisonous mushrooms and slip them in with the mushrooms we normally eat. They would not be tasted or smelled. Before they would even be suspected, the victim would be dead."

"Do you believe that's what might have happened?"

"It's a likely possibility."

"So my road ends here, but I won't give up. I shall take other steps to find proof of malice. Thank you for your help."

As Zarill parted from his friend, he thought to himself, "I must apprise Joseph of the need to control the easy acquisition of harmful plants and poisons. I wonder how many people have died by poison who were considered to be ill by natural causes?"

---

"They have started building your house. Have you seen it?" The king smiled.

"Yes. It's magnificent," Joseph said.

"Do you think your tour was successful?"

"Even now the provinces are planting the seeds that will yield the harvest of our first year of plenty."

"What do you think of Egypt? You have now seen all of it, haven't you?"

"I've seen most of it, and I love it more than ever."

"What of the people?"

"They were warm and cooperative. I learned much from them. I also learned something new about Egypt. In one of the cities we visited, they were celebrating a water festival. The songs and dances told the story of the discovery of Egypt. Before the ceremony, I knew that it was discovered by a woman, but not that it was under water at the time."

"Yes, that is the story. Most of the cities still celebrate water festivals. While you were gone we had a water festival of our own. Once a year we take the priests, put the statue on the royal vessel, then sail to On and have ceremonies in the temple there. Then we sail back here to Memphis."

"That sounds interesting. I wish I'd been here to see it."

"You'll see it next time. What was the other thing you wanted to tell me?"

Joseph looked at Pharaoh and thoughtfully said, "I've just come from talking with my commander, Zarill. I set him to searching out the affairs of Kenah, but he has found nothing. He's been persistent, but there's no real information yet—unless you consider murmuring against the king a crime."

"I consider it a crime, but the law doesn't. Still, we must watch him. He may stir up more trouble than we wish to handle."

"We'll continue on the course we've begun."

"Thank you. And Joseph, I don't want to burden you with more than you can bear, but—"

"I'm here to serve. If God put me here, then he'll help me—help us—to do whatever is necessary."

"During your absence, I held my monthly hearings for the public as usual. That's the time when any subject in the kingdom can bring his grievances before the throne and be heard. But it bears more heavily on me than ever before. I understand now why the previous pharaoh held his public courts only once a year. This time when I sat in judgment, I found myself wishing you were here to share the load."

"Yes, of course. I'll help you anytime you need me. I should observe your next hearings."

"Thank you. If we share the duty and give audience twice monthly, it will be easier."

"Let it be so."

"I'll tell my scribe to write it so it may be law. Also, we'll be giving a banquet soon to honor some visiting dignitaries. You'll be present of course, but I want you to take over most of the conversation. Your responsibilities also include relations with foreign lands. I'll be there to prompt you, although I doubt you will need prompting."

"Thank you for your confidence. It will be a challenge for me to speak my mind without giving offense. I've always spoken my thoughts as they come into my head."

Apophis laughed. "Yes, I've noticed."

"Sometimes my words have caused trouble. I'll do my best to use diplomacy."

<hr />

"It's been several months since Joseph has been in office," Yrameesa said. "Are you pleased with him? Are you pleased with yourself for discovering him?"

"I'm delighted with him—and myself. Yet really, I had nothing to do with it."

"You believe his God is responsible? Well, maybe I believe that also, even though we must wait fourteen years to test his prophecy."

"Yes, and I hear of discontent over that fact." The king looked sad.

"You mean the old priest? My servants talk of his remarks in the palace and on the square."

"He's trying to frighten people into believing the gods of Egypt are jealous. He tries to rouse them to rebellion. But I believe his true motive lies with what he calls the Ultimate or Supreme Sacrifice. If he could entrap Zana-panea and offer him to the gods, he would have obtained his crowning success."

"Shouldn't you condemn him?"

"In due time. I'm waiting for him to expose his intentions. I must be sure before I accuse him. He has a large following among the priests and in the court. Joseph is pursuing the search for evidence against him."

"Then he must be careful not to show his intentions."

"What do you mean?"

Yrameesa laughed. "I've watched him at the palace dinners. He becomes engaged in conversation and at times his speech is reckless."

Now the king laughed. "It's not so much reckless as honest. He tries to be tactful, but in the end he pours out his real thoughts. The curious thing is that his manner is so genuine that no matter what he says, no one ever takes offense. He's actually drawn most of our tributary kings closer to us. Only the truly evil would be offended by Joseph."

"Does it worry you?"

"Not at all. Do you see the looks of adoration he receives? The more the people come to know him, the more they love him."

"If you can just stop Kenah before he gathers too many followers."

"Yes—and we will."

---

The duty Joseph liked least was that of judge. Once every two weeks the floor of the throne room was teaming with supplicants, there to obtain justice for some grievance. After first observing the procedure, he decided he must always have his trusted friends at every hearing. Moesha stood on the side,

Wama and Punt on either side of his chair, and palace guards stood on every stair.

One such hearing was typical. Two peasants stood before the chair. Joseph stepped down to the third level, and the presenter said, "This man sets a claim against his neighbor who he says has stolen his ox."

"Let him be heard," Zana-panea said.

"I'm an honest, hard-working man. I try to keep watch on my oxen, but they have their own way and one wandered into my neighbor's field where he damaged some seedlings and ate his fill."

"Did you make restitution?"

"I will when I can, but I only have enough to feed my wife and children. I have promised that when my crops grow, I will replace the loss."

"Is that satisfactory?" Joseph asked the neighbor.

The second man said, "I, too, have a family to feed and I cannot wait. It seems fair that I keep the ox as payment. Where will I find food to replace that which was destroyed? I won't have enough to pay one fifth to the store house. I won't even have enough for myself."

The other spoke. "But I can't repay the damage unless I can irrigate my fields. I depend on my ox for the watering."

"I see both your sides." Joseph turned to the second man. "Let me assure you that you will have a crop more abundant than you have ever seen. I will have seed given to you. It's not too late to plant, and the crops will grow rapidly. So that you will both enjoy abundance, you will take turns using the ox until you can share in the purchase of a second animal."

He motioned to Moesha and whispered into his ear. "See that a supply of food is taken to each of their homes."

When Apophis found out what Joseph had done, he rebuked him. "Charity can be good, but not in foolishness. Word of what you have done will spread, and others will pour into the court."

"I gave them from my own stores."

"You don't have stores enough—nor do I—to sustain the many requests that will come to us. I see that you are sorry, but you must balance your decisions with good sense from now on. I'll send out an edict to halt a run on the palace."

"I will do better, but what about setting up a plan where we take from our abundance each month and put it into storehouses as a reserve for the poor, to aid them with just enough to get them through a setback."

Pharaoh was nodding his head. "Let it be done."

———

"Come with me, Aseneth." Yrameesa was out of breath. "I guess our husbands have ignored our wishes."

"What do you mean?" Mahta asked, hurrying behind.

"You'll see."

In one of the empty rooms adjoining the nursery, mats had been laid out to accommodate wrestling. Magron and Manasseh were deeply engaged in trying out the arena.

"Apophis ordered this after being told of the persistent wrestling of our sons."

Mahta sighed. "I'd hoped it would pass, but Joseph says it is in his blood."

"Pharaoh has even engaged a wrestling master for the two." The women watched for some time.

"I can't detect any real pleasure on their faces," Mahta said. "Why do they love to do it?"

"Come now, Magron," his mother said. "That's enough for today. Let's clean up and have some juice."

The boys came and stood by their mothers, who dried their hair and wiped their brows. "Are you happy to have a room in which to wrestle?" Yrameesa asked.

"Yes," Magron said, keeping his eyes on his opponent.

"Very happy," Manasseh said.

"Why do you like it so much?" Mahta asked.

Manasseh shrugged, but Magron said, "I have to."

"What do you mean, you have to?"

"I must be the best at all I do."

"And you think that includes wrestling?"

"Doesn't it?"

The mothers looked at each other.

"But if Manasseh is better than me, he'll be Pharaoh when we grow up."

"Is that it?" Yrameesa said.

Mahta said, "Magron, Manasseh's father is not to replace Pharaoh—or anybody. He is only there to assist. We Hebrews have no ambition to wear a crown. Manasseh is being taught to love God and serve his own people. He will never ascend the throne of Egypt."

"Don't you want to?" Magron asked his friend.

Manasseh shook his head. "I just want to wrestle."

The women laughed. "So you don't have to fight Manasseh again if you don't like it," the queen said.

Magron looked relieved but tried to keep the dignity of his calling. "That will give me time to learn more important things so that I may be a great and powerful ruler." The young princes were given affectionate hugs by their mothers.

When Mahta reported the incident to Joseph that evening, he said, "Very well, we'll provide some challengers. We'll let Manasseh act out his inclinations and see what he's made of."

After a time, Wama and Punt each took on the role of tutor until Punt became the chief trainer of the combative young Hebrew.

In subsequent days, however, Magron did not relax his wary attitude toward Manasseh.

# Chapter Thirty-six

# Design for Storage

Joseph knelt in his room. "Dear Lord, it's been some time now since I promised the granaries. Soon the first crops will be harvested and in need of storage. Forgive my mortal sins, O God, and consider thy servant. Show me the way to preserve these people." He did not sleep well that night.

"I wonder why nothing is coming to me," Joseph said to Mahta. He fasted and continued to pray for two more days.

On the third day, Moesha came to him. "One of the designers is here to see you." The man was one of the quiet ones, not the spokesman who had designed his house.

"How is the work going?" Joseph asked.

"Your residence is taking form, and the healing house is almost finished."

"Good," Joseph said. "What can I do for you?"

"Please forgive my boldness, but I've been thinking of something that won't stay out of my mind. I heard that, because of Pharaoh's dream, you've been preparing the country for seven years of plenty and seven years of famine. I began to wonder how I would build storage bins for such a vast project—if I were ever consulted. I finally decided that I must share with you what I've put down—if I may."

"You may explain your plan."

"The grains will be confined much the same as in a honeycomb. We have developed a strong clay, poured into frames and dried. After each cell is filled, the ends are sealed. Each cell is two cubits high, two cubits wide, and twelve cubits long. They can be laid end to end and stacked one on one. They will be built near waterways to be accessible to barges for input or output. It will require many thousands of workers and much upkeep with materials and food. If done correctly, millions of buckets will be accessed from our stores."

"Yes, yes, of course!" Joseph looked at the designer. "God has answered my prayers in the most logical way possible."

"I beg your pardon?"

"Never mind. You're a good man. You've done an important thing today for Egypt. I see that your plan is the right plan. Thank you very much."

Joseph left the much-relieved designer and went immediately to Apophis to show him the plans. "We must start building immediately."

The necessary steps were taken, and within days the work was begun throughout all the land.

"So you learned something new about the way God works," Mahta said after hearing the story.

"I have. How arrogant of me to think that everything has to be done by me. Doesn't God have capable children with talents He has given them, ready to be used at His bidding?"

"But what if they don't respond?"

"There will always be humble men and women through whom God's work will be accomplished. If one doesn't listen, another will. God's plans will not be thwarted."

That night the family knelt in prayer with an outpouring of gratitude. "We thank thee for showing us the greatness of thy ways. And thank thee that we may be observers of thy works and servants in thy hands."

The year of the first harvest saw an abundance never seen before. Crop after crop yielded excellent produce. The granaries were sufficient to accommodate the plenty. "We'll build more if they're needed," Pharaoh said. "The Hebrew God is the God of goodness.

"Do you have anything new to report?" Zarill asked his officer.

"No, it's the same routine as usual. The holy man speaks his mind against the rulers at every opportunity. The only thing I've noticed that bears mention is the girl."

"What girl?"

"On two or three occasions I've seen him talking with the same maiden. I don't know who she is, but I'll try to find out. She wears the clothing of a serving maid—from the palace, I think."

"Let me know the next time you see her and I'll come at once to look at her. It may be nothing, but we must be sure. You did right in telling me. Don't relax your watch on the priests."

# Chapter Thirty-seven

# Celebration and Intrigue

"The festival of the gods will be in a few days—the new year festival," Joseph said to Mahta and Manasseh. "Perhaps you'd like to watch it with me. I know a place on the roof where we can see everything."

"Won't you be involved?"

"I'll be free that day. I have nothing to do with Egyptian gods. Pharaoh will be the center of attention."

"Do you want to watch?"

"Yes, very much. I want to know more about how the people believe."

"All that stuff is just silly," Manasseh said.

"Don't say that," Joseph said. "It may seem like nonsense to us, but it has roots of genuine doctrine. You must always respect others' beliefs that are different from your own."

"Besides," Mahta said, "your grandparents are devoted to the Egyptian beliefs. They are good people because they are sincere. They were kind in allowing me to believe as I wanted and to teach you accordingly. In fact, they even discouraged me from observing their ceremonies. Now, however, I believe I can watch them with interest. How about you, Manasseh?"

The morning of the festival the family awakened early. "We must be on the roof before the sun comes up." They made their way to the spot Joseph chose, a good place to watch. They could see the front of the palace and the balcony where Pharaoh would stand. The pavilion below was also in full view. The priests assembled below, standing in distinct order, about sixty in all. Around the square, commoners were gathering to observe.

Soon Apophis appeared on the balcony with Magron. The boy's head had been shorn, displaying the royal side lock in duplication of his father.

"Oh, the young prince is going to participate in the ritual," Mahta said.

Joseph explained. "Pharaoh and his son have been washed and dressed by the priests just before their appearance on the terrace. Pharaoh wears the royal robe, the right shoulder draped and the other shoulder bare. His son is his mirror image, with his robe over the left shoulder. Watch now. The sun is about to rise."

In one breathtaking moment, the first rays of light from the solstice sun shot across the horizon and caught the gold cap high on the obelisk that stood before the palace. The gold pinnacle reflected a beam back at an angle that lighted the balcony and its occupants.

Pharaoh stood, his arms outstretched, and Magron imitated the actions of his father as strong golden light bathed the two. Everyone fell silent as the king chanted. "Amon Re, god of light, send thy beams upon my face. Light my eyes, my ears, my mouth, that I may be renewed. Bathe my body in the fire of life and keep the darkness from me."

From below, the priests in unison chanted. "Amon Re, god of light, sail to us to stay a short time and give us life. Instruct the chosen of Osiris, who will use the gift of light to see and hear and speak."

"This light from the sun comes only once a year at this precise moment," Joseph whispered. "The power it gives is supposed to last one year."

The golden spell on the balcony lasted only a few moments and was gone. Pharaoh and prince disappeared back inside with the passing of the shadow.

"Why do the priests hold the green boughs?" Manasseh asked.

"They hope to catch some of the magic light on the symbolic branches so that the plants will be green for another year also."

The chanting continued for a time as the priests moved in procession back into the temple.

"What happens now?"

"The holy men are inside the temple preparing the gods for the procession this afternoon. In the eighth hour of its rising, the sun will flood through the pylons of the temple. The procession will begin there and move out onto the colonnade where the sun, at its fullest, will fall on the gods that have been carried there. The gods in turn will bless the onlookers."

"I want to go down there," Manasseh said.

"We can see it from here," Joseph said.

"No, I want to get close."

"So do I," Mahta said. "That was a beautiful ceremony. I think I want to observe the rest of the festivities down among the people."

"If we were to go down there," Joseph said, "I'm afraid there will not be as much observing as being observed."

"Couldn't we take Wama, Punt, and Zarill to protect us in the crowd? You would be recognized, Joseph, but Manasseh and I could dress as commoners and go about unnoticed."

"That would still be too dangerous."

"No one would look at our faces. They would be too busy watching. Please, Joseph." And Manasseh added his plea to his mother's.

"Let's go to our morning meal. We'll see."

In the end, they had their way.

There was excited laughter as Mahta, with Hegis's help, found her nomad clothes that she had used on the tour. "I can use some of my wraps for the prince." They soon looked as inconspicuous as any travelers on the commons. Mahta even used a veil to cover her face.

"There you are," Hegis said, as she put the finishing tucks on their outfits. "May I go and watch also?"

"Yes, of course. Manasseh and I will be down shortly."

They showed Joseph how they looked. "Be careful," he said as he kissed both his loved ones. As soon as they left the room, he motioned to Wama and Punt. "Go down and follow them about. Try not to be too obvious, but I'll feel better if I know you're watching them." Joseph turned to some work at hand.

A short time later, Zarill came hurrying in. "I know who it is!" he said.

"Who?"

"One of my men saw the woman at the temple door with the old priest. He came immediately to get me. I went with him to the courtyard where I saw Hegis leaving the temple door."

"Hegis?"

"Your wife's handmaiden."

"She's the one who has been meeting with Kenah?"

"Yes. Now we're sure."

"I can only guess what she's been trying to find out." Joseph was thinking quickly. "Go down, Zarill. Find Wama and Punt. They're watching Mahta and Manasseh. Bring them all back here."

Joseph went to the roof as Zarill hurried to the square. The procession had started and the crowds were thick. People were pushing to get close enough to see and to receive the blessings from the gods. "He'll never find them in those crowds," Joseph said to himself. "Father, please take care of them. Keep them safe."

From the roof, he could hear the song of the priests. Leading the band of men was the high priest, set off by the leopard skin he wore over his robe. All the rest were dressed alike in their priest clothing.

"Thoth, guardian of the good, guide of all the needs of man..."

---

Mahta and Manasseh had gone to the other side of the pavilion to get a better look. The statue of Thoth had just passed.

"What is the golden bull for, Mother?"

"I don't know. I think it stands for Ptah, god of Memphis. Sometimes they show him as a man."

The song continued.

"God of Memphis, god of strength, to all the artists and artisans send your will and release the powers of creation..."

Next, they saw a polished black stone carving–a Cippi of Horus– standing on a bed of crocodiles and holding snakes, scorpions, and other deadly things. Behind the statue, the priests carried a large basin of water.

Mahta tried to explain. "The water has washed over the statue and is supposed to now contain the power of protection Horus promises."

The priests were dipping small branches in the water and sprinkling the crowd, who clamored to be the recipients of its virtue. Their song was of protection.

"I don't know what the vessel being carried between the poles represents," she said.

The vessel had pictures painted on the sides and streamers flowing from it.

The priests sang, "Hathor, god of air, blow the wind of life inside my body, that from the breath within, wisdom will flow from my mouth."

The people reached out to touch the streamers.

At this point the priest of Kenah came by. He walked holding a bough on the outside edge of the group. Mahta stiffened as she felt his eyes search through the crowd and stop on her. He seemed angry. He looked past her as if he were looking for someone, then back to her with fire in his eyes. He passed on.

The feeling of terror came back to Mahta, her head swimming. She could hardly hear. She dimly recognized that Amon Re was symbolized by a large, pure gold disk, carried high on a tall pole in the middle of the procession.

Of Osiris, son of Amon Re, she heard them sing as though through a fog.

"We look to your example...who formed man on the potter's wheel..."

Mahta wanted to go to her room. She looked around for a passage.

"...Isis, daughter of Amon Re, giver of life and health..."

Carved Ma'at feathers carried by the priests were touted to and fro.

"...give purity from the queen of heaven..."

A crocodile, an ibis, a fox, and some other animals representing gods came by.

Mahta was distracted by someone tugging at her cloak. "Oh, Hegis! I'm glad to see you!"

"Isn't it wonderful?" Hegis said as she loosened Mahta's veil and kissed her on the cheek.

"Yes, very beautiful," Mahta said, a little flustered at Hegis's actions. She turned, but Hegis was lost again in the crowd.

There was shoving, and a man selling fruit from a covered cart bumped into Mahta. She reached for Manasseh, but he was gone, and she panicked and started thrashing through the crowd. The man with the cart held up a cloak as if to cover her with it. Everything seemed to be happening so slowly.

She looked about for someone she knew, but saw only pairs of eyes that seemed to focus on her. The faces came closer. She felt a strong hand on her arm and opened her mouth to scream.

"It's all right, Mistress. It's all right." It was Wama. "Come with me."

He pushed through the crowd, protecting her in his arm as they went. "Punt has your boy. We'll take you home."

Safe in Joseph's arms, she wept. When she could talk, she said, "For a long time I've thought it was my imagination, but I believe that old priest means to do me harm. I meant to tell you many times before, but it always seemed so silly compared with the real problems you face every day." She told him of the time she was lined up with the other virgins. She told him of Jain, and wept bitterly. "I always get sick now when the festival comes."

She told him of the many times the eyes of the priest reached into her soul and left her cold. "And then today I felt that someone was trying to grab me."

"They probably were." Joseph told her what he had learned about Hegis.

A short time later, Hegis came in. She looked surprised to see her mistress, but quickly composed herself. "Did you like the festival?" she asked.

"Come with me," Joseph said. Hegis followed him into a room where they stayed for some time. When they came out, she was crying. She went to her room, gathered her things and left.

"Aren't you going to restrain her?"

"No, she'll suffer enough, being in league with the evil of Kenah. Besides, I want him to know that I know what he's been about."

"Did you reprimand her?"

"I questioned her. I tried to get her to talk about herself."

"What did she say?"

"Nothing. She is more terrified of the priest than anything else. I held out the hope that she could change, that I could help her, but she refused."

"What will become of her?"

"I told her she could come to me for help at any time."

"Poor Hegis. I know what it's like to be an orphan. I feel sorry for her to have allied with the wrong sort."

Sunset was nearing. From below the balcony, they could hear the final singing of the celebrants. The family went out on the terrace and listened to the song.

"Amon Re is mighty. Heaven and earth reunite once more. God is in his House. Our joy is complete."

The priests and all their array disappeared behind the temple doors. The festival was over.

# Chapter Thirty-eight

# Resolution

The next day Mahta urged Mizrel to give up her position in the nursery and be her handmaiden. Nuni was reluctant to let her trusted assistant go, but finally relented. "As long as it's to be with Mahta's family," she said.

Mizrel was grateful. "I'll serve you well. You'll see."

"Of course you will. I'm delighted you can be with us."

It was easy to settle into a routine with Mizrel. She was never in the way, but always there when needed. In Joseph's presence she was giddy and girlish. There was no mistaking the effect he had on her. One day she broached the subject she had been mulling in her mind. "Mistress, if your husband ever wants me, I mean...what am I supposed to do?"

"Mizrel," Mahta said, "I don't think Joseph has ever thought of having a concubine. If he did—and your position would make you a possible choice—you would know what to do."

When Mahta spoke to Joseph about Mizrel's question, he said, "I suppose I'm expected to have concubines, but for now I'll forego that custom and devote myself to my wife and son."

"Thank you, Joseph. How is it that you always say just what I want to hear? And if I'm right, your devotion may soon be shared by three. Do you have enough love for one more?"

Joseph hurried to his wife and gathered her close. "Do you mean—"

"I'm not certain, but I think I carry life within me."

"My cup runneth over!" he said, as he sank into a chair and pulled Mahta onto his lap. "God is good to us."

"The moon will be full tonight."
"Then we must have our walk by the garden."

━━━◦◦◦━━━

Joseph had barely arisen the next morning when Moesha announced that Zarill had come to see him.

"Come in. Have some fruit and seed cakes with us."

"I have urgent news and must speak with you immediately."

"Then we will go to my private chamber."

When they were alone, Zarill said, "My captain who has been following Kenah was on duty last night. He's not allowed within the temple, yet he knew something strange was going on. So he crept along the river to find a spot where he could observe. They were having a ceremony of some sort in the funery, chanting some mystical verses as if to the full moon. Then he saw on the lion couch a young woman, the same girl who had been meeting with the old one."

"Hegis."

"She appeared to be in a stupor of some sort. When the chanting ended, they drove a knife into her heart."

"No! I shouldn't have let her go. I didn't know it would come to this." Joseph dropped into his chair. "Such rituals have been forbidden."

"That's not the worst. They did unmentionable things."

Joseph sat with his face in his hands. "I should have known. I could have prevented it." He got up and paced, then stopped at the table and slammed his palms down with an agonizing groan.

Zarill said, "I know they do these things in the name of religion, but the captain said it was horrifying."

"It is horrifying, but not all the priests are corrupt—only these three, but they'll be stopped. Thank your officers for me; they did well. I'll require their presence in a meeting with Pharaoh. He must hear everything from the beginning.

Apophis listened quietly to the report of Zarill's secret guards, including that of the moonlight sacrifice.

"We've heard enough now, haven't we?" He turned to Joseph. "I will not call my counselors to hear this; we'll confront the three priests ourselves. The guards will repeat in their presence what they've told us."

"Where was the night priest who was supposed to be on duty?" Joseph asked.

"That's right," Apophis said. "He is my trusted friend. We'll send for him right away."

The runner had been gone only a few minutes when he rushed back into the room. "The night priest is dead. They just found his body in the temple, in the Hall of Shu. He appears to have been poisoned."

Pharaoh stood up. "We will hear the three priests immediately. Send for them—now."

"What can you do?" Joseph asked.

"Normally I would have them beheaded. But these evil men, who call themselves holy, gained such a strong hold before my reign that I must act with caution. The test has come to this: the people will choose to believe either the priests, or me."

The three priests kept the secret council waiting for two hours. They finally arrived with an air of confidence—even arrogance. Kenah looked over his accusers, then eyed Joseph with a sneer of contempt.

Pharaoh spoke. "We are met here because of a grievous report. The law is written that the offering of humans as sacrifice has been suspended."

"Does Pharaoh think that mere writings can subdue the will of the gods?" the priest asked.

"The gods show no evidence of displeasure," Apophis said.

"Yes, because we have kept them appeased."

"What do you mean?"

"Because the gods are pleased with our last Supreme Sacrifice, they have granted more abundance than ever before."

"What Supreme Sacrifice?"

"The royal sacrifice, the pharaoh before your usurpation. We had agreed that if he could not serve the gods of Egypt, he would be sacrificed for the good of everyone."

"But I saw him as he lay in state," Apophis said.

"You saw his body after we administered potions. We then took him to the temple, purportedly to be embalmed, and offered him to the gods. Then followed one of the most fruitful years we have ever seen."

Joseph spoke. "So now you have hoped for another Supreme Sacrifice—another person of royalty—so you can take credit for the coming years of plenty that you already know will last seven years."

"We know of no such thing. Your claim to answer the king's dream is cunning in that we must wait fourteen years to prove it. I say that the gods of Egypt have given us a good year, not some Hebrew god who does not exist."

Joseph persisted. "The girl you sacrificed last night—was she offered as a proxy for my wife?"

"It would have been better to use royalty—even pretentious royalty such as yourself. But the girl looked enough like your wife to pacify the gods."

"But what of the other despicable acts?" Apophis asked.

"You know little of offerings. Why do you think we look for virgins? The gods cannot act for themselves—that is what priests are for. We must act for them."

Joseph was appalled. He said, "You twist the ordinances of the true God to an evil end. He never intended that sacrifice should come to this. God has asked for the first fruits of the fields, and the firstlings of the flocks—and nothing more. How can you even think of treating human life so disdainfully?"

"And what about the night priest?" Pharaoh asked.

"Human life is nothing to the gods," Korash said.

Apophis shook his head. "This matter will not be debated here, neither before the court. Three days from now, you will be called before a council of your peers, a conclave of all the priests in the territory. To be sure you are there, I will have you detained in the royal prison until then. Take them, Zarill."

"You cannot lay hands on a holy man!" the oldest priest shouted.

"You see that I can and will," Zarill said. They were escorted away.

Word was sent out to all the priests, and they began to gather to the city amid rumors of what had happened.

On the morning of the third day, Zarill came to Joseph. "You need not come to the council," he said. "The three accused were found dead this morning—of poison."

"Did someone at the prison do it?"

"There's no way to tell. They probably did it themselves; although I don't know where they got the poison."

"Well, now they shall have a look at what is beyond. Their stone gods will be of little use to them in the real kingdom of God. I pity their wretched souls."

# Chapter Thirty-nine

# Leading to Battle

Joseph and Mahta watched the sunset whenever they could and they now stood on the highest balcony of the palace looking west over the white city. They could see the great desert beyond and the horizon where the sinking red globe would soon disappear. As they looked they saw a rider far in the distance. He was on horseback and coming fast toward the gate closest to the palace.

"I believe it's a soldier from the border guard," Joseph said. "I'll go down and receive him; his message must be important."

By the time Joseph left their chambers, the palace runner had intercepted him. "A messenger has come with an urgent request. You're summoned to meet Pharaoh in the reception room."

The messenger, a courier from the king's guard, was out of breath. "I've ridden all day, the second of two riders with news from the border. The elders of the Ishmaelites beg help from the armies of Egypt. The soldiers of Tarshish have been spoiling the lands of Havilah on which the children of Ishmael dwell. They lay siege to their cities and overrun their villages. The elders fear that they'll be consumed if the invaders are not stopped."

Apophis turned and asked Joseph, "What do you know of the Ishmaelites?"

"They are a peaceful people. Ishmael was the brother of my grandfather. He went to live in the desert with the promise from God that his people would be mighty and inherit the lands designated to them."

Pharaoh nodded. "That's all I need to hear. I have respect for the God of Abraham. I will not defy him." He offered the messenger food and rest, then sent for his scribe. "We will send this reply back to the Ishmaelites:

"'The armies of Egypt will depart shortly. They will subdue the soldiers of Tarshish and return the land of Havilah to the Ishmaelites. The king of Egypt will require allegiance and tribute from the king of Havilah if we are successful.'"

He sent off the message, then took Joseph by the arm. "Come with me." In the king's private quarters, Apophis faced his friend and looked at him soberly. "When I was newly on the throne, I always went personally into every battle. I wanted to be at the front of my army so that the people would see that I would defend Egypt with my life. For several years, I haven't gone to war. I have sent my captains to fight for us."

Joseph said, "I understand. You think it's my place to lead the army now."

"It would be a great move, politically. The factions in the government that resist you might be won over. The people would rally behind you."

"You're so sure we would win?"

"From a strictly military view, yes. But we also have your God on our side. Do we not?"

"I don't know. I hate the idea of war."

"Why do you hesitate?"

"All my young life I watched my brothers go away to skirmishes and wars. I even saw my father return weary from battle. I was taught that fighting was a last resort, to be engaged in only if there was no other course."

"So how do you feel about this cause?"

"To safeguard the Ishmaelites' land of inheritance is justification enough. While it isn't our quarrel, we should help our neighbors.

"Yes, I hesitate to order you to go, but—"

"I'll call on the blood of Israel in my veins and try to think like my brothers."

"Good. I hope to have you lead the men. I'll expect your preparation. In the meantime we'll gather the army and supplies. Two days from now, all should be ready to set out."

When Joseph was alone, he asked God, "Father, if it be thy will, let us go in willing submission to put down this act of warmongering."

Joseph sat with his family and held his wife in his arms. "I know you feel like crying, Mahta. I feel like crying myself."

Through her tears she said, "Forgive me. I know you must go."

"I've had assurance from the Lord. If we go in righteousness, we will not be harmed. I've also asked Him to comfort you in my absence."

"Thank you. Do you know how long it will take?"

"No, that depends entirely on how the fighting goes."

Manasseh perked up. "Can I go with you, Father? I'm the best fighter around here. Wama says so."

"No, my son. You are much too young."

"I'm already ten."

"Someday your skill in body combat may be used to the Lord's advantage—but not yet."

---

The troops were lined up as far as the eye could see. Pharaoh stood up with Joseph in a posture of review. "They look good," he said. "They'll serve you well. I've received the count and they number 40,600 men."

Joseph said, "I've been in conference with the leaders. They appear to be skilled and capable."

"Goodbye, Zana-panea. If you should not come back, I want you to know how highly I esteem you."

"But I will come back. Don't lose your confidence in me or my God." He laughed. "You must exercise more faith. Goodbye, dear King."

Traveling was slow because of the vast numbers of soldiers. Since Apophis had been in office, he had commissioned war chariots barely large enough for two soldiers, built so that one would drive while the other used weapons. One horse pulled each vehicle. There were square wagons loaded with food, water, and weapons.

The weapons consisted of swords, shields, and javelins. Those skilled with the use of the bow and arrow made up a troop. The cavalcade of horsemen were allotted the swords and javelins. Foot soldiers with nothing more than slings and stones marched proudly in their rows. The charioteers and horsemen slowed their pace to keep in step with the foot soldiers. Each fighter was issued a cap and a leather vest. Almost all would carry a shield.

Joseph felt a surge of fatherly love for the display of men before him. "Father, protect each one and let our fighting be just."

They spent the second night camped across the river from On. Each night, Joseph met with the leaders. "I don't really have knowledge of your methods. I've never received military training," he said one evening.

Zarill explained. "Your only role is that you remain visible. The men will follow you into hell if they think you're going there first. The captains and leaders will be at your side. You'll see. You'll know what to do."

On another occasion in camp, Joseph talked about the methods used by his brothers. "When I was young, I knew some mighty warriors. Each one was equal to fifty of a regular fighter. They were never defeated. One of their winning tactics was to roar mightily with each attack—not just the normal battle cry, but a giant roar. This greatly subdued their foes and gave advantage to the attackers."

"Do you know the roar?"

"Probably not as well as the originators, but I can teach it as I can remember." So on a quiet evening in the desert, if anyone had been near they would have heard a series of frightening sounds emanating from the center of camp.

At the border crossing, they were apprised of the latest conditions. Some of the Ishmaelite representatives were there to meet them, obviously tired and hungry. "We've been in battle many months," they explained. "Our supplies are gone and nearly our will. Fortunately the enemy sustains the same hardships. We'll direct you to the core of the battle. There, the prince of Tarshish holds sway. It is he who seeks to overrun us and confiscate our lands. He's a formidable enemy."

In a few days the army reached the outskirts of the lands of Havilah. Evidence of desolation was everywhere. Fires were still burning. Hardly a dwelling was left standing. Blood stained the earth. Now and then, straggling soldiers still battled one another. "We'll leave a portion of our troops here to divide and clean up any hostile pockets that may remain."

The main body of men pushed on, troops dispatched to areas as needed. It went on like this for many days—minor skirmishes with stragglers. Then almost without warning they found themselves deep in the middle of battle.

Joseph tried to assess the situation. Before he could think, an arrow struck his shield. A javelin missed its mark and took his horse from under him. With his first retaliation, he forgot to roar.

Then, when he heard his men plunging to their duty with the Israelite roar, he took heart. It heartened the Ishmaelites as well. With renewed vigor they rose to face their enemy with one final, terrible exertion and a chorus of yells.

Joseph lost himself in desperate swordplay. He had plunged and hacked and overcome many foes, and it seemed as if they had been fighting for hours. *Why is there no rest?* It became an effort just to hold the sword. *How can the men keep on? How can I be an example?* He called up strength from deep within himself and began again to swing the blade.

Then, in one pivotal moment, he saw before him the menacing face of the enemy bearing emblems of royalty. It was as if the prince had sought him out.

*So you are the one whose greed has nearly laid waste to a nation.* Joseph ducked to miss the first swing of the sword of Tarshish, whose skill with the blade was evident. Joseph staggered back and lost his footing. Soon the glaring enemy was upon him. Joseph rolled over and with all his might, pulled himself up to face the prince.

*How would Simeon do it?* He side-stepped and traded blows. Then seeing an opening, and with a mighty roar, he raised his sword and swung with all his strength. The head of his enemy rolled away, his lifeless body fallen in its own blood. Such was the fate of the aggressor, son of the king of Tarshish.

Joseph felt sick and stood with his head bowed, trying to regain composure. He came to himself with the awareness of cheers all about him. The soldiers of Tarshish had dropped their weapons and run away. The weak, emaciated soldiers of Havilah, almost in unison, knelt on the ground around Joseph as he, himself, fell to his knees and thanked God for the victory.

The way home seemed to go much faster than the journey out. As the troops neared home, they sang of the king Zana-panea. They sang of glory and of victory. Pharaoh rode out to meet the army and receive the report from his commander. "Do you realize, Joseph," he said as he rode by his side, "that not one of your men was killed? Some were wounded—and they'll be hailed as heroes—but no one died."

Joseph didn't feel like a hero. "It was sobering. My stomach is sick and I feel I'll never be the same. I have the greatest esteem for the professional soldiers. I can't help but think of my master, Potiphar. War is a terrible master. I'll make it a point to visit each of the wounded and thank them."

Instead of rushing to their homes and villages, the soldiers stayed by Joseph to walk in tribute and praise behind him as he came into the square of Memphis.

Apophis led Joseph to the balcony where everyone could see him. Mahta and Manasseh stood with him. The people shouted and threw kisses and knelt in homage to their victor. Flowers were strewn everywhere.

Pharaoh sent out a summons. "Tonight we'll celebrate in the colonnade. Everyone may pay tribute to Zana- panea."

The large dishes were lit with fire. Thrones of gold and jewels were placed on the platform by the Obelisk—the same platform where Joseph and Mahta had been displayed as slaves.

Now, as the honored family sat there, all the people of the region gathered to them. Neither Joseph nor Mahta wore their crowns on this occasion. Joseph wore his battle raiment without the helmet. Since his hair had grown back, he wore it cropped close to his head. His dark waves contrasted with the long golden strands of his wife, and the pair were dramatically handsome. One by one the people bowed before them and placed an item of tribute in front of the stand.

Joseph was uncomfortable, but as Apophis had advised, he knew he must make himself visible. It was the people who needed thanking.

There was music and dancing in the square. The crowd was ecstatic and would not be subdued. That they loved the new royal family was evident. Many who spoke dialects of the remotest regions spoke to Joseph personally and he understood all of them.

As people came and went, one woman drew attention to herself, a weathered peasant who stood near the items of tribute and mouthed something toward the royal chairs. With the din of the noisy throng, they could not tell what she was saying.

Mahta left her seat and walked down to the woman, who embraced her. Mahta inclined her ear and the old woman said something to her, then struggled to remove a single gold band from her finger. She placed the ring in Mahta's palm, then closed both her hands over the queen's. Mahta looked up at Joseph.

"Thank you," Joseph read from his wife's lips to the giver. She took the ring and placed it on her own finger, then said something in the ear of the peasant. They embraced, and the old woman went away smiling.

"What did she say?" Joseph asked, as Mahta took her seat.

"She said, 'Tell the king thank you for bringing my son home alive.'"

"What did you say to her?"

"That I'd wear her ring always and cherish it in my heart."

As they went to their beds that night, Mahta said, "We have come a long way from that slave platform."

"Yet we are still the same, you and I."

"And may we never change."

# Chapter Forty

# Birth and Blessing

Manasseh sat on the steps with his chin in his hands. "Oh, I'm not sad," he said to Zarill. "I'm happy. I just have no place to go right now so that I'm not in the way."

"And what are you happy about that sends you to the palace steps?"

"My mother is getting ready to have her baby."

"I see. And why are you not in the nursery with the other children at a moment like this?"

"I was there, but I didn't feel like playing."

"Come with me, then." The commander took Manasseh by the hand. "We'll go to the arena and I'll teach you some soldier skills. We will pass the time there until news about the birth comes. We'll tell the runners, so that they'll know where to reach us."

"Will you wrestle with me?"

"Wrestling is not my sport. Let's see how well you can learn to joust."

———✦———

The midwife had just arrived, but Mahta was frightened. The birth pains had been coming for two days, though they had not intensified until the last few hours. Now they were getting progressively more severe.

"You are bearing up well, my dear, and will soon have a new one to care for," the midwife said. As she felt her belly to determine the baby's position, she watched Mahta and asked, "How long have your pains been this forceful?"

"I don't know. It seems a long time. My first birth did not take this long. Is something wrong?"

"Every birth is different, but the baby is not in the proper position and is going to need our help to get it here."

Mahta's eyes widened as she turned to her husband. "Joseph, please pray for us."

"I have been praying, Mahta. But I should have done this sooner." He laid his hands on his wife's head and said, "By the power Thou hast given me, I ask Thee, Father, to intervene in this birthing. Please help us know what to do. Thou canst affect the life inside the womb. Please let it proceed as it should. Bless Mahta that she may have some relief from the pain and find the strength to function as she should. Amen."

The midwife looked at Joseph with wonder. She saw concern, faith, and strength in his face. She turned to Mahta whose muscles tightened as another wave of pain began. She touched the queen's arm. "Quickly now, I need you to be strong and get to your feet."

"My feet?" She heaved herself up and stood.

All in attendance rushed to aid her, but the midwife waved them off, saying, "We must help the baby position itself with your movement."

As she walked around the room, Mahta sensed the wisdom of this move. With the next pain, she leaned with her arms against a table. Twice more she did this, then told the midwife, "I felt a shifting. It feels different now. I think the baby turned."

She was exhausted but eager as she lay in the birthing position on her side. "Now I can feel the pressure pushing the baby down—it's coming!" She grabbed Joseph's hand as she felt the unmistakable desire to bear down. Her body seemed to take over as she felt it working to bring the baby into the world.

"The top of the baby's head is visible," the midwife said. "When you feel that pressure again, I want you to push."

Gratefully, when the next pain came, she pushed and groaned with the relief of finally being able to proceed. She felt a burning sensation and warm fluid.

"Good! The baby's head is out. Now wait—take some quick breaths and wait for the next tightening."

While Mahta paused to prepare for the next pain, the midwife wiped the baby's nose and mouth as it miraculously turned itself to deliver the shoulders. At the next pain, Mahta again bore down and felt the baby leave her. She closed her eyes and smiled in relief and joy as she regained her breath and finally relaxed. Joseph was cradling Mahta's head and wiping her hair from her face. The sound of the baby's cry filled the room.

"That's it, he's here!" the attendant said.

"He?" the father asked.

"Yes, it's a boy."

"Is he all right?" Mahta asked.

"A little out of shape from the ordeal, but healthy and hearty. He'll be fine."

She wrapped the fussing boy in soft cloth and handed him to his mother, who was laughing through her tears. Mahta placed the baby's cheek next to hers and talked to him softly. He quieted quickly as though listening to a voice he recognized and knew.

"He is beautiful. Oh you dear, sweet baby. We were so hard on you. Thank you for being brave and strong. You will like it here, you'll see. We will take good care of you. Isn't he wonderful, Joseph?"

"He is wonderful," Joseph said through his tears. "How blessed we are—two sons."

"I am so happy, Joseph. We must thank our Father in Heaven for this miracle. Now I am very tired. I think I could sleep for two days."

In spite of her fatigue, Mahta found she could only sleep for short periods of time. Once when she awakened, Manasseh was standing by her bed. Ramieth and Rena had been there, fussing over the new one while Mahta slept. Joseph was sitting nearby, holding the baby and singing his lullaby.

Mahta asked Manasseh, "Did you see your new brother?"

"Yes, I saw him. He's little."

"Well, he's very young."

"But can he do anything?"

"Not yet. All he can do right now is eat and sleep. He'll grow soon enough."

"When can I play with him?"

"You may hold him."

Joseph brought the baby, and as Manasseh sat on the edge of the bed, the baby was placed in his arms. The ten-year-old sat very still and gazed with awe at the new life. "Look at his fingers," he said. The baby tightened his grip over one of his fingers.

Mahta uncovered the rest of the baby. "And his toes. They are so little. Look, he is yawning." They all laughed and marveled at each little action of this incredible new life.

Mahta hugged Manasseh and said, "You are a fine big brother. There will be much for you to teach the little one."

"I think he's going to cry," Joseph said as he was taking him from Manasseh.

Mahta smiled. "He is probably hungry. Here, give him to me." The baby began sucking immediately and settled into a position of comfort. Mahta felt the tightening reaction of her womb as her body began its natural course of recuperation.

"He acts like he knows just what to do," Manasseh said with a sound of disbelief.

"That's part of the miracle." The family spent as much time together with the baby as they could for the next few days. Joseph watched his new son as if he didn't want to miss one moment of his existence, as if he wanted to compensate for the time he had lost with Manasseh.

Only a week had passed when Joseph told Mahta, "Tomorrow will be the eighth day, the time when the male children of Israel receive their blessing and circumcision."

"Of course. I remember. I'm so pleased that you're here this time to fulfill the covenant."

The family gathered in a large room. Pleoris, the physician, was invited to perform the cutting.

Manasseh had been taught by his father for two years now of the ordinances and blessings that accompanied the doctrines he espoused. This was a special occasion.

The baby cried out as the foreskin was clipped, but he settled down afterward at his mother's breast. Then Joseph laid his hands on the tiny head and prayed. His words were well-chosen, his voice full of the emotions of a new father.

"And I bless you to the end that you may enjoy the privileges and responsibilities that go with the covenant. You are today blessed to uphold the ways of the God of our fathers. Even the same God and the same blessings partaken of by Adam. You are hereby set apart from the world of unbelief. You are set on a course to incline away from sin. May you fulfill the path God has foreseen for you. To this end I give you this father's blessing, and with it, I give you a name. The name by which you shall be known is *Ephraim*, which means fruitful. I give the name and the blessing by the power of the God of Abraham, Isaac, and Jacob. Amen."

---

"That was a beautiful ceremony this morning," Mahta said as they went to their beds.

"We are a family."

"Is it enough, Joseph?"

"What do you mean? Of course it's enough."

"You know what the midwife said."

"Yes, that it looks as if there could be no more children. Does that trouble you greatly?"

"I can be this content always if you don't desire more."

"I'll leave it to God. If these two sons are our blessing, then so be it."

Mahta turned her back to her husband and would not let her voice betray what her face conveyed. "You may have concubines, and all the children they could bear for you. All you have to do is—"

"I told you before, Mahta. I won't take a concubine. You are all my joy. If our family is to be small, I'll still consider my cup to be brimming over."

She turned to him with tears in her eyes. "Oh, Joseph, how could God have loved me so much to have given me you?"

"I'm sure he loves you very much. I know I do."

The family of Pharaoh came to see the two-week-old baby. Manasseh and his parents stood proudly by, smiling as the onlookers made their comments and adulations.

"We'll have a palace feast to commemorate this high birth," Apophis said. "I'll order the preparations right away."

At the celebration, Pharaoh raised his cup. "We've seen two years of great abundance and have entered the third year of the prophecy of Zana-panea. He's made changes for the better in our city. A victor in battle, he has brought our troops home unscathed. We are indebted to our ruler. Now he presents us with a second man-child. Let's drink to the health, power, and continued wisdom of this great man and his family." A loud chorus of cheers rose from the gathered guests. They stood in unison and raised their cups.

Mahta looked carefully over the congregation. *There were once a number of deadly enemies in this group. I wonder if there are still those who nurture hatred for Joseph?*

If so, they were not evident.

When next Pharaoh and his second-in-command met to discuss matters, he was pleased with the report. "You say you have received an assessment of the cities on a regular basis?"

"Yes. The officers I've placed over the gathering give me detailed reports of the progress. So far the storage bins seem able to accommodate the plenty of these two years, with room for five years more. The extent of the planting and harvest exceeds even my anticipations. Where I suggested they dig canals and extend the waters of the river, they have gone great distances beyond the obvious boundaries. Everywhere the waters have been diverted, the land yields green treasures."

Pharaoh sighed and shook his head. "I cannot believe my great good fortune. I'm well-pleased with your leadership, my friend. All my confidence in you has been confirmed."

"What's your opinion of the infirmary?"

"I've been intending to go there and see it for myself. Will you accompany me there now for a review of the premises?"

The architects had done well in laying out the healing place. The physician, working with the architects, had planned carefully for every detail. In addition to planning the physical layout of the place, Pleoris had been successful in training qualified workers. A number of eunuchs took over the primary responsibilities with several young women to assist them.

The use of the herbs and compounds that Joseph had taught his friend in prison had been adopted and generously administered with good results. The physician had honed his skills in the treatment of various injuries and was an expert on eye, ear, and nose ailments. He even did some work on teeth from time to time. His apprentices were learning his fine talents to be passed on.

As they looked over the main room, Joseph and Apophis saw row upon row of beds with clean linen. The attendants were busily going from patient to patient. Joseph noticed one eunuch in particular and went to the man. "Pardon me, you look like someone I should know. I'm trying to remember if we met before."

The eunuch looked into Joseph's face and said, "I knew you in prison."

"In prison? Why...you're Lym."

"I am. I wasn't sure we would actually meet here."

"You knew of my promotion?"

"The physician informed me when I came to seek a position here. But I feel uncomfortable. I don't know how to talk to you now."

"You need not fear me. I'm still your friend. I've thought about you and wondered if you went through with your decision."

"You can see that I did." Lym was still nervous.

"I admire you for holding strong to your convictions. Are you happy?"

"It's been a long road, but yes. I'm finally really happy." He still did not smile.

"Tell me about it," Joseph said. He took Lym by the elbow and led him to a quiet place in the room where they could sit and talk.

Apophis saw that Joseph wanted the moment of privacy with his friend and moved on with his entourage of guards and aides to finish the inspection.

"Now, my friend. Tell me how your life has gone since you left the prison."

"Well, first I went back to the pleasure house. I had to. That was the only place I could go, the only life I had ever known. For a time I ignored the vow I made to become a eunuch and tried to resume the life without conscience I had lived before. It came to a point, finally, when I realized that there was no quality of life in the behavior I had chosen. I came to recognize, too, that even though I was a victim of my past, I could still determine my future. To tell you the truth, I often thought of you and the way you treated people. I set up that kind of benevolence as my goal.

"Without telling my comrades, I secretly had the castration done. When I tried to go back, however, they treated me vilely. I thought I could continue working there as an attendant, or housekeeper. Eunuchs are numbered as employees in the pleasure house and I knew they were highly esteemed. But it was as if the other hosts felt like I was passing judgment on them. It couldn't be the same. I had to leave. I wandered for a time. I tried to get other work. I was even reduced to begging. On the streets, I saw the kind of misery I had seen in prison. I tried to help, and little by little I learned to give of myself. When word spread that the infirmary was opening, I came immediately and the physician remembered me, impressed with the change in me. So here I am. And yes, I am really happy. I discovered a secret."

"What would that be?" Joseph asked.

"That thinking of others and giving service to those who need you is far better than living just for yourself. Relieving suffering is much more rewarding than wallowing in self pleasure."

"That's commendable, Lym, and I greatly admire you. I'll remember your example of service. You've helped me to be a better person just for having known you."

Now Lym was smiling. "Will you come again?"

"Yes, and when you can, please come and meet my family. Come to my house and Moesha, my steward, will see to your meeting."

"Goodbye, Joseph...my king."

"Goodbye, dear friend."

---

The splendid house adjoining the palace was finished. The family of Joseph was ready to move into their own home. All of the palace servants were enlisted to prepare the new house. Joseph's staff, along with the bustling crew of Pharaoh, began the work at hand.

Joseph and Mahta took Manasseh by the hand while Mizrel carried Ephraim and they walked through for the final inspection. The house was laid out much like the palace with the large reception room containing the stairs and throne in the front part of the building and the living quarters behind. Polished granite was laid for all the floors on the main level. It was also used for the pillars and stairs. Wood had been imported for use in the structure and adornments in every room.

Gold was Egypt's chief resource, and the designers were told to spare nothing in the embellishment with gold. The thrones were artfully carved golden structures covered with precious gems. Fine brocades and silk veils were hung in the appropriate places designated as room dividers. There was no kitchen. It had been decided that Pharaoh's ample food facility would serve both houses.

To access the palace, a walk had been constructed joining Joseph's room upstairs with the palace balcony close to Pharaoh's quarters. On the lower level, the side doors of both buildings could be reached within a few short steps.

"I didn't think it would be so big," Mahta said.

"We'll need the room—you'll see. We have many servants to house, and maybe Ramieth and Rena will come."

"Maybe your family will come some day, Joseph." Mahta saw by the look on his face the effect of her remark. "I'm sorry. I didn't mean to hurt you, but really, they might come—don't you think?"

"That world is far away, as if it happened in a dream. Yet I want to see them. Yes, Mahta, they might come."

"This is our first night in our own home. I love the smell of the new wood. It feels good. Do you feel it, Joseph?"

"Yes, it does feel good. I hope I don't come to love the feel of luxury so much that I forget."

"We won't forget," Mahta said. "My greatest blessing was born in the dusty path of the slave caravan. I'll never forget. I remember the first time I saw you. There you were, covered with dirt, your head hung low, sullen and grim."

"I was miserable."

"Yet there was a kind of magic about you. I wasn't the only one who felt it, but I did feel it. My heart leapt within me. Then, when you finally spoke, I felt as if in the presence of someone mighty."

"Mighty scared," Joseph said, "and trying to bluff my way into bravery."

"No, I don't suppose we must ever forget. But let's be grateful for all we have now. How will we teach our sons what we've learned?"

"We'll tell them our stories and teach them to love God."

"Let's make our house one of prayer and of learning."

That day, with his family and closest staff, Joseph conducted a ceremony of dedication in which he covenanted with God to use all his abundance in the service of God and his fellowman.

---

Mizrel came to Mahta one morning. "I have a special request to make of you, Mistress. I don't know whether you've noticed or not, but Wama and I have grown close."

Mahta laughed. "How could I have missed it? If I didn't see you touching in the hallways, I couldn't mistake the looks on your faces when you see each other."

"Yes, Mistress, you're right. We like each other very much. We want to be married and move into a room together."

"Does Joseph know?"

"Wama is asking permission of the master at this very moment."

"You know the palace rules, don't you?"

"Yes. I know that Pharaoh doesn't allow his palace servants to be married. He employs only eunuchs or single people so as not to overrun the palace, I suppose. For many years I worked as a single woman in Pharaoh's nursery."

"And now you want to end your life as a single woman. I'll talk with my husband."

"Thank you, Mistress."

Joseph was smiling as he came to Mahta and pulled her aside. "Well, what do you think of Wama and Mizrel?"

"I think it's wonderful. I wouldn't deny them their happiness for anything in the world."

"Yet Pharaoh's rule is a good one. Single people make more efficient servants."

"Maybe they do, and maybe they don't. Rather than dismiss them, I'm willing to find out."

"Yes, I suppose I'm at liberty to make my own house rules. But if we set a precedent with this couple, we may start a practice we cannot control."

"Let's take our chances."

"We do think alike, you and I. Shall we make a celebration for them?"

"If they want it. Let's ask them."

In the end the couple was quietly married and they carried on as routinely as possible.

One day Mizrel confided in Mahta. "I don't think you have to worry about us filling our quarters with babies."

"What do you mean, Mizrel?"

"When I was young, I was violated many times and severely abused. There was a dead, unformed baby once. I don't think there can be anymore."

"I'm so sorry, Mizrel, and I hope you may have as many babies as your love can produce. We'll prepare new quarters for you if we must. Just give Wama all the love you have in your heart to give."

"Thank you, Mistress. You are a good woman. For now, I'll have great joy in giving my motherly love to Manasseh and Ephraim.

---

The granaries were filled to capacity. Provisions were hastily collected and stored for short-term consumption as well. The seventh year of plenty had just been harvested. Without speaking it aloud, some people seemed to hold their breath to see what would happen next. Many had followed the program of Zana-panea just in case. Others, confident in the integrity of their leader, had no trouble carrying out the seven-year plan. Still others who could not bend their pride had done things their own way. One such was Opeph.

Opeph was the leader of the city of On and considered himself to be experienced and wise. He had not liked Joseph from the beginning. When Zana-panea had come to install the new program, Opeph had resisted. "I'll do it my way," he had said. He engaged a builder and ordered a storage facility of his own design to house a great deal of food. He didn't believe he would need it, however. "Seven years of plenty and seven years of famine," he scoffed. "Who could foresee such a thing anyway?"

Now the fat years were at a conclusion and everyone's bins were full, even Opeph's.

# Chapter Forty-one

# Assessment and Preparation

There had been scarce years before. Egypt and her neighbors had suffered hardships many times. On those occasions people from all over had come to Egypt to buy her surplus.

When Mahta and Joseph were anticipating who might come to Egypt for grain, she mentioned Ahkmar. "I suppose even his sorry band needs sustenance."

Joseph said, "I used to see Kumash at Bazaar, but he hasn't come for the last several years. I wonder what became of him."

The end of the eighth year of the prophecy of Zana-panea was not like any year before. No one could remember such a dramatic decline in moisture. The earth was baked and cracked. Fields that had born billowing grains now lay parched and dead. Orchards where fruit had bent branches with over-laden produce now stood like skeletons, stretching out their wasted arms. The mighty river once spread a layer of fertile silt over her banks. Now the flow had shallowed to a streamlet, barely enough to float a barge or to offer drinking water. The reservoirs were filled, which offered hope that the animals and people would be sustained, but the hearts of the people were humble.

"Were it not for the dream of Pharaoh and the wisdom of Zana-panea, we couldn't have survived even this first year of drought. Now we must abide with our stores and weather six more seasons."

The neighboring countries fared no better. While there was barely enough water to drink, the efforts to water the vegetation had been futile. A blight was on the land, and crops would not grow.

After that eighth year, people began to gather to Memphis and to the governor of Egypt to plead for food. Among the first petitioners were citizens of Egypt.

"Why are you here?" Joseph asked. "Did I not warn you and teach you how to lay up your own stores?"

One man said, "I believed you, but I had a storage bin already. I used the one I'd used before."

"And what happened?" Joseph asked.

"For a few months we were able to use our food stuffs, but as we dug deeper, we saw that the inside had rotted and that vermin were attracted to it. Now there's nothing but a smelly pile of garbage and pests where our storage should be."

"I'll give you from our central stores," Joseph said. "This first time you need not pay inasmuch as you donated one-fifth part of your harvest to the center. Next time you come, a high price will be required. You may wish in the end that you'd listened to the counsel."

Each Egyptian who came was dealt with in this same manner. Eventually Opeph, leader of On, came.

Joseph allowed an audience with him. "How is it that you come to Memphis to get grain? Are you not from the land of plenty? Did God not show you how to store up against this day?"

Opeph stood defensive. "How is it you talk to me as if I were an errant child? I have had experience in these matters. Have I not overseen the city of On in judicious rule these many years?"

"You may be a good leader and you may have had much experience, but when God sends a word of significance, one must listen."

"I have always done my duty by the gods of Egypt."

"Yet now you come seeking food for yourself. And what of all the people of On? They contributed one-fifth of their harvest to the central storehouse and trusted you to its preservation. What has become of their donations?"

"I had my builders erect a fine storage unit, grander than most. We put away enough for seven years. But when we began to draw from its supply, the whole of it from the core outward was moldy. It was too dense. No one can lay in that much for seven years and expect it to last."

"The granaries of your neighboring towns have lasted. Those who followed the design shown them have not suffered."

"So what am I to do? Go hungry?"

"No, we won't let any man of Egypt go hungry. Your townspeople will be supplied, but since you have elected to act contrary to counsel, you must pay a high price for your grain."

"You are not fair."

"I am more than fair. Because of your obstinance, you should be required to go without until all the obedient are fed. Go now, and next time it will cost you even more."

Opeph was put out of his office as leader. In his years of power he had acquired much wealth. He owned several houses and much land. By the seventh year of famine, he had relinquished all of his wealth, his houses, his lands and cattle to get food for himself and his family.

All the Egyptians were handled in this manner. Those of wealth, who had been too proud to listen, ended up being in debt to the king. Pharaoh, as a result of the wise dealings of Joseph, ended up a wealthy king, owning most of the land of Egypt. Those who followed the counsel and stored accordingly were well cared for.

---

At this session of Pharaoh's court they were to decide the course of the lean years. Apophis and Joseph sat in their thrones. The men of learning stood in their respective places on the steps.

"Confusion has already started. How are we to handle the masses of people who will pour into our city?" The feelings of most men of the court were being expressed by the chief priest.

Pharaoh answered. "Zana-panea himself has been interviewing each of the supplicants. It will be too much for him soon. We must devise a plan."

One of the counselors asked, "How can we prevent pilfering or unfair overloading by some?"

Zarill responded. "Right now each visitor to the city is being searched for weapons and questioned at the gates. But if a group wanted to attack a granary, they could enter in small numbers through the ten separate gates, then join up and overcome the guards at the food sites."

"Yes," Pharaoh said. "Hungry men may be willing to risk desperate dangers to get supplies."

"Should we place more guards at each site?" Zarill asked.

"They may not even need to attack," one of the stargazers said. "If a wealthy man has many servants and many pack animals, he could send each servant through the gates to gather stores as if for his family. That would not be just, for a less wealthy man may have no servants."

"So how do we care for the hungry in fairness while safeguarding our security?" Pharaoh asked.

"This is Zana-panea's plan. What does he have to say about this?" one of the architects asked. All eyes moved to Joseph.

"I've been thinking on these very issues," he said. "I have, at least in part, come up with a program. A sentinel would be placed with the guards who examine the visitors at each gate. He would record the name of each entrant. The entrant's name, his father's name, and his grandfather's name would be required. A proclamation must also be sent out to inform all lands that only the head of a household or his male children would be allotted grain. That way they could not send extra servants to stockpile goods."

"We could limit each portion to that which can be carried on one donkey," Apophis said, and the court applauded. "Let the scribes make it law by writing our words."

Joseph stood up and said, "We will need help from all the king's court. You may be called upon to help monitor as the crowds grow thicker. We must expect more sick to be brought to the infirmary. The magistrate will need help in hearing and sentencing lawbreakers. Many without money will be tempted to steal. We must be ready for all contingencies. This time of hardship will make us stronger if we make ourselves equal to the situation." Again, the court applauded.

"Let us all see to our tasks," Pharaoh said.

"Does the famine reach into Canaan?" Mahta asked, as she and Joseph shared their evening meal.

"It reaches there and far beyond."

"Does your father have resources against such a hardship?"

"My father is wise; he plans carefully for all conditions and has his servants store all sorts of foodstuffs. He buries roots in the deep ground. He dries fruits and vegetables. His bees produce great quantities of honey that it may be put in jars and kept. He dries the meat of cattle and fowl so that it can last a long time. My father's wells are many—filled to sustain against a drought. He even has granaries to house the surplus grain of their fields." He paused for a moment. "But he doesn't have a means of storage sufficient for more than two years. If the animals are to be kept alive and fed, his stores would be used up in less time than that."

Mahta sat quietly and watched the face of her husband as he spoke with a depth of feeling she'd never seen before. His father must have been much on his mind. "Are you thinking they might come?" She asked.

"It was so with my father, and grandfather, and his father."

"What was so?"

"That they came to Egypt when there was a famine in Canaan."

"So you are expecting someone to come?"

"I expect someone, but my father is too old to travel. He will probably send my brothers."

"How does that make you feel?"

"Anxious. I want to see my brothers, but I wonder if they still hate me. When I left them, I had the broken heart of a seventeen-year-old. I've had nothing else to relate my feelings to since then."

Mahta was thoughtful. "I, too, am anticipating a visitor."

"You—a visitor?"

"Not to me personally, but to the city."

"Yes, of course—your uncle. Do you think he's still alive? If he is, he too must come for food. Well, we must not pass this up. I'll share my plan with you. I am having the sentinels at each gate record the family names of every visitor who comes to the city. The gates will admit people only during the daylight hours. At night I will have the lists brought to me so that I may study the names written there."

"And you will know who is here."

Joseph nodded. "I will have those whose names I select brought to me for an audience the following morning."

"Where will you interview them?" Mahta asked as she fought to hide the emotion in her voice.

"I've been sitting on the platform in the square, but I'll turn that over to others. From now on, those whose names I select will be brought to my throne room where I can question them privately."

Mahta asked, "Then on occasion, would it be possible for me to sit on my chair and quietly watch the proceedings?"

Joseph smiled. "Yes, of course. I'd welcome you by my side."

"Well, when you come across the name Meshca, son of Hador, son of Ammon, I'll sit with you for the interview."

"Is there anyone else you wish to see?"

"Yes. If our old master, Kumash, comes, please make it known to me so that I might greet him."

"I, too, would love to see Kumash. But I wonder why he hasn't come to Bazaar these many years."

"Perhaps he'll come now."

# Chapter Forty-two

# Tension in Hard Times

Ephraim was five years old. Manasseh had just had his sixteenth birthday. By now it was obvious that Ephraim would have light hair like his mother, but he had the same blue-colored eyes of his father. Manasseh had dark hair like his father, his eyes also blue. Both carried a full, thick head of cropped curls. The boys were a source of great joy to their parents. Manasseh, following his early inclinations, was an athlete of superior abilities. While gentle with his younger brother and soft-spoken in company, on the arena floor, he was a strong competitor. Wama and Punt had been good teachers. Zarill also.

Joseph, on occasion, tussled on the mats with Manasseh. One day Wama came to Joseph and said, "That boy is plenty strong. If he wanted to, he could take me down. I think he holds back his true power in respect of age."

"Is that right?" Joseph said. "Well, I must test out this theory myself."

So one afternoon, at his invitation, Father Joseph found himself engaged in friendly combat with his son, Manasseh. "Show me your skills," he said. But he, too, felt that his son was holding back. "Don't be afraid of hurting me. Do not limit yourself." A short moment later, Joseph was pinned in an uncompromising hold. He laughed with pride as he later told Mahta about it.

Ephraim followed his brother's pattern to some extent. Already he displayed good muscle coordination. He was skilled at sports and wrestling, but his main interest lay in the arts. He liked to sing. From the beginning of his life he had responded to his parents' songs. He listened avidly to the court musicians. Now, at five years of age, he was always found singing and making up his own little songs as his mother used to do. Even at his young age he found pleasure in seeing pieces of fine weaving or carving. The artists that painted the glyphs on the pillars and walls of the temple and palace were commissioned to decorate Joseph's house with wall pageants. Ephraim was entranced with the process. He found beauty everywhere. He loved to walk with his mother and have her explain the paintings and carvings on the buildings. Both boys liked to do that.

Both seemed also to love learning. Because no others believed in God as Joseph and Mahta, the responsibility of religious instruction fell to them. Lessons of other subjects were taught by the men of the court. Joseph was always on hand to inquire into the lessons taught. Sometimes he laughingly corrected a point on which he differed. He often told the boys the story of his ascension. They were enrapt by the telling and would ask many questions. They asked again and again to be told by both Mahta and Joseph the stories of their slavery and Joseph's imprisonment. They liked to learn of their ancestors and relatives far away.

"Will you teach us all the answers so we may climb up the steps?" Ephraim asked.

"No, you will never sit on the throne of Egypt. Your paths lie in a different direction."

"But we are your sons," Manasseh said.

"Yes, but I am here only by the will of God to carry out his plans."

"Does God have plans for us?"

"Yes, he does. You are to be leaders of your people."

"Where are our people? How can we lead people we haven't seen?"

"It will come about—in time. God has said so. Be believing. Trust me and the God of our fathers. You'll see many things that you do not see now."

"How can we believe something we cannot see?" Ephraim asked.

"It's called faith," Manasseh said, answering for his father. "It was faith that put our father where he is now, Ephraim. You and I must learn to be like our father. We must learn faith." A parental smile was shared between Mahta and Joseph over Manasseh's mature answer.

"I'm afraid that much of what we'll see will not be pleasant," Joseph said. "We are only into the second year of the famine."

———◦◦◦◦———

"I've closed the temple." Ramieth stood in the doorway looking dejected.

"Oh no, has it come to that?" Rena said, going to her husband. She led him to a chair.

"There's so much turmoil. Last night someone attacked the night priest and bound him just so they could eat the food that had been set out for the gods."

"But no one's allowed in the temple but the priests."

"Tell that to the starving man."

"What will we do?"

"We cannot stay here."

"No. I didn't want to tell you, but even if we tried to stay and finish the scant food left in the garden, we couldn't because someone stripped our trees of the last figs and dates hanging there. Every nutritious vegetable or leaf that was not yet shriveled was cleaned out."

"Gather a few items of clothing. We'll go to our children."

"But I don't want to be a burden to them."

"We won't be a burden. They've told us repeatedly they want us. They even had chambers built for us in their new house, and we can always make ourselves useful. Besides, there is food there."

"Very well. Let us hurry then. I don't feel safe in On; too many things are happening."

The two servants that the priest and his wife employed had been sent back to their families. The only animals left in the shelter were two horses. A few precious things were hurriedly packed. Ramieth harnessed the horses and hooked up their chariot.

"If we have a clear path, we should be able to be in Memphis by nightfall."

They looked one last time at the house and gardens they had loved. Ramieth wheeled the chariot past the temple.

"It's so beautiful," Rena said. "What will become of it?" Ramieth didn't answer.

They weren't the only ones leaving the city. Many had already gone to Memphis. Some had gone, collected their rations and come back to try to maintain their homes.

Because of its location near the mouth of the river, and being the last bastion of civilization before Memphis, On was vulnerable to marauders. It was not safe to leave a home untended. The Egyptians themselves posed less threat, however, because of their moral traditions—they would not take that which was not theirs. If a farmer had only one chicken left, he would share it with his neighbor. But the mixture of foreigners coming to the city, dismissed servants with no place to go, and those on the verge of imminent starvation had turned On into a city of chaos. "All because that prideful leader, Opeph, went against counsel," Rena said as they drove out of the city.

The streets were full of people heading toward Memphis and the hope of food. There were only a few chariots on the road and the couple was making good progress. Most of those on foot were now behind them. But in the road ahead a man lay in the path of the wagon.

"We must help him," Ramieth said. They pulled up and he got out. Before they knew what had happened, the man in the road leapt up as another man knocked Ramieth down. Another pushed Rena out of the cart, and the three attackers rode away in the chariot.

"Are you all right?" Ramieth asked, limping over to pick up Rena.

"Yes, but my sensibilities are offended and I'm angry. Why must people act like wild beings?"

"There are always those who rob and steal. Now I'm afraid. Times have turned many hearts to evil. Can you walk?"

"I am only a little bruised. I can make it. How far must we walk?"

"We are not far from the barge, but we may not make it in time to cross. I'm sure it shuts down at dark."

"But look, people are crossing over there. There is barely enough water for the barges. We can wade across."

After watching for a little while, they decided it was still too deep and dangerous to push through. They traversed the road by the shore, feeling tired, hungry, and battered.

"If I weren't so angry, I probably couldn't keep going," Rena said. "The thought of those men drives me on." They passed the night huddled together under a wasted palm tree.

In the morning light, they could see the white city in the distance. Weak and spent, they came to the barge and crossed. When they approached the city gate they were slowed by the numbers of people being questioned and searched. As they stood to wait, Ramieth said, "Look."

Outside the city wall, a distance from where they stood, lay their abandoned carriage on its side. "The horses were probably sold," Rena said.

They made it through the gate, then continued to Joseph's house. Inside, they were immediately recognized. Servants scurried to their aid. They were soon put in a room to rest where hot broth was brought to them. Mahta came running in, concerned yet relieved to see they were all right.

Later that evening they felt much better and told Joseph and Mahta the details of their misadventures.

Joseph said, "It appalls me that Memphis must be host to such thieves."

"Never mind. We're going to be all right," Rena said. "It's good to be with you."

"What about your home?" Mahta asked.

"It will always be theirs," Joseph said. "Egyptian law states that all land given to priests is theirs forever without taxation."

"Yes. It also says the priest's family will be fed and cared for," Ramieth said. "But I can't tell you how fast a city can fall to ruin under a hostile crowd. Do you know that every day Rena carried buckets to the river to collect water for her garden just so she could sustain the meager food that grew there? But then someone came at night and stripped everything away."

"Let's wait out the famine here, together. I'll have the scribe note the title to your land. When it is all over, we'll see if there's anything to go back to."

"Is this what will happen in other cities?" Mahta asked.

Joseph considered that thoughtfully. "As far as I know, Opeph was the only leader who didn't comply with instructions. Some individuals went contrary, but I don't think the panic you experienced today will be far spread. We're watching carefully the distribution of food all over Egypt."

"Thank the gods for a man such as you," Ramieth said.

―――――∋⊙∘⊙⊂―――――

As Joseph had predicted, the infirmary was full of sick people. The prison was bulging once again. Day after day the square was thronged with people either petitioning for their share of food, or begging, unable to prove they were of a household. Tents were set up outside the city walls. People languished on all the streets of Memphis.

In better days Bazaar or Festival would have brought people there. Now, it seemed as if the whole world were coming to Egypt. Bargaining and trading went on in a spirit of despair, the happy days of a few years ago now gone.

Each night Joseph gathered the lists and perused each one. Finally one evening he went to Mahta and held up the papyrus. "The name *Meshca, son of Hador, son of Ammon* is on this list."

Mahta paled slightly and drew a breath. "So it's happened at last. I don't know whether I'm happy or sad, whether I really want to see my uncle."

Joseph put his arms around her and held her tight. "You can think about it tonight. I'll have him brought before me in the morning."

The following morning found both thrones occupied. As always, Wama and Punt stood by Joseph, Zarill and a number of his guardsmen nearby. Several supplicants for food had already been heard. Now, Zarill said in a loud voice, "Meshca, son of Hador, son of Ammon will now be heard." A sickly-looking man with a graying beard bowed prostrate on the floor at the bottom of the stairs.

Joseph reached over and took Mahta's hand. "Is that him?" he whispered to her. The man remained in a prone position on the floor, for he had not yet been given permission to rise.

"He doesn't look the same. My uncle was a large, robust man."

"It's been twenty-two years since you saw him."

"Have him stand."

Joseph said loudly, "You may rise and make yourself known."

The man struggled to get up. "I am a humble farmer. My name is Meshca. I come from the land of Ammon. Everyone in Ammon is starving. I come to petition for food."

Joseph said, "Tell me about your family."

"My wife of many years died last year. My son is crippled and awaits me at home. I have few servants and hardly any beasts left. I beg your generosity, that I might return home and save my household."

The room was quiet. Joseph didn't speak, but looked at Mahta. "Should I give him supplies?" he whispered.

She had tears in her eyes. "Yes, of course."

Joseph said, "Give this man a double portion of food. One for himself and one for the male child at home. If need be, supply an extra donkey on which to carry it home."

The man was bowing and nodding and looking bewildered as he thanked Joseph repeatedly.

"And let Meshca, son of Hador, son of Ammon, know that it is because of the goodness and generosity of his niece, Mahta, that he is blessed this day. Now go."

The man could not understand what was happening to him. He turned and looked about as if to bring reason into his disoriented mind. "Ma...Mahta?" he muttered, looking into several faces as he left the room.

"See to his needs. Fix his load and lead him safely out of the city," Joseph said.

# BOOK THREE

# REUNION

# Chapter Forty-three

# Hunger Drives Brothers to Egypt

"Behind you, Dan!" shouted Zebulon. Beyond the ridge! Take care!"

Dan turned just in time to see the crouching lion spring squarely onto its intended prey. The sheep struggled to get away, but after only a few minutes of resistance, the lion tightened its jaws on the helpless victim's throat. He shook it as if to test his grip, then began to skulk away, the sheep dangling from his mouth.

Zebulon didn't hesitate a moment. He bounded over the rocky terrain, joined Dan, and together they converged on the lion as it loped back up the ledge. First Dan, then Zebulon threw with precise aim the spears they carried. The lion went down.

Zebulon was on the animal immediately. He retrieved his weapon and sank it again and again into the beast until no evidence of life remained. As they looked at the lifeless form, Dan said, "It's getting to be too risky out here. They strike now in broad daylight, out in the open. They aren't even put off by seeing the shepherds."

Zebulon said, "This famine is changing even the nature of the wild ones."

Reuben and Asher had heard the commotion and came running from the far side of the flock. "This is the second time this week," Asher said. "Those we don't lose to animals, we lose at night to thieves."

Reuben said, "I'm not going to wait. Father would approve, I'm sure. It's senseless to keep the flock out here. They try to graze on dead grass and get thinner each day. We must drive them back to Hebron."

Asher agreed. "We can pen them in the fold there and hand-feed them grain and hay. We'll also need to feed them leaves or grass. They can't live on grain alone."

"But this famine can't last forever," Dan said. "Surely we'll get some moisture soon."

"We'll take counsel at home. Zeb, go tell the others to bring their flocks to the place of the three peaks. We'll meet them there."

When the ten brothers were gathered and the sheep and goats accounted for, Reuben said, "Simeon, you take Judah and Naptali with you. Go through the hills and hunt whatever wild game you can find. We'll need all we can gather. The rest of us will lead the flocks back to Hebron. We'll pick whatever edible leaves and brush we can find along the way and meet you at home."

---

The sheep were gathered in the fold and the servants were standing guard. Jacob had led the family in prayer. They were conserving food, so the humble meal was finished and cleaned away. He said, "Take the little ones to their rest. I'll have a conference with my seven sons."

He looked into the eyes of each of the men facing him. "Times are bad. We don't have enough in the shelter to feed the animals. Already the cows have gone dry. There'll be little more milk or cheese from the goats."

Isacar asked, "Can't we live for a long time on the meat of the farm animals?"

"We could live for a short time on the sheep and cattle, if we fed them all our grain," Jacob said. "But our children need porridge, and our families must have bread. We'll surely use up everything in our storage long before this famine ends."

Just then Judah came in, carrying a mountain ram over his shoulders. Simeon held several hares in one hand. Naptali held nothing.

"We searched all the terrain between Shechem and here. There is little to be found. Everyone hunts," Simeon said.

Jacob motioned to Judah. "Take the ram to the servants to be dressed and dried for later use. The hares also. You have done well."

Reuben asked, "Father, can you ask God what we must do?"

"Yes," Asher said. "God must know how long it will be dry."

Jacob answered, "I anticipate this spell to be a long one. God has confirmed it."

Zebulon asked, "What will you have us do, Father?"

"In past years of famine, we found relief in Egypt."

"Is there no famine there?"

"Yes, but even though the mother river has lost her succor, I understand that provisions have been stored up. I hear there's enough there for all the afflicted countries."

Dan jumped to his feet and said, "Then we'll go."

"Yes," Reuben said. "We'll take our fiercest men and many servants and go down to Egypt."

"No," the patriarch said, "The proclamation forbids any but family males to receive an allotment."

Asher said, "Well, counting you, Father, we have twelve family males. That should get us a fair supply."

Jacob said, "But they must be there in person to be counted. I can't make the trip. I'm too old and too tired. The grief I've suffered in my life has rendered me weak."

They knew he spoke of their brother, Joseph.

"And though I hesitate to let any of you travel—I would shelter you in my arms if I could—I won't allow Benjamin to leave my sight."

Reuben said, "Then the ten remaining sons will go. We'll go with God in strength. You can be reassured, Father, we'll return unharmed and with food."

"Yes, my son, I have faith in you. You must go."

Early the next morning the ten men filled their pockets with staples needed for the trip. Their servants brought the pack mules around and loaded them with provisions. Jacob joined his sons.

Zebulon said, "Tell us what we must know for our journey, Father."

Jacob stood thoughtfully watching the preparations. "When I went to Egypt many years ago, it was also because of famine in this land. I went there to live for the duration of the blight. I took a great many provisions with me."

"We won't go there to stay any length of time," Reuben said.

"No," Jacob said. "You'll be there only long enough to gather the grain and return as quickly as possible."

"What are you trying to tell us, Father?"

"I was wondering if you might be able to buy donkeys in Egypt. If you can, then maybe you should."

Reuben said, "You mean we should carry what we need ourselves?"

Judah added, "That's a good idea. That way we could run a good portion of the way—not bother with the slow animals, or worry about how to feed them."

Naptali said, "We can run faster than the animals could go, anyway."

Zebulon, joining the spirit of the conversation, said, "We can live off the land. We'll take our weapons."

Their father nodded his agreement. "You'll need to carry one water bag each. You may find a place or two to refill them along the way. Take only one change of clothing and your best sandals. You'll want to present yourselves fresh when you enter the city. Once there, you can buy whatever you need. They'll be asking a high price, but right now, we have more money than supplies."

They stuffed their inside pockets with dried meat. A small pack for their backs carried the clothing and bedroll. Naptali, Judah, Gad, and Levi slung a bow and quiver over their shoulders. Reuben, Simeon, and Dan strapped a sword to their waists. Asher carried a spear. Most of them, from the skills of being a shepherd, carried a sling in their tunic. Isacar, Zebulon, and Judah kept the flutes they had whittled while tending sheep. The water bags were brought and each man strapped one on and tucked it under his arm.

"Can you travel with all that weight?" their father asked.

"It's no more than a fat sheep," Isacar said. "We've run up and down mountains carrying more than this."

As he saw them off on their journey, Jacob advised his sons, "Go in peace. Refrain from combat on the road. When you come to Egypt, remember that they look down on shepherds. Abide the law and be inconspicuous. Perhaps it would be well if you each enter separately into the ten gates of Memphis so as not to call attention to yourselves. Get the grain we need and hurry back. Your father will watch and pray for your return."

The travelers reached through their legs, gathered their robes to the front and tucked them with their belts. "We'll gird up our loins and run the faster. Goodbye, Father!" and they were away.

They covered a great distance that first day. They were still fresh, the weather was not as hot as it was going to be later on, and they were eager to get the distance behind them. The setting sun found them on the shore of the sea.

"We'll camp here tonight and rise early to resume our errand."

Asher speared some fish. They made a fire and ate their first real meal since setting out. Along the way they had chewed a little dried meat and stopped only long enough to drink and take brief rests.

"How satisfying food can be when you earn the right to the appetite."

"We certainly earned it today."

"But that was the easy part of the trip. We'll see what tomorrow brings."

They said their evening prayer, then formed a circle and sang a song of gratitude to God.

The next morning they finished their portion of fish. In Gaza they filled their water bags and set out again.

It took them three days of hot, difficult going to cross the Sinai. They found a hare or two to sustain them, but by the end of the third day, they supped on snake and lizard meat or anything they could find. When they tried to sleep under the cloudless sky, they heard wolves howling in the distance.

# Chapter Forty-four

# King of Gaash

The fourth day in the desert saw the end of their water supply. By the following day, when they were able to buy water from a vendor, their lips were parched and swollen, their throats dry. They were walking, not running now.

The border guard on the outskirts of Egypt had been relaxed. No country had enough strength or food to sustain an army. Mother Egypt opened her arms to all comers. Pharaoh's guard had been gathered to Memphis to patrol the city, stand by the storehouses, and guard the granaries.

As they camped that night, they chose a spot where many other travelers were resting. By morning light the men from a nearby caravan approached and said, "We're servants of King Elan of Gaash. Our master in the royal conveyance beyond wishes to speak with you."

"I'll go," Reuben said.

"We'll all go," Simeon said, placing his hand on his sword. The ten men walked to the covered carriage.

The servants laid down carpets and motioned the brothers to sit, but they remained standing. The curtains were drawn back to reveal a man wearing a crown. He turned and sat facing them.

"Greetings to you! I am Elan, King of Gaash, from the land of Canaan. We have met before."

"If you call being engaged on a battlefield having met, then yes, we've met," Reuben said.

"Please sit down. I apologize for not providing a tent for privacy, but we're traveling as simply as we can and we must do without some of the comforts."

"How did you know who we were?" Reuben asked. They still stood.

"Everyone knows the sons of Israel. You wear the garment of a common shepherd, but you're known by many as the princes of Israel, and surely, if I'm king of a city, then your father, Israel, must be king of all Canaan. It's whispered up and down the road that you're going to Egypt. Your reputation puts fear and respect into the hearts of all who know you."

"Why did you wish to speak with us?"

"I want to offer you some refreshment. I see that you carry only a few implements, while I have enough provisions to care for me and my entire entourage of servants."

"We're on our way to Memphis to get grain."

"And so am I," the king said. "Although by the edict they sent out, I believe you'll be able to get much more. You are ten, and I and my son count only for two in my household."

"They probably make exceptions for kings."

"We'll see. But aren't you numbered more than ten men in your family?"

"Our father chose to remain at home and to keep our brother with him."

The servants were pouring ten cups of goat curd and laying out some bread and fruit. Reuben looked at the food, then at his brothers and sat down cross-legged on a rug. The others followed.

"I hope you'll tell your father of my hospitality and convey to him my good wishes."

"You wish to be remembered to him?"

"I wish to be allowed to live."

"Why do you say that?"

"Do you remember when I joined two other cities and went to war against your family? We were trying to gain more land and wells."

Reuben nodded.

"I shall never forget how fierce you all were. Your smaller forces completely brought us to our knees. I was taken captive as were my people. You led us back to your father and carried the spoils of victory."

The brothers ate and kept a silent tongue, watching carefully for any sign of trouble as they listened to the king.

He continued. "It was your father's right to keep all our goods and cattle, put me to death and enslave my people."

"He doesn't want your kingdom."

"No, indeed. Instead, he returned the spoils and sent us back to our homes."

"With the promise that you would no more go against him."

"Yes. He did that to me and to almost every other king in Canaan. As a token of peace, I have since sent him gifts. Each year I send five hundred core of wheat, five hundred baths of oil, and five hundred measures of wine as tribute to Israel."

"We thank you for our father."

"But now, I'm in fear of retribution."

"How say you?"

"This year and last, because of the famine, I haven't sent my portions. I'm in the debt of your father and I put myself at your mercy."

The brothers had finished eating. Reuben stood up. "We're all in need of food and all in need of God's mercy. Go your way in peace and do not fear us. If the times become favorable again, you may resume your tribute."

Now the king was bowing to the ten men who stood before him.

Reuben said, "Thank you for the repast. We'll tell our father. Goodbye."

The next day the brothers came to the land of Goshen, and although it had lost its abundance to the drought, it was still a haven of rest. They washed and drank and bought food from peddlers. They spent the night beneath the palms, the most peaceful of the whole journey. They chose a spot well away from the other traveling petitioners, who were enjoying the hospitality of the trees. When they were by themselves, they set up their circle, prayed, sang, and relaxed into quiet contemplation. Isacar brought out his flute and played tunes, soft and melodic, into the night air.

When it was quiet for a moment, Reuben said, "I watched your faces yesterday as we sat before King Elan. I saw a mask of calm that hid the inclination of belligerence."

"Are you concerned about our behavior?" Asher asked.

"Very concerned. You showed restraint, but you weren't tested to any great extent. We've lived a free and open lifestyle. If anyone or anything ever comes within our circle, we instinctively react to protect what is ours. We've enjoyed the gifts of strength the Lord gave us. Almost every man here has wrestled a wild beast and felt the thrill of victory. In fighting a bear or lion or wolf, we know how to handle ourselves.

"From now on we'll face a new and different challenge. We've never been in a city before—not like Memphis. There'll be temptations of every sort. There are clever thieves and conniving merchants in the city. These are desperate times and we're novices in the sophisticated world. We'll pray for God to accompany us into the city and that we may be wary and wise." Reuben finished speaking and it was quiet.

Then Dan said, "Are you worried for us, or for yourself? Do you anticipate a weakness in yourself if a harlot entices you?"

"That's not fair, Dan," Isacar said sharply. "Reuben's suffered enough for his indiscretion."

Levi added, "And wasn't he physically ill and close to death for seven months because of it?"

"But she was my mother—even if she was just a servant." Dan put his face in his hands, and Naptali kept his eyes on the ground. This subject had not been broached for twenty-seven years. Emotions were now being exhibited that had been shut inside.

There was a stirring among the brothers. Some moved to stand up, but Reuben raised a hand to motion silence. "No, it's well for this to be voiced. I need to reassure all of you, as well as myself. Yes, I committed a grievous sin when I lay with Bilha. To you, Dan and Naptali, I can never make restitution, but because of my sin, I'm aware of what can happen to a man when he sees a beautiful woman unclothed. I can tell you how the image sears itself into the brain and stirs up emotions and thoughts to an uncontrollable kind of sickness. That's how it was when I came upon Bilha naked and drunk with wine. She was not to blame. She was asleep and not answerable.

"I can pass on to you the experience of my pain and grief and the peace of my repentance. As a result of that moment of weakness, I lost my inheritance." He paused. "But now I'm on my guard. I've pledged my future moral conduct. If you can benefit from my experience, then more to the good."

"None of us is without sin," Judah said, "except maybe Isacar and Zebulon."

Isacar and Zebulon looked at each other and shook their heads. "We struggle daily with thoughts and actions just like the rest of you."

Judah continued. "Some of us are impulsive and quick of temper."

"You're talking about me," Simeon said. "Reuben's transgression is resolved—it's behind him. The greater sin is in me, for because of me our brother is lost."

Again, murmurs rose around the circle.

"You didn't act alone," Gad said. "We've been silent on this matter these twenty-two years, but you must know that not one day passes that I don't think of what we did."

"Nor I," Dan said, followed by the others.

"I think the more hate was in me," Gad said. "Do you remember the time I took the sheep from the lion's mouth and finished killing it—the time Joseph was with us and he came upon me in the act of dressing the dead sheep?"

"I remember," Asher said. "He went home because of heat sickness and told father you had killed a sheep in violation of the counsel of Reuben and Simeon. They'd told us not to slay one of our herd. We were only to eat what we could hunt."

"Yes," Asher said. "I, too, was angry with him for having informed on you unjustly."

"That was a little thing," Gad said, "but I let it prey on my mind and sour my insides."

Levi said, "Then, when he revealed those dreams of his..."

"That we should all bow down to him? I must admit that even I, who loved him, had trouble brushing that off," Naptali said.

Simeon spoke again. "But it was jealousy that ate at me. Secretly, I believed that Reuben's loss of the birthright would allow me to receive it."

"I had the same wish," Gad said, "being the firstborn of Zilpa."

"And being the firstborn of Bilha, I might have been considered," Dan said.

Simeon continued. "When he walked boldly into the camp that day, wearing the coat symbolizing that *he* was Father's choice, I lost all sense of reason."

"I've relived that day over and over in my mind, too," Judah said.

"So have we all," Reuben said. "But I think I've repented and found some semblance of peace in my soul."

"I'll never have peace until I know what's become of Joseph," Dan said.

"I try to imagine seeing him again and wonder how I'd feel," Gad said. "If I'd still feel any hatred."

"I wonder, too," Simeon said. "I went through a terrible battle inside myself. My bitterness caused a malaise in me that resulted in my hand becoming rigid and lifeless. That frightened me into submission to the Lord. I repented and after seven days regained the use of my hand. Since then I've felt free of hate, but..."

"Seeing Father's grief daily weighs so heavy on my heart, I don't think it will ever be resolved," Reuben said.

"Perhaps God has had a hand in our coming to Egypt," Levi said.

"What do you mean, Levi?" Zebulon asked.

"As long as we wear the remnant of the coat next to our hearts, and as long as we wonder what has happened to Joseph, we will have no rest. But what most likely happened to him?"

After some thought, Judah said, "He would have been sold— and the central slave market is in Memphis."

"So you think we might find him in Memphis," Zebulon said.

"But then what would we do with him?" Simeon asked. "We still have the problem of facing up to Father for our actions."

"But I'm ready for that," Levi said, "if our brother might be redeemed to us. Let's try to find him."

Reuben nodded. "I think you're right. If we're all in accord, then we must make a plan and ask God to help us find our brother. We'll sleep now and make our plans before we enter the gates."

The following evening the brothers had gathered outside the wall of the white city where many who had come at dusk waited for the morning's passage. At dawn, Reuben gathered his brothers for one last council. "I've been thinking about what we should do," he said. "Father was right in that we should enter separately through the ten gates. That way we won't draw attention to ourselves."

"Yes," Judah said. "If the king of Gaash is here, and he remembered us, surely there'll be others."

"I was thinking," Reuben said, "that we could each search a part of the city for Joseph. It won't be easy, though. He may not look the same. He was seventeen when he left us. He would be thirty-nine now."

"Where should we look?" Dan asked.

"The most likely place would be the pleasure houses," Judah said.

"Perhaps," Zebulon said. "But he was strong, a good worker."

"Yes," Reuben said. "We mustn't overlook any position a slave could occupy."

"How much time will we allow ourselves for the search?" Naptali asked.

"Three days. We'll meet in the central square three days from now when the sun is at midday." Reuben paused, then added, "When they ask for our father's name for the permit, use the name Jacob—Israel is too well-known."

The ten men dressed in their finest tunics and loose robes, then put on the sandals saved for special occasions. They kept only the patch of the priesthood robe and their bags of silver in their inside pockets.

"I'll see you in three days," Reuben said, and he stepped forward to the sentinel of the gate to be issued his permit."

"I am Reuben, son of Jacob, son of Isaac from Hebron of Canaan," the brothers heard him say, as they parted to go to their assigned portals.

# Chapter Forty-five

# Brothers in Memphis

At the second gate, Simeon gained admission. At the third, Levi, and so on, each son of Jacob going by age from eldest to youngest through the ten gates of Memphis. Zebulon, being the youngest, entered the extreme side of the city, the arch closest to the house of Zana-panea. Having satisfied the sentinel and obtained his permit, he stepped into the dazzling city. He didn't want to appear as the innocent that he was, so he squared his shoulders and walked confidently toward the colonnade and all the activities that awaited him there. He gazed at the splendor of the palace and marveled at the alabaster lion that guarded the once-beautiful flower garden of Pharaoh. He ran his hand along the smooth marbled pillar.

As he came to the pavilion, he was immediately attracted to the food items being sold. Except for chewing on some dried meat, he hadn't eaten since they left Goshen. He purchased some dried dates and figs, then a drink of water from a colorfully costumed water vendor who served it in a fancy brass cup. He then purchased some flat bread, one loaf to eat immediately, the other to nibble on as he strolled about to orient himself to his surroundings.

Zebulon was educated. Israel had seen to it that all his sons were taught the essential knowledge of the well-bred. The lessons in the Egyptian language, however, were not absorbed as well as they might have been. Now Zeb found himself struggling to understand the words filling his ears. He could speak the tongue well enough to buy the necessities, but beyond that, his skills were dead from disuse. "How am I going to ask questions that will help me find Joseph if I can't communicate?" he asked himself.

That entire first day he wandered the pavilion, trying to take everything in. In the center of the square surrounding a huge obelisk, elevated stands held bags of grain brought from the granaries across the river on the east side. Members of the royal guard stood to monitor the allotments of food as the sentinels sat at their desks, checking permits. This was one of five such places of distribution. The lines forming in front of the desks extended far along the colonnade as men representing their families waited with one donkey each to obtain their life-giving portion. In pairs, more guards patrolled the city to keep order as the bags of grain were transported from the ferry to the square.

In other parts of the city and the square people were milling about in the business of everyday activities. Zebulon stood watching a brass smith pound his plates of metal into pieces of art. While Zeb watched the artisan at work, someone else was watching him.

Immediately to the right of the gate he had entered, Reuben saw the rows of priests' houses ahead and the looming magnificence of the palace. He walked toward it and saw the large homes of the king's court facing the central square. "This is where I'll search," he decided.

After he had purchased food to satisfy his hunger, he walked back around the first house, hoping to find the servants' quarters, but found only that the stables and carriage ports paralleled the square. For a long time he wandered up and down that first street, looking at the rear side of the great houses, hoping to encounter a servant he could speak to. At the end of the street, he saw Isacar coming around a corner toward him.

"I am glad to see you," Isacar said. "This is a large, lonely place for an outsider."

"Yes, we'll join forces. Maybe we can accomplish something together."

They stopped a stable man who was leading a team of horses onto the street. In his best Egyptian, Reuben asked, "May I inquire something of you?"

The man laughed. "You may speak to me in the tongue of Canaan. I perceive that you're Canaanite, are you not?"

"We are," the surprised brothers said.

"I'm from the land of Shinar. I was taken many years ago as a captive in battle and sold as a slave to this house. My use of the language of Canaan is awkward after these many years, but it's better than your Egyptian."

"Thank you for your indulgence," Reuben said.

"What is it you want?" the servant asked.

"We're looking for a Hebrew slave. He would have been sold here some twenty years ago. He is comely and strong."

"I don't know any Hebrew slaves. I'm sorry."

Can you tell us where we might look?"

"The slave market was saturated twenty years ago. Some were sold to the shipowners. Some to the officers of surrounding cities. Many were taken into the palace. Others like me were picked up by the privileged."

After considering these alternatives, Reuben said, "Thank you. We'll move on in our search. Come, Isacar." They slept against a wall on a narrow street their first night in the city.

Asher and Simeon met up on the square as they were getting the feel of the city. Being reticent to ask any questions in an awkward language, they contented themselves with looking at every likely person they saw, scrutinizing every servant or slave that passed them as they wandered the streets.

Judah met Gad on the street as he came through his gate. Judah, having a better grasp of Egyptian, went boldly about the pavilion asking questions of all the merchants.

Naptali, Dan, and Levi found each other late in the morning of the first day and committed themselves to search the pleasure houses, three in all. They were surprised to find that here, for a price, they could obtain food, drink, and lodging. Interpreters were on hand to overcome the disparate language barriers.

Harlots were not forced on them, and the eunuchs were hospitable and accommodating. They found that they could easily lounge in the reception area and watch the comings and goings of all sorts of people. Thus they passed a comfortable day and had a good night's sleep.

Before they slept, Dan voiced the fear they all had. "What if they made a eunuch of Joseph?"

"Don't say it. It can't be," Levi said. "We'll continue to hope otherwise."

<hr>

"Are you in Memphis to obtain grain?" a voice said to Zebulon. The man spoke in Canaanite.

Zebulon turned. "Yes, I'll get my portion in good time, but I have other business first."

The stranger bowed to Zebulon. "I am Shala, son of Ishaman, out of Shiloh. We are fellow countrymen, are we not?"

"Yes, I'm also from Canaan—from Hebron."

Shala continued. "I've been here many times, for I was a trader in the good times when I came to Bazaar. I wonder if I could assist you since you appear to be in unfamiliar circumstances."

"Is it so apparent?"

"Not to everyone, but my eye is trained. I've encountered every sort of man." He then whispered, "I know the stance of a shepherd."

Zebulon stiffened and backed away.

Shala laughed. "You needn't fear me. I'll aid you, if I can, for a pittance of your silver."

Zebulon looked at the man carefully. *How does he know I have silver?* "No, I'll fare by myself, thank you," he said.

"I know the city. I can help you find anything you desire. For example, you'd probably like a refreshing bath and perhaps some appetizing food and a soft bed."

"I'm looking for someone," Zebulon said.

"I speak many languages. I could aid you in your queries."

Zeb relented "Very well, I'll hire you, for a pittance, to assist me in my search."

"Good," Shala said. "Let me begin with the bath. I know a pleasure house nearby. Come with me."

Shala was as good as his word. The pleasure house where he took Zebulon was as accommodating as he'd said it would be. Zeb didn't even have to talk. Shala arranged everything. At Zeb's instructions, he even asked the knowledgeable eunuchs if they'd ever heard of a Hebrew slave named Joseph.

Relaxed after his bath and meal, Zeb slept soundly and awakened the next morning refreshed. But Shala was gone along with Zeb's permit and bag of silver.

A eunuch approached him. "Will you pay me now for your services?"

"I can't pay you. My silver is gone."

Zeb was escorted by the king's guard to the prison at the corner of the palace. *How could I have let this happen? What will become of me? What will I tell the others—if they ever find me?*

Upon seeing the handsome Hebrew, the prison keeper looked closely at him. *Ah, he reminds me of my Joseph.* To Zebulon he said, "You'll be confined here until a magistrate can hear your case. There's an overload because of the times; it may take many days."

---

Joseph had gathered the lists that the runners brought to him each evening from the gatekeepers. He sat down and began to read the names. On the first list, he found the name *Reuben* and jumped to his feet, his heart pounding as he read it again. *Reuben, son of Jacob, son of Isaac from Hebron and Canaan.* He swallowed hard, sat back down, and searched the list again. "Just Reuben," he said.

He searched the second list. *Simeon, son of Jacob, son of Isaac from Hebron of Canaan,* he read. Quickly then, he studied each of the ten lists and found the names of ten sons of Jacob.

"Benjamin's name is not here," he said aloud. He searched the lists again. "Why isn't Benjamin here? And why is there one name on each?" He sent for Zarill and said, "My brothers have come." His voice broke as he spoke.

"Joseph, I know you've long hoped for this day. What would you have me do?"

"First, I want no one except those in whom I have confided to know of this. Close all the stores except one so that my brothers must seek their grain from that one source."

"But they've been here one day. Perhaps they have their grain already."

"No, not yet. I have checked the store lists. Besides, the lines are long. You shall be on hand to check off each permit as they approach the desk. Bring each of them to me. I'll receive them as the governor of Egypt. For my own reasons, I don't want them to know who I am—not yet. Please, help me keep the confidence."

"Of course. I'll go now and make the arrangements."

Joseph hurried into his private room and fell on the bed. Mahta, seeing his actions, quickly dismissed the servants and went to her husband's side. He wept quietly. "They have come," he said.

"Your brothers?" Mahta asked. He nodded.

"Oh, my dear. What is this burden you have borne these many years?"

Joseph sat up. "Benjamin is not with them."

"What does that mean?"

"I don't know. I have no way of knowing their hearts. I wonder if they hate Benjamin as much as they hated me."

"That was a long time ago, Joseph."

"Yes, but he's not with them. I won't be satisfied until I know that he's all right. He's the one I've longed most to see."

"What will you do?"

"I've made plans to have them sent to me. They weren't in the lines today, so we should be able to intercept them tomorrow."

"And will you face them?"

"Only as Zana-panea. I won't reveal myself to them until I am satisfied that Father and my brother Benjamin are well."

"Or that they won't seek your life?"

"That too." Joseph sat quietly with his head bowed.

"Does it occur to you that your brothers might recognize you?"

"I don't think they'd expect to see me on a throne. Besides, my hair will be hidden under the crown—and it has been twenty-two years. No, I have no fear. I'll keep my distance."

——————

The second day in the city was much the same as the first for Simeon and Asher. They continued to search the streets for any servants who looked like Joseph.

Naptali, Levi, and Dan moved from the first pleasure house to go to another. They settled themselves to study all the occupants and visitors as they'd done the day before and heard the eunuchs talking about the traveler who had cheated them and had just been taken to the prison.

Reuben and Asher still watched the rich houses and inquired of the servants when they could.

Judah and Gad were becoming more bold in their queries. They went from one stall to the next and from one merchant to another, asking if they had ever known a Hebrew slave named Joseph. As the question was posed to a wine vendor, a nearby eunuch overheard and turned abruptly to face the inquisitors. "Who wants to know?" he asked.

"We are Hebrews," Judah answered. "We are looking for our brother, who was mistakenly sold as a slave many years ago."

"What is your name?" the eunuch asked.

"I am Judah. My brother's name is Gad. We are the sons of Jacob out of Hebron in Canaan. Do you have news of a Hebrew slave?"

"No," the eunuch said. "I knew one once, but it was not he." The eunuch walked away and made his way quickly through the crowd. Soon he was running to the house of Zana-panea.

Joseph had been pacing all morning, waiting for news from Zarill. He was interrupted by Jaeb rushing in. "Master, I thought you should know. I just came from the square."

Joseph felt tense, not knowing now what to expect. "Yes, Jaeb, what is it?"

"There were two men who said they were from Hebron. They were looking for their lost brother."

"What did they say?"

Jaeb told Joseph everything he had heard. "Would they be looking for you, Master?"

"Yes, Jaeb. They are my brothers. You did well to conceal your knowledge of me. I will send for them and deal with them in my own way."

"Is there anything I can do?"

"Yes. Go to the square. Find them again, but do not let them see you. I want you to keep an eye on them until I am ready to have Zarill bring them to me."

Jaeb laughed with a conspiratorial nod and said, "I am going already."

As Jaeb was leaving, one of Zarill's men came hurrying in with a message. "At the open store, the name of Zebulon, son of Jacob, son of Isaac from Hebron of Canaan, has been noted."

"Are there no other names to report?"

"Just the one."

"Very well. Tell Zarill to bring Zebulon to me."

Joseph's thoughts raced. *I want to see Zebulon, but I hesitate to face him one on one. Where are the others? Why did they ask for me? Do they still want me dead?* He was still pacing and fretting when Zarill appeared.

"I have the one," the commander said.

"Very well," Joseph said. "Give me time to prepare." He sent for Mahta, then sat down on his throne beside her. Moesha, who knew of Joseph's situation, stood beside him. Wama and Punt stood behind each chair. Some guards were on the steps.

Zarill came in with his captive. Joseph stood and walked quickly down the steps. "This man is not Zebulon. Where did you get this permit?"

The man began to mutter.

"Search him," Joseph said. The guards produced a bag of silver coins.

"Where did you get this silver?" Joseph turned aside and said to Zarill. "I know the workmanship of this pouch. I can safely say that neither the silver nor the permit belongs to this man."

Zarill turned back to the man. "What became of the man you stole these things from?"

"I left him at the pleasure house—please have mercy on a poor, hungry, miserable beggar."

"Take him away," Joseph said.

Mahta came to Joseph's side. "I'm sorry Joseph. This must be disappointing, but at least we know where he was."

"Yes, and now I know what we must do. Zarill, have your men spread out over the entire city and encounter every Hebrew or Canaanite they can find. Inspect the permits, and when they find the sons of Jacob, have them brought to me."

"The store is closing now; it will be sundown soon. Do you wish us to seek them in the dark?"

"No, wait until morning. When they are gathered, bring them here. I will not give them audience until all ten are together before me."

Zarill personally escorted the thief to the prison. As he turned him over, the prison keeper said, "There is a Hebrew here who reminds me of Joseph."

"Let me see him," Zarill said.

The keeper pointed. "The one sitting alone, over there."

"Keep him here until morning. I will send someone to collect him. Say nothing to him."

"Well, that takes care of one of the ten," Zarill said to himself as he went back to Joseph's house.

# Chapter Forty-six

# Audience with Zana-panea

"What do you want with us?" Simeon demanded.

The guards were not being forceful. They were told to be polite. "You are summoned to the palace of Zana-panea. He wishes to talk with you."

"Why did you single us out?"

"We search for the ten sons of Jacob."

"Very well, but we will not be dealt with unjustly." Simeon turned to Asher "This is not what Father meant when he said to be inconspicuous."

As they neared the large doors leading to the hall of Zana-panea, one of the guards said, "You will undo your sandals and leave them here. You are not allowed before Zana-panea with your shoes on."

Simeon and Asher looked at each other and at the sandals already left in the hall. A twinge of guilt overtook them as they loosed the footwear saved only for special occasions. Expensive and well-made, these were the sandals they had purchased with the silver obtained from selling Joseph some twenty-two years earlier.

They left their shoes by the others and followed the guard into a large room. A series of fifteen stairs led to a dais holding a pair of ornate thrones. Two impressive guards stood behind the empty seats, a number of other guards on the steps. A man in official dress stepped forward. "My name is Zarill. You shall wait here."

Simeon was glad to see that Zebulon, Naptali, Levi, Dan, Judah, and Gad were in the room ahead of them, waiting for the rest to be brought in. The men did not know what to do nor what to expect. They gathered together and in hushed voices tried to determine why they were there. Soon Reuben and Isacar were let into the room.

"At least we are all well," Reuben said, "and together again."

Zarill stepped up to the dais. After a short time, a gong sounded and Zarill said, "The great ruler Zana-panea and the queen Aseneth."

Through the curtain stepped the royal couple, their bearing splendid and imposing to the shepherds. A steward stood beside his master.

The brothers, overcome by the majesty of the moment, fell to their knees and bowed their heads to the floor before the kingly pair.

———◦◦◦———

"The sons of Jacob, of Hebron of Canaan, will be heard," Zarill said, his voice commanding.

At this point Mahta slipped behind the curtain to allow Joseph privacy with his brothers.

In Egyptian, Reuben said, "We are flattered to be in the presence of such a high man of Egypt, but—"

"This will not do," Joseph broke in, playing the role of ruler in his most austere manner. "Call someone who can speak Egyptian and the language of Canaan so that these men may be understood."

Punt looked over at Wama with a puzzled look on his face. Wama smiled but played along with the ruse. It was amusing that the man who knew forty-nine languages would call for an interpreter. The wait was uncomfortable. The longer the brothers stood, the more restless they seemed. Finally a man from Pharaoh's palace came in with Zarill.

"I want these men to know that they have nothing to fear from me," Joseph said through the interpreter. "I desire only that they speak truthfully."

"We come in peace," Reuben said. "Our only purpose is to get grain and return home as quickly as possible."

"You have been here three days, yet did not approach the desks. That does not appear to be quick."

"We were looking for someone."

"Your permits state that you are the sons of Jacob."

"Yes, we are the ten sons of Jacob."

"Why did Jacob not come with you?"

"He is too old to travel."

"Is Jacob not also called Israel?"

"Why, yes."

"And are not his sons mighty and undefeated in battle, whose names strike fear in the hearts of kings?"

Reuben replied. "We once retaliated in our sister's defense and we defend that which is our own. We do not initiate terror."

"That may be," Joseph said, "but we guard against those who might send their soldiers in separately through the gates only to join up inside and overtake a sentinel at the grain desks."

"We have no such intentions!" Simeon cried.

"We have silver," Asher said. "We're not beggars."

"Then perhaps you come to spy, to see the conditions of our land. Maybe you would report back to your king that we have vulnerable areas."

"No, no! We do not have a king," Levi said.

Reuben said, "We don't aspire to power."

"We did not come to fight," Zebulon said.

"Then why were you found in the prison?" Joseph asked directly to Zebulon.

All nine of the brothers turned their heads sharply to look at Zebulon. Palms out, he shrugged, looked at his brothers and said, "I was tricked." Then to Joseph he said, "You must know that, because the man who robbed me was imprisoned by you. You knew he was not a son of Jacob."

"You're right. I perceived falseness in him. I retrieved your silver and your permit. It will be returned to you." He turned back to Reuben. "But that does not satisfy my curiosity about the unusual nature of your brothers nor why they are really here."

Reuben said, "We're not spies. We are humble shepherds, not learned in the ways of the world."

"How can I know this?"

"Our father, who did not want us to get into any trouble, told us to enter separately through the ten gates."

"Are you used to getting into trouble?"

"No. Our father worries about us."

"Why?"

"It would be hard for you to understand."

"You shall explain whatever I bid you."

Reuben bowed briefly. "He is a man of God. He has always had great dreams for his twelve sons."

"Twelve sons?"

"Yes."

"I wish you hadn't said that," Judah said in a low voice, yet Joseph heard it.

"I see only ten men. Where are the other two?"

"Our youngest brother remains at home with our father."

"Why is that?"

"He is kept near our father because he is the youngest and is a comfort in the man's old age."

"How old is the lad?"

"He's twenty-nine years old."

"And you say he is too young to leave his father?"

"We didn't mean it that way."

"What did you mean?"

"Our father cherishes his children more than anything on earth."

"Egyptians value their children. Why do you imply that your father is greater than others?"

"He teaches us to obey God and to be sober in our habits."

"Is that why they found some of you in the harlot's house?"

"We were looking for our lost brother."

"Oh, so...one is lost?"

"Yes."

"Might he be dead?"

"We don't know. He's the one we were seeking in your city."

"Why seek him in the pleasure house?"

"In his youth he was beautiful. We thought perhaps he would have been sold—"

"How did he come to be sold?"

Just then a courier from Pharaoh came with a message for Joseph. He held up his hand while he turned aside to talk with the runner.

The brothers looked at each other. In Hebrew Judah said to his brothers, "I would rather be fighting a bear or a lion on the hillsides of Canaan than trying to match wits with this high ruler."

"We're no match for him," Levi said.

"Didn't I tell you that someday God would exact his punishment on us for what we did to Joseph?" Reuben said.

Joseph heard what his brothers said in their own language and was overcome. He made an excuse, as if because of the messenger, and went behind the curtain to regain his composure. Mahta had stood behind the curtain listening to it all, for she, too, understood what they were saying. She looked at Joseph with encouragement, but remained strong in bearing until he went back in.

"Well," he said. "I am not satisfied that you are not spies. To prove your words, you must bring your youngest brother. That way I might believe what you say."

"Our father will be against his coming," Reuben said.

"Then I shall imprison all of you as spies."

"But we must return with the grain. There are many mouths to feed in the large family of Jacob."

"How many?"

"We, with our wives and children, add up to seventy souls," Levi said.

"And there are many servants," Isacar added.

"All under one roof?" Joseph asked.

"No, we have houses close to the house of our father, but he is still the patriarch," Reuben said.

"You mean king."

"No, we do not believe in kings," Simeon said.

"Yet we respectfully acknowledge your rule," Reuben hurriedly added.

"Tell me about your children," Joseph said.

Reuben began, "I have four sons."

Simeon said, "I have six sons."

"My sons number three," Levi said.

"Two of my sons died," Judah said. "I have three living."

"I have seven sons," Gad said.

"Four sons and one daughter," Asher said.

Dan said, "I have only one son."

"There are four for me," Naptali said.

Isacar added, "Mine also number four."

"And I have three sons," Zebulon said.

"And your youngest brother?" Joseph asked.

"Benjamin is the father of ten sons," Reuben said.

Joseph tried not to show his smile. Then he said, "I will allow you to go to the home of your father that you might return with your brother. I will keep one of you here as an assurance that you will keep your word." He looked them over as if trying to decide which one. "I will keep that one," he said, pointing to Simeon.

"Oh, no," the brothers groaned.

"Keep me," Zebulon said.

"No, I'll keep him," Joseph insisted. The guards on the steps moved to take the hostage by the arms.

No one had ever laid hold of Simeon's arms and he reacted with instinct. As soon as the soldiers reached toward him, he whirled. His arms and feet seemed to strike a hundred blows. Before they knew what was happening, the soldiers were picking themselves up and looking toward Zana-panea for orders.

He held up his hands to motion that they were to do nothing. Then he looked back at Punt and Wama, who then rushed down the stairs and moved to overtake Simeon.

This time Simeon was reacting to the rush inside his body. He let out an Israelite roar and Punt and Wama found themselves embroiled in a fight as if with a wild animal. Whether out of deference to Joseph, or whether they were genuinely outdone, both Wama and Punt soon found themselves on the floor, Wama sprawled with all fours extended, and Punt facing down with Simeon's foot planted firmly on his back. Simeon raised his arms and gestured victory.

Manasseh had come running when he heard the roar as if he couldn't help but respond to something in his nature. He stepped through the curtain.

Joseph began to feel twinges of real fear because he knew his brothers could dispatch everyone in the room if they decided to. At the same time, he remembered the feeling of deep admiration for his older brother, which he had known as a child. He wanted to see this through, but had he allowed something to begin that could not be finished short of calling out the entire guard of the palace?

He felt a hand on his shoulder and looked up to see Manasseh looking questioningly into his eyes. No words were spoken, but Joseph nodded.

The men in the outer circle were murmuring among themselves in an uneasy awkwardness. What could they do? Reuben knew the situation had to be remedied. He was about to speak when he noticed Zana-panea's nod.

Manasseh walked slowly and deliberately down the stairs, removing his outer garments as he went. He stepped onto the floor, which had now become the arena, eyes holding fast to their intended target. Simeon was still breathing heavily. Punt and Wama, aware of the impending confrontation, got themselves up and out of the way as quickly as they could.

This was Manasseh's first real challenge. He had never had to face anyone in a match that really mattered.

Everyone else in the room moved back, widening the circle. A hush fell over the room. Simeon, flushed from his heady victory and cooled from his rage of temper, now watched in disbelief as this large, young Egyptian prince approached in an attitude of combat.

Collecting himself again, and striking the pose of the fighter, Simeon met the gaze of his opponent. For a few long moments the two men looked deep into each other's eyes as they slowly moved sideways in a circle, then reversed their steps. Suddenly Simeon gave a giant roar and sprung forward, but Manasseh, unaffected by the yell, swiftly jumped out of the way. Again they crouched and stalked until Manasseh made a move to grab Simeon's arms. The grasp was quickly broken and Manasseh reached to get a headlock. For several moments the older fighter struggled to free his neck from the vise-like grip. His strong legs found a sure footing and in a quick move, the boy was on the floor with Simeon on top of him. Manasseh rolled and was pushed again to his back. The battle displayed a great deal of rolling and crushing accompanied by groans and grunts. Just as Simeon was about to pin Manasseh, the younger opponent rolled, found a place to put his knee, then jumped to his feet in the offensive stance. This time it was Manasseh who gave the Israelite roar, and Simeon stopped abruptly as if jarred by some realization.

Joseph, watching Simeon's face, swallowed hard, his heart pounding. *Does he see something in Manasseh's eyes? Does he realize he might well be looking into a mirror and seeing his younger self?*

Simeon regained his composure and again positioned himself to an advantage. From there he thrust forward, grabbing Manasseh around the middle. It took the youngster off his feet, but Simeon's usual opponents would have found themselves tossed a fair distance with the plunge. Manasseh quickly struck Simeon a blow to the side of his neck. Simeon let go, and while he was trying to recoup, Manasseh quickly brought up a knee to his groin, grabbed an arm and turned it to force Simeon onto his knees. Manasseh then forced him to the floor and left him prostrate in defeat.

Simeon was subdued, and the moments he lay quiet on the floor seemed long to Joseph. Manasseh had his foot on his captor, signaling victory. As the guards picked Simeon up off the floor, he leaned toward Reuben and said quietly, "Please don't tell father I was taken down by an Egyptian. Tell him it was an Israelite." The men of Israel were left in shock at what had just occurred.

"Who is he?" Judah asked.

"He is my son," Joseph said.

———❦———

"Go in haste," Joseph told the brothers. "Even though one brother remains here, his share of the provisions will be sent along with the rest of you."

As much as could safely be piled on one donkey was carefully packed by the servants under the directions of Moesha, who had specific instructions from Joseph. Oats were supplied for the animals. Lentils, rye, and barley were packed, but wheat was most abundant to assure food for the family Israel. To their surprise, the men found that one extra donkey had been provided to carry water. The nine brothers and the eleven beasts began the trek homeward.

———❦———

"What do you suppose it all meant?" Levi said as they gathered for their first night's rest.

"You mean the hearing?" Judah asked.

"Yes, and the generous supplies we were given to take home."

"I don't know," Reuben said. "I have never felt so misunderstood in my entire life."

"It bothers me still that our character was impugned so," Asher said.

"It was as if the Lord were chastening us and making clear our sins," Isacar said.

"Yes, or why would Simeon have been taken down?"

"I will never understand that."

"Surely God punishes us."

Zebulon said, "I can't help but wish we had found Joseph in the city so that we might have finally resolved that issue."

"I agree, Zeb," Reuben said. "We will never be free of that darkness until we know what became of him."

Judah said, "Now we have to face Father with the news about Simeon."

"Maybe we should go back and try to snatch him from his captors," Dan said.

"And have all of Egypt after us?" Reuben said. "We are brave and mighty, but we would be uselessly killed in such an attempt."

Levi said, "God is with us to fight our battles when our cause is just, but this time it is our own reckoning we must abide."

"What will we tell Father about Simeon?" Gad asked.

"We'll tell him the truth," Reuben said.

# Chapter Forty-seven

# Report to Jacob

Early the following morning a loud cry awakened the brothers. "What is it?" they said as they jumped to their feet.

"Look here," Levi said. "I opened my sack to get some oats for the animals and found my bag of silver inside."

"Oh, no. Now he will have cause to accuse us of being thieves."

Reuben hurriedly ran to the other sacks and, to his dismay, found all ten bags of silver.

"Now the man on the throne will call us not only liars and spies, but thieves as well," Gad said.

"Should we take it back?" Zebulon asked.

"No," Reuben said. "We'll return it later. For now, we must hurry home. We will ask Father what we must do."

---

The old patriarch listened carefully to the full account by all nine of his sons. He sat still for a long time.

"You say Simeon willingly submitted to being imprisoned?"

Reuben answered. "He will not be so much a prisoner as a hostage."

"What matter? If my son is lost to me, am I to be comforted by the terms of his confinement? Am I to be bereft of two sons now?"

"I have never seen Simeon like that, Father," Levi said. "In experiencing defeat, his whole demeanor changed. He was no longer belligerent, but went meekly with his captors."

"He did it for us," Isacar said. "He knew we would not get food unless he stayed."

"He must be restored to me along with his true spirit. How is it that the sons of Israel can be called spies and thieves? There is something awry in Egypt."

"What would you have us do, Father?" Judah asked.

"We will wait out the famine, then go peaceably and reason with the man on the throne. What did you call him?"

"Zana-panea."

Jacob gave a thoughtful nod. *One who knows the mind of God. What manner of man might this be?*

As if they knew his thoughts, the sons began to extol the grandeur of the ruler.

"No king is his equal. His bearing was regal."

"His garments were exquisitely beautiful."

"He wore a towering crown of gold."

"His mind was sharp and insightful."

"Yes, and he was generous and kind."

"We will wait," Jacob repeated.

"But Father, it was voiced by all in Egypt that the famine would last seven years," Dan said.

"How say you?" Jacob said.

The brothers told Father Israel the story of Pharaoh's dream and of the mysterious dreamsolver who had accurately predicted seven good years.

"And now he sits on the throne?"

"Yes."

"And he predicts seven bad years?"

"Yes, sir."

"We have begun only the third year of famine," Levi said. "We will not be able to make do with the portion we have received."

"No, we will not," Jacob said. "We surely need more food from Egypt—unless the man is wrong. I'll ask God."

During the weeks and months that followed, no more was said of it. Everyone tried to resume as normal a lifestyle as possible. The sons did everything they could to make things run smoothly. Israel loved his children and knew their hearts were heavy. He also knew that they would soon have to go again to Egypt. He had asked God and learned that the dreamsolver was right.

# Chapter Forty-eight

# Watching Simeon

The first few days after the confrontation, Joseph was on edge. He knew what Simeon was capable of doing. He had seen to it that he was secured, not in Pharaoh's prison, but in the specially-built cell in Joseph's own house.

"Go to him, Moesha. Tell him I prefer that he consider himself my guest rather than my prisoner. Tell him I hold him only to assure that his family will be fed."

From behind the gate, Joseph watched. He could see Simeon, but he could not be seen.

Moesha was kind and gentle in his handling of the man of might; he seemed to enjoy ministering to him. Moesha had experienced the worst kind of confinement and gave Simeon an element of mercy unknown to the common man.

Moesha did the talking. Simeon listened and said nothing. Behind the gate, Joseph stood tentatively. *Oh, Simeon, if only you knew how much I love you. The feelings of my boyhood return to me. I see you as my hero, my champion. For one look of approval from you, I would have done anything. Yet by my honest actions, you came to hate me. Do you hate me still?*

Joseph shifted his weight and his foot caught the grating with a soft clang. He stood rigid in his position.

Simeon looked toward the hiding place. Joseph could not be seen, but for a long time Simeon stared, his gaze steady, his face inscrutable.

*What are you thinking, Simeon?*

One day Moesha said to Simeon, "I am instructed to leave the cell door open. Our master thinks you are wise enough to know that your family's safety depends on your behavior here. We'll furnish a chamber for you and make it as comfortable as possible. You may roam about as you desire."

Joseph was watching. He expected Simeon to retort as to the injustice of his detention, but he said nothing.

"I'm worried about him," he told Mahta. "He's becoming lethargic. Confinement is robbing him of his innate temperament."

"Should I go to him?" Mahta asked.

"No, he could not endure the humiliation. You make men want to be heroes in your presence."

Manasseh and Ephraim, with permission from their father, went down to Simeon's quarters. "We thought we could cheer you up," Ephraim said. Manasseh nudged him, embarrassed.

"Is there anything we can do for you?" Manasseh asked.

Simeon didn't answer.

"We just made it worse," Manasseh said in reporting to his father.

Wama decided to try brightening Simeon's world. "You are plenty strong," he said, smiling. "You certainly defeated the governor's personal guards." He talked and laughed for a long time as if Simeon were responding and enjoying the conversation as much as he. He told him about his life in the south. He told him of his imprisonment. At one point, he almost slipped and told too much about Joseph.

The next day he went again and took Punt. He told Simeon everything he knew about the speechless man.

This time Simeon softened. He looked into Punt's face and searched his eyes as Wama spoke. From deep within, the compassion of a true man of God awakened. His own trials were nothing when measured against what Punt had endured. As the two giants left, Simeon said, "Will you come and see me again, Punt?"

Joseph was delighted. "Have him go alone. That way it will be Simeon who is forced to talk," he said.

It worked. Soon Simeon was telling Punt about herding sheep on the hillside in Canaan. He described how he and his brothers had dispatched marauding lions and bears. As he talked he reveled in his memories, and the telling brought healing. Day after day Punt visited downstairs.

Then one day Punt motioned Simeon to follow him outside. "Are you sure this is all right? Do they trust me?" Simeon said.

Punt nodded and pantomimed that they needed exercise. Within a few days they could be seen in the early morning running around the outside wall of the city. Punt even smiled, and so did Simeon.

But most gratifying to Joseph was that one day, he found the two men wrestling.

# Chapter Forty-nine

# Another Trip

"The time has come, I'm sad to say," the old man told his assembled sons. "Our little ones will soon be crying for bread. You must go again to Egypt."

"We'll go, Father, but you know what that means," Reuben said. Jacob looked solemn and slowly shook his head.

"The governor will not receive us unless we have Benjamin with us," Levi said.

Tears were in the eyes of Jacob. "My heart is broken. My son in whom I stored my prophetic hopes is lost to me. I wear his blood-stained cloth next to my heart. My son in whom God put the strength and spirit of lions and who made me proud is restrained in a foreign land among strangers. Now I'm asked to relinquish the lad whose presence is the brightness of my lonely world."

Benjamin stepped to his father and knelt before him. "Father, I'll be all right. God will watch over us. We have strength and goodness on our side."

Jacob placed his hand on Benjamin's thick curly hair and thoughtfully patted his head. The brothers looked at one another.

Reuben spoke. "If we were skilled in the debate of kings, perhaps we could convince the ruler of Egypt that we are true men. But even though we're cunning in speech in our own land, before him we become inept and speechless."

"There's nothing we can do but prove ourselves by presenting Benjamin," Judah said. "And I'll keep him in my constant vigil. I promise, nothing will happen to him."

"You may hold my two sons in our absence," Reuben said. "If I don't bring Benjamin back, you may do with them as you will."

"Yes," Father Jacob said, "I see that Benjamin must go, but I want to tell you, my sons, what God has shown me in vision.

"Many years ago it was made known to me that my twelve sons would become twelve mighty nations. I am a man of faith. My joy is in serving God. But how can there be twelve nations if there are not twelve sons?"

The room was quiet, and Jacob continued. "It's my hope that each of you fill the measure of your existence, for a man is not complete who does not fulfill his destiny. A prophet is ineffectual who does not carry out the wishes of God."

"You always told us, Father, that God's purposes cannot be thwarted by man," Isacar said. "And that our ways are not His ways."

"You've done nothing wrong," Levi said. "God doesn't expect you to keep us secluded under your roof in order to bring to pass his plans."

Jacob bowed his head. "Yes, of course. Your words humble me. I must rely on the arm of God and submit my will to his. My sons have this day taught me what I should be teaching them. We'll make preparations for the trip."

When the family next gathered in a circle for prayer, Father Jacob raised his arms to heaven and said, "Deliver my sons in safety to Egypt. Touch the heart of the ruler, that he'll deal justly with them. In thy mercy, Lord, return all my sons to me."

The wives and children echoed the words of the prayer and wept.

As the men prepared to set out, their father said, "Take the gifts I have made ready for the ruler. Here is a measure of gum and some jars of honey. Take this storax and laudanum for incense and perfume. There are almonds and other nuts also.

"You will take the silver from your last journey plus a double portion for this trip. Most importantly, here is a message I have written to the high man. Give him my respect and conduct yourselves properly. May you find honor in his eyes and in the eyes of the court."

They took the donkeys back with them in case of a shortage; they even took extras.

This time when the sons of Jacob of Canaan approached Memphis, they all went through the first gate. As they strode across the square, heads turned, but they did not go to the stores on the square. They went directly to the house of Zana-panea. At the door of the house, they asked to speak to the steward. Moesha came.

The brothers presented him with their bags of silver. "We found this silver in our sacks," Reuben said. "Do not think ill of us. We return it to you. We did not know it was there."

Moesha said, "It is of no consequence. Keep your money. Zana-panea does not accuse you. Come, we must make you ready for your audience."

Moesha sent a runner to alert Joseph that his brothers had returned. He sent another to bring Simeon. Servants appeared to wash the men's feet. Attendants bustled about them and saw to their every need.

Dan laughed. "One can never be sure of what to expect in this place."

"Well, don't let yourself be caught unguarded," Judah said.

"No. The difficult part is still ahead of us," Levi said.

Just then, Simeon came hurrying into the room, accompanied by the large black guard they had seen him take down.

"You look well!" Judah said to him.

"I feel well. How good it is to see all of you! This is my friend, Punt." He told them as much as he knew about his new friend as Punt left to occupy his place by his master. The men talked as fast as they could to share the experiences of their time apart. The reunion was short-lived, but joyous. The men were still apprehensive, even Simeon. No one knew what to expect as they were shown into the throne room.

Joseph and Mahta were watching the lesson of Ephraim and Manasseh when they received word that the brothers had returned.

"Make them comfortable," Joseph said. "Tell them that we will join them for a noonday meal in the great hall."

"Is Benjamin with them?" Mahta asked.

Joseph peeked through the curtains into the great hall where the brothers had been set to rest on some oversized cushions.

"Yes, he is. And he's a wonder to behold. Come and look. Do you see him?"

"Yes," Mahta said. "He is wonderful. Just like you. I'll be in my quarters if you need me."

Joseph closed his eyes and drew in a deep breath. *Now I know my brother is whole. What shall I do next?*

When the appropriate time came, the tables were set up and laid with succulent foods. The servants of the court took their respective places. The sons of Israel stood up.

The ruler made his entrance, as awe-inspiring as the first time. The men bowed low before the throne.

In Egyptian, Joseph told the servants how to seat the brothers at their table. He had them placed in order from eldest to youngest, facing the dais. Beginning with Reuben, they sat in a row and ended with Benjamin. Joseph could not take his eyes from Benjamin's face.

The interpreter had been brought in again.

"May I address the ruler before we eat?" Reuben asked.

"What is it?" Joseph said.

"Our father sends gifts and a message to the high ruler of Egypt." The brothers brought out the gifts and laid them on the steps at Joseph's feet.

"This is a generous gift considering the hard times that afflict your home in Canaan," Joseph said. The message was handed from Reuben to Moesha and then to Joseph. He took the message and tried to sound unaffected. "Is your father well?" he asked.

"He is well for one who grieves much over the well-being of his sons," Reuben said.

"Is this your younger brother of whom you spoke?

"Yes, this is our brother, Benjamin."

Benjamin smiled and bowed.

"Please begin your meal. I'll see to this message."

The men returned to their seats, and the servants began presenting the food. Joseph's heart was pounding. He opened the message and hoped his hands were not shaking too much. He read:

"From thy servant Jacob, son of Isaac, son of Abraham the Hebrew, the prophet of God, to the revealer of secrets, ruler of Egypt, greetings."

Joseph read that much and was overcome. He gave brief instructions to carry on, then slipped behind the curtain. Through his tears, he read on:

"When the famine made it necessary for me to send my sons to Egypt to buy food, I sent them in good faith. I told them to enter separately the ten gates of Memphis so that they might not draw attention to themselves. They thought to look for my son, Joseph, who is lost to me. That you should accuse them of spying is a mystery to me, for a man who can know the mind of God and correctly interpret the king's dreams can also correctly look at my sons' hearts and know that they are not spies."

Joseph smiled, took a deep breath, and continued.

"If you would study the history of Egypt you would know that my fathers are not unknown in your land. You would see how God put a curse on Pharaoh when he tried to take Sarah from Abraham. You should also know of the reputation of my sons in battle. They are greatly respected and have never been defeated. I did not want to send my son, Benjamin, to you. But because you kept Simeon, I had no other choice. Now will you look on my sons and know that they spoke the truth? Please restore all my sons to me. I wish you peace."

Joseph finished the message and wept. Then he washed his face, composed himself, and joined the banquet in progress.

Moesha whispered, "Are you going to tell them who you are?"

"Not yet. I still don't know the intents of their hearts, but I think I now have a plan. I'll trick them into thinking that I'm going to keep Benjamin. If they let me have him without a struggle, I'll know that they have hard hearts. If they argue and fight to my satisfaction to take him away from me, I'll know they are truly concerned for him and the feelings of their father. I'll know that their hearts are good, and I will reveal myself to them."

In a loud voice of concern and hospitality, he asked, "Are you enjoying your meal?"

"We are," Reuben said. "You are generous."

"Why do you not eat the delicacies or drink the wine?"

"Since our brother, Joseph, became lost to us, we made a vow that such things would not touch our lips until he was found."

"Is the rest of the food to your satisfaction?"

"More than we deserve. If it is not too impolite, we have a question for the wise and learned man."

"What is your question?" Joseph said through the interpreter.

"How did you happen to seat us in the order of our birth?"

Joseph suddenly saw how he could implement his plan. He pushed his ornate goblet of silver and jewels to the front edge of the table in full view of everyone. "Do you see this goblet?"

"Yes, it is beautiful."

"Its function for me is more than one of beauty or to satisfy thirst." He paused, looked at the men's faces, and continued. "This is my divining cup. In its depths I can see the mysteries that elude the common eye."

Moesha stifled a gasp and stood curious, waiting to hear what Joseph would say.

"Then why didn't he know we were not spies?" Levi said, in high Hebrew.

"Or that we truly had a young brother?" Asher said.

Joseph heard them, and as if continuing his thought, he said, "The trouble with a divining cup is that one can only see what it wishes to show. I saw in the cup the order of seating and didn't know it was by age."

322    The Coat and the Crown

"Can the cup see what has become of our brother, Joseph?" Judah asked.

Joseph drew the cup to him and looked deep into it. "Is your brother strong and of goodly appearance?" he asked.

"Yes—or he was when last we saw him."

"I see that he is alive, but the cup does not show me where."

The brothers murmured among themselves.

Joseph watched them. *Do you want your brother alive so that you can kill him, or that he might be restored to the family?*

The meal was finished and the servants followed instructions to provide the necessary supplies for the family Israel. Moesha was told Joseph's plan. When the sacks were secured, he slipped the silver goblet into the one belonging to Benjamin. The brothers offered their thanks and departed.

Zarill waited until the Israelites were well away from the city wall and then, with his soldiers, overtook them. "The governor's divining cup has been stolen," he said.

"We didn't take it," Reuben said.

"We are instructed to search through the sacks on your beasts to see if it can be found."

"We are not thieves," Simeon said.

Judah shrugged. "Go ahead and search."

"Zana-panea gives the edict that if the cup is found, the one who possesses it must stay and be his slave."

"So be it," Reuben said, confident in the integrity of his brothers.

The soldiers searched every bag and came last of all to Benjamin's animal. The brothers stood in a stance of assurance, their arms folded. The last bag was opened and the silver goblet was held high.

"No!" Reuben cried.

"It can't be!" Judah shouted. They all looked at Benjamin, who was standing dumbfounded and wide-eyed. "I— I don't know how it came to be there," he stammered.

The brothers went with much hostility back to the hall of Zana-panea. Joseph was waiting as the Israelites were ushered back into the hall. The other members of the royal family were absent on the dais this time.

"Why did all of you come back? My instructions were that only the possessor of the stolen cup should be brought."

"The cup was not stolen. Of that we are certain," Reuben said. "How it came to be in the sack of my brother is a mystery to us."

"We came because we are determined that Benjamin should not be left behind," Judah said.

"I have no desire to enslave your entire family. As the ruler I must see that justice is done on this matter, and I have decreed only that the one be detained."

"We cannot—we will not leave him," Reuben said.

"We will forfeit our lives in battle before we depart without him." It was Simeon who spoke thus, taking on the position of combatant, his face grim as he scowled at the guard and all who occupied the room.

Following Simeon's lead, the brothers instinctively assumed their positions with their backs together, forming a circle of defense, their arms and bodies ready to be used as weapons. They were a formidable band.

The sight of the fearless and mighty force struck fear in the hearts of everyone in the room. The soldiers, almost in unison, reached for their swords. Wama held his great reserve of strength at the ready. Moesha, knowing he would be of little use, was nonetheless ready to defend his master regardless of the consequences. They had all seen what one Israelite did to those who tried to restrain him. Now eleven mighty ones stood ready.

Joseph's heart pounded. He knew what these men were capable of doing. "Hold, hold! There is no need to do battle. We must discuss this matter as reasonable men."

As Joseph spoke, Punt left his place behind the throne and walked deliberately and soberly to the circle of men. He went directly to Simeon, raised his arms in a gesture of surrender, then slowly lowered his arms and lovingly encircled them about his friend. Simeon reciprocated the embrace.

Judah, mistaking the act as one of offense, let out a mighty roar.

Terror struck the hearts of all who heard. The cry resounded past the walls of Joseph's house and into the palace of Pharaoh.

Pharaoh, having been apprised of Joseph's dealings with his brothers, was aware of the imminent danger. Guards hurried from every quarter toward the direction of the frightening yell. Pharaoh himself set off immediately to Joseph's house. He would go to the private residence and secrete himself behind the curtain.

"It's all right, Judah!" Simeon said. "This is my dear friend, who only sought to comfort me."

As the soldiers poured into the hall, Joseph signaled Zarill, who ordered the men to put away their swords and back away. He motioned Punt to return to his place. The room became quiet once again. Still, everyone was alert and cautious.

"I have great respect for the might of the sons of Jacob," Joseph said. "Let me continue with my inquiry. We will try to reach a satisfactory solution."

"Our father counseled us not to fight, but to conduct ourselves with good manners," Reuben said. "But we are men of the hills, trained to react in threatening circumstances. In our natural setting, we would have by now easily dispatched a bear, or a lion, or a hostile king's army. But as you can see, we use restraint."

"Thank you for using restraint," Joseph said, smiling.

"We didn't come here to fight," Levi said. "We came only to get food."

"We aren't thieves," Zebulon said.

"Will you hear our side of it?" Reuben asked.

"I will," Joseph said, settling in his chair.

Reuben began, "We were twelve sons and one daughter of our father, Jacob living in Canaan of Hebron. One sorrowful day, which we have long regretted, our brother Joseph, the chosen of our father, was lost to us by our foolishness. We believe he became a slave in Egypt. We repent his loss, and have sought to find him and return him to our father."

Levi interrupted. "So when our brother was taken from us, our father drew to himself the younger brother, son of the same wife as Joseph. This was his comfort."

"When it became necessary for us to come to Egypt, our father was reluctant to let us come because he did not want to lose any more sons. As you know, by misunderstanding we had to return with one less brother to our aged and beloved parent. When it became necessary to return to Egypt, we reasoned with our father that we must bring Benjamin, that our true status might be verified."

Judah interjected. "I pledged my life that I would safeguard my brother and return him safely back home."

"And I gave two sons in assurance that on their lives, we would return all eleven sons to Hebron of Canaan."

The noise had not only brought Pharaoh and soldiers to the throne room, but Mahta and her sons had also run to see what was happening. As they approached the throne room, they saw Apophis listening behind the curtain. When he saw Mahta and the boys, he put his finger to his lips, and they nodded and waited behind the veil. The four stood there now, listening to Reuben's story.

Joseph did not know what to do. Satisfied that his brothers were sincere, he did not hide his tears. In Hebrew, he said, "Benjamin, will you come forward please."

Without realizing that Joseph was speaking his language, Benjamin obeyed and walked hesitantly up the steps. Joseph motioned him forward.

Levi and Reuben noticed the change in tongues, however, and looked quizzically at each other. All the Hebrews noticed the ruler's tears and wondered at their cause.

"Sit," Joseph said, pointing to the empty throne beside him.

Benjamin seemed perplexed. He looked at Wama, who smiled and nodded. He looked at Moesha who said, "Yes, sit down." He sat.

Joseph handed him the silver cup. "I give this to you as a brother." He kissed Benjamin's forehead, then said in a loud voice, "I wish to be alone with these men."

"He is quite mad," Judah whispered. "What does he want with us alone?"

Zarill said, "But Master..."

"Yes, Zarill. Take your men and go. I will be fine now."

# Chapter Fifty

# Joseph's Disclosure

Pharaoh, satisfied that the reconciliation was imminent, motioned through the curtain to Moesha. "Tell Zana-panea that when he has had sufficient rejoicing, I want to see him for a brief meeting." Moesha whispered the message to Joseph and left along with all of Joseph's staff.

The Israelite men backed away from the throne as Wama and Punt disappeared through the curtain. When they were alone, the ruler took off his crown, laid it in his chair and walked down the stairs. He stood before the men. They studied him as he stood there. Without a crown, he looked quite different. *Why does he descend to us?* Simeon narrowed his eyes as if to study the handsome man with the full head of hair.

The ruler extended his arm to Simeon. "Your brother, Joseph, is here," he said emotionally. It was difficult for him to speak. This man who had skillfully done combat with words from the throne now choked on the effort to reveal himself.

The men began to look around the room. Simeon kept his eyes on the face before him.

"Where?" Reuben said. "Did you find him?"

"He is here," he said again, spreading his arms.

Some of the brothers reacted defensively as if afraid of some residual vengeance. Some stood rigid. Simeon automatically placed his hand where his sword was usually sheathed.

"I am Joseph." He stepped closer to them, then walked over and stood in front of Zebulon. "Don't you know me, Zeb?"

Zebulon stared. "Joseph? Is it really you?" He shook his head. "Is it really you?" he said again, then fell at the feet of his brother as they wept together.

Reuben also realized the incredible truth of the moment. "My brother, how can it be?" He sobbed and wrapped his arms around Joseph. "Have we really found you?"

Benjamin, more willing to believe than the others, ran down the stairs, grabbed Joseph and wheeled him around while they both laughed and cried. "We did not think to find you here."

The rest of the men, seeing the reciprocal embrace, slowly realized what was happening. They looked hard into the face of the man who had tormented them. "It is him! I see it now," Levi said and moved slowly forward.

"But how did you come to be on the throne?" Asher asked.

"How can this be?" Judah held Joseph at arm's length and looked deep into his eyes. "Why did you torture us so? No—never mind, we had it coming."

Joseph answered, "I had to be sure you did not still hate me—or Benjamin."

"Oh, Joseph, forgive us," Judah cried.

Most of the men rushed forward to embrace their lost brother, but Dan and Gad hung back, fearful that the memory of their hate would lessen their acceptance in Joseph's mind. Asher was also timid about stepping forward, but the great surge of love and relief he felt overcame his shyness and he stepped up and warmly enveloped his brother.

Joseph looked toward Gad and Dan, smiled and reached his arms toward them. They came to him then for a bone-crushing hug.

Only Simeon stood back, wearing the same sober face Joseph had so intensely studied in the past months. They approached one another slowly. Joseph offered his arms. Simeon grasped the arms, smiled and nodded his head. The fear and doubt in both of their minds prohibited any further show of affection.

Mahta and the boys had waited behind the curtain for the initial shock to be over. Then Joseph extended his hand toward Mahta and said, "My brothers, I would like you to meet my beautiful wife and queen. In Hebrew, she is Mahta. On the throne, she is known as the queen Aseneth.

Mahta had removed her crown and warmly moved to embrace her new-found family. The Israelite men, taken by Mahta's beauty and bearing, responded like docile kittens.

"This is Manasseh, who is seventeen, and Ephraim, who is six, almost seven."

"Didn't I tell you he was an Israelite?" Simeon laughed as he reached for Manasseh's hands and shook them vigorously. He felt Manasseh's arms and muscles, feigned a wrestling hold, and laughed unrestrained.

The men spent the next while getting acquainted with Joseph's family. One at a time, almost all of them came contritely to Joseph to beg his forgiveness, and he, in turn, begged to be pardoned for his torturous inquisition.

Reuben signaled everyone to be quiet. "I have something to say. I speak for myself and for my brothers when I say to you, Joseph, that we could not have known the outcome of your dream when you saw the wheat stalks bow down to you, and the stars also. Today we acknowledge the fulfillment of what God showed to you. And so, humbly and gladly, we now ask forgiveness."

"I'm afraid I still speak with unbridled restraint," Joseph said.

The wonder of the moment and the incredible culmination of circumstances was expressed over and over. For about two hours they asked questions and talked, eager to hear the account of Joseph's life since he left them.

"Come, we will make ourselves comfortable in my house." They all went into the living quarters and settled down to listen.

Joseph briefly shared the events of his life, told of his slavery, of Potiphar and Zelica, and of the eight and a half years he spent in prison. When he told of ascending Pharaoh's steps, he explained it in careful detail.

"Forty-nine languages you say, Joseph, and you needed an interpreter for us?" Levi teased.

In telling his tale, Joseph delighted in drawing the expected responses from his enrapt audience. "And of the dreams of Pharaoh, you have heard."

Reuben looked at Joseph and smiled, shaking his head. "So here you are, the dreamsolver whom Pharaoh put in charge of the affairs of Egypt. My little brother."

Gad added, "Second only to Pharaoh himself."

"I may not let you live down the divining cup," Zebulon said. "Divining cup, indeed."

Joseph sounded the gong. Moesha came in immediately. "This is Moesha, my best friend in prison," he told them. Wama and Punt were also introduced. He spoke to his servants, "It is time for another meal. Will you see to the needs of my brothers? I must meet with Pharaoh."

---

Apophis was deeply touched by Joseph's account of the reunion. "I would like to present my family to your brothers," he said. "But first we should send for your father and the rest of your family. I would invite them to spend the duration of the famine as my guests in Egypt."

"That is kind of you," Joseph said. "I think they would welcome the security of your hospitality. Do you know the family numbers more than seventy members? And I don't know how many servants there are."

"They are herdsman, aren't they? We will give them the verdant valley by the mouth of the river, the land of Goshen. I give it freely as a gift to the great family of Israel. The Egyptians don't value it. They think they are above shepherding."

Joseph embraced Apophis. "Thank you, dear friend. I will tell my brothers."

"Wait, Joseph. I know your father is old and ill-prepared to travel. Send for him. Send your brothers home to collect him in our finest chariots. Send wagons of supplies to see them safely back here. Take some of our finest clothes from the royal wardrobe so that your father may be honored as is his due. Have Zarill appoint a guard to go as escorts."

Apophis was more and more pleased with himself as he spoke. His gestures became larger and his voice louder. "Take presents for the children and wives." He laughed, as if enjoying his idea. Then he sobered. "But you must wait here. These times are too dangerous to risk having you cross the border. Just send your brothers and soon your whole family can be here with you for a proper celebration."

Joseph reported Pharaoh's words to his brothers. Orders were soon given and the plan of Apophis was carried out.

---

The ground shook as the cavalcade of wagons, chariots, horses, and men thundered along the route from Egypt to Canaan. Onlookers rushed out of their houses to observe the array.

It had been decided.

Reuben said, "When we come to within distant view of the family home, we must halt the caravan. Judah and Naptali will run ahead. Father must be prepared."

"What will we tell him?" Judah asked. "How can we ever explain?"

"Tell him lovingly and gently that we are again twelve sons," Levi said.

"The rest he will learn when we arrive," Reuben said. "Warn him of the imposing spectacle Pharaoh sends."

The old patriarch received it better than they had expected. Not even his sons knew of the capacity of God's servant, Israel. He responded to Joseph's experience with a dramatic sigh, as if a great weight were taken from his shoulders. He was left tearful from gratitude and resolute in his aim to fulfill God's wishes.

He embraced Judah and Naptali, then stepped aside for a moment in quiet contemplation. *At last I understand. Even though I wearied Him by the asking, God could not reveal Joseph's whereabouts to me else I would have thwarted His plans to have Joseph save our people and our world.*

He turned toward his sons, straightened his shoulders and said, "Let the host of Pharaoh approach. We will make ready our sojourn."

The entourage of Israel made a wondrous sight as they moved toward the city of Memphis. Pharaoh's chariots and horses and the people bedecked in the royal garments gave pause to those travelers who shared the route seeking food.

As the band neared the land of Goshen, they separated in two groups. Some of Zarill's men escorted the servants and children into Goshen to set up tents and prepare dwelling places for the Israelites after they made reunion with Joseph. The brothers and their wives would be presented at court and introduced to Pharaoh.

"We will bring Joseph and his family back here to mingle with you as soon as our business is concluded," the children were assured.

# Chapter Fifty-one

# Patriarch and Sons

The impressive caravan stopped at the end of the pavilion before the palace and Joseph's edifice. Servants ran to attend the honored guests.

"It is much the same as I remember it," the old patriarch said as he stepped onto the polished floor. He shrugged away the offer of help as he climbed the stairs and walked with bearing into the royal house. When the doors to the reception room were opened, he stepped inside and saw before him the son he had prayed to rejoin for so many years.

The embrace between Joseph and Jacob was poignant and unrestrained. Jacob wept with the love of years as Joseph melted into his father's arms as a small boy needing nurture. The family stood reverent and weeping in the privilege to witness the reunion.

Joseph's father reached inside his robe, drew out the patch he wore next to his heart and handed it to Joseph. Reuben, seeing the gesture, reached for his piece, but Jacob held up his hand.

"Joseph's coat will not be restored to him. You will each keep your portion until such time as your appointments will be made known. This day a new order of the priesthood is ordained from Heaven. There are to be twelve patriarchs, not just one."

Then Father Israel called for a prayer, and each of his sons, with his wife by his side, gathered in a circle. Manasseh and Ephraim watched from the side. The old man, with all the glory and honor he possessed, stood in the center, raised his arms toward heaven and began in his still-rich voice to supplicate his beloved God, his posterity repeating the words.

"God of our fathers, who created heaven and earth, we praise Thy name. Thy name is holy. Thou hast power to cast away our sins. Thy mercy will lift us up.

"Know, oh Lord, that we bow in gratitude. We are a family reunited to serve Thee. Our hearts are contrite. In Thy pardon we seek redemption, that we may dwell with Thee in Thy house of joy and light forever. Amen."

As soon as the prayer was ended, the group, as by lifelong habit, began to sing and dance in their traditional way. Into their second song, Manasseh and Ephraim joined them.

El Shaddai, El Shaddai,
Look down from Thy throne on high.
Thou art strength. Thou art light.
In Thy arm is heaven's might.

El Shaddai, Almighty King,
Bend to save this helpless being.
Lift me up with Thy great power.
I need Thee every passing hour.

El Shaddai, El Shaddai,
Hear my cry, O hear my cry.

Suddenly Joseph broke the circle and motioned silence. Apophis had heard the music and come to welcome the family. He stood in the doorway as the circle parted and politely bowed to welcome him into the room. Pharaoh walked directly to Jacob, looked into his eyes, then dropped to his knees before the prophet-patriarch, the acknowledged man of God.

Some in the room drew in their breath, but not Father Israel. He reached as a man of his position would, laid his hands on the head of the kneeling pharaoh and gave him a blessing.

After the blessing, he gave his hand to help Apophis to his feet. The humbled king looked around the room until his eyes met Joseph's. "May I join your circle?" Once again the songs and dances of joy filled the hall of the house of Joseph.

———————

The family Israel was soon settled in the land of Goshen. Their servants had laboriously driven their herds from Hebron to the new home. A new life was taking shape.

Ephraim and Manasseh found an affinity with their cousins and spent all the time they could with them in Goshen.

Punt was given his freedom and he chose to live in Goshen, close to his friend, Simeon. Now the two could work side by side in the fields, building a place for themselves. Whenever Simeon went to Memphis for a celebration or a visit, Punt went also, where warm and gracious friends always received him. Usually on such visits, Manasseh worked in a bout or two on the mats, and Punt smiled often now.

———————

The seemingly endless seven years of famine finally ceased, the first fruitful year giving every heart joy. As by a miracle, the waters ran clear and pure and full. Trees that looked long dead burst into leaf, and forgotten flowers bloomed and sent their perfume into the air. The land turned green with pasture for the animals and meadows full of blossoms.

The people of the land, no longer doubting that Zana-Panea was inspired, freely gave their hearts to him. Of all the kings who had ever sat on the throne of Egypt, none were more loved than Apophis and Zana-panea.

With the foresight of a prophet, Joseph also foresaw the redressing of the land. Now the grains were allotted to the inhabitants of Egypt as seed, every man given equally his share. A whole new era of planting and harvest began, and a feeling of well-being accompanied it.

The men who worked the land of Goshen prospered. They knew how to work hard and their efforts were blessed. None of the sons of Israel seemed eager to go back to Hebron of Canaan.

Joseph had spent as much time as he could with his father, having yearned to once again sit at his feet in discussion of all they had not shared. Jacob was eager to discourse on all the facets of doctrine and philosophy the two could conceive. They discussed the question of why God had not told Jacob that Joseph was alive, and both agreed that it was kept from him to fulfill God's purposes.

One day Joseph came with his carriage to pick up Jacob. "I want to show you something," he said. He drove the carriage out to a lone spot on which stood a beautifully designed, well-built edifice.

"This is the burial place of my friend, Cephas. I wanted you to see it." He told his father of his love for the high priest and of the many adventures they had shared. Then they drove back to Goshen and sat in the shade of the trees and talked.

"Father, I am in a position to offer you a tomb of magnificent design. You and I both understand the lost skills that produced the great pyramids. If you wanted, I could—"

"No, my son. It is important to me that I be buried in the cave of Macpelah. I must be laid next to my father and mother, and with my wife Leah, and my grandfather Abraham."

"The Egyptian priests have great skill in the art of embalming—" Joseph stopped. From the look on his father's face, he knew the man was adamant in his decision. "Why is it so important to you, Father?"

"I don't know exactly, Joseph. I know that it was by divine instruction that Abraham purchased the cave for his burial place. I have since reasoned why it was of significance to God."

"Yes, I have wondered why God would have a special place for his servants to be buried."

"You know that the coming years will bring the advent of the Redeemer."

"Yes, Father. We used to talk of it often. I saw in a dream that he was to be the Messiah. I saw his life and his death."

"As did I, but it is his death that is my subject now. When the Son of God gives up his life, He, and only He, will have the power to reunite His body and spirit. He will be a glorified being."

"Resurrection, yes."

"By that godly act, he will have the right and power to begin to raise up the rest of us mortals." He sat quiet for a few moments, a feeling of reverence surrounding them.

"I see what you're thinking. If his servants are worthy of exaltation, and close to His burial place, might they not be the first whom he raises up?"

"Is it presumptuous to want to be worthy enough to qualify for such a place of honor?"

"It is enough to make a man want to live a life without blemish. Do my brothers know of your wish?"

"They do, and they are as resolute as I in their choice of place to make their graves."

"What a glorious wish. I, too, will request a place among you, and I will see to it that your plans are carried out. I promise that when the time comes, we will take your body to the burial place of your fathers.

It was only two years after the burial discussion that Jacob sent for Joseph and his other eleven sons. "Bring Manasseh and Ephraim also," he told them.

When the twelve men and Joseph's sons were before him, he said, "The time has come. Soon I will go to rest with my fathers. It is my prerogative to choose the legacy I leave my sons. I have decided to give each a father's blessing. I will also bless the sons of Joseph."

One by one, the beautiful, strong, and mighty offspring of Jacob knelt before him. He evoked in carefully chosen words God's wishes for the twelve tribes of Israel. Each one was promised the blessings that would accompany a righteous compliance with the mind of the Lord.

He also drew Manasseh and Ephraim to him. "Come stand between my knees as a symbol that you are to be my adopted."

Joseph nodded his assent. He had already had the discussion with Jacob and understood what was in his mind. Then Father Israel bestowed a promise on their heads. When the blessings were at an end, he said, "I will tell you now of my wishes regarding my death and burial." He carefully explained the details of how he pictured it to be accomplished.

Two days later, he died, having lived 147 years.

His family mourned him, as did all of Egypt. In Pharaoh's house, the affairs of government halted to pay tribute and honor to the great man, now deceased. Apophis told Joseph, "Make sure the most skilled embalmers see to the necessary procedures." They discussed the plans that had been decreed by Father Israel.

With the passing of their father, some of the brothers' deeply-buried fears awakened.

"Do you suppose that now he'll expel us from Egypt?"

"Has he been showing us favor out of deference to Father?"

"Has he really forgiven us?"

It was Simeon who confronted his brother at his home in Memphis. "It's time for us to talk," he said, gazing into Joseph's eyes with that same unreadable stare.

"I'm here for you," Joseph said.

"Some of us wonder if you are waiting for a time to exact revenge for our wrong doing."

"Oh, Simeon, I'm sorry that any of you must be burdened by doubts. No. I fought the battle of my feelings long ago. I didn't find peace until my forgiving was complete. God could not have shown me his wonders if I had nurtured ill feelings."

"Then you do not hold our sins against us?"

"Simeon, if only you could have known. You were my hero, my model—"

"No, Joseph. I can in no way measure up to what you are."

"You have, and you always will."

This time, the embrace was complete—nothing held back.

"I love you, my brother."

"And I love you, my king."

———————— ·oo· ————————

The time arrived for the procession to begin, which would culminate at the burial place in Canaan. For over a month Israel had lain for all of Egypt to honor.

"We shall do it this way," Joseph said. "Two lines will be formed beside the casket. On the left will walk Reuben, Simeon, Judah, Dan, Naptali, and Gad. On the right will be Asher, Isacar, Zebulon, Benjamin, Manasseh, and Ephraim. Thus twelve places will be filled. Levi will walk behind the casket since his inheritance will be the privilege of ministering among all the nations of Israel. I will follow on horseback since my destiny was foreseen by God and I was taken from the twelve to sit on the throne of Egypt. My two sons will walk in my place and in Levi's. This was my father's wish."

He finished speaking, and the twelve each put his hand on the carrying rod. Together they lifted the casket and began the walk.

Jacob had been laid out magnificently. The casket was gold, covered with precious stones. His clothes were the finest that could be found. He lay with only a veil for covering so that all might see him.

Before the walk began, Joseph approached the casket, leaned over and kissed his father. Then he took the crown from his own head and tenderly fitted it on the head of the dead prophet.

As the procession moved out, it seemed that all of Egypt drew toward the funeral group. Many joined in and walked behind. Some threw flowers; others knelt in honor of the father of Zana-panea.

Upon leaving Egypt, a new following began. Word of Israel's death had spread and many people in all the lands that knew of Israel turned out to give their homage.

When they crossed the border into Canaan, they saw that the high king of Gerar, Abimilech, was waiting to pay respects. In a gesture of true honor, Abimilech took off his crown and placed it in the casket at Jacob's side. The king's troop then followed the procession.

Next came the king of the Hivites, who followed Abimilech's example and also put his crown at Jacob's side. The king of the Heitites did the same, as did the king of the Chorites.

Jashub, king of Tapach, gave his crown.

Elan, king of Gaash, happily followed.

Thuri, king of Shiloh; Parathon, king of Cazar; Susi, king of Sarton; Labon, king of Beh-o-ran; and Shabir, king of Othnaymah each relinquished his symbol of authority to surround the untitled, but real king of Canaan.

Joseph's heart was full. He bowed his head in humble acquiescence to the God who had shown him this picture. For there before him lay the one great prophet with a crown on his head. Encircling him were twelve crowns, and holding tight to his casket were the twelve princes of Israel, who carried him home.

The End

# Epilogue

The children of Israel stayed for many years in the land of Goshen. They prospered greatly and had many offspring. When Manasseh and Ephraim wed, they took their brides and went to live in Goshen with their people.

Joseph reigned on the throne of Egypt for eighty years. In all that time, he was adored as a just and benevolent ruler. Zanapanea was, of course, given a magnificent burial place along with the other kings of Egypt. It was many years later that the children of Israel, led by Moses, finally left Egypt to go back to Canaan. They took Joseph's bones with them. He was buried in Shechem in the area of the Holy Land apportioned to the tribes of Ephraim and Manasseh.

Let all these blessings be a
Crown upon the head of Joseph,
The man who ruled Egypt
And was his brothers' glory.
The birthright,
The kingdom,
The honor...are Joseph's.
—*from the Targum*

# Sources

*Atlas of the Bible*. Pleasantville: Readers Digest, 1981.

*Bible Manners and Customs*. New York: Flemming Ravell Co., n.d.

*Book of J*. New York: Random House, 1991.

*Book of Jasher*. J.H. Parry Co., 1970.

Breasted, James Henry. *Ancient Times*. Chicago: Ginn and Co., 1916.

*Great Events of Bible Times*. Garden City: Doubleday, 1987.

*Great People of the Bible and How They Lived*. Pleasantville: Readers Digest, 1974.

Holzapfel, Richard N., Dana M. Pike, and David R. Seely. *Jehovah and the World of the Old Testament*. Deseret Book, 2009.

Horton, George A., Jr. *Studies in Scriptures*. Vol. 3. N.p. Randall Book, 1985.

*Josephus*. Grand Rapids: Kregal Publications, 1978.

*King James Bible*. 1979.

*Lost Books of the Bible, Testament of Patriarchs*. N.p., n.d.

Merkley, Marion G. *Old Testament Stores*. Deseret Book, n.d.

*Nelson and Phillips Pictoral Bible.* New York: 1874.

*New English Bible and Apocrypha.* N.p. Oxford and Cambridge Presses, 1971.

Nibley, Hugh. *Temple and Cosmos.* Deseret Book, 1992.

*Old Testament Student Manual.* 1981.

*The Pearl of Great Price.* 1981.

The *Qur'an.* N.p., n.d.

Rohl, David M. *Pharaohs and Kings.* New York: Crown, 1997.

*Spirit of the Old Testament.* Deseret Book, 1970.

The *Torah.* N.p., n.d.

Wallace, Arthur. *LDS Roots in Egypt.* Los Angeles: L.L. Co., 1981.

Zobell, Hans J. *Observations of Joseph's Granaries.* Alexandria, Egypt: 1868, 2005.

# Acknowledgements

First of all, my daughter Barbara; if not for her assistance, the book would not be.

George Horton, tour guide, teacher, and source.

My sister, Helen Beaman, who gave help at every turn. My other siblings, Karen Gibson, Wayne and Lon Keith for believing in me.

Pat Sheranian and Phyllis Gunderson for nagging me to publish.

Steve and Donna Stewart for their aid.

Dorothy Jensen and Donna Mackert for their red pencils.

Penny and Larry Humphries, my angel neighbors.

Sue Brown, Markay and Nad Brown, Linda and Ron Martin, and JoAnne Wilson for encouragement.

Brenda Winegar and Mallory Mackay for being at my elbow in time of need.

Boyd Craig and his assistant, Victoria Marrott, for hours of work and patient endurance.

Keith Yorgeson for his granary papers.

Karen Heckman for her Egypt papers.

Lynn Aaron for her brilliant insights and the loan of her antique Bible.

Jonah Duffin after whose words I patterned young Joseph's words.

Larry Barkdull, facilitator; Jerilynn Carter, editor extraordinaire; Brian Carter, typesetter, advisor, and guide; Boyd Tuttle, publisher, printer.

Connor Martin, sketch artist (in an earlier edition).

# About the Author

Mary Keith Boyack raised her family in Los Angeles, California, attended University of Southern California and Los Angeles City College. She has always loved music, storytelling, and gardening. She is published in five books of poetry and has written fifteen children's stories. *The Coat and the Crown* is her first novel with more in the offing.